Hot Sex and Sudden Death...

Just Looking by Bill Pronzini

"Her eyes shifted back and forth between him and the phone, her face all scrunched up and hot-eyed, and she wasn't the most beautiful woman he'd ever seen anymore, she wasn't even pretty, she was getting ready to have him arrested, put in prison—He lunged at her. . . ."

The Gold Fever Tapes by Mickey Spillane

"Why some women look naked with their clothes on is beyond me, but with Cheryl I finally figured it out. She was what I called posture-naked. She always did those damn things that made a man look at her, like bending stiff-legged over the bottom drawer of the filing cabinet so that her miniskirt hiked up to her hips. . . ."

Pickup by Martin Meyers

"She was driving me crazy. I knew what I wanted from her. What did she want from me? I was aware of the answer; I just didn't want to admit it. Killing another human being was too high a price for a piece of tail. . . ."

Top of the World by Bill Crider

"I'd seen the way she fondled pistols like a lover, and I'd seen her nearly delirious with excitement after we did a job. I'd heard her voice, full of breathless exhilaration after she shot Sam. And then there was the way she acted with me, the way she talked, the things she made me do. . . ."

Erotic Tales of Crime and Passion

FLESH
AND
BLOOD
DARK DESIRES

EDITED BY
Max Allan Collins and Jeff Gelb

Published by Warner Books

An AOL Time Warner Company

Copyright © 2002 by Max Allan Collins and Jeff Gelb
All rights reserved.

Mysterious Press books are published by Warner Books, Inc., 1271 Avenue of the Americas, New York, NY 10020.
Visit our Web site at www.twbookmark.com.

An AOL Time Warner Company
The Mysterious Press name and logo are registered trademarks of Warner Books, Inc.

Book design by Fearn Cutler de Vicq
Printed in the United States of America
First Printing: May 2002

10 9 8 7 6 5 4 3 2 1

Library of Congress Cataloging-in-Publication Data

Flesh & blood, dark desires : erotic tales of crime and passion / edited by Max Allan Collins and Jeff Gelb.
    p. cm.
  ISBN 0-446-67858-9
    1. Detective and mystery stories, American. I. Title: Flesh and blood.
II. Collins, Max Allan. III. Gelb, Jeff.

PS648.D4 F58 2002
813'.087208—dc21   2001044572

To our parents,
who instilled in us our love of reading and
our interest in writing

Contents

Introduction

Response to *Flesh and Blood* volume one was so immediate and gratifying that the good folks at The Mysterious Press of Warner Books have granted us another opportunity to travel down these mean, mysterious streets.

So what's the appeal of noir, anyway? Maybe it's as simple as, "Some poor shmuck's got it worse than me." Every day, we have a multitude of choices to make. Every one of them could take us down a dangerous, even dead-end road. We've all thought, "what if . . . ?" *Flesh and Blood* offers us the opportunity to safely navigate those poorly lit boulevards and find out exactly how lucky we are that we didn't obey our erotic or criminal impulses.

But what is noir these days? Is it a PI on the prowl? A gritty police procedural? An unwholesome whodunit? For that matter, what defines an erotic story? Is it hardcore or something less direct? These are questions we've wrestled with in accepting stories for the *Flesh and Blood* books, and they have no simple answers. But one thing's certain: We know a *Flesh and Blood* story when we read it.

Finding stories has been a fascinating, fun task. Many mystery writers have been clamoring to try an erotic noir story. *Flesh and Blood* offers them a quality environment to stretch beyond normal boundaries they may encounter in their usual stories. Writers appreciate the opportunity to tell a tale that will keep us guessing about who the hero or heroine is, and whether he or she will even survive until the story's end.

As with the first book, we've cherrypicked a combination of great names, starting right at the top with an ultra-rare reprint from Mickey Spillane himself. We've selected both known and new writers to titillate and terrorize you.

You'll find plenty of sensual suspense in these pages. So come along for the ride. Just be careful: slippery when wet!

FLESH AND BLOOD
DARK DESIRES

Lily and Men

John Lutz

Lily was in her usual back booth in the bar at the Royal Roman Hotel in Miami near South Beach. It was one of the newer, plusher hotels masquerading as twenties renaissance, all pink and blue pastel Art Deco. A hard place to find a sharp angle.

Hard to find a sharp angle on Lily, too. She was a month past her thirty-fifth birthday but looked like a twenty-five-year-old high-fashion model who had put on a little too much weight in the right places. In fact, she told her customers who weren't regulars that she was a model. They believed her. They believed whatever they wanted about her. Fantasy was part of the deal.

Anyone glancing at Lily wouldn't have guessed. The slender, coolly attractive blonde in the back booth looked more like a traveling conservative businesswoman than a prostitute. She had her long hair swept back severely and pinned in a bun and was wearing a pale gray pinstriped business suit with tailored slacks and jacket, white blouse with mock bow tie, virtually no makeup. The kind of woman who might own her own company, which in fact she did, though she accepted work contracted out by Willis Gong.

When she'd begun this business ten years ago as a student at the University of Miami, Lily hadn't thought of herself as a prostitute. She'd been simply a college girl in need of cash, making some temporary concessions and rationalizations.

It turned out to be easy money. Even easier than she'd imagined. And nothing like she would have guessed from watching TV or movies. A girlfriend named Doris had introduced her to a bartender at one of the convention hotels who for a small percentage would let her sit in the lounge where men would make contact with her. Lily had a chance to size them up, decide for herself whether she'd trade sex for money, before going upstairs with them to a room the bartender somehow managed to supply even when the hotel was fully booked.

Lily and Doris sometimes worked as a team. Both had been psychology majors; they knew about fantasy. Both were young and unspoiled and attractive, which translated into so much money that both of them dropped out of school to devote more hours to their newfangled occupation. Lily had stayed away from the drugs that were offered free and for sale. Doris hadn't. Now Doris was dead. Lily was bruised.

That was where the years had left them. They hadn't left Lily financially comfortable, but she was close.

Close enough, she thought, to do something she'd been considering since her work had become less fun and more . . . well, work. And since Doris had been found strangled to death in a hotel linen closet.

Willis Gong arrived, smiled at Lily, and slid into the booth to sit opposite her. They talked here from time to time. It was dim where the booth was, well beyond the bar in the long, hazy lounge, and far enough away from other customers so that conversation was private.

Lily, no longer an idealist, thought of herself as a prostitute now, but she still didn't think of Willis as a pimp, even though he arranged with employees of half a dozen hotels to allow her and several other prostitutes to operate from their restaurants or lounges. He was an amiable, middle-aged man with thinning white hair and kindly blue eyes, given to faded Levi's and plaid shirts. At first Lily had thought his gentle nature might conceal something ugly, but it turned out that the thoughtful and soft-spoken man who maximized and shared in her profits was exactly as he seemed. Lily couldn't remember Willis ever getting angry or raising his voice, and some of his clients had given him plenty of reason.

He ordered his usual glass of white wine, then looked at Lily more closely and frowned. There was a cut near the left corner of her mouth, and bruises around both wrists.

"The fella from Kansas City?" he asked.

"Yeah," Lily said. She decided not to mention the similar bruises around her ankles, or the welts on her thighs and buttocks. When she'd gone to the hotel room she brought her valise of tricks that included her leather restraints; the client had insisted on using ropes. She'd brought her cloth belt; he had a leather belt. Lily felt the pain again from last night. "He turned out to be a son of a bitch."

"Didn't seem the type," said Willis.

"Neither do we."

Willis smiled. "You got a point."

"I'm gonna quit, Willis. It's time."

"You sure?"

"I don't want to find myself with somebody like Kansas City who won't know when to stop. I don't want to end like Doris."

"Understandable." Willis sipped his dry white wine, unperturbed. He'd been here before. "So what'll you do?"

"Go into business for myself. Another kind of business."

"Need money?"

"No, thanks to you. I've got enough for a start somewhere else. In some other city."

"I don't wanna sound like a pessimist, Lily, but most new

businesses where the owner doesn't have previous experience fail."

"I'll be working with something experience has taught me a lot about," Lily told him. "Men."

Willis took another sip of wine, then he grinned and squeezed her hand. "Let me know when you go public. I'll wanna buy stock."

———————

A year later. Another booth, another hotel bar, this time in Sarasota.

Lily was seated alone, coincidentally wearing the same conservative businesswoman outfit that had been a turn-on for Kansas City. She was sipping a daiquiri and watching a man at the bar. Brad. Lily knew about the Brads of the world. She was waiting until he got halfway through his second drink and would be feeling the effects of his first.

Two days before in Lily's office, Brad's fiancée, Joan Marin, had smiled nervously at Lily and said, "You have an unusual occupation."

Lily smiled back. "But a useful one."

"That's why I called you," Joan said. "You saved a girlfriend of mine."

Still smiling, Lily shrugged. "I save as many as I can. Here's the deal, Joan. I choose the time and place and make myself available to Brad. I don't exactly come on to him, just make it clear that I could be agreeable to what he might suggest."

"Can you do that?" Joan asked.

"It's a subtle thing, but I've mastered it," Lily said.

"I never could flirt," Joan said, "even though I've worked at it."

Lily looked at her—this attractive enough brunette who'd gone to the right schools and had the wrong hairdo—and thought, not in a thousand years, sweetheart. But she widened her smile and said, "It's my business. If Brad does proposition a stranger a month before your wedding, you've got a right to know about it. And I'll see that you do know."

"Will you . . ." Joan twittered nervously ". . . I mean, go all the way?"

"No, no," Lily said tolerantly. "Ours is a business arrangement, and sleeping with your fiancé isn't part of it."

Joan looked down, looked up. There was a glint like a diamond chip in her eye. "But what if I wanted it to be? I mean, there's only one way to have actual proof."

Surprised, Lily nodded. "I understand. I can supply you with a videotape, if it comes to that. But of course my fee will be increased accordingly."

Joan agreed, and didn't find Lily too expensive. But she did ask meekly if she could pay 10 percent of the fee up front, the rest after Lily's report. Lily told her that would be okay, thinking how the rich really were different from the rest of us, but very much like each other.

———

This Brad, Lily thought, watching him at the bar, was also rich. Joan had told her that, but it wouldn't have been necessary. Lily could figure it out from his obviously expensive blue blazer, Italian loafers, the glitter of his gold watch and diamond ring when he lifted his arm to sip from his glass. A young, good-looking guy over six feet tall, with dark eyes and a head of black curls. He was well built enough that he made his tailored jacket look even more expensive.

He glanced over and saw Lily staring at him. Didn't smile, but didn't look away immediately. Lily averted her eyes precisely when he did, so he would know she'd also looked away. Lily knew how to flirt the way an artist knows how to prepare to paint.

When Brad was finished with his second drink, he hadn't

come to her, so she went to him, standing close and asking the bartender for a bowl of peanuts.

When she'd returned to her booth and sat down, she saw that Brad had followed her. Big surprise.

"Do I know you?" she asked coolly.

He smiled white and wide, aiming his charm like a gun. "Would you like to?"

Lily waited a couple of beats. "I don't know. Would I?"

Brad sat down opposite her.

He was obviously experienced, and very good. Lily had to admire how adroitly he played her while she was playing him. It took him only about ten minutes to ask if she'd wait while he went to the desk and got a room, then go upstairs with him. Lily dropped the coy act. She told him that wouldn't be necessary, she was staying at the hotel and had her own room.

He was good all the way. No violence or disrespect, only gentleness combined with blatant lust. Lily's style.

Afterward she lay back with her fingers laced behind her neck and smoked a cigarette. Apparently Brad wasn't a smoker himself, but he registered no complaint. Lily watched him watch a bead of sweat she could feel finding its way around the nipple of her left breast. The expression on his face almost made her want to reach for him, but that would hardly do when she showed Joan Marin the videotape of her fiancé thoroughly enjoying the last half hour with a stranger he'd picked up in a hotel lounge. The camcorder was set up between the wardrobe and desk, concealed in the shadows and focused on the bed, with a piece of tape over its red power light. A small voice-activated recorder was taped to the back of the headboard so it could pick up words uttered even in a whisper.

Brad reached across her for the glass of scotch poured from the bottle he'd brought up from downstairs. Lily gasped and sat straight up as the glass slipped from his hand, spilling ice and diluted scotch over her bare stomach and crotch.

"Damn!" Brad said. "I'm sorry." He leaned down and began to lick her stomach.

Not in the mood, Lily shoved him away. "It's okay," she said, "really." The mattress was wet and cold beneath her. "I'm gonna get up and shower."

"Okay," Brad said. "I'll wait for you. Then I'll buy you a big dinner so you'll forget my awkwardness."

Lily thought, why not? She liked the guy, and Joan wasn't going to marry him after seeing the videotape. Lily had even gotten Brad to say he loved her, always the end of an engagement.

She showered quickly then dried off with one of the hotel's towels from a heated rack, thinking maybe she'd found the right occupation for a woman with her skills and a realistic attitude.

When she wrapped the towel around her and returned to the room to get dressed, she found Brad still nude and seated on the edge of the bed. He was going through her purse. Lily forced herself to be calm, fighting back her anger. She'd had Brad wrong. Now she wondered how wrong.

"Private investigator, huh?" he said, holding up the copy of her license.

The hell with this guy, Lily thought. He was the one with the problem. "Knowing that will hardly make any difference now." She dropped the towel and stepped into her panties.

He smiled at her, his own coolness disturbing, making her wonder all the more. He should be furious, threatening. "Notice that smell?" he asked her.

For the first time she did, the acrid scent of burned plastic.

"I burned the videotape in the wastebasket while you were showering," he explained. "I figured Joan might hire someone to test my fidelity. It's the thing to do for women in her crowd. So when I saw you I could hardly believe my luck."

Lily continued dressing, staring at him curiously. He wasn't simply a sneak thief caught rooting through her purse. Something else was going on here.

"I recognized you," Brad said. "You're Lily from Miami. When you came on to me, I knew you were a working girl one way or the other, so I decided to take my chance and hope you were hired by Joan and not still . . . er, working your other profession."

"I decided on a new, honest profession. A new start in another city."

"You should have chosen a city farther from Miami."

"I like Florida and don't want to leave. But I won't miss Miami. Are you a former client of mine?"

"No, I only recall you from someone telling me about you at a convention in South Beach. I admired you enough to remember your face."

"Then you don't really love me?" she asked wryly, using humor to stall for time while she finished dressing, trying to figure out what this was about, how she should deal with it.

"I meant it when I said it. And I'm glad you turned out to be you, because it makes what I'm going to ask a lot easier."

Lily felt better. He wanted something from her he couldn't simply take. Something he had to ask for. She bent forward to display her cleavage while she fastened her bra, looking at him to let him know she was waiting.

"You see, Lily, I have a prison record, and I'd rather not have Joan find out about it. What I'm asking is for you to give her a clean report on me."

"She only has my word anyway, now that you destroyed the tape."

"But I want you to go beyond saying I didn't betray her. I want you to tell her you checked out my past and it's unblemished.

That way she won't hire someone else to check it. Rich women are suspicious."

Lily couldn't resist grinning at him. "You don't think they have good reason?"

He gave her a sheepish look and nodded. Lily didn't buy into it.

"There's something more, isn't there?" she said.

He gave her a level stare that went right to her, surprising her with its effect. Joan would be crazy not to marry this guy even if he murdered his last five wives. He said, "You're no fool, Lily, which is why I think you'll go for what I'm going to propose."

"You already proposed to Joan," she pointed out.

"I'm being sincere now, and not about marriage. I'm marrying Joan for her money."

"Shocking," Lily said, zipping her skirt. "I would have guessed you had money of your own."

"I did, and now I don't. But I will again. Joan's."

"Unless she finds out about your past," Lily said. She knew how to play the Brads of this world.

"That's true. Especially my recent past."

Here it comes, Lily thought. "How recent?"

"As long ago as the New York Diamond District robbery."

Lily sat down in a chair near the bed, not bothering to button her blouse. She remembered the multimillion-dollar jewel heist from when it was all over the news about six months ago. Four men had held up separate shops in New York's Diamond District simultaneously, then somehow faded into the throngs of pedestrians on the sidewalks. Later the police theorized they'd worn the dark clothes of Hasidic Jewish diamond couriers beneath their coats, then placed hats or yarmulkes on their heads and passed for diamond merchants themselves. Lily recalled thinking the robbers might just as easily have dressed as cops, but the cops would never advance that theory unless they had no choice.

"You were one of the robbers?" she asked.

He nodded. Didn't seem to be kidding.

"Then you should be rich. None of you were ever caught."

"All of us got away," Brad said, "but when the four of us split up, only three of us had diamonds."

"Your partners robbed you of the robbed diamonds?"

"Yes. I was stupid enough to give them the chance. That leaves me just about broke. Which is why I need Joan." He fixed her with that dreamy stare again. She felt it. "I'm being honest with you, Lily."

"That doesn't seem to be your pattern."

"It is when my back's to the wall, like it is now."

She finished buttoning her blouse, then bent over and reached for her shoes and slipped them onto her feet.

"You didn't say no, Lily."

"Since we're being honest with each other," she said, "I'm wondering, if I report to Joan that she's about to marry a saint, what's in it for me?"

"You get half."

"Of what?"

"Millions. Joan's not very careful with her financial records. Her first husband died five years ago and left her over four million dollars. It's grown since then."

"If you get half after the divorce, that's a million for me. All that just for giving Joan a favorable report about you?"

"Well, there's more. I want you to befriend Joan, keep building me up, make sure she doesn't do any more checking into my background. Right up to the marriage and beyond."

Lily was thinking ahead. "I guess part of my job would be to talk her out of a prenuptial agreement."

"Not necessarily," Brad said.

"Then what makes you think you'll walk away from the marriage with a couple of million dollars that you'll then split with me?"

"More like six million," he said, watching Lily closely now. Knowing it was the kind of money that shortened her breath.

"How six million?" she asked, thinking this is just the sort of stupid but simple plan that might work, only there has to be a catch because there always is.

He gave her his handsome smile. "The inheritance . . ."

"Uh-huh . . ."

"Plus the life insurance."

"Oh, Jesus!" Lily said.

––––––––

The wedding was a small one, with only a few family members and friends. Joan's old college friends were a snooty lot, but they seemed to accept Lily easily enough. It helped that Joan introduced her as "my very dearest friend."

The reception was at one of the best hotels near the marina and downtown Sarasota, less than half an hour's drive from Joan's luxurious home on Longboat Key. A portable dance floor had been set up, and there was a four-piece band playing softly enough that there could be conversation.

When Lily and Brad were dancing, Lily found herself feeling good in his arms. She resisted the temptation to press herself against his lean body in front of everyone. Instead she moved just close enough so she could whisper to him. "Mr. and Mrs. Brad Masters," she said. "Is that even your real name?"

"Real enough. Want some punch?"

"I want you," she said. "And as soon as possible after the honeymoon is over."

––––––––

During the next two weeks, Lily tried not to think about Brad and Joan in Hawaii.

The distance from Brad gave her time to do some reconsidering, and she drove to Miami and met with Willis in the bar at the Royal Roman Hotel. Like old times. It didn't feel good.

"I'm glad you're doing okay," Willis told her, leaning across the table and patting her wrist. He was wearing Levi's and a long-sleeved plaid shirt despite the eighty-degree temperature outside. "You said on the phone you needed a favor. If I can help you, I will."

"I need to know about a guy who calls himself Brad Masters. Whatever you can find out about him."

"That his real name?"

"I doubt it."

"I thought your new business was finding out things like that."

"This one's over my head, but maybe not yours." She paused, but she knew Willis would keep her secrets. He had in the past. "He was involved in that big New York diamond theft last year."

Willis's expression changed to one Lily had never seen before. It gave away nothing. "I've got lines to it," he told her. "I might be able to learn something for you. But it would help if I knew his real name. Or at least what he looked like."

"Here's his photo," Lily said, handing him a copy of a snapshot taken by Joan. A smiling Brad at the wheel of her vintage Jaguar convertible.

"Nice-looking guy," Willis said. He looked closely at her. "You involved in a romantic way?"

"'Fraid so."

Willis smiled and wagged a finger. "You of all people should know what they say about mixing business with pleasure."

"He's not in the detective business."

"I didn't mean the detective business. You're supposed to be smart about men, Lily."

"That's why I want to learn more about this one."

"This is a favor I'm glad to do," Willis said. "It might save you some heartache."

"To tell you the truth, I'm surprised I still have a heart."

He patted her wrist again. "I'm not."

———————

The day before Brad and Joan were due back from Hawaii, Willis phoned.

"Your Brad is Bradford Colter from Buffalo, New York," he said. "He's got a police record, but nothing violent if you don't count blowing the doors off safes. He's an expert at it. That's what he and the others did in New York, used plastique explosives to blow open safes so they could get at where the real value was in those shops. Did it in broad daylight when the sidewalks were crowded. The sounds of outside heavy construction in that block masked the noise of the explosions."

"Clever."

"The word is, if you're involved with this Brad guy, you can trust him. We're talking honor among thieves here, though, not necessarily honor in romance."

"Honor among thieves will do, Willis. Thanks."

"Trust is relative, Lily."

Lily told him she knew that. And she did. That's why she'd kept in her safety-deposit box the audio tape that matched the video Brad had destroyed that night in the hotel room. Though she was reassured about Brad, she decided to hold on to the tape.

After all, he was deceiving Joan.

———————

Lily met Brad and Joan at the airport the next day, kissed them both on the cheek, and welcomed them home.

The three of them went out to dinner that night at Sharkey's down the coast in Venice, and a glowing Joan hung all over Brad and couldn't stop talking about their time in Hawaii. Lily kept smiling and playing along, Brad's leg resting against hers beneath the table.

They didn't have a chance to be alone together, to make love, until almost a week later at the house on Longboat Key, in Joan and Brad's bedroom.

Brad made love to Lily in the controlled violent way she'd learned to enjoy. He was the only man she trusted, the only man she'd let out all the stops for in years. The intent way he looked at her while he drove himself into her again and again, when he released in her. And afterward, even as he rolled off her onto the other side of the bed. She'd seen enough of fantasy to know this was real. He wasn't like the other men. In his way, he loved her. His way was enough for her.

Exhausted, she lay back perspiring on Joan's pillow, listening to her own ragged breathing in counterpoint to Brad's.

She wasn't surprised when he chose this as the time to tell her how Joan was going to die.

"I'm an explosives expert," he began. "It's my specialty and you're going to have to trust me on that."

She lay quiet, staring at the ceiling and pretending this was news to her.

Brad continued: "I'm going to place in the gas tank of Joan's Jaguar a small detonating device that can be activated by a plastic timer beneath the seat. I've substituted some old wiring near the tank with the insulation worn off, so that it will look like electricity arced and ignited fumes from the tank. This is most likely to happen just before or during a thunderstorm. It will be assumed that lightning struck nearby, momentarily spiking the voltage and causing the arc."

The first question Lily asked was a practical one. "What happens to the timer?"

"It will melt and be unrecognizable. Likewise the detonator it-self. I know explosives, Lily, and I know cars. Trust me, this will look like an accident."

She rolled onto her side and looked into his eyes. "Are you re-ally that good at your specialty, Brad?"

"Let me show you," he said, and pulled her to him.

————

It was the time of year for storms in southwest Florida. They struck all around Sarasota, but not there. While the city lay dry in heat beneath low dark clouds, a tornado destroyed three houses in nearby Punta Gorda. Lily sat in the evenings with Joan and Brad on the verandah behind Joan's house and watched dis-tant chain lightning illuminating the sky and sipped margaritas and prayed for rain.

She was surprised one morning after spending the night at Brad and Joan's, as she often did, when Brad gave her a wicked look and a nod. Lily glanced outside. The sun was shining.

Joan came downstairs already dressed and carrying a small overnight case. "I'm driving over to North Palm Beach to visit an old college friend who just moved there. Moira Brent. Remem-ber her from the wedding?"

"I think so," Lily lied. She'd already prepared some coffee and buttered toast, just about the extent of her cooking skills. "Aren't you going to eat breakfast?" she asked, seeing Joan kiss Brad good-bye.

"Gonna skip it," Joan said. "I want to get on the road and beat the morning traffic. Got a long way to go."

Neither Brad nor Lily said anything as they watched her gulp down half a cup of coffee, then start for the door.

With a backward glance at Lily, Brad followed her outside.

Lily watched from the window as Brad opened the Jaguar's door for Joan, then bent down as if he'd dropped something, his body blocking Joan's view as he leaned into the car. Lily's heart accelerated as she realized he was setting the timer that would activate the detonator. She watched as he kissed Joan good-bye again, more passionately. Then he smiled and waved as she drove away. His head was bowed as he trudged back toward the house.

"Done," he said, when he was inside.

"It isn't raining," Lily pointed out.

"It is in south central Florida," Brad said. "The weather channel even has tornado warnings out. Joan's taking Highway 72 east and will be driving right through the center of the storm activity. I don't think we'll see my wife and your best friend again."

Lily walked over to stand directly in front of him, close to him. Her heart felt as if it were trying to escape from her chest. "How do you feel about that?"

"Elated," he said. "What are you feeling right now?"

"Turned on," she told him.

"It'd be better if you and I were in two different places an hour from now. That's another reason I chose this morning. I've got a job interview in forty-five minutes."

"A job interview," she said. "That's wonderful."

He kissed her, she judged even more passionately than he'd kissed Joan good-bye.

"What will you be doing while I'm gone?" he asked when they'd separated.

She smiled up at him. "Watching the clock."

———

At 10:06 A.M., two minutes before Joan's scheduled departure from the world, Lily was seated at the kitchen table sipping her fourth cup of coffee. All that coffee had been a mistake. She was nervous enough to scream.

She calmed herself by envisioning Joan in her Jaguar speeding along desolate Highway 72, probably with the radio on high volume. By now she'd be in the rain, would have the car's top up and the wipers scything across the windshield. But in less than a minute . . .

The jangling phone propelled Lily up out of her chair and almost did make her scream.

She lifted the receiver and said hello, trying to keep her voice level.

"Lily, it's me, Joan."

Lily almost dropped the phone. She kept her composure. "Are you in Palm Beach already?"

"No, I'm calling from my cell phone in the car."

Lily considered this. They'd be talking when the gas tank exploded, when Joan died. Despite herself, Lily felt a warm, tight knot in her stomach. The heat spread to her groin. It was terrible of her, she knew, but she was actually going to enjoy this. How many people had this kind of opportunity?

"I have something to confess, Lily. I hope you won't think too poorly of me when I do."

Not that it matters, Lily thought. "Why, go ahead, Joan. You can trust me not to turn on you."

"I'm a terrible person, always have been. I have what some people call a checkered past. Evil lives in me, Lily, and I have the police record of a confidence woman to prove it. There's enough money in the bank to pay rent for the house till the end of the month, then nothing. I fooled Brad into thinking I was wealthy so he'd marry me."

Lily sat back down, feeling light-headed now. Cold despite the warming morning.

"I hope you won't think too poorly of Brad, either. He's no more what he seems than I am, Lily. I've known from the beginning he was part of a gang of robbers who stole millions of dollars worth of diamonds in New York last year. He never told me he was rich, but because of the diamonds I assumed he had hidden assets. I only married him for his money, Lily."

Lily sat stunned, not knowing what to say. "Joan . . . Ah, Joan . . ."

"I hate to tell you this because you've been so sweet, but I haven't reformed, Lily. There's only one way to turn my marriage into money now, and that's to hand Brad over to the police for the reward. A consortium of diamond merchants has offered over a million dollars to anyone who can furnish information leading to the arrest of any of the thieves. Brad is in Sarasota now, three blocks away at a job interview. I can send the police directly to him. I know Brad will hate me. I hope you won't, Lily."

"Joan, don't call the police! Please!"

"I'm not going to, Lily. I didn't drive toward Palm Beach. I just drove around getting up my nerve to do this. I'm parked on Ringling Boulevard in Sarasota, right in front of police headquarters. When I hang up I'm going to walk inside and—"

"Joan!"

The receiver emitted what sounded like a loud animal growl, then the static of a disconnected line.

An instant after she slammed the receiver back in its cradle, Lily knew the questions that would be asked: Why had a car, parked with the engine off and miles from any electrical storm, suddenly exploded in front of police headquarters? What was actually known of its dead driver, Joan Marin-Masters? Of her new husband, Brad?

Of their good friend Lily?

The eventual answer to all those questions would be murder.

On numbed legs, Lily staggered outside to sit in the fresh air on the verandah. Her mind was whirling in tighter and tighter spirals, as if boring deep into a black future.

She'd figured right—she knew men. It was a woman who'd fooled her.

She couldn't catch her breath. In the direction of the mainland, she could see a dark plume of smoke in the clear blue sky over downtown Sarasota.

The breeze seemed to be carrying it her way.

Just Looking

Bill Pronzini

He hadn't had a woman in so long, he'd started carrying a picture of his right hand around in his wallet.

Everybody he told that to, the guys he worked with at Mossman Hardware, his buddies at the Starlite Tavern, thought it was a pretty funny line. He laughed right along with them. But at night, alone in his two-room apartment, he didn't think it was so funny anymore. Thing was, it was the plain damn truth. He'd only had a couple of women in his entire life—thirty-four years old and been laid just twice, both of those times with hookers. Last time had been over eight years ago. He was just too embarrassed to get undressed in front of some hard-shell whore in a lighted room, have her look at him naked and see the contempt and laughter in her eyes. Too painful, man.

The way he figured it now, he'd never have sex again unless he paid for it. Never get married, never have the kind of relationship other guys had with a woman. He was too butt-ugly. No getting away from that—he had mirrors in his apartment, he saw his reflection in store windows, he knew what he looked like. Big puffy body on little stubby legs, not much chin, mouth like a razor slash, knobby head with a patch of hair like moss growing on a tree stump. Somebody'd said that to him once, in the Starlite or someplace. "You know something, man? You got a head looks like moss growing on a fuckin' tree stump."

Most of the time it didn't bother him too much, being a toad and not having a woman. Most of the time he was a pretty happy guy. He liked his job at Mossman Hardware, he liked drinking and shooting pool with his buddies, he liked baseball (even if some of the players nowadays with their billion-dollar contracts were assholes), he liked bowling at Freedom Lanes and playing draw poker at Henson's Card Room and watching martial arts flicks on the tube and now and then reading a Louis L'Amour western if he was in the mood for a good book. And when he got horny, well, he had his collection of porn videos and he could go on the Net and surf through the porn sites. Looking was the next best thing to having, right? Just looking could be pretty damn good.

But sometimes, some nights, not having a woman really bothered him. Some nights he felt like busting down and bawling. Life sucked sometimes. When you had a face and a body like his, when you looked like you'd been whupped with an ugly stick, life really sucked sometimes.

He figured things would go on pretty much as they always had, the good and the bad, right up until he croaked. One day the same as another. Weekdays he went to work at the hardware store, knocked off at six, headed to the Starlite or Freedom Lanes or Henson's, went home and watched a video or fooled around online and then went to bed. Weekends he took in a ballgame, holed up in the Starlite, played poker, played pool, played with his computer, played with himself. Boring, sure, but he was used to it and mostly it suited him. He was better off than a lot of poor jobless schmucks living on the streets or on welfare or hooked on drugs, wasn't he?

Yeah. Sure he was.

Only then, all at once, everything changed.

Then he met Julie Brock.

Well, he didn't really meet her. More like he ran into her, almost. It was on a Saturday morning and he was in Safeway buying a couple of six-packs and some TV dinners and other stuff.

He pushed his cart around into the frozen food aisle, and there she was, not two feet away, so that he had to veer off to avoid slamming his cart into hers. As soon as he got a good look at her, it was like he'd been punched in the belly. He couldn't catch his breath, couldn't stop staring. He must've looked like one of those cartoon characters, Wile E. Coyote or Bugs Bunny, when they got surprised—tongue hanging loose, eyes bugged out so far it was like they were on the end of stalks.

She was a blonde. Not your ordinary blonde, not your Marilyn Monroe type. Sort of a tawny blonde, dark and light at the same time, he'd never seen a color like it. And tall, real tall, almost six feet, with perfect bare legs that went up and up and up. Nice little rack, nice tight ass. Oh, she was gorgeous, man, the sweetest piece of sweetmeat he'd ever feasted his eyes on. She knew it, too. Walked slow and lazy, like a cat, her head up and her nose up. Haughty. Sweet and haughty and twice as sexy in a pair of shorts and a blouse as any of the naked broads on the Net or humping in one of his porn flicks.

She didn't pay any attention to him, didn't even glance at him. She stopped pushing her cart and opened a freezer case and bent over to get something off one of the lower shelves so he had an even better view of her ass. He stood there staring until she moved on. Then he started pushing his cart after her. He couldn't stop looking, he couldn't just let her go away. He felt like he'd died and gone to heaven. He felt like . . . he didn't know *what* he felt like, except that he was all hot and cold inside and his johnson was half standing at attention in his shorts.

He followed her around the store, not real close so's she or anybody else would notice. He got in the same checkout line she did. He trailed her out to the parking lot, to a little red Miata. His own beat-up wheels were in the next row. He hustled over there and threw his bags in the backseat, and when she pulled out of the lot he was right behind her.

This is crazy, he thought after a few blocks. Me following a woman around, any woman, let alone a stone fox like her. But what the hell, it wasn't like he was a pervert or anything. He didn't mean her any harm. All he was doing was *looking*.

So he kept on following her, all the way home. And it turned out she lived in a bungalow on Acacia Street, five blocks from his apartment. He parked across the street and watched her carry her groceries inside, and he had a big urge to go over there, offer to help so he could see her again up close. But he didn't give in to it because he knew what'd happen if he did. She'd take one look at him and tell him to bugger off. She probably had a dozen handsome guys sniffing after her every day, she might even be married or living with somebody. She wouldn't want anything to do with a butt-ugly toad with a head that looked like moss growing on a fuckin' tree stump.

She took the last grocery bag into the bungalow and didn't come out again. He stayed put for a while, but he couldn't keep on sitting there all day waiting for another look. That was just plain stupid. So he drove on to his apartment and put his groceries away and sat down in his recliner. He'd planned to go to a ballgame today, Giants were playing the Dodgers, but now he didn't feel like it. Didn't feel like bowling or going to the Starlite or doing anything else he liked to do on Saturdays.

He couldn't stop thinking about the blonde. It was like she was lodged inside his head, big as life, that tawny light-and-dark hair and that gorgeous face and that hard body.

Oh, that fine, hard body!

———

Sunday morning he drove over to Acacia Street again. He'd dreamed about her that night, damn near a wet dream, and woke up with her, and wanted to see her again in the flesh so bad he couldn't think about anything else.

Damn, though—her Miata wasn't in the driveway. He parked and waited a half hour or so, but she didn't come home. He got tired of just sitting and walked over in front of her place, casual, like a guy out for a Sunday stroll. Her bungalow was small, painted a bright blue with white trim, trees and bushes growing thick along both sides. When he squinted down the driveway he could see a jungly backyard, too—part of a lawn, more trees, some tall oleanders. He knew this neighborhood almost as well as his own and he was pretty sure the yard butted up close to Miller Creek.

Back in his car, he drove around the block. Two blocks, matter of fact, because what was behind her place was a grammar school. Nobody was at the school today except some kids playing basketball on the courts behind the classrooms. He walked past them, across a soccer field and another acre or so of lawn. A chainlink fence made up the far boundary. On the other side of that was Miller Creek, and on the other side of the creek was the blue bungalow. He could see part of its ass end when he got to the fence, but the rest was hidden by the trees and oleanders.

Another thing he could see was that it was a short distance down the bank, across the mostly dry creekbed, and up the other bank into those bushes. Be easy enough to find your way in the dark if you were careful. You wouldn't need to climb the fence, either. There was a gate about twenty yards away. Why they'd put a gate in the fence here was anybody's guess, but there it was. The padlock on it was an old Schindler. He grinned when he saw that. Hell, with one of the passkeys they had at Mossman Hardware, you could open that puppy up in about two seconds flat.

———

Eight o'clock Monday morning, he was back across the street from the blue bungalow. He didn't have to be at work until ten and he was hoping the blonde would leave for whatever job she had long before that. Sure enough, she came out at about eight-twenty. All dressed up in a tan suit, that tawny blonde hair piled high on top of her head. Sweetmeat for a treat!

He followed her red Miata downtown. She stopped for coffee and a doughnut or something at a bakery on Fourth and then she went to the Merchants' Exchange Bank on Hollowell. The bank wasn't open yet, but somebody let her in and she didn't come out again. So that had to be where she worked.

He took another ride to the bank on his lunch hour, and this time he went inside. He saw her right away. She wasn't a teller—she had her own desk and she was tapping away on a computer, her lower lip caught between her teeth. He tried not to stare too hard as he walked by. There was one of those little nameplates on her desk and that was how he found out her name was Julie Brock.

————

Over the next week he found out some more things about her, just by hanging around the bank and her neighborhood. Turned out she wasn't married or living with anybody. She did have a boyfriend, handsome football player type who drove a fuckin' Mercedes. The boyfriend stayed late at her bungalow a couple of times, but not the whole night. Which maybe meant *he* was married, or maybe it didn't mean anything at all. Guy didn't come over every night, either, only on Friday and Saturday. During the week, she turned out her lights and hit the sack before eleven. Probably because she had to get up early for her job.

The following Monday night, he left his apartment a little before ten and drove to the grammar school. He made sure nobody was around before he went into the schoolyard, across to the chainlink fence. He was scared and excited, both. He knew he was taking a real big risk, he'd had a lot of conversations with himself about that, but he hadn't been able to talk himself out of it. Crazy, sure, but it was the only way he'd ever get to see her alone, up close and personal.

He slipped through the gate, picked his way across the creek and up into her yard without making enough noise to carry. The rear windows and back entrance were dark, but he found a lighted window on the far side. The curtains were open and the room inside was plain as day. Oh, man, it was her bedroom! She wasn't in there, but the covers on the bed were turned down and more light was showing behind a partly open door in the far wall.

He stepped into a patch of tree shadow, his mouth dry and metal-tasting. It was a perfect spot for looking, only about twenty-five feet of lawn between him and the window. He waited there, so damn excited he had trouble catching his breath.

And then he heard the sound of a toilet flushing and she walked out of the bathroom, and all she was wearing was a bra and panties. Bug-eyed, he watched her move around here and there, arranging clothes and stuff. And then she started doing a bunch of exercises, bending over, stretching, jumping, twisting, all that fine glistening flesh shaking and quivering.

He didn't think the show could get any better, but pretty soon it did. As soon as she stopped exercising, she reached up behind her and unhooked her bra and let it fall. A couple of seconds later she was out of her panties, too. Natural blonde! He couldn't believe he was seeing her like that, all of her, naked. Hot and sweaty and naked, right there in front of him, rubbing her hands under her breasts and down over her hips . . .

Man, oh, man, oh man oh man oh man ohmanohmanohman-ohmanohman—oh!

———

He kept going back there. After that show the first night, he wouldn't've stayed away for a million bucks. Didn't go Friday or Saturday, but most every other night. Once the boyfriend was there even though it wasn't the weekend, the two together in the sack, but the only light was in the bathroom and he couldn't see much of what they were doing. Another time she had the curtains closed for some damn reason. The rest of the nights it was showtime. Into the bedroom she'd come in bra and panties, fuss around, do those exercises for about ten minutes, get naked, rub up that hot sweaty body for a minute or so, then go take a shower and get into bed and shut off the light. Man, it was better than any video he'd ever seen, porn or otherwise.

Then one night, a real warm night, she had the bedroom window open for some air. She came out and did her number, and he must've shifted around and made a noise or something because all of a sudden she quit exercizing and moved to the window and stood peering out. He was pretty sure she couldn't see him out in the dark, but he froze anyway. She stood staring for a few seconds and then, quick, she shut the window and went and turned out the light before she got into bed.

He should've taken that as a warning and not gone back for a while. But he didn't. He went back the next night at the same time.

And that was his big mistake.

————

The lights were on in her bedroom, same as usual, but he didn't see her as he slipped through the oleanders to his ringside spot. He figured she was still in the bathroom, which was always a relief because a time or two he'd got there a little late and missed part of the show. He eased forward into the patch of tree shadow, licking his lips.

And all of a sudden a bright beam of light hit him square in the eyes and a voice, her voice, said hard and angry, "You dirty damn pervert!"

He almost jumped out of his skin. Panic surged in him and

he'd've taken off, run like the fuckin' wind if she hadn't said, "Stand right there—I have a gun, I'll shoot if you move."

He froze. Heard himself say, "A gun?" in a voice like a frog croaking.

"That's right, and I know how to use it. You don't think I'd be out here waiting for you unarmed, do you?"

"Listen, I'm sorry, Julie, I didn't mean nothing—"

"Oh, so you know my name. Well, I know *you*, too, you fat creep, I've seen you before. What were you planning to do? Sneak in some night and rape me?"

"No! Jesus, no, I never would've done nothing like that, I never would've hurt you . . ."

"You just like to watch, is that it? Well, your Peeping Tom days are over right now."

"What . . . what're you gonna do?"

"Call the police, that's what I'm going to do."

"No, wait, you can't—"

"Can't I? You just watch me. Go on, get moving."

"Moving? Where?"

"Into the house, where do you think?"

He didn't want to go into the house. He still wanted to run, but what good would that do? She could identify him, she'd sic the cops on him anyway—

"Move, I said. If you don't do what I say, if you try anything, I'll shoot you. I mean it, I will."

For a few seconds more it was like he was paralyzed. Then he wasn't anymore, his legs were moving and taking him out onto the lawn. The flashlight glare slid out of his eyes—she was over on the other side of the tree—but he was still half blind. He stumbled and heard somebody make a little moaning sound . . . him, it came out of *him*. She told him to walk around to the back door and he did that. She told him to open it and go inside and he did that, too.

Kitchen. He stood there blinking, trying to focus, so scared he was shaking all over. She came in behind him, looped around to one of those breakfast bar counters a few feet away. She had a gun, all right. Little silver automatic that caught the light and seemed to be winking at him.

"Sit down at the table over there," she said.

Still blinking, he started over to the table. Then he stopped and swung his head toward her again. Now she had a cordless phone in her other hand. Her eyes shifted back and forth between him and the phone, her face all scrunched up and hot-eyed, and she wasn't the most beautiful woman he'd ever seen anymore, she wasn't even pretty, she was a hag as ugly as he was getting ready to have him arrested, put in prison—

He lunged at her. Didn't think about what he was doing, just did it. She swung the gun up and squeezed the trigger point blank. She'd've killed him sure, shot him down like a dog, except that the little automatic must've jammed, it didn't go off, and in the next second he was on her.

He knocked the fuckin' gun out of her hand, yanked the phone away from her. She opened up her mouth to scream. He jammed his hand over it, dragged her body in tight against his. Even then, even after she'd tried to blow his brains out, he didn't have any idea of hurting her, only wanted to keep her from yelling somehow so he could get away. But she fought and squirmed, kicking his shins, clawing his arm, it was like he had hold of a wildcat. She got one arm all the way loose and those long nails slashed up and ripped furrows in his neck. That hurt, really hurt. Made him mad and kind of wild himself. He couldn't hold her, and she twisted her body and pulled loose and tried to break his balls with her knee.

The next thing he knew he was hitting her with the phone. Hitting her, hitting her, hitting her until she quit making noises and quit fighting and fell down on the floor on her back. There was blood all over her face and head and her eyes were wide open with a lot of the white showing. He saw that and he wasn't wild anymore. He stared at her, stared at the blood, stared at the bloody phone in his hand. He made the same kind of sound he'd made outside and dropped the phone and went down on one knee beside her. Picked up one of her wrists—limp, no pulse—and put his fingers against her neck and didn't feel any pulse there, either.

Dead!

Then he ran. Ran like there was a pack of junkyard dogs on his heels. Out of the kitchen, across the yard, through the bushes, across the creek, through the fence gate, across the schoolyard and out to where he'd parked his wheels. Not caring how much noise he made or if anybody saw him, not caring about anything except getting far away from there.

He didn't remember driving home. He was running and then he was at the car and then he was in his apartment putting on the dead bolt and the chain lock. He was shaking so hard he could hear a clicking sound, his teeth knocking together or maybe the bones rattling inside his skin. When he put on the light he saw blood on his hands, on his shirt and jacket. He ripped all his clothes off and got into the shower and scrubbed and scrubbed, but he couldn't make himself feel clean. He couldn't get warm, either, not even lying in bed with the electric blanket turned all the way up.

He lay there in the dark, his head full of pictures of her lying on her kitchen floor all bloody and dead. But it wasn't his fault. She'd tried to kill him, hadn't she? Clawed him, tried to break his balls? He hadn't wanted to hurt her—she'd made him do it in self-defense. Her fault, not his. Hers, hers, hers!

He kept listening for the doorbell. Waiting for the cops to come. He'd tell them it wasn't his fault, but he knew they'd take him to jail anyway.

Only the cops didn't came. He lay wide awake the whole night, waiting, and in the morning he was amazed he was still alone.

He called up his boss, Mr. Mossman, and said he was sick, he wouldn't be in today. Then he put on his robe and sat in his recliner with the TV going for noise and waited for the cops to show up.

All day he sat there and still no cops.

At six o'clock he switched over to the news and pretty soon he heard her name, saw her picture flash on the screen. Julie Brock, twenty-seven, found dead in her rented bungalow on Acacia Street, bludgeoned to death with a cordless phone. Neighbors had heard noises, one of them saw a man running away but couldn't describe him because it'd been too dark. The TV guy said the police were working on several leads and expected to make an arrest soon. Maybe that was the truth and maybe it wasn't. All he could do was sit scared, wait scared to find out.

He waited four whole days, there in the apartment the whole time. Told Mr. Mossman he had the flu and Mr. Mossman said take care of himself, get plenty of rest, drink plenty of liquids. He drank plenty of liquids, all right. Beer, wine, scotch, every kind of alcohol he had in the place. Watched TV, drank, threw up most of what he ate, and waited.

The cops never did show up.

On the fifth day he wasn't so scared anymore. On the sixth day he was hardly scared at all and he went out for the first time to buy some more beer and booze. On the seventh day he knew they weren't going to come and arrest him, not ever. He couldn't say how he knew that, he just did.

The furrows on his neck were mostly healed by then, but he put on a high-necked shirt and buttoned the top button to make sure the marks didn't show. Then he went back to work. Mr.

Mossman said it was good to have him back. That night, when he went to the Starlite Tavern, his buddies said the same thing and bought him a couple of rounds of drinks and he won eight bucks shooting pool.

Things settled down to normal again. He worked and went to the Starlite and Freedom Lanes and Henson's Card Room, the same as he used to, and the whole crazy thing with Julie Brock faded and faded until he wasn't thinking about her at all anymore. It was as if none of it ever happened. Not just that last night in her bungalow—all the nights before it, the whole crazy business. He couldn't even remember what she looked like.

A lot more time passed, and his life was just the way it'd been before, good sometimes, boring sometimes, lonely sometimes. And then one day he was working behind the counter at the hardware store and he looked up and this babe was standing there. A redhead—oh, man, the most gorgeous redhead he'd ever seen. His eyes bugged out like they were on stalks. Young, slim, that red hair like fire around her head, white skin smooth as cream, a great rack poking out the front of her sweater, her mouth big and soft and smiling at him. He stared and stared, but she didn't stop smiling. Real friendly type, wanted to buy a space heater and some other stuff for her new apartment.

He showed her around, helped her pick out the best items, wrote up her order. She wanted to know could she have it delivered, and he said sure, you bet, and she gave him her address along with her credit card. He watched her walk out, the way her ass swung under her green skirt, and his mouth was dry and he felt all hot and cold inside and his johnson was having fits in his shorts.

He couldn't stop thinking about her all day. She was the most beautiful, exciting woman he'd ever feasted his eyes on. Before he got off work he packed up her order so he could deliver it himself, personally. He had to see her again, see where she lived. There wasn't any harm in that, was there?

Just looking?

Desire in the First Degree

Mary Kay Lane and Wendi Lee

Bud hadn't thought I was smart enough to get on a jury, but here I was, one of twelve people sitting in judgment of a man accused of first-degree murder. It was a big responsibility, but I welcomed it.

Normally I spend all day in the trailer waiting for Bud to come home from work at the feed plant. He didn't want me to have a job or friends—he wanted me to take care of him only. So I spent most of my days reading romance and true crime— books about people with more exciting lives than mine, people with passion.

Bud didn't like the idea of me being away from home, but he couldn't get me out of jury duty. The night before, he petted my long brown hair like I was a dog and said, "They don't need you. What they need is people with brains and opinions. No offense."

"None taken," I lied.

I quit thinking about Bud when a door opened and a guard led the defendant into the courtroom.

What can I say about him except that the moment I saw him, I felt like all my bones had dissolved in my flesh? I felt like my heart had burst open and my blood was gushing uninhibited throughout my body. He wasn't handsome, not like Bud is, but I still could hardly take my eyes off him.

He towered over the bailiff by at least a foot. And he was too thin, his face long and pale, his long, dark hair curled about his ears and collar. His nose was straight and strong. The handcuffs looked useless around his slender wrists. His hands were so soft and elegant that I couldn't imagine how he could have allegedly committed such a gruesome murder.

But what struck me most were his eyes—they were so dark as to be almost black—and they were unafraid. His lips curved into a half smile as he looked each of us in the eye. I could have sworn when our eyes met, he lingered slightly longer.

The judge began to instruct us about jury duty, but no one was paying attention until he said, "As you are aware, there is anticipated to be a tremendous amount of media coverage of this case. Because the victim was a well-known member of our community, and because the crime was particularly heinous, the jury is to be sequestered until a verdict is read."

The other jurors moaned and complained, but I quietly let out a sigh of relief.

––––––––

We were allowed to call someone to bring what we needed to stay several nights in the Mark Twain Hotel. I called Bud at work and left a message on his voice mail explaining that I couldn't be home for a while. I asked him to bring me a nightgown, a toothbrush, and some changes of clothes. I told him I loved him.

I never heard from him and he didn't bring me my things.

––––––––

I told myself that being chosen to sit on a jury was an honor. I had been trusted enough to decide the fate of a man. I had been viewed as intelligent enough to distinguish fact from fiction, truth from lies. And I tried to keep that in mind every day we met in the courtroom. Yes, this could be the defining moment of my life . . . the part I would look back on with pride. I had not let myself down, or my fellow jurors, or my country.

It sounded very grand, this mantra I recited to myself every morning. But there was one problem: Ethan Beall.

The first time I had seen him, I felt like I was cresting the hill of a roller coaster, just before being hurtled downward at a tremendous speed. The second time I saw him was like that, too. And the third and the fourth and the fifth. The only difference in my reaction to him was that the hill each time was higher and steeper.

Was I fascinated by the man or his crime? Were the two inseparable? I had listened as the prosecutor told the jury that the defendant's lover had been the wife of a prominent doctor. Dr. Unterreiner had been the head of neurology at the State University. His wife, Jennifer, who was not allowed to testify because of conflicts with her own trial, had asked Ethan Beall to kill her husband, who had refused to divorce her. Ethan had agreed.

That alone fascinated me. To kill for love? To be so in love that you would kill another person? Sure, I loved Bud—at least I thought I did—but I wouldn't kill for him.

Jennifer had told Ethan—allegedly told—that if her husband were dead they would run away together to someplace exotic, like Mexico.

Ethan pushed the doctor out his office window into a courtyard below. Only, despite numerous broken bones, Dr. Unterreiner survived the fall. In a panic, Jennifer urged Ethan to finish him off and dismember the body for disposal. Ethan went outside and cut off his head with an antique surgical saw from the doctor's office. The medical examiner testified that Dr. Unterreiner was likely still alive when the decapitation occurred.

When Ethan spied campus security nearby, he ran and would have escaped if it had not been for Jennifer, who turned Ethan in to save her own skin. She cried that Ethan had been stalking her for months, that he had killed her husband in a fit of jealousy.

I didn't believe that for a minute.

Mr. Gunderson, the defense attorney, was very good at confusing us, making Ethan look like the victim. But the prosecutor, a sleek blonde, was very good at reminding us who took a saw to a man's neck and splattered his blood all over campus. She waved the saw in front of us. There were bits of dried blood and hair and other stuff on it. I had to look away. I looked at Ethan instead—his expression was inscrutable.

I know the prosecutor was trying to get members of the jury to feel horrified by the act of killing someone in such a gruesome manner, but all I could think of when I looked at Ethan was, "You loved her that much?"

————

We spent evenings in our separate hotel rooms, but we were allowed to take dinner together. A guard was posted in the room to make sure we didn't talk about the trial.

Still, I had already figured out who stood where regarding the trial. It was clear to me that the other jurors, for their various reasons, wanted to convict Ethan, and that some of them would vote for the death penalty if they could.

When we met in the courtroom every day, the hate and disgust emanating from eleven of the twelve jurors when Ethan walked into the courtroom was almost as palpable and suffocating as the sensation I got when I looked at him.

Yes, and he at me.

————

There were three other women jurors—Jane, a mother and housewife who acted like jury duty was a paid vacation from her two hellions, Jared and Josh; eighty-six-year-old, blue-haired Millie who muttered the Hail Mary every time Ethan Beall walked into the courtroom; and a fifty-two-year-old divorcee named Nancy who chewed gum and snapped it between her too-red lips. Nancy read romance novels. During the trial. And when she wasn't doing that, she was making eyes at the defense attorney.

One night during dinner, the guard took a long bathroom break and we finally broke the cardinal rule of not talking about the trial and the defendant.

"I can't stand to look at him," Jane said. "He gives me the creeps. Looks like a living corpse."

"You mean a walking corpse," I said. "Living corpse is an oxymoron."

"You bet he's a moron," Nancy said. "Did you see his reaction when that lawyer showed a picture of the body?"

"You mean body parts," Jane said.

"Whatever." Nancy waved a manicured hand, blood-red nails making red streaks in the air. "Anyway, I looked at him and . . . nothing. He didn't even blink. There were people puking in the back of the room and he sat there like he was watching the Home Shopping Club."

"That doesn't mean anything," I said, surprising myself. Maybe being away from Bud was making me braver, more inclined to speak my mind.

Three heads swiveled my way. Nancy raised her perfectly arched eyebrows. Jane frowned disapprovingly. Millie began to pray, her thin dry lips moving rapidly.

"I'm just saying, we can't be too quick to judge."

"Are you insane?" Nancy asked, her voice going up a notch or two. "If you think there's any way he can be innocent, you're crazier than *he* is."

"I'm just trying to keep an open mind," I said. "I think we all should."

"Do you now?" Jane asked, giving me a withering look. "I suppose you also think we should invite him to tea after the trial. And please rape us and chop off our heads!"

"Girls, girls," Millie said. "Lord knows there is enough vulgarity in the world without it coming from the mouths of ladies. We are all here for the same purpose—to see that justice is done. Danielle has led a quiet and sheltered life, and I'm sure she will come to the same conclusion we all have by the end of the trial."

Millie peered over her glasses at me and suddenly I felt like I was on trial.

"What . . . what do you know about me?"

"I remember the circumstances that led to the deaths of your mother and sister."

I swallowed hard.

Jane put on a concerned face. "What happened?"

Millie answered as if I suddenly wasn't there. "Danielle's mother and sister were killed in a fire. A neighbor, Bud Brinkman, was able to save only Danielle."

It had been a horrible night. I still lost sleep thinking about waking up to acrid smoke in my nostrils, stinging my eyes, blinding me. I still heard Stephie, my ten-year-old sister, crying and coughing, calling for me. I had tried to break the small window in our shared bedroom, but I was too weak from smoke inhalation. The window had been painted over years ago and it wouldn't open. I crawled on the floor, found Stephie, and dragged her over to the window. I passed out before I could give the window another try.

The next thing I knew, I was out on the lawn, the trailer a burned mass of twisted metal and wreckage. I was lying in Bud's arms and he was gently brushing hair away from my face. He visited me every day in the hospital while I recovered and asked me to marry him a month later.

Ever since then, I had grown my hair. Bud had forbidden me

to cut it, actually. It seemed a small concession to make for a man who had saved my life. It now reached down past my knees. Bud had a thing for hair—he liked to be wrapped up in it when we made love.

"I knew Bud when he was just a lad," Millie was saying. "I taught fifth grade and he was one of my students." Her eyes glinted as she leaned forward and added, "Do you want to know something interesting about Bud?"

I knew I'd regret asking, but I did anyway. "What?"

"He liked to play with fire when he was a boy. I caught him one day on the playground, setting fire to a pile of garbage. I boxed his ears and sent him home. But I don't think my intervention did much good. I heard there was a bit of trouble when he was in middle school as well, but I thought he'd grow out of it."

I felt like I was going to pass out. Is this what Bud meant by me not being smart enough? After all the reading I did, I still don't know anything about people? After all these years, I'd never figured out that it was him? Was that the real reason he cut me off from the world?

I found myself shaking my head in disgust at my own stupidity, but Millie misunderstood. She thought I was in denial.

She looked at me slyly. "Don't you think it was awfully convenient that he was there to save you, but didn't get your sister out as well?"

Amid the murmurs of Nancy and Jane, I excused myself and went to bed. I lay with a book in front of me but couldn't read.

For years Bud had made me feel like I was the lucky one. Now I didn't feel so lucky.

In the morning, there was a letter for me at the front desk. I thought at first it might be from Bud. I hadn't talked to him in

three days, since the trial began. But when I tore open the envelope, I knew immediately it wasn't from him. Bud's handwriting
looks like a nine-year-old's. This handwriting was tiny and neat
with a few flourishes like the swooping D in Danielle.

Danielle,
I know that you defended me. Thank you. Do not mention
this note to anyone. In fact, it would be in our best interests if
you destroyed it at once. I'm sure you realize how grave the
situation would be for me if anyone discovered I had contacted
you. You can imagine I've had difficulties finding people I can
trust, and my heart is less aggrieved knowing I may have an
ally after all.

E.

Were there words spoken that day at the trial? Were there ar-
guments? Witnesses? Evidence? I cannot remember. I only remember Ethan, feeling his presence, feeling his need. I marveled
at how composed he remained under such scrutiny. How he
stood aloof from the hateful glares of others. How strong he was.
How beautiful. How in need. He had been hurt deeply by Jennifer's betrayal. Any idiot should be able to see that. And, God,
how my heart went out to him. He had committed a horrible
crime in the name of love, and then had been betrayed. Which
was worse?

Even before receiving his note, I had known what he needed
more than a prison sentence. He needed compassion. He
needed to be shown that a woman can love and love well and be
devoted. He needed me.

I imagined what our first meeting would be like. The way he
would trace my cheekbones with his long, tapered fingers. The
way he would tilt my head as his soft lips met mine. The way his
body would feel on mine.

The gavel pounded. A recess for lunch. I was startled and a little disappointed. I would miss Ethan while we were gone.

I walked with the others to the cafeteria and filled my tray with food I wouldn't eat. I didn't quite get to the table when I felt a rough hand on my elbow. It yanked me around so that the food went flying.

Bud. He hadn't shaved and he looked like he'd lost weight. His hair was a mess and his eyes were bleary.

"I need you back home, Danni. Now." His voice was thick, hard to understand.

The sight of him filled me with disgust and rage. Before me was a sick man, a murderer, much more ruthless than Ethan because Bud killed out of selfishness.

"Bud," I said in a low voice, "I'm just doing what I have to do. By the law. I can't come home till it's over. Don't make a scene." Too late. I was aware of the stares of every other person in the room.

"Please come home. We can tell the judge that this was all a misunderstanding."

"You can't make me quit, Bud. You're not above the law."

"God, this doesn't even sound like you. Don't you miss me, Danni?"

Miss him? I tried not to smile. I should be flattered that he needed me more than he'd ever admitted before. But his need was scary. I compared Bud's need to Ethan's—Ethan was in control, Bud was out of control. I saw that Bud's need for me had been so overwhelming that he had set fire to the trailer, killing my mother and Stephie so that he could rescue me. So that he'd be my only family. So that I'd be grateful to him forever. Did I miss him? I suppose I missed him—like I would miss a wart that I'd removed.

I kept my voice low and hissed, "Frankly, yes, I missed you the other day when I needed fresh clothes."

His eyes softened and he reached out to touch me. I steeled myself. "See how much you need me? You can't even get dressed properly without me. They're eating you alive, aren't they?"

"I'm doing okay. And it's not that bad washing my underwear in the sink."

"I just want you to come home. And then we'll make some changes, so this doesn't happen again."

I swallowed. "Changes?"

"I can't have you being away from home. You need to be there. With me."

"What for? I don't do anything there."

"What do you need to do? Don't you have everything you need?"

Everything, I thought, except a life, love, passion, dreams, a future.

"No. Not anymore. I thought I did, but I don't now."

Bud lashed out, knocking over a plastic chair. I winced. Out of the corner of my eye, I saw a uniformed police officer heading our way.

His voice rose a notch. "Damn it, Danni! I saved your god-damn *life*! And for what? To be treated like *shit*? You ungrateful bitch."

"Bud, listen—" I was going to try to calm him, tell him that he was my knight in shining armor. I also wanted to tell him that it was time for me to try to save my own life. But I didn't get the chance.

"I should have let you burn," he hissed as the officer grabbed him from behind and escorted him from the building.

He couldn't have said anything more perfect—it burned the last bit of love for him out of me.

I hung my head and was afraid to look up. But when I did, I saw Ethan, watching me from out in the hall, his eyes full of compassion.

That night, there was another note for me at the front desk. My fingers stumbled over the envelope and I had trouble getting a grip.

Danielle,

I do not hate Jennifer. Does that surprise you? I do not think of her fondly, or at all, but I do not hate her. For she gave to me a gift that I intend to give to you. I know you need me. I felt your despair. You will only know life when you know what it's like to want someone so badly, you are willing to do anything for that person. I am willing to do anything for you, Danielle.

E.

I do not believe I heard a single word that was said at the trial the next day. I could only think of the letter, which I had, of course, destroyed after memorizing it. When Ethan walked into the courtroom and his eyes met mine, I felt at the same time such a hollowness and fullness in my heart, I could feel or hear nothing else. It was as if, when he walked into the room, my life until that moment . . . my life with Mother and Stephie, my life with Bud . . . was drained away and refilled with Ethan. And though we were separated by forty feet, I could feel his breath, I knew that his black hair would feel like silk beneath my fingers, I could almost smell his scrubbed, almost sterile aroma. I knew the muscles beneath his skin would be wiry and strong, his belly flat, his hips narrow.

And even though I did not yet know what made Ethan write to me, I was beginning to understand why he had killed Dr. Unterreiner. I was beginning to understand what people do when they are truly in love.

Even if Jennifer had double-crossed Ethan, it made him no

less guilty. But it did make him less responsible. For who can be responsible for anything when he or she is so in love?

I did not listen, but I watched carefully. I watched Ethan as he wrote on the yellow legal pad of Mr. Gunderson. I knew in my heart, even though he did not look my way, that the letter was to me. I could hear the sound of his pen scratching on the paper, when I couldn't even hear the words of the lawyers, the witnesses.

> *Danielle,*
>
> *Did your heart beat faster when you saw me? Mine did. I can't stop thinking about you. I can tell by your eyes that you are the only person on the jury with any compassion . . . any passion, at all. I feel safe when I think of you and I know I will never have the need to explain myself to you. I think you understand better than anyone. Better than myself, perhaps.*
>
> *I hope I have not frightened you. I long each moment for a word in return. Simply give a note, if you are so inclined, to the messenger who delivers these to you. He has been well paid for his silence by my attorney and myself and is trustworthy.*
>
> *E.*

I ran my finger over the letters that he printed so meticulously. I imagined his long, graceful fingers doing such intricate work.

"Danielle!"

I looked up to see Nancy approaching. I slipped the letter into my purse.

"I don't know how to put this, Danielle, so I'm going to come right out with it."

I knew what was coming and I didn't care. I had more important things on my mind.

"The other jurors think that you're thinking of voting 'not guilty.'"

"I don't think we should talk about that now. We haven't received our instructions from the judge."

"We don't need instructions. We know what to do. At least most of us do. As soon as it's over, you can go back home where you belong. We all can."

I frowned, thinking her words sounded fatalistic and horrible. "Listen, Nancy. I know why you all want to get this over with. You have to wait till the trial's over before you can start hitting on the defense attorney. Jane is having an identity crisis without her kids around to tell her who she is. And Millie wants to get back to her church so she can pray for my soul. This is not about concern for me, but for yourselves."

Nancy's face turned red. She turned abruptly to the elevator where she jabbed the button so hard she broke a nail. I smiled and sat down in an overly soft chair to compose my own note and wait for the messenger.

————

The next day the defense rested its case.

————

"Guilty. Guilty. Guilty. Guilty. Guilty. Guilty. Guilty. Guilty. Guilty. Guilty. Guilty. Not guilty."

Four heavy sighs. Three hands banged on the table. One Hail Mary. And three cuss words.

"Goddamn it, Danielle," said Lurvy Ossian, the foreman. "You going to keep us here all night?"

"My responsibility is not to you."

"You're goddamn right it ain't. It's to the rest of society. You want to let that faggot psychopath out on the streets?"

"I do not believe Mr. Beall is a homosexual or a psychopath. If anyone is psychotic, it's Jennifer Unterreiner—"

"She's not on trial here! *He* is. There is no doubt he killed Dr. Unterreiner. Do you agree?"

"Yes, but I don't believe he was responsible for his actions. He was under Jennifer's influence. She exploited his love for her. Have you ever been in love, Mr. Ossian?"

"I love my wife, but I wouldn't kill someone just because she says to."

"Then maybe you don't love her enough."

"Don't judge me and my wife. We're not on trial here, either."

"I'm just saying that if you haven't felt about a woman like Ethan—Mr. Beall—felt about Jennifer, you can't possibly know what he was thinking, what his intentions were, if he even knew what he was doing. I've a feeling a love that powerful can overwhelm the senses. Even common sense. So do we convict a man for being in love?"

Mr. Ossian stared at me like I had just sprouted horns and a long pointy red tail—as did the other ten jurors.

I shrugged. "I'm sorry if this is all an inconvenience for you, but a man's life is at stake and I can't take it lightly even if it means I have to miss tonight's rerun of *Walker, Texas Ranger*."

He stood up and pressed his bulbous nose close to my face. "We're finished, Ms. Brinkman. I've had enough of your insults."

I took a deep breath and stood up as well, staring him in the eye. "And I've had enough of your ignorance and intolerance. Call the bailiff."

————

Hung jury.

I had done it. For the first time in my life I stuck up for myself. I saved a life. Maybe two.

I couldn't look at Ethan when the judge read the verdict. But

I felt his eyes on me, almost as if they were a source of heat, penetrating my thin dress, my skin, my heart, my *soul*.

I left the courthouse and fought my way through the throng of reporters. They lined the courthouse steps and thrust microphones in my face. I walked as quickly as I could, pushing the microphones out of my way as if they were the dangling branches of a bush. I noticed, however, that Lurvy Ossian, red in the face, was talking animatedly to a group of reporters.

I went back to the hotel, not sure why—I had nothing there—but also unsure of where else to go. I had no money, no clothes, no friends.

I entered my room and lay down on the bed. I turned on the TV to block out my own thoughts and fell asleep.

I woke an hour later to a soft knock on my door. It wasn't an urgent sound the way I imagined Bud would knock. I slid off the bed, stretched, and went to open the door. A hand shot out from the opening and grabbed my wrist.

Ethan.

He stepped inside, still holding my wrist in his impossibly cool hand. His eyes locked with mine. I couldn't look away from the depth of them. Up close, I could see they were not black, but the deepest blue I had ever seen. My breathing grew shallow as though there were a weight on my chest, and my legs felt weak. He pulled gently on my wrist. I took a step toward him and my body melted into his.

Though I could hardly catch a breath, I whispered, "How did you . . . ?"

He put a finger to my lips. "I have a lot of money, Danielle, did you know that?"

I shook my head.

"And there are a lot of corrupt people in this town."

"That, I knew," I said.

"They are easily blinded."

"Do you have to go back?" To prison, I meant.

He shrugged. "Not if I can help it."

"Won't they come looking for you?"

He brought his face close to mine. His breath, too, was shallow. His lips touched mine, then moved down to my neck, my chest, touching lightly, feathery. I shuddered. He pulled the shoulder of my dress down, exposing one breast to the cool night air. I longed to feel him take me into his mouth. My nipples ached for him.

He stopped there, cupping one breast in his hand, the other hand in my hair. He kissed me again, back up my neck, flicking his tongue gently in and out. When he reached my mouth, he kissed me tenderly and fully, finally. His mouth was soft and sweet.

Onto the bed, on top of him, I could feel his narrow hips under mine. He pulled my dress over my head. I unzipped his pants.

"You saved my life," he said.

"You saved mine."

———

Making love to Ethan, I never felt like I was paying back an insurmountable debt. I never felt like I owed it to him, or he to me. For the first time in my life, I was making love to a man because I wanted to.

———

He wanted to know about Bud . . . how he wouldn't let me cut my hair, how he didn't want me to leave the trailer, how he expected me to spread my legs whenever he wanted.

"And he says he saved your life?" Ethan said. His voice was as soft and as much like a caress as his kisses. He was plaiting my hair into one long thick braid.

I smiled. "I used to think he did."

"What changed your mind?"

"You."

"I knew that," he said with a smile. He was as endearing as a child when he smiled. He fastened my braid at the end with an elastic band and let go of my hair. His smile faded and he looked suddenly sad, more serious than when he was on trial for murder.

"You can't go back to him."

"Where else is there?"

"I can take you anywhere you want to go." He ran his hand down my stomach and between my legs. I was already wet and waiting for him. "Technically, we don't even have to get out of bed."

"As lovely as that sounds," I said, trying to keep my voice steady, "I think we have to leave sometime."

"Sometime," he said softly, letting soft kisses fall on my breasts.

———

Near dawn, we fell asleep in each other's arms. I had been sleeping with Bud forever and never felt as complete as I did now. I had always felt like Bud had most of me hidden away somewhere. But with Ethan, I was complete and free.

I had a dream and in it, I watched Ethan saw the head off of Dr. Unterreiner. Amazingly, I wasn't afraid or repulsed. I was fascinated, inspired. He turned to look at me and there was blood on his face, his hands, his clothes. I could see that it hurt him to do it. But I could also see the reasons he had . . . the love, the desire to be desired, the obsession.

When we both turned back to look at the body, it was no longer Dr. Unterreiner. It was Bud and he started to scream my name.

"Danni? I know you're in there!"

The pounding on the door pulled me out of my sleep.

"Danni! Let me in before I break the fucking door down!"

I looked at Ethan. He was already awake, staring at the ceiling.

"I think you have a gentleman caller."

"What am I going to do?" I whispered.

"You heard him. Let him in before he breaks down the fucking door."

"But he'll see you! You've got to hide!"

"God, this is tedious," he said with a sigh.

"It may be for you, but I'm not quite as used to this as *you* are. What should I do?"

"I think you should make up with him."

"What?" My heart turned to a lead lump.

"I think you should make up with him and fuck him and then kill him."

"Danni! I'm going to kick open this door on the count of three! *One!*"

"Kill him?"

"If you don't, he'll kill you and me."

"*Two!*"

"How will I do it?"

"You'll think of something."

"I don't have anything. You didn't happen to grab that saw on your way out, did you?"

"Very funny," he said with a slight smile.

"*Three!*"

There was a loud thud. Of course the door didn't budge.

"Go open it."

"Will you help me?"

He shook his head. "I'm done killing, Danielle."

"But—"

He took my hands in his and pulled me down on top of him. "Do it for me. For us. It will set you free in a way you can only imagine." I could feel him getting hard again against my thighs. "It's the only way we can really be together, on *every* possible level. Do you understand?" His eyes, searching mine, were impossible to resist.

I nodded. "Perfectly."

He kissed me again. "You are so much stronger than Jennifer," he said, mentioning her name for the first time. "I've no doubt you won't let me down." He got up, and walked into the bathroom.

"Danni!" Bud yelled.

I pulled my dress over my head. My braid was still in place from earlier when Ethan had put it up for me.

I took a deep breath and opened the door. I gasped. He looked worse than before. "Bud, I was in the bathroom!" I grabbed his hand. "Come inside. You need to sit down."

He yanked his hand out of mine, but came in. When he walked past, I could tell by the odor he hadn't showered in a while.

"Bud, are you all right?"

He sank onto the bed and glared at me. "Why didn't you come home? Everyone else went home last night."

He was pitiful.

"I didn't think I was welcome," I said, lowering my gaze. "Oh, Bud, you were right. I don't know what got into me. It was the trial. The stress. I *never* should have done it."

His gaze softened, then, and he held out his hand. "Do you mean it?"

I nodded. He pulled me onto his lap. I tried not to grimace at the smell. He put his hand up under my dress and grabbed my breast, his hand so rough, his grasp too tight. I could only think of Ethan and his gentle touch, his soft caress, as though I were made of glass. A moan escaped my lips, but it was from the pain, not pleasure. Bud didn't know the difference.

He buried his face in my hair and said, "Oh, my pet. My darling little pet."

I shuddered when he called me his pet. Again, he mistook my revulsion for ecstasy. He kissed me roughly on the mouth, his three days of beard growth scratching my cheeks, his breath sour. Ethan's skin was soft and smooth.

"Tell me you'll never leave me again. Tell me you'll always be at my side." He lay back on the bed. Sitting right on his pelvis, I could feel him growing hard. He dropped his hands to my waist, and then lower. He was so rough when his fingers entered me, I cried out, thinking all the while of Ethan hiding and waiting. This was the hardest thing I had ever done in my life . . . let a monster make love to me while the man I loved waited in another room. But I was doing it for Ethan, for my freedom.

I unzipped Bud's jeans, which were grimy from days of wear. His eyes closed and whispered, "Do me with your hair."

I raised my eyebrows and paused in consideration. "Okay."

His eyes were still closed. He was so pathetic I wanted to throw up.

I took the tip of my braid and tickled him on the chest. "You like my hair, don't you, Bud?"

He nodded, an idiotic grin on his face. Suddenly I realized this wasn't going to be as difficult as I'd thought.

I tickled the braid up to his neck and in his ear. He opened his eyes.

"No, no," I said softly. "I want this to be a surprise." I touched the tip of the braid to each eyelid as he closed them.

I brought my head close to his and carefully slid my braid around the back of his neck. I flicked my tongue around his ear, just to keep him diverted. Then I quickly threw the end of the braid over his neck and looped it into a makeshift garrote. I moved my head to the side and pulled tightly.

I didn't feel a thing.

Bud's eyes popped open in surprise. He tried to get his hands free to push me off, but they were tangled in the folds of my dress. By the time he got them out, he was too weak to use them effectively. I pulled tighter from the top of the braid and the tip. The gasping noises and choking noises he made were close to my ear. I felt something in his throat give way. After a minute, he stopped struggling, but I knew it would take longer to kill him. I kept pulling until my arms were sore from the effort. Finally, I felt his last hot, rancid breath on my cheek.

I climbed off him, smoothing my dress. I felt weightless, free.

The bathroom door opened and Ethan came out. He looked like an angel compared to the slob on the bed. He took me in his arms.

"I heard everything," he said. "I think you're a genius." He kissed my forehead, my nose, my mouth.

"What do we do now?"

He took my hand. "We've got to get out of here . . . somewhere farther away than Mexico."

"Okay, but there's one thing I need before we go."

"What's that?"

"A haircut."

Ethan smiled. "I'm no good with scissors, but I'm handy with a saw."

Hard R

Richard S. Meyers

A life of shame is a fate worse than death.
—Anonymous

I didn't know Ruby was choking. You can never really be sure with the good ones. It's easy with the bad ones. Any sound of actual emotion amid their fake squeals is a sure sign that something's wrong. But with girls like Ruby, a fake gasp pretty much sounds like a real choke.

"Hard R" video rule number one: Don't damage your models. We left that to the slasher movies, not to mention the mythical snuff films, which we felt were terrible wastes of female flesh. "We" is me, Andy Baltimore, the dilettante writer/director, and Jonathan King, the thin, dour rope master who had been single-handedly shepherding the bondage-oriented Tyler Publications for nearly twenty years.

"Cut," I said quickly, lurching forward to yank the duct tape down and drag the cloth out of her mouth before she turned blue. "You okay?"

"Untie me, would you?" she gasped quietly, tears dripping silently down her otherwise placid face. Tears . . . that was new.

I worked and worked on the knots around her wrists, but it was slow going. I finally turned to reach for the bandage scissors, locking gazes with King. There was no missing his expression; the slight rolling of the eyes, the semi-exaggerated leg stretching, and the resigned camera lowering. It was the same teasing epithet he'd been giving me for years: "time-wasting amateur."

I couldn't help but smile because we both knew our leching overlapped. He liked being the mustache-twirling villain. I liked being the voyeur whose guilt was assuaged by the rescue. But he was a lot better at it than I was. To him, cutting rope was wasting rope. It's like he always said: "When I tie 'em, they stay tied."

The way I look at it, though, after twenty years of the same thing, why not waste a little rope trying something new? That's supposedly why I was invited to join the company after a few months sending fan mail to King, commending him for his dedication and talent. The distributors didn't care, as long as the work wasn't too good. Quality meant attention outside the steady customers, and attention invited a sanctimonious local, state, or national crackdown. And with politicians in full bellow, defenses like "porno is an eight-billion-dollar-a-year industry, it can't be four psychos with two billion each" won't cut it.

Besides, what we did was "pervo," not "porno." There was no sex or even full frontal. We toiled in the realm of the "Hard R"— that wide, profitable space between the "R" and "X" ratings, where people's pet perversions went to play. So why did it seem so much dirtier?

Case in point: Ruby lay on the carpet patch in the makeshift office set in tan lace-topped thigh-highs, black patent leather high heels, a short black skirt, open white shirt, and black demi-cup bra—an overtime secretary waylaid by the night watchman. It was pure d.i.d. (damsel in distress) and what was so bad about that? The big boys at the studios did it all the time . . . but those were usually for "audition tapes". . . which stayed in their voluminous personal collections.

Anyway, I wasted more time untying Ruby, but I didn't mind. It was sexier than anything we published: her great shape, her little contortions, the smoothness of her flesh, and even an unwilling moan or two. I tried to stay professional by again admiring

King as an artist in rope, to whom the hemp's neatness and severity were celebrated with the seriousness of a sommelier. No sloppy, loose "television tie" for him, which is why Tyler was still the best-selling company in the subgenre.

I finally got the ropes off Ruby's wrists, and as I moved to her legs, she put a hand on my shoulder. That got our attention. Ruby was easy to work with, seemingly guiltless, and one of the best-looking veterans of the business, but like all the other models, novice or otherwise, she kept a thick wall up between who she was and what she was doing.

Considering the job, there's a strong separation of libido and state here. As much as I enjoyed the mags and vids when we were finished, we took pride in pretending we were professionals just doing a job. And the models took pride in pretending they weren't working in the crotch of entertainment.

"I'm sorry," Ruby said, as if choking on the material she allowed us to wedge in her mouth was somehow her fault.

"That's okay, Ruby," I assured her, glancing at King, who looked from me to her as if discovering a new species. When I finally got the last rope undone, I couldn't help but stare at the marks it left in her skin. Taking her contact as a signal, I even ventured to rub her ankles a bit to help recirculation.

I expected a rebuff or at least a subtle evasive maneuver, but all I got was a quiet question. "Could we take a break?"

I deferred to King, who gave me a deep, personal, sardonic look of hopeless pity, before stating, "Whatever . . . we got time before the next one arrives." We were pulling an all-dayer at our agent's dingy photo studio, situated in the back of his storefront office on a low-rent stretch of Melrose. We had Ruby for the morning, then some tattooed, pierced newcomer for the afternoon.

We adjourned to the tiny office in front, where the "Master of the Hard R," William Randall Thurston, lorded over his shabby yet overstuffed domain. He had covered the windows with shades, bars, and cages, so the only light came from fake Tiffany lamps that made his threadbare pate glow.

This friendly, aging ex-actor ran WRT Limited, *the* casting agency for girls and boys willing to do everything but Triple X. As such, his coffers and casting books were filled with Skinimax and Playboy Channel possibilities. But when that wasn't happening, the frustrated models could take off their shoes for foot-fetish videos, pretend to be knocked out for sleepy-time flicks, get tied up by the likes of us in the B/D realm, or scissor their legs with another model for muff wrestling. But wait, there's more. If they were really hot for much bigger wads of quick cash, or even were actually into it, the hopefuls could try their luck getting whipped or pierced in the S/M world, or even use their acting chops pretending to be shot, stabbed, or strangled for pseudo-necro sagas. Big Will cast them all.

He was sitting at his desk to the left of the entrance, surrounded by his big client books filled with Polaroids. He looked like an Arabian genie, only with an open, short-sleeved shirt and polyester pants. Ruby sat by the door on the easy chair refugee from one of the better Salvation Armies, while I perched on a folding chair by Will's desk. Given the room, we were all no more than three feet from each other.

Knowing better than to share Thurston's coffee, she spoke almost immediately. "I'm worried."

"What about?" I grunted, trying not to stare into her still-open shirt.

"You remember the pictures I asked for?" I nodded, but I didn't really. "I sent them to my father," she confessed.

I looked at Thurston, but he gave me a silent shrug, as if to say "Who knows?" He kept me and King away from the ones with serious substance abuses, but none of us knew a Hard R model/actress without daddy problems.

Ruby looked down at her hands guiltily. "I think he's really mad."

I thought, "Well, what did you expect?" but said nothing. If there was one thing I had learned from talking with the models, it was that abusive fathers were capable of anything . . . as were vengeful daughters of wealthy parents who ignored them. I couldn't help wondering which Ruby was.

She pinioned me with her big eyes. "I mean, *really* mad."

"Okay," I replied cautiously. I'm not big on mental minefields. Actresses usually had daddy problems. Perverts often had mommy ones. "So?"

"I don't know," she said distantly. *"That's* what I'm worried about."

Reality creeping into our well-fortified fantasy was making me feel a bit greasy and giddy. "Maybe you'd better not send him any more photos," I suggested slowly. Considering her workload, he might have enough bondage pics to paper the playroom by now.

"I think it's way beyond that," she said. "I'm getting weird calls, and I think I'm being . . ."

The door took that moment to open and in came the semi-welcome Marv Denninger. Marv was a nice, middle-aged husband and father with a very bad case of the sugar daddy syndrome. Nothing new: A "nice" guy fixates on a "bad" girl, with visions of stardom dancing in both their heads. So he pays for all sorts of things and she goes along with it, but any way it played, he's out a chunk of change and no body fluids are ever exchanged.

"I thought you were working until noon," Denninger said almost accusingly to Ruby.

"We finished early, Marv," I said. "Hello, Marv. How are you, Marv. Nice day, isn't it, Marv."

"Hey, Andy," he said absently before returning his attention to Ruby. "You ready, then?"

She smiled apologetically, making me wonder yet again why so many Hard R photographers made their models leer. "See you next time, guys," she said, and went off with Marv to his SUV.

I looked at Thurston. Thurston looked at me like a cross between the Cheshire Cat and the Dalai Lama. "They come in by the dozens every week, Andy," he reminded me again, letting his eyes wander over the groaning bookshelves filled with photos of the hundreds that were hunting dreams and dodging nightmares.

Young men, yes, but mostly girls. Not quite beautiful girls, not quite ugly girls. Skinny girls, chubby girls, tall girls, short girls, white girls, black girls, Asian girls. Girls with nervous or brassy smiles that combined hope with disbelief, longing with despair, desire with depression, optimism with fear, and occasionally trust with stupidity. Girls with breast jobs that looked like waterballoons or baseballs shoved under their nipples. He took pictures of them all.

"Yeah, I know," I said.

"Every week, Andy," he went on, still grinning. "They come, and they go just as fast. By bus, by plane, by car, by train. All with desires . . . and bills to pay . . ." Thurston stopped his mock chiding. "He came in here before, while you were working, looking for her."

"Who?" I asked. "Marv?" He nodded. "He's harmless," I said.

"Her father isn't," Thurston replied. "And the combination of the two . . . ?"

"Look, look," I said, waving my hands dramatically. "I just touched her ankle!"

"It's not what you do," he said with a knowing smile. "It's what you feel."

"Stop it." I laughed. "She's Marv's headache."

Suddenly Will got serious. That was so rare I paid attention. "Be careful, Andy," he told me. "She's not acting normal. What do you think this performance was all about?" He motioned to the chair she had been sitting in. "And that's not all. I've thought a long time about telling you this, but . . ."

At that moment the next model showed up with a fairly standard anxious/apprehensive look, so it was into the back, where King and I had to decide whether she would make a better biker chick or stripper. To tell you the truth, I was glad for the interruption. I have a tough enough time dealing with my own guilt without taking on other people's secrets.

Yeah, yeah, toiling in the Hard R can be fun and exciting, but Jon had been doing it for so long that the fantasy bondage was rubbing his loner reality raw. Still, he took pride in his photography, and, as long as I limited my more laborious experiments, he seemed happy with my company. When we finally finished for the day, I had neatly forgotten what Will started to say, and Thurston himself didn't bring it up again.

We paid our biker chick two hundred, headed into the rush hour traffic, and didn't give it another thought until Will was killed.

But that was still a few days away. In the meantime, King and I drove to Westwood to take in the latest Hollywood release, then had dinner. Despite being a good ol' boy from Florida whose best buddies were Jack and Jim (Daniels and Beam), Jon was a nice, interesting guy who really seemed to appreciate my friendship. But as much as we talked, planned the magazines, filmed the videos, went shooting in the mountains, went to restaurants, and watched TV, just about the only personal thing I knew about him was that he had all the respect in the world for women, and none at all. The feeling, apparently, was mutual. He lived in a self-created vacuum that I was only visiting.

The vacuum was broken the following Monday when I reached the squat, cement Tyler Publications "building" on a side street between West Hollywood and Santa Monica. Jon sat down to read the paper while I went to my side of the windowless, paneled office to complete the copy for the "Her Big Mistake" and "Right Girl/Wrong Time" pictorials in the next issue of *Gagged*.

It's a living.

Seemingly in a trance, Jon showed me a headline on page eight: "Man Found Shot to Death Inside Porn Business." It read: "Police investigators discovered the body of a man who was apparently shot to death. The sheriffs homicide bureau is investigating the apparent suicide. The shop belonged to WRT Limited, believed to be an adult-entertainment business. The victim is believed to be the owner, but no suspects have been arrested."

"We're not porn," I said vacantly, in shock.

"It's porn to them," said Jon. His expression also hinted at feelings long kept under a cement lid.

I'd like to say that all thoughts of bound girls left my head, but in reality, every single one we ever tied came back—their eyes accusing above their mouth-filling, lip-mashing gags.

"What the hell happened?" I finally said.

"Don't ask me. What were you and Ruby talking about the other day?" After I told him, he wanted to know why I hadn't informed him.

"Hey," I replied defensively, "you're the one who told me not to take anything they say seriously!" King called it the "hooker mentality." They made up lies to make themselves feel better about what they did, and the more you bought it, the bigger the lies got. That way you would be the fool, not them.

"Not Ruby," he said. "Will."

"Oh," I reminded myself regretfully. "Yeah."

"Oh, Christ," Jon moaned, putting his long hands over his eyes. "Callistro."

I cringed. I had only met Callistro, no-first-name, once, and I didn't want to meet him again. He was a sleazy, ambitious "actor's agent" with the narrow-eyed look of a genetic socio. He was full of big ideas about the "bondage industry" that clearly masked the desire for his own sadistic playground. We tried to explain the difference, but it was obvious he didn't have a clue, and didn't want one. The guy was scary and he wanted Will's client list.

I felt sadness for Will, suspicion for Ruby, and pity for myself. I snapped out of it when the phone invitation to Thurston's memorial service came in. I left a still-brooding Jon to buy some suitable clothes for the occasion, then drove over in my own car, which I kept in the building parking lot.

The wake was a revelation. I had only known Will as a kind-hearted satyr who supplied girls, and occasionally boys, to our fantasies. I had no real idea of the friends he had kept from his mainstream showbiz days or his family. I numbly shook hands, murmuring condolences, before gravitating to my own kind in what was rapidly becoming the Hard R section.

It was kind of entertaining to see the range of mourning clothes in darker shades of Lycra/spandex, with three-inch heels instead of four. And, although we exchanged commiserations, I couldn't stop picturing them as I usually saw them; squirming in duct tape, cord, and leather. But considering our working conditions, or maybe because of them, they were actually all pretty nice people. Sure, we had our share of back-stabbing and even suicide, but for the most part it was better than marketing departments.

Then Ruby came in, wearing a wraparound, v-necked, black dress with matching high heels. I walked over to her quickly.

"Where's sugar daddy?" I asked quietly. Her eyes flashed while her brow furrowed in confusion. She was not used to me acting the tough guy . . . nor was I much good at it. "I mean Marv," I added.

"He's going to be late," she said.

"Then how did you get here?" Everybody knew Ruby didn't drive.

"Callistro brought me." And before I could completely assim-
ilate that, there he was. Callistro, in his "I-don't-care-what-the-
occasion-is" silk sports coat, white shirt, slacks, and loafers. He
looked like a cut-rate Kirk Douglas at his psycho best.

"Andy," he said as if we were old friends. "Love your work."
He held out his marble-colored hand, which I took with dismay.
"What a shame," he commented unconvincingly. "They say he
was in a bad way. They found some doctor's bills. . . . Well, looking forward to working with you." Having established his territory
and my subservience, he went to crush someone else's digits.

"He acts like he already owns Thurston's client list," I grumbled, making an exploratory fist.

"Who else?" Ruby said, then laid her hand lightly on mine.

She ignored my "I'm-not-the-guy" expression, so I asked
pointedly, "Ruby, do you think your father is capable of doing
something like this?"

She reacted as if she hadn't even thought of it. "Oh god. He
might be . . ."

Now I was really nervous. It would be a lot easier to believe
that Callistro had killed Thurston for his territory than that there
was a vengeful parent offing anyone he thought had corrupted
his little girl.

Before I could pursue it further, Marv showed up and the service started. Ruby seemed to want me to sit alongside, but I was
just as happy when Callistro and Marv sandwiched her. Instead
I sidled over to Jon.

"Where have you been?" I whispered.

"Man, you will not believe it," he hissed.

I looked at him. He wasn't one for word games. And he usually didn't start drinking until after work, but this was no longer
a workday. "What? Where were you?"

"I had to stop off at my place," he said conspiratorially. "Man,
you will *not* believe it!"

I already didn't believe that he had made a ninety-minute trip from his condo and back. "What already?"

"I went to Thurston's." I stiffened. I knew that King had keys to the studio's back door, but what the hell was he thinking going there now? "I wanted to see if I could get some of my stuff before the cops confiscated it all," he explained.

"Are you *nuts?*"

"The place was torn apart," he continued as if I hadn't spoken, "but I knew where he kept his stuff."

"What stuff?" I asked reluctantly, vision of air flights out of town dancing in my head. "You mean, in the safe?"

He made a dismissive face. "The safe was gone. So were the actor photo books. But the safe was a decoy. Will actually kept his secrets under one of the floor tiles."

I didn't know whether to put my face in my hands or my fingers in my ears. "What the hell are you doing?"

"You don't want to work with Callistro, do you? I was trying to find the Thurston client list so we could deal with them directly."

Suddenly he noticed that our whispering was drawing unwanted attention, so he shut up. And no matter how many times I poked him or tried to get him alone afterward, it didn't work. Everyone wanted to pay respects to the rope king. I was finally about to corner him in the parking lot when Ruby and Marv appeared behind me.

"We've got to talk," Denninger said.

I looked helplessly at Jon, who merely smiled. "Meet me at my place tonight," King said. "I've got something you have to see."

Then the coy bastard left me alone with the sugar daddy and daughter. "What?" I asked Denninger as King drove away.

I thought he'd discuss Ruby's father or at least his concerns about having his charge in Callistro's clutches, but instead he said, "I was hoping you'd give Ruby a ride."

"What about Callistro?" I blurted in surprise.

"Not Callistro," Ruby said darkly. "Not again."

"How about it?" Marv pressed.

I was unable to keep from noticing the swell of her chest or the way the high heels accented her legs. "Uh . . . sure, I guess. What's the emergency?" It had to be an emergency if Marv was going to hand her off to Callistro *and* me on the same day.

"No emergency," he replied. "I just have to take care of something." Before I could come up with a clever or desperate retort, he turned away.

I was left to stare down at Ruby, who trained her big eyes on me. Was the v-neck of her dress wider and deeper than it had been before, or was that just my imagination?

"Where to?" I managed to say.

She named an address near Culver City and I opened the passenger door for her. My four-year-old Honda wasn't impressive after Marv's SUV and Callistro's limo, but it was relatively clean. And I sure beat them for gas mileage. As I got behind the wheel, visions of sickeningly sweet romantic fantasies clashed with hot monkey sex scenes. I managed to keep it together by mentally starting a letter to *Penthouse Forum*. "I had the hottest thing on two open legs in my car . . ."

Guccione would be disappointed. We both seemed dazed for several awkward minutes later before I finally asked, "Heard anything from your dad?"

She made a negative sound, without turning from the window. Her face in the glass's reflection was infinitely lost. I turned back to watch the road, getting increasingly upset. Someone had strip-searched Thurston's place, taking the safe and the actor books. Thurston was dead and maybe murdered. And here I was, having schoolboy fantasies—both G- and X-rated. What the hell was wrong with me?

We finally arrived at a small house at the bottom of a hill. I

said something like "here you go," and she said something like
"thanks." There was one second when she leaned down and we
locked eyes. But then my eyes slipped down to her cleavage and
it was over.

We said something like "take it easy," then I drove into the
congestion, taking it all personally. What was that all about? The
only thing I could figure was that she was supposed to come on
to me on the orders of either Marv or Callistro or both. But she
couldn't, and I didn't know whether to like or hate her for it.

The real reason occurred to me as I cursed the endless rush
hour traffic. I prayed I was wrong, feeling increasingly ill as I
made my way to King's place. I finally reached Jon's condo-
minium complex, which stood at the edge of a redevelopment
amidst a mountain range. I knocked on his door, but there was
no answer. I tried the door. It wasn't locked. The shades were
drawn and no lights were on, but the sunset still infused the large
room with a golden light. Jon looked like a paratrooper whose
chute hadn't worked, landing across his favorite chair in front of
the TV.

The King was dead.

His head was back, thankfully, so all I saw was what looked
like crushed hamsters covered in strawberry preserves splattered
on the wall behind him. One of his rifles lay between his legs.
His belongings were strewn everywhere, but a bunch of pictures
surrounded the chair. They were of his favorite black model,
naked, bound, and gagged so tightly part of her skin was turning
white. Her big eyes looking pleadingly up toward the camera.

I closed the door behind me, fighting panic and the desire to
vomit. What a set-up. I could hear the hypocritical cops now . . .
just another Hard R suicide, by another pervert overcome by
guilt for what he had done. Maybe they'd even try to pin
Thurston's death on this "remorseful sicko". . . if they hadn't already closed the Thurston case as a suicide.

I looked around, trying to think rationally. Somebody had wanted something Thurston had. What could he have had that was so important? King had reacted like it was all some kind of joke. But if it had been under a tile, it couldn't have been very large. And whoever had killed Jon didn't know him the way Jon knew Will.

Will's life was pictures. Jon's life was booze.

I found it in the freezer. There were three bags of cracked ice, but only one tray. I looked into the cubes. I could make out a small discoloration inside each. I lowered the tray and found myself staring at two bottles that stood near the ice crusher. The amber liquid inside reminded me of amber-colored film.

Before I left with one bottle and the ice tray, I used a kitchen towel to wipe all the surfaces I had touched. As I drove back to town, I considered leaving an anonymous tip so the cops could find King. I told myself Jon wouldn't have wanted me to, but I'm a coward and a liar. Still, I hate feeling trapped more than being trapped.

More than anything I wanted to play this out like a tough guy, but I finally had to stop the car. I vomited and cried in a ditch on the side of the highway. I still don't know whether or not to be proud of that. I have these little emotional episodes every ten years or so. The last time was when my wife and I decided to divorce. But each decade I'm glad. It reminds me that I'm not totally controlled by my head or crotch.

Getting Ruby into the car was no real problem. It was late at night and I found her waiting on her porch with two suitcases. When I masterfully told her to get in, the expression on her face changed so quickly and so often that I stopped trying to interpret it after surprise, confusion, and conniving.

"This won't take long, will it?" she asked. "I'm being picked up in a few minutes."

I held up an envelope. "No, not long," I replied. "Look what

I've got." Then, simple as that, off we went. It wasn't until we were on the highway heading north that I hazarded another look at her fresh-scrubbed face and her form in a white v-neck t-shirt, black jeans, and cowboy boots. I concentrated on a tiny red cloth rose at the base of the v-neck. "Don't you want to know where they were?" I asked.

I've got to hand it to her. She stayed silent and calm, but then again, what was I expecting? "They were in the ice tray and booze," I continued. Ruby still didn't say anything, but I was aware of her face in the moonlight and the shape of her body in the seat next to me.

I waited. If she hadn't gone for it, I'm not sure what I would've done. But no use thinking about that now, because she said, "So you got them, huh?" I couldn't speak. I nodded. "So how much do *you* want?"

Nausea started clawing up my throat again. I fought it off. "I don't know," I answered honestly. "First, one question. Do you even have a father?"

She looked at me in surprise, as if it were the last thing she was expecting. "Yeah." She almost laughed. "I got a father. I don't send him pictures, though. He might get off on them too much."

I couldn't tell whether that was true any more than anything else she had ever said. "So you were working me with those stories of the mystery dad you could blame everything on."

"It didn't have to be my dad," she reminded me almost proudly. "Remember I nearly got out that stuff about being followed. Any mystery man would do."

"As long as you got pity. If Marv, Callistro, or Will wouldn't give you what you wanted, there was always me."

She shrugged. "King was too much a hard-ass."

It was then I realized she probably didn't know Jon was dead. Or care. "When did you know about the pictures?" I asked, swallowing my anger.

Her voice, when it came, was sharp and knowing. "Thurston showed me them last month," she said. "When the cable stations and men's magazines started to show an interest in me. I was going to look for another agent, so he wanted to impress me."

I felt like lowering my head between my legs, but I just kept driving north. Luckily the traffic was getting lighter. "He was going to cut you in?"

She laughed. "The asshole wasn't going to do anything with them! He just wanted to show me how famous some of his clients could become!"

But she had seen gold in the old photos. The faded pictures of the young, naked man who would become one of the most popular children's show hosts on television.

The world had gotten more sophisticated, if not more mature, but if there was one thing Pee Wee had proved, it's that children's television was still susceptible to shame. And this wasn't even an alternative comic satirizing kids' shows—this was a man beloved and trusted by millions of parents as well as children. If these photos got out, he was ruined. Worse than ruined, he would become a pitiful, despised joke.

"When did *you* find out?" she asked in return.

I hazarded a glance at her. I had to turn away quickly. As sick and sad as it was, she wore my mother's face . . . or at least the expression when the sham of the sitcom mom fell away to reveal the cunning, mean-spirited drunk beneath. I started talking as fast as I could, holding the wheel until my knuckles went white.

"I knew something was up today when you 'needed a ride.' You were supposed to play me, right? Anything to buy time. But silence worked as well, so why bother, right?"

"You had your fun," she said knowingly. She may have made a derisive sound.

"So did you. When Will hid the pictures from you, you had

sugar daddy tear the place up. It wasn't Callistro because he'd have taken the girl photo books too. But you got nothing. So when you heard what Jon was whispering to me in the funeral parlor, you had to keep me away from Jon's place until Marv was through. But he didn't find the pictures, did he? So what were the suitcases for? Callistro hot to get you in his clutches? Marv's wife putting on the pressure to cut you loose?"

She moved like a striking python. She snatched the envelope from my hand, tore it open, looked inside, then stared at me. The envelope was empty. "Andy," she said with incredulous sarcasm. "What do you want?"

I felt a flash of anger and despair. I felt the same kind of rush of power and fear I felt when I pulled the trigger of any gun Jon and I used in our mountain target ranges. I was actually going to do this.

"Ruby," I said. "I want a way out." Then I twisted the wheel violently to the right.

The car slashed across an empty lane and skidded on the gravel as I tromped on the brake. Nobody stopped. You didn't help another driver if you wanted to live in LA.

By the time her head bounced off the window I had the handcuffs tightened around her wrists. It's sad what a man can do when he's not afraid to hurt someone.

I drove back onto the highway. I was still shaking and my head was pounding, but I noticed that the traffic was even thinner now.

Ruby's hands were cuffed behind her and her elbows were cinched by a plastic pull-tie, the cloth flower on her t-shirt straining toward the windshield. Her ankles were duct-taped together, and a red rubber ball was shoved into her pried-open mouth, sealed with more duct tape.

With her jaw pried open like that, all she could do was grunt and squeal. There was nothing she could tell me that I wanted to hear and there was nowhere she could go with the door locked and her seat belt on.

"I don't want to blackmail the poor guy," I finally said. I couldn't continue for a while. Their target had been in the same boat as Ruby, only he got a lucky break . . . or maybe he didn't hate himself, and everyone else, as much as she did.

"You put this in motion," I said slowly. "After all these years of pretending to be helpless, acting out other people's perverted fantasies, you wanted to feel powerful. Had Marv's money run out? Is that why he agreed to go along with you?"

I looked at her then, but quickly turned away, unable to face her expression of both fury and pleading. "You liked the feeling of control, so you started trying to play everyone, just to see if it would work. But once you found out about the pictures, you saw a big score. But it all went so bad, so fast. You couldn't find the pictures, no matter who died . . ."

My eyes started to tear. I blinked furiously. "Amazing. You'd think Callistro was the killer. But he just likes hurting women. It's the quiet, desperate guys like Marv who can't handle it once their dreams gets so near . . ."

I stared out the windshield, watching the lights of the valley flick out and the gloom of the mountains rise like a tidal wave. "What did you like more? The lure of the money or the feeling when you had them killed?"

She moaned, trying to get me to look at her, trying to get me to see how pitiful and pleading and promising her eyes were. Instead I tried to think of another way out. I couldn't.

"I sent his pictures back to him," I finally said. "Back to the guy on the kids' show."

She grunted in disbelief and frustration.

"I used Marv's return address."

She tried to scream and swear at me as I turned off the highway and headed deep into the desert.

Maybe someone will find her in time. Maybe my powerful and famous guilt will get the best of me and I'll go untie her before I leave town. But right now I'm just trying to deal with how I felt when I left her.

Maybe Callistro will think Ruby simply had enough and skipped town. Happens all the time. Every week, as Thurston told me over and over. Maybe the kids' show host will have something happen to Marv, just to be on the safe side. Won't be the first time something like that happened either.

All I know for sure is that Ruby won't be playing me or Marv or Callistro or the cops or a jury anytime soon.

When I tie 'em, they stay tied.

My Lolita Complex

Max Allan Collins and Matthew V. Clemens

On my second night in the house, sitting in the hot tub with Kelly, I agreed to kill her father. Sweat poured down my face and whether it generated from the steaming water, Kelly rubbing against me beneath the surface, or what I had just promised to do, I couldn't tell you.

Her arms still around my neck, her heart-shaped face inches from my spade-jawed own, her breath sweet and warm, her pert young breasts pressing hard against me, she said, "Uncle Joe, you're a lifesaver. I can't tell you how I've prayed for this moment." Then she kissed my cheek, her lips lingering a second too long.

The shit I was getting into, like the water I bobbed in, was about neck high. My first day in that brick mansion had been slightly less eventful, but as I thought about it, murder had been in the wind even then.

I'd made the trip to Davenport, Iowa, for the funeral of my sister, Rachel Forlani. Two years older than my forty, Rachel had still had that jet-black mane even if my Beatle mop had already begun to gray at the temples. She was one of those women who aged slowly and well . . . and now she would never look old.

A freak accident, her husband Jason had told me on the phone: Rachel had somehow gotten drunk while bathing and drowned. Jason Forlani and Rachel had been each other's second spouse. Stepdaughter Kelly's mother—a woman I never met and Jason never spoke of—had divorced him years before he met my sister. Rachel's history had been little better: Her first husband, Peter, had dropped dead of a heart attack ten years ago while still in his early thirties.

Peter, a successful investment banker, had left Rachel with a great deal of money. I knew Sis pretty well, and she would have traded the whole pile to have him back. The world doesn't work like that, though, and Rachel seemed to be searching for Peter at the bottom of every vodka bottle on the planet. That was pretty much the story until she met Jason Forlani. Somehow he broke through her vodka fog, and before long Rachel turned up at my front door and to my surprise, she was sober.

She stayed a couple of days and told me everything about the new man in her life. At the end of the visit, Rachel invited me to come to Iowa for their impending marriage, which I did. My sister seemed genuinely happy and I liked Forlani immediately. Affable and low key, he appeared the perfect bearer of the quiet life I thought Rachel needed.

Now, barely two years later, Jason was meeting me at the front door of the brick mansion they had purchased in an old money section of the town that lay in the crook where the Mississippi ran east and west.

Several inches shorter than me, Jason stepped out onto the stoop and put his arms out. Laptop slung over my shoulder, I let my suitcase drop to the ground and accepted his embrace. A frail man, he seemed to be hanging off me, his weight sagging against me as if he had used the last of his strength to attach himself to me.

"Joe, I'm so glad you're here," he said, his voice a hoarse whisper in my ear.

I stood there patting his back awkwardly.

"Rachel could always depend on you," he went on. "She'd be happy to know that you came so quickly."

Still locked in the clumsy embrace, I said, "We all loved her."

That broke whatever emotional dam still remained for Jason. He sobbed into my chest, arms gripping with more strength than I would have given him credit for. He was small, but damn strong. His tears soaked into my shirt, and I felt like a fool standing at his doorstep for the whole neighborhood to see.

"Maybe you should go in and sit down," I said, trying in vain to steer him through the door.

"I'm just so glad you're here," he blubbered between sobs.

"I know, I know, me too."

Slowly, Jason allowed me to lead him inside the house. A wide foyer opened to the heavy oak staircase that led to the second floor. Doors to the right and left led to the living room and dining room respectively. I helped Jason ease down onto one of the lower steps and returned to the porch to retrieve my bag, kicked the door shut, and turned to face the emotional wreck that was my host.

I hadn't seen Jason in about six months, since Christmas, and in that time he seemed to have aged twenty years. His skin sagged, almost as if his face were melting. His eyes, red-rimmed and bloodshot, bugged behind Coke-bottle wire frames. I knew Jason was diabetic, and that he took insulin shots, but he looked like an old man. He was barely seven years my senior, but strangers could have mistaken us for father and son.

"You look like shit," I said, adding a grin as punctuation.

He flashed a weak smile. "You don't pull any punches, do you? Rachel liked that . . ."

"How much sleep you getting?"

"Some."

"Not much, you mean."

"Not much," he admitted.

I sat next to him on the stairs. "Find out anything else?"

Shrugging a little, Jason said, "The coroner's ruled it an accidental drowning. She was drinking in the hot tub, coroner's opinion, fell asleep and drowned. The vodka bottle was still on the floor next to the tub."

I shook my head. "She'd been sober for what . . ."

"Almost five years, since we first started dating."

"Damn," I said. "Had she been depressed? Stressed?"

Jason thought for a moment before answering. "I don't think so—anyway, she seemed fine to me. I thought we were happy. But you knew her, Joe—Rachel kept a lot inside."

I nodded. "She was always hard to read."

We got up, Jason absently brushing off his butt despite the fact that the stairs were immaculate. "I'll show you to your room."

He reached for my suitcase, but I got there first. "Better let me get that," I said. "I brought my anvil collection."

Nodding, he led the way up the stairs. "The first bedroom is Kelly's, the second one'll be yours. Bathroom's right across the hall and I'm down at the end."

I remembered the layout from the single night I'd spent in the house right after Rachel and Jason were married.

He opened the door, and I passed him and entered the bedroom.

"You need anything else?" he asked.

I shook my head.

"Go ahead and rest up, then—dinner will be about seven."

"Sounds fine," I said.

Jason started to go, then turned back. "I'm sorry we lost her."

He wasn't going to let this be easy. He seemed to need to wallow in it every second. "Me too."

Jason nodded and shut the door behind him.

Not quite claustrophobically small, the bedroom had about as much personality as a Holiday Inn room. The hardwood floors peeked out from under the edges of a massive area rug that created a beige island in the middle of the room. A chest of drawers with a twelve-inch TV on top sat against one wall, a double bed with a pastel floral print comforter squatted against the opposite wall. On the wall to the left of the entrance was a sliding door that hid the closet. The final wall contained a window that over-looked the backyard. Beneath the window a low bookcase held Clancy, Parker, Grisham, Cornwell, and even a couple of my books.

I pulled *River of Death* off the shelf. A small-press true crime book I'd done when I first became a full-time writer, the copy looked as though someone had actually read it. I leafed through the title page where I found my inscription to my sister, "Stay on land and avoid the River of Death—your lovin' brother, Joe."

What had seemed cute at the time now seemed macabre.

"Reading your own book?" a voice chirped from the doorway.

I jumped halfway out of my skin. I hadn't even heard the door open, yet Kelly, Jason's seventeen-year-old daughter, stood there as nonchalantly as if it were her own room. Something inside me stirred, much as I tried not to let it. Five-five, maybe five-six, her longish blonde hair bleached from time spent in the early sum-mer sun, Kelly sported a tan that made me wonder if there were bikini lines beneath the denim short shorts and the tight white t-shirt that accentuated the firmness of perky breasts and allowed just a teasing glimpse of tan stomach and belly button.

"Hi, Kelly," I managed.

She swept into the room, brushed by me, lifting the book from my hands on her way by, and plopped onto the bed. "Am I interrupting?" she asked.

"Nope, I just got here."

Sitting up straighter, her eyes met mine. "I'm really sorry about Rachel, Uncle Joe."

"Thanks."

"I know you two were close."

I nodded. "Has it been hard for you?"

Kelly looked down at the book in her lap, studying it for a long moment. "Even though she wasn't my real mother . . ." her voice trailed off as tears rolled slowly down her high pink cheeks.

"I know," I said, then she was in my arms.

She'd set the book aside, gotten to her feet, and hugged me before I knew what was happening. "It's just that I miss her so much already. She was so cool, so good to me."

"I know," I said, patting her shoulder.

"And Daddy, she was always good to him whether he appreciated it or not."

"What?"

"I'm sorry," she said, backing away, blinking her big blue eyes. "I shouldn't have said that."

Kelly practically left a vapor trail, she went out of the room so fast. She didn't bother closing my door, and before I even completely realized she'd gone, I heard her door close.

What the hell had she meant, "Whether he appreciated it or not"?

Plopping onto the bed, I picked up the book and settled back. As I read the dedication, "To Rachel, my sister, my hero," I felt tears pooling, then spilling. And to my dismay, I noticed that I could still smell the sweet aroma of Kelly where she'd pressed against my chest. I shifted the erection in my pants and willed it to go down.

The next sound I heard was a soft rapping on the bedroom door. I awoke slowly, my tongue thick in my mouth, my eyelids heavy, my throat dry. "Yeah?" I croaked.

Kelly opened the door and stepped into the dusky bedroom. I could barely see more than an outline, but she seemed to be wearing a short dress now instead of the t-shirt and shorts. "Daddy says dinner's ready."

"Okay," I said. "I'll be down in just a minute."

"I'll tell him," she said, then disappeared.

I got to my feet, ran my fingers through my hair, and decided I better make a stop across the hall before I went downstairs. As I crossed the room, I again noticed Kelly's sweet scent hanging in the air.

The aroma of dinner filled the first floor. Coming down the stairs, I found Kelly waiting for me at the bottom. She leaned against the newel, her long blonde hair now pulled back in a loose ponytail, a very short floral dress showing off her tan, slimly muscular thighs. I tried not to notice.

She looped her arm in mine and led me through the door into the dining room. Jason sat at one end of the table, and a short broad Hispanic woman trundled in and out of the room, carrying dishes in from the kitchen.

"Joe, I hope you like baked chicken," Jason said, waving me to a chair at the end of the table.

I nodded my approval as Kelly let go of me and took the chair to my right between her father and me. I looked at the table awash with dishes. Steam rose from the huge plate of baked chicken, as well as from a bowl of mashed potatoes, a tureen of gravy, and a huge bowl of corn. Two kinds of rolls and a huge bowl of tossed greens completed the setting.

"Expecting company?" I asked. "Like maybe the Oakland Raiders?"

Jason smiled. "Conchita comes from a large family. She cooks a lot. We've always got leftovers in the fridge, so help yourself. You're family, Joe—what's mine is yours."

"Thanks, I'll remember that."

The food was excellent and we ate mostly in silence. We avoided talking about Rachel and had little else to discuss. It wasn't until the plates were cleared and dessert, cherry pie à la mode, sat in front of us, that Jason finally got around to bringing up my career.

"Working on the next great book?" he asked.

I knew he was trying to be upbeat, but considering the condition of my career, it sounded like sarcasm. Those first two books, *River of Death* and *Torso: Catching the Chainsaw Killer*, had each sold moderately well in the Midwest, where the crimes occurred, but stiffed throughout the rest of the country. There'd been a few magazine articles and some freelance newspaper work, but for the most part, it had been my teaching job that allowed me to write at all. Then, when I lost that, handouts from Rachel had become my meal ticket.

I shook my head. "Working on an article for a magazine," I lied. Truth was I had no jobs, and an equal number of prospects.

Jason's eyebrows raised with interest. "Really? About what?"

Fuck, I thought. I put on my tap shoes and continued the lie. "Uh, it's a followup to *River of Death*."

"Really?" Jason asked.

"Yeah, you know, interview with Lane five years later."

Jason nodded.

Donald Lane, the man who had drowned his entire family in the Mississippi, had been the subject of my first book. He was now serving a life sentence with no possibility for parole in Iowa's maximum security prison at Ft. Madison. Saying it out loud, it really didn't sound like a half bad idea. I wondered if I could peddle it. I looked up to see Jason and Kelly staring at me. Obviously, one of them had spoken and I'd been caught not paying attention.

"Sorry."

Jason repeated his question. "Have you spoken to Lane yet?"

I shook my head. "Still doing the preliminary background and trying to get past his lawyer."

This sounded so good it was beginning to feel like I wasn't lying. I definitely had to look into this story.

"Do you think he'll even talk to you?"

"Can't hurt to ask," I said with a shrug.

The conversation sort of petered out then as we settled in to work on our pie and ice cream. After dinner, we moved into the living room. Kelly excused herself to go upstairs and phone a friend. Jason and I sat mostly in silence, pretending to watch some show on television. After the local news, he too excused himself and went up to bed.

I was drifting off to sleep somewhere in the middle of *Letterman* when I felt a warm hand running down my cheek. I opened my eyes, blinked several times and finally focused to see Kelly standing over me. She again wore the white t-shirt and denim shorts.

"You were asleep," she said, her voice soft and sweet as marshmallow.

"Just resting my eyes."

She smiled. Her teeth were large and white, her lips soft and a deep red, with just the tip of her pink tongue showing through. "You always snore when you're resting your eyes?"

I chuckled. "If you want to really get rested you have to snore, didn't you know that?"

She laughed too, the sound bubbling up from inside and coming out rich and captivating.

I stared at her, fighting the desire to take her in my arms. Kelly reminded me a great deal of Heather, the student I'd lost my job over.

That was what I got for trying to relate to my kids, being too close to them, too friendly—who else my age listened to Christina Aguilera and Britney Spears, for Christ's sakes? Thirteen years of teaching high school shot to shit because some well-intentioned counseling got too personal.

Which is horseshit, right? Boils down to, I couldn't keep my hands off one of the students. The affair had cost me my wife as well. Marion hadn't even bothered to listen to my side. As soon as I admitted the truth, she tossed me out on my ass.

Now I was having those same feelings again, with my niece, my goddamn niece! Of course, she was only my niece by marriage, and legal in this state, but still, I didn't think that would fly with Jason—and it sure wouldn't have with Rachel, if she were still alive.

Which, of course, she wasn't . . . I shook my head trying to clear away those thoughts.

"You okay?" she asked.

I nodded. "Tired."

"Too tired to go for a walk?"

She turned and looked up the stairs like she was afraid Jason would hear us.

"I think so," I answered, not wanting to tell her the truth, which was that I was afraid to be alone with her.

"I need to talk to you," she said, her voice turning breathless as she again glanced toward the stairs. "It's important."

This seemed like a really bad idea, but Kelly seemed seriously troubled about something and maybe all she needed was someone to talk to—somebody older who could listen, and help.

"I'm your uncle," I said. "You can always talk to me."

Once we were outside, down the front walk, and strolling through the peaceful neighborhood, Kelly seemed to relax a little, though she still hadn't said a word about what was bothering her. The June night air contained a little more bite than I'd anticipated and I wished I'd brought along a sweater. Glancing at Kelly, I couldn't keep myself from noting pencil-eraser nipples poking under her top. Getting to the corner of her block, Kelly took a right and I stayed even with her, allowing the silence to continue.

Finally, she turned to me, her hands on my biceps stopping my progress. "He killed her, Uncle Joe," she said—her voice so hushed I figured I hadn't heard right.

"What?"

"He killed her," she repeated, her voice a more insistent whisper.

"Who killed who?" I asked, searching her face. The streetlight at the corner was behind me, my head keeping her face in shadow as if I were part of an eclipse of her face. When I tried to move to one side she followed. When I moved the other way again she stayed in front of me. If any insomniacs were looking out their windows, we probably looked like a drunken dance team.

She bounced now, still holding my arms, her frustration strangely electric, but she kept her voice low. "Daddy killed Rachel."

"Bullshit." The word leaped from my throat unbidden.

"It's not," she said, her voice high-pitched, urgent.

I shook my head vigorously. "No way," I said, struggling to keep my voice low so as not to alert the neighbors. "No fucking way. That's not funny, Kelly. That's a bad, bad joke."

Her face grew pinched, her grip tighter, her eyes pleading. "It's not a joke, Uncle Joe. He did it."

"I'm not going to listen to any more of this," I said.

And I tore myself from her grip and marched away.

She followed close behind. "Joe, I can prove it."

I stopped, spinning to face her, anger rising in my voice. "How?"

Kelly almost ran into me, took a step back, then looked up at me with the eyes of a scared animal. "Wuh . . . well," she stammered, "I can . . . can't exactly prove it."

"Why would you even say such a thing about your own father?"

She grabbed my face in her hands, our eyes locking. "Joe, he makes me have sex with him."

My hands went to her wrists to pull her hands away, but I paused as I looked into her eyes. Something I saw made me think that somehow these unthinkable things she was saying might be true. Her eyes never wavered, no sign of anything but innocence and honesty on her face.

"He's been doing it ever since . . . you know, since my boobs came in."

"Kelly . . . you can't say these things unless—"

"They're true, Uncle Joe. He's been raping me and raping me and I can't do anything about it, he looks scrawny but he's so strong . . ."

Slowly lowering her hands from my cheeks, I said, "We've got to take this to the police."

She shook her head. "They'll never believe it."

"Sure they will. You'll talk to doctors, and counselors, and—"

"No one will believe me. My father is an upstanding citizen, and I've been in all kinds of trouble . . . and I've been with a lot of boys. If they investigate, I'll be the one that looks awful."

I didn't know what to say.

"We should head back," she said.

"Wait a minute," I said, grabbing her shoulder and stopping her. "Let's say I believe you . . . at least about the incest. We've got to do something!"

"There's nothing to be done," Kelly said, her voice as matter-of-fact as if she were ordering drive-up at MacDonald's.

We walked, and I said, "Tell me why you think he killed Rachel."

"Two reasons. First, I finally told her about him, what he'd been doing. And she believed me. I think she suspected, before."

"When was this that you told her?"

"The night before he killed her."

"Shit!"

"And then there's the other reason—her money."

"You know about the money?"

"Yeah, from her dead first husband—my dad and Rachel sat me down and explained it to me. She thought it was important that I know about stuff like that, you know, just in case."

I nodded. Truthfully, Rachel had given me the same speech, or at least something near it.

"How did he do it?"

"Kill Rachel?" Kelly trudged wearily toward the house, pondering my question. "She was crying, all upset, and drinking . . . she must've conked out and he injected her and put her in the hot tub."

"Injected her? With what?"

"Shit, Uncle Joe! He's diabetic! The easiest thing in the world for him to get is insulin."

I tried to wrap my brain around the words that Kelly spoke. Quiet, unassuming Jason, the man who had wept in my arms earlier this afternoon, a rapist and killer? He'd seemed so broken up when I'd arrived—was it possible he'd been play-acting? But if it wasn't true, that meant that Kelly was lying, and what possible motivation could a seventeen-year-old girl have to lie about her father raping her?

The rest of the night passed in fits and starts as I tried to sleep and failed. I just couldn't stop thinking about what Kelly had told me, and the more I considered the accusations, the less sense the situation made.

When I came downstairs the next morning, dressed in my best (and only) black suit—since we were, after all, about to go to my sister's funeral—Jason and Kelly were already at the dining room table, although neither of them seemed to be eating. Jason nursed a cup of coffee, his own suit a dark-gray pinstripe, his shirt white, the tie a conservative gray with narrow stripes the color of dried blood.

"Morning," I said, fighting to keep both my voice and face neutral. I wanted to shout at Jason, "What the hell are you doing fucking your own daughter?" But I didn't say it. If I confronted Jason about the incest, I'd get tossed out on my ass, and Kelly and I would never get the evidence that he killed Rachel. Yet I still couldn't believe Jason had killed my sister . . . though if he had, I was determined to see him put away for the rest of his life.

"Good morning," Jason said, his eyes downcast, studying his coffee.

Kelly glanced up from her glass of juice, an untouched plate of toast in front of her. She didn't smile, she just met my eyes for a moment, then looked away.

We got through the funeral somehow—that's all you can do with any funeral. Jason seemed more in control than he had when he'd met me at the front door yesterday. Tears trickled down his cheeks, mine too for that matter. The minister said some nice words about Rachel. I spent the entire service looking at only two things: Rachel's casket sitting in the center aisle to my left and Jason's profile two seats away from me.

Kelly sat between us. I touched her knee with mine and she glanced over at me. I mouthed the words, "We need to talk," and she nodded.

After the service, we hosted a church luncheon for Rachel's friends, most of whom I didn't really know, and members of Jason's family, none of whom I knew. I had many conversations with many people that afternoon, but it's all a blur in my memory; hell, it was a blur, then.

Anyway, as soon as we were back in the house, Jason bid us good night, even though it was barely 5:00 P.M., and he disappeared into his room.

Kelly knocked on my bedroom door around seven and we went down to the kitchen where she made us both chicken sandwiches from last night's leftovers. She nuked the remaining corn and mashed potatoes and it served as a decent enough dinner. I started to broach the subject of Rachel's death, but she shooshed me and told me we could talk about it later when she was sure her father was asleep. I agreed and retired to my room.

She came to fetch me shortly after ten. The white string bikini she wore filled in most of the small gaps my imagination had left about Kelly's figure. "Why don't you put on your trunks," she said. "We'll go down to the hot tub—it always relaxes me."

I shook my head. "No trunks."

Pointing at the dresser, she said, "Top drawer."

I opened the drawer and pulled out a pair of black trunks that looked to be approximately my size, and held them up. "Where'd these come from?"

Kelly shrugged. "I think Rachel bought them for when you visited. You just didn't visit."

"Oh," I said.

I pulled off my shirt and looked up to see Kelly still standing in the doorway, an appraising smile settled on her pretty face. I guess I was in pretty good shape for an old fart.

"I . . . I'll meet you downstairs," I said and eased her out of the bedroom, closing the door behind her.

When I arrived downstairs, Kelly was nowhere in sight. I remembered Rachel phoning me in early March to tell me about their installing a hot tub in the backyard. Quietly, I made my way through the house and went out the back door. The yard was surrounded by a seven-foot privacy fence. The neighbors weren't close enough to see over the fence from their bedrooms.

Kelly had already entered the water. She floated in the huge tub, hair streaming and drifting on the surface like blonde seaweed, her head leaning against the edge, her arms bracing her against the bottom as the rest of her body shimmered through the torrent of bubbles and rising steam. "Come on in," she said, her voice turning into that husky whisper again.

I got into the water slowly, the heat coursing deeper inside me with each step down.

"Feels good, doesn't it?"

Nodding, I eased myself onto a seat across from her. "I can see how this would help you relax."

"Best thing," she said. "I love it here."

"About your dad," I began.

Suddenly, she sat up and moved closer to me, pushing against my arm until I raised it so she could huddle against me, my arm around her, her soft flesh against me. "What do you think we should do?"

"I think we should go to the police."

Kelly pulled away, her mouth open, her eyes wide. "We can't."

"Trust me," I said. "No—trust them. They'll get to the bottom of whatever's happening."

Shaking her head, she rushed back into my arms. "Don't make me tell the cops. They'll never believe me and . . . and the humiliation . . ." Her voice trailed off.

"We've got to go to the police," I said, trying to sound adamant even though I could feel Kelly against me, every inch of where she touched on fire with desire.

"There is another way," she said, her voice practically a purr, her head resting on my shoulder.

I pulled back a little to see her face. "What other way?"

"You could take care of it for me."

The look in her eyes didn't allow me to mistake the intention of her words. But still I asked, "Take care how?"

"Do to him what he did to her."

"No fucking way! What are you, nuts?"

"They'll never believe me, and if they do, I'll be this dysfunctional incest person, to everybody in the world, for the rest of my life—you gotta take him out, it's the only way."

"No chance."

She moved closer, her warmth infiltrating me, her arms around me, her tongue flicking my ear. "I would do anything to repay you, Uncle Joe . . . just anything."

Nothing on earth would have given me as much pleasure as saying yes at that moment. If she was right about her father murdering Rachel, I would do it happily, joyfully, even—I glanced down at the tan body in the water next to me—without such a generous reward. Still, I managed to say no.

"We've got to try my way first," I said. "It has to be right."

Soft tears trailed down her cheeks. "You're right, Uncle Joe," she said. "You must think I'm horrible and evil for even thinking such a thing."

I patted her shoulder, wiped away the tears, ran a hand through her blonde hair, moving damp tendrils off her face. She still cried softly, tilting her face to mine. I kissed her softly on the forehead, then both eyes. Kelly looked at me for an instant, her face an unreadable mask, then she pressed her lips to mine—softly at first, then more urgently. Her tongue slid into my mouth, then mine into hers. Immediately, we tore off each other's bathing suits and my kisses moved from her mouth to her long neck to her supple breasts.

Beneath the water, her hand found me, stroked softly, her legs moving around down there until she straddled me. Our heat rocketed through me as she guided me inside her. We rocked and bucked, water slopping over the sides of the hot tub, her moans like music.

As we lay in each other's arms, she said, "The only way we can be together is to have my father out of my life—forever."

"That's what jail will do."

She shook her head. "What if he's found innocent?"

"We'll still find a way."

"Do you love me, Joe?"

The question took me by surprise but I nodded.

"I mean, did you love me before this, tonight?"

"Sure, Kelly, you're a very special young woman. I've always seen that. Of course I love you."

I mean, she was my niece.

"You believe me, that my father's been fucking me?"

"Kelly . . ."

"Do you believe me?"

"Yes."

"Did you believe me when I told you all of this last night?"

I shrugged.

"Did you?"

Slowly, I shook my head.

"Then what makes you think strangers will believe me?"

Damn it, she made sense.

She reached into a towel wadded up next to the tub and came out with a small-caliber automatic pistol. "This was Rachel's gun."

"Rachel's gun . . ."

"It has to be now, Joe. While he's still asleep, before he can hurt me again. You heard terrible sounds and caught him raping me and you went nuts and got your sister's gun and . . . and that's what happened."

Things were moving too quickly. I jumped out of the hot tub, staying as far from the gun as I could.

Climbing out carefully, making sure not to get the gun wet, Kelly followed me. She stood before me, the moonlight bathing her nudity in an eerie white light.

I wanted to tell her she was crazy, that this whole idea was fucking insane, but I just kept staring at her body there in the moonlight, not saying a word.

Then she pressed against me again, her body hot, her kiss ardent and eager.

I felt her press the gun into my hand. "Just this one little thing and I'll be yours forever. You can do anything, anything you want."

She pulled away then and like a zombie I walked toward the house. I couldn't believe I was doing this. I went in through the back door and climbed the stairs. My nudity didn't even feel out of place. This would be pure, just me and the man who had killed my sister, raped the woman I loved. I crept down the hall, even as a voice in my head shouted, "Stop, this is insanity!"

I continued to move forward, silently twisting the doorknob. The room, pitch black, felt cold, the air prickling my naked skin. I eased forward, Jason's breathing coming from just ahead on my right. He slept soundly, his breathing even and regular. Each time he exhaled I moved another step closer. On the fourth breath I leaned over his bed, his body a lumpy silhouette in the bed. His face, upturned and placid, showed no shadow of the guilt he must feel for his crimes.

Letting my hand come forward, I softly touched the barrel of the pistol against Jason's temple. At that precise second, just as his eyes popped open in shock, I heard a siren in the distance. I don't know why I heard that when I heard no other sound save for Jason's breathing. The breaths came faster and shallower now that he was awake. Just as his eyes found mine in the darkness, I pulled the trigger.

The report did not explode, as I expected, but sounded more like a cap gun going off. My arm jerked slightly from the recoil, and a small clump of Jason's brain blew out the far side of his head. It wasn't at all like these things appeared in the movies. Of course, having written true crime I knew that, but it still surprised me a little.

Jason's blood appeared black on his skull and the pillow. I said nothing, just turned and walked out. When I got to the end of the hall and looked down the stairs, Kelly stood at the bottom, a flimsy robe clinging to her damp skin. She seemed to be watching out the small window next to the front door.

What was she looking for, lights going on in the neighbors' houses?

I came down one step, the gun dangling from my hand.

"We . . . we have to get our stories straight," I said.

Suddenly, Kelly jerked open the front door and two policemen entered with their guns drawn.

They saw me, and the bigger one, a rangy white kid who looked like a college linebacker, pointed his nine-millimeter at me and yelled, "Drop it now."

His black partner dropped to one knee, aimed at me while sweeping Kelly behind him out of the line of fire.

"He raped me," she screamed. "And he murdered my father."

Then it all became clear. Now I knew that Rachel really had been murdered—injected with insulin, all right; it was just that Jason hadn't been the one to do it.

"Wait," I said, my hand coming up automatically in a stop gesture. I realized I was still holding the gun just as the first bullet ripped into my chest. The force knocked me backward and I was about to fall, my feeble hands trying to toss away the pistol, then the second bullet hit higher than the first and I crumpled to the floor.

It would have been better if I'd died then, I suppose. Certainly better for Kelly, who would have inherited not just her father's share of my sister's estate, but the portion meant for me as well. Instead, I'm in Ft. Madison, serving a life term, in the company of two murderers I wrote books about. My presence amuses them.

Anyway, this is the book proposal. It would flesh out easily— I could do a whole section on being a teacher and the girl who seduced me. And if we want to go for a cheap irony, I could do a few chapters about prison life, and how one night in a hot tub led me into hundreds of nights of terrible sex in the showers.

Not that I'm complaining. They're letting me write in here, so at least I can still pursue my craft, and I'm over my Lolita complex, even if I can see the warden's daughter from my high, barred window.

Mercy

I've always appreciated women who can say *fuck* without the word sticking in their throat. Whether it is said in anger or in lust, the word *fuck* from a woman's lips is far more potent than from a man's. A woman who can say *fuck* boldly is a woman who can conquer the world.

I'd heard Mercy Palmer say *fuck* on more than one occasion, and whenever she said it, it always made me want her more.

For some men there are many women. For me there has always been only one. I don't mean to say there haven't been women with whom I've had sex. While I hardly have a Ph.D. in carnal knowledge, there have been several times when the words *I love you* have been whispered desperately through my lips. In reality, however, the sentiment meant little more than *can we have a quick shag while your old man's not around?* No, the difference between loving someone and being *in love* with someone cannot be gauged in temporal measures.

Although I was no Casanova, my problem with women was not necessarily getting them into bed. Once I'd had them, once the adventure of the conquest was gone, I lost interest. This hardly made for strong, long-term relationships. However, I believed my obsession with Mercy was different. Here was a woman you could have again and again and never lose the lust for more.

When I was ten and Mercy was eight, she called me a fucking little wanker, and I was hers forever. I gave her back the jam pastie I'd snitched from her school lunch tray and marveled at the worldliness of women and how they would always know far more than men.

I *was* a fucking little wanker. In fact, even at ten I was having a good wank several times a day. How Mercy Palmer found out was beyond me, but if she knew, then certainly she'd take pity and help me out from time to time. I was ten going on eight. She was eight going on thirty. She never helped out.

Time only changes some things.

I was now thirty going on fifty. Mercy, however, could still say *fuck* with wanton abandon, and I was still a *wanker*, although I was now closer to the figurative definition than the literal.

"For fuck's sake, Peter. Why do you let that bastard treat you that way?"

She just had to say the word, and the little head that rules my big head perks up and takes notice.

"It's no big deal, Mercy," I said.

"Of course it is. If you let them treat you like shit, then you're no better than shit."

Her black skirt was tight across her curved hips. Sitting next to her in the grotty, but noisy pub, I couldn't help noticing it was short enough to show the tops of her black stockings if she made any movement at all.

"Okay, I'm no better than shit. But at least I'm shit with a job."

Mercy's green eyes flashed. She shook her head as she ran her fingers through her shoulder-length black tresses. Her large, natural breasts rose and fell as she sighed. She wasn't wearing a bra under her scarlet silk blouse, and her nipples poked out like tenpenny-nail heads. "Holy crap, Peter. How do you ever get laid?"

"I get by," I said, stung by this latest slight.

"What? A quick touch-and-tumble in the back of your beatup Peugeot?"

"Well, only if I've paid out sixty pounds for dinner and another twenty on drinks."

Mercy laughed. A full, rich, vibrant guffaw. She just threw back her head and let it rumble out.

Oh, sweet Mary, a woman who could say *fuck* and laugh till her panties fell down. I could die happy just having known her.

She was upset with me because I had let Reginald Morton take the credit for a new storyline on *Breaker's Heart*, a reasonably successful cops and robbers shoot-em-up showing Tuesday nights at 10:00 P.M. on BBC 1. Both Mercy and I were *Breaker's Heart* staff writers. I was just a hack, but Mercy was looking to get her own show on the air—a show we were convinced would be far better than the crap we were currently turning out. Crap sells, however, and until the world came to its senses and became literate, Mercy and I were doomed to the purgatory of recycling American cop dramas as English originals.

Before I had a chance to argue my case, good old Reggie slid into our booth and planted three pints on the scarred wood table—all of them for him. The cell phone, keys, and large leather wallet-cum-scheduler he had trapped under his arm fell out and scattered across the table.

He sat with an explosion of air from his lungs and planted a hand on Mercy's thigh. She leaned over and plunged her teeth into the meat of his left arm. Good old Reggie damn near tore his suit jacket getting free.

"Right little cannibal, aren't you," he said, aggrieved.

"A man-eater," Mercy concurred, and ran her tongue lasciviously around her lips.

The pub was filling with Friday night just-a-quick-one regulars, studio hacks who didn't want to go home right away in case somebody said something behind their back. Slot machines and sports on two large tellys passed for atmosphere. However, the proprietor—a part-time character actor with no character—drew a fair pint and a full measure of spirits when the occasion arose.

Already more than half cut from sipping at his gin flask all day, Reggie finished his first pint in one giant quaff. He picked up the second pint and drained half of it. "Fucking sods at the network have had me chasing around so much I almost disappeared up my own bum hole," he said, after pausing to catch his breath.

When Reggie said *fuck*, it didn't have anywhere near the same effect on me as when the word tippled over Mercy's bee-stung lips. Reggie Morton was the producer of *Breaker's Heart*, the *show runner*, as he liked to be called ever since his last trip to Hollywood. He wrote six scripts a year for the show, not one of them based on ideas from his own alcohol-soaked imagination. He relied on weak-willed staff writers, such as myself, to provide him with the inspiration, which he then slapped into one of four script variations. Notwithstanding this repetitiveness, his episodes always drew the highest ratings of the season. The BBC loved him. I despised him.

"I hear Sheila MacIntyre has old man Eversham wrapped around her little finger," Reggie said. Eversham was the BBC programming chairman. "Word is he's going to give the go-ahead to her *City Lights* series."

"If that slut has Eversham wrapped around anything its her legs," Mercy said. "*City Lights* is the biggest piece of crap to float down the Thames since Maggie Thatcher's last official bowel movement."

"Oooh, meow," Reggie said, mock swish. He finished his second pint and immediately started his third. "I forgot you were hoping to get some ratty little program off the ground with Eversham. What's it called?"

"You know damn well it's called *Crescent Row*."

"That's right," Reggie said. "Some kind of Dallas rip-off set in Bath, right?"

Reggie was taking the piss something fierce. The problem was, our usually give-as-good-as-she-gets Mercy did not have a sense of humor where *Crescent Row* was concerned.

For over a year Mercy had been working to create the concept of a modern *Upstairs, Downstairs,* set in Bath, the Beverly Hills of England. She had six prepared scripts, interest from several popular actors for the lead roles, and had done everything but bring her knee pads into a meeting with Eversham to get the show off the ground. She probably should have brought the knee pads, because old man Eversham was vacillating—which was probably better than masturbating, but not by much.

"You really are a shit, Reggie." Mercy was pouting. I wanted to bite into her protruding bottom lip and suck out the blood.

"Don't be mad, sweetie." Reggie was still in swish mode. He signaled the waitress with his third empty pint glass. "*Breaker's Heart* will be back again next season. If you're nice to me, you'll still have work."

"Give it a rest, Reggie," I said. He was hitting the booze hard even for him. I didn't know how he was going to drive home. Didn't care, either.

He looked over at me, "You, on the other hand," he said, "will be a victim of corporate downsizing."

I felt my scrotum shrinking. "What do you mean?"

"Didn't I tell you, old boy?"

"No, you didn't."

"I'm so sorry, but the network is cutting our budget for next season by 10 percent. What with the raise Marcus will expect, cuts are going to have to be made somewhere else."

Marcus Tanner, the star of *Breaker's Heart,* already had more money than a Swiss bank. Still, he'd never consider starting a new season without holding out for a substantial raise. There were too many other producers waiting to pounce on him should *Breaker's Heart* be canceled.

I still couldn't believe what I was hearing. "So, you're cutting the writing staff?"

"Have to, dearie," Reggie said, downing half of another pint. "It means I'll be forced to write several more episodes, but we all must make sacrifices."

"When does this become official?" I asked.

"Oh, you'll be kept on through the end of this season's production."

"But that's only two weeks away. How am I supposed to find another job by then?"

Reggie swilled down the last of his refilled pint. He slammed the glass down on the table and accompanied the noise with a satisfied belch. "Not my problem, old boy. My problem is keeping the network sweet."

"Mercy is right," I said. "You are a shit. What about the storyline for the new episode? Will you at least give me credit for it and let me write the script? I need the money."

Reggie gave me a dark look. "That idea is mine. I have the outline all prepared to send to the network. You wouldn't want to take credit for something you didn't create, would you? If that's your attitude, perhaps you should be terminated now."

I held my tongue despite the anger building inside me. The storyline was my idea, but I needed the two weeks of work. "Sorry, Reggie," I said eventually. I saw a look of disgust cross Mercy's face.

"Fucking worm," she said.

Reggie assumed she was talking about me.

"Yes, quite," he said with a laugh. "Well, must be off. Have a script to write this weekend, don't you know." Open wound, insert salt.

Reggie, the pompous git, stood up, wavered for a second and sat back down. He burped and went a little cross-eyed.

"Shit," Mercy said. "Look at the state he's in."

Reggie grinned. "I could still give you a quick tumble." His words were badly slurred. He reached out toward Mercy's thigh, but she brushed his hand away.

"You couldn't tumble a load of washing," Mercy said.

Reggie's eyes turned mean. "That pussy you're sitting on isn't made of gold, you know. Pussies like yours are a penny a pound in this business." His voice was getting loud, gathering attention from the pub's other punters. He tried to stand up again. "If you don't get your fucking priorities right, you'll be out on your fucking ear like the stupid toe-rag sitting next to you. Then you'll damn well spread your legs in a hurry."

"Oh, fuck," Mercy said, fending off Reggie as he staggered and almost fell over her. "Peter, get him out of here and into a taxi."

"Not me," I said. "He can sleep on the floor for all I care."

Pushing Reggie back to a sitting position, Mercy threw her keys on the table. "Look, I'll get him outside. Just get my car and bring it around the front," she said, leaning forward to rub her hand across my thigh. I wasn't so far gone I didn't take the opportunity to gaze into the depth of her cleavage. "Come on," she said. "It's not the end of the world. We'll get the bastard home, and by tomorrow he'll have changed his mind. He needs you. Where else is he going to get storylines from?"

I didn't believe her.

Mercy got up and pulled Reggie to his feet without waiting for my answer. With his arm over her shoulder and hers around his waist, it looked as if they were off to an illicit tryst. There were several knowing glances and rude noises from the voyeurs in the pub. Mercy gave them two fingers and told them all to "Fuck off!" How she loved that word.

I waited a minute before following, still considering my situation. My Peugeot had been running rough lately so I'd taken the tube to work. What finally decided me was the hope I could persuade Mercy to give me a lift after we'd dropped Reggie.

I gathered up Mercy's keys. I then picked up Reggie's keys, his wallet-cum-scheduler, and his cell phone, all of which he'd left behind. I stuffed the items in various pockets and headed for the car park.

Mercy had guided the ambulatory but drunken Reggie around from the front of the pub, cursing me for taking my time. In the rear car park, we stuffed Reggie into the backseat where he immediately began to snore. Mercy took her keys back, slid into the driver's seat, started the engine, and accelerated almost before I could get in myself.

Her car was a semi-new green Trident, and Mercy shifted easily through the gears as she pulled out of the car park in front of an overburdened lorry. Ignoring the sound of tortured brakes, she flew into traffic like a demon on a rampage.

Lying on the backseat, Reggie was moving around. He was mumbling to himself something about, "Gonna show you what your pussy is missing."

"Shut up, shithead!" Mercy yelled at him.

After we'd driven several miles in silence, Mercy finally said, "I can't spend another season writing the crap we produce for *Breaker's Heart.*" I could tell she was fuming. "If that bitch Sheila MacIntyre gets the go-ahead for *City Lights,*" she continued, "all the work I've done on *Crescent Row* will be for naught. I can't believe that old fool Eversham has allowed MacIntyre to turn his head."

"It is all about you, isn't it, Mercy?" I said in a bit of a snit. "What about me? At least you've got a spot on *Breaker's Heart.* I've been given the push. How the hell am I supposed to keep up the payments on my flat? Hell, everything I own is on the *never-never*. I'm so far in the red, I'll never see black again."

"Don't worry. You can work for me on *Crescent Row*."

"Putting me on the staff of a nonexistent show is not going to pay my bills."

Mercy let out a loud sigh. "You *are* a fucking little wanker, Peter. We'll just have to do something to make sure *Crescent Row* gets on the schedule."

There was the *f*-word again. The sound of Mercy's voice when she said it brought me back to my senses. I looked over as she drove and saw her skirt had risen above her stocking tops. The white of her thighs shone like a beacon under her garter straps. I felt my throat closing.

"Like what?" I forced the words out.

Mercy turned to me with a smile. Her skirt shifted even higher. "We're writers," she said. "We'll think of something."

Within twenty minutes, we were slipping down the driveway between the secluded Georgian monstrosity Reggie called home and the high hedge separating him from his neighbor.

"Would you look at this," Mercy said in disgust when she opened the Trident's back door and half dragged Reggie out of the car. I took a gander and saw Reggie had his pants down around his ankles. He was semi-stuporously playing with a purple erection.

"Ha, ha," he said. "Gotcha!" As sperm exploded from his penis, I jumped back. The thick, white fluid sailed through the air and striped across Mercy's dress.

"Shit! Fuck!" she said.

I laughed, she swore again, and Reggie passed out completely.

Finally, huffing and puffing, we dragged Reggie out of the car, used his keys to unlock the door, and hauled him inside.

"Too bad the bastard lives alone," I said, as there was nobody to help us with Reggie's increasingly heavy bulk.

"Who in their right mind would live with this fucking wanker?" Mercy shot back. We dumped Reggie on the closest settee and left him there.

Back in her car, Mercy glided through the quiet neighborhood as if she couldn't wait to be away from its influence. After a few short miles, the terrain was still upscale, but of a decidedly trendier nature. I'd been so deep in my self-misery, I'd not noticed where Mercy had been driving. I was surprised when she suddenly pulled in to the rear of Grove Mews, where she lived.

"Hey," I said, perturbed. "I thought you were taking me home."

"I told you I'd give you a lift, but if you think I'm fighting the traffic to your little piece of suburban squalor, you don't know me as well as I thought you did." She slipped out of the car and leaned back in to talk again. Inside her blouse her breasts swayed free and gently in front of my eyes. I felt an almost irresistible urge to reach out and caress them. "You coming or not?" she asked. The double-entendre was no mistake.

I unbuckled in a hurry and followed Mercy's swaying bottom up a short flight of steps to her flat. The view was marvelous. I felt myself getting hard. I'd wanted this woman so badly for so long. Right at that moment a mercy fuck from Mercy was at the top of my priority list.

Inside she kicked off her shoes and moved into the small kitchen. I stood, self-consciously looking at the tapestries and throw pillows with which Mercy had decorated, and tried to catch my breath. I put a hand in my jacket pocket and cursed. I still had Reggie's wallet and cell phone.

Mercy came back with two large glasses of wine. I could have sworn she'd undone another button on her blouse.

"What are you waiting for?" she asked. "Sit down. Make yourself at home."

I *uhmm*ed and *err*ed turning around until Mercy set down the wineglasses, pushed me onto an overstuffed settee, pulled my shoes off, and curled up at the other end with her feet tucked under her. She handed me a wineglass and took a big swallow from her own, as if bracing herself for what was ahead.

Exactly what was ahead? The brain in my head asked the question, but the brain in my penis ignored it. I was mesmerized, watching as Mercy's breasts struggled to free themselves from their silken prison with every movement she made.

"Peter," Mercy said. "We are upfucked unless we do something fast."

I gulped and looked sheepish.

"Not *that*," Mercy said with a resigned sigh. "When we do *that*, it will be anything but fast."

Showed you how much she knew. But wait a minute—she was talking about *when* we did *that*. I didn't even think we were going to do *that*—ever. What had I missed?

"I'm talking," Mercy said, trying to focus my attention, "about doing something fast to save ourselves from turning into television sluts. We've got to get off *Breaker's Heart* and do something different if we're ever going to get somewhere. We've got to do something about Reggie and that bitch Sheila MacIntyre before we're both made redundant."

"I've already been made redundant," I said. "I'm not like you. I'm a hack. I can't devise any of my own series ideas that are worth a crap. All I'm good for is putting new spins on somebody else's creations." It was a harsh truth, but true nonetheless. If somebody came up with a good idea, I had a knack for turning it into a great idea.

"But you are so good at putting on those new spins," Mercy said, moving forward to place a hand on my leg. One beautiful breast spilled free. She made no move to restrain it. "That's why I need you on *Crescent Row*."

My heart was pounding so hard I almost didn't hear her. My penis was twisted in my Y-fronts, throbbing painfully, begging to be set loose. "There is no *Crescent Row*," I squeaked.

"But there could be," Mercy said. Her hand moved up to my thigh. Her other breast spilled out.

"How?" I was frozen with desire. I'd dreamed for years of getting my leg over Mercy. Now she was coming on so strong, I couldn't grasp what was within my reach.

She backed off slightly. "Your new episode for *Breaker's Heart*," she said.

"What about it?"

"Reggie is claiming it's his idea."

"So?"

"So, think about the premise."

I tried to organize my thoughts. How had I pitched the idea to Reggie? "Breaker investigates the accidental death of a woman as the result of an autoerotic session," I said. "So what?"

Mercy smiled invitingly. "But Breaker," she said in a mock serious voice, "is convinced it's murder because, unlike men, women very rarely engage in autoerotic play by themselves."

Autoerotic was the term applied to the techniques used to voluntarily cut off the blood supply to the brain in the moments leading to orgasm. Many men died from tying themselves up to cause this sensation, only to go too far and pass out, strangling themselves. Very embarrassing for the family member or friend who discovers the scene.

Couples had been known to engage in similar fetish-play, as there was safety in numbers. Still, accidents occurred, but my research had shown there were almost no cases of women accidentally dying from singular autoerotic practices.

"And how does Breaker catch the suspect in the end?" Mercy asked.

I shrugged. "He has to trick him into a confession, doesn't he? There was no other way to prove it."

"A bit lucky, don't you think?"

"Everything Breaker does is lucky."

"Yeah, but he does it with such insincere sincerity, doesn't he?"

"And the public love it, damn them. But what does this have to do with Reggie?"

"You still have his cell phone and wallet, don't you?" Mercy was smirking now.

"Well, yes," I admitted sheepishly. She knew me too well.

"Of course you do. You're a silly little wanker, but you're my silly wanker." Mercy was back to massaging my thigh.

"Agreed," I said. "But I'm also a thick little wanker because I still don't know what you're on about."

Mercy smiled. "Our friend Sheila is into autoeroticism."

"And how do you know?"

Mercy smiled. "I'm not just a one-way girl, you know."

That threw images into my head. Mercy with Sheila MacIntyre?

"Okay. But what does that do for us?"

Mercy grabbed me by the crotch. I yelped.

"Don't be stupid, Peter," Mercy said, half angry. "If Sheila were to die tonight of an autoerotic incident, and Reggie's wallet and cell phone were found at the scene, he'd be in no shape to deny any allegations brought against him. They'll find the notes for the script idea Reggie has prepared for the network. They're being presented under his name, not yours, since he stole them. It's the ultimate set-up."

"You're out of your mind," I started, but Mercy squeezed my prick until I yelped again.

She kept talking. "With Sheila gone her show would be defunct. And even if Reggie wasn't prosecuted for anything, the scandal would ruin him for running *Breaker's Heart*. With no *City Lights,* and Reggie out on his ear, *Crescent Row* would get the chance it needs, and we'd be on our way."

She was expertly unzipping my pants, freeing my prick and taking it into her mouth. I sighed this time as she moved her lips smoothly up and down my shaft. Then, with a plopping noise, she pulled her mouth free and captured my prick between her breasts. From somewhere, a magician's conjuring trick, she produced a condom in a foil package. She tore the package open with her teeth and expertly slid the thin rubber into place.

"Got to put its nightcap on," Mercy said. "Don't know where it's been."

She was right. I was a silly little wanker, but I was her silly little wanker. At that moment, I would do anything for her.

Even commit murder.

Mercy pushed herself away from me and flopped back on the settee. She squirmed lewdly, causing her skirt to rise up higher and higher, revealing she wore no panties, her black stockings held up by a frilly black garter. She spread her nylon-clad legs wantonly.

"Come on, Peter. You know you want me," she said. Her voice was husky, but at least she could speak. From my end of the settee, I was unable to do anything but make inarticulate noises. She held her arms out, beckoning me. "Put it in me now, Peter. Please, Peter. Fuck me."

I was going insane. I thrust forward, fighting to get clear of my pants and Y-fronts. It's always easier in the movies. Shoes caused a problem, but I finally kicked them free and damn near across the room.

I fell on her like a demolished building coming down. I entered her in one movement, crying out in ecstasy and lust. She wrapped her legs around me, locking her heels across my buttocks, and bucking as hard as a rugby forward diving into a scrum.

Her fingers were buried in my hair, her lips next to my ear. "Kill Sheila," she said between gasps, "and you can fuck me again and again." There was that word. Four little letters in Mercy's voice that obsessed me. As I exploded inside her for the first time, my world felt as if it were shattering.

Once would never be enough for a woman like Mercy. Before I had time to catch my breath, she had dragged me from the settee to her bed. She tore my tie and shirt free, and then used her mouth and her nails to bring me quickly back to life before slipping on another rubber nightcap. Did she have a never-ending supply? Where did she keep the damn things?

I tried to lose myself inside her again, but there was something wrong. Internally, I was suddenly struggling with the same demons that plagued all of my relationships. I wasn't tired of Mercy, but she was now tainted with tarnish—a new car with its first nick. I'd had her. I'd finally conquered the one woman I thought I could never have.

The big brain was finally taking over from the little brain. As thrilling as she was, as gymnastic, as lewd, as rude as she was, Mercy was just another fuck.

As she whispered of sexual desires and murderous plots, the genius of my hack skills kicked in. I could always take somebody's good idea and make it a great idea.

Mercy ground her pelvis hard against my pubic bone. She mumbled about Reggie's wallet and cell phone. *Yes,* I thought in a remote part of my brain, they could easily be used to implicate him.

As the little death of orgasm swept through her again, I saw she was right about the police following up on the script notes Reggie claimed were his own work. Somebody would have to tip the coppers the wink, but they would do the job.

Finally, worn out, Mercy lay sleeping in my arms. I embraced her, my eyes wide open, creative juices flowing in the wake of the exhaustion of more natural lubricants.

The chances were still slim of *Crescent Row* getting on the air even if *City Lights* flickered out. Old Eversham could pick any of two dozen other shows all set to jump onto the schedule.

Breaker's Heart, on the other hand, was a sure thing. With my bills, I needed a sure thing. If Reggie was dumped, the show would go on with a new show runner. Mercy maybe?

Wait a minute—why not me?

Take a good idea and make it a great idea. That was my forte. Reggie had been heard making loud, sexually suggestive comments to Mercy in the pub. They had been seen leaving together. There was nobody in the back parking lot who saw me help Mercy lay him down in the back of her car. And if anybody saw Mercy driving away, it was dark enough they would have only seen two bodies in the seats—Reggie and Mercy would be what they thought.

Nobody was at Reggie's house. He was now passed out for the night. Nobody saw us getting him into the house because of the high hedges. Reggie's sperm was on Mercy's skirt. I'd used a condom. This was getting brilliant.

If it was Mercy who died of autoerotic strangulation, the wallet, the cell phone, the sperm, and the script notes would damn Reggie to hell.

Such were the ratings and star power of *Breaker's Heart* that the show would go on without them and not even skip a beat. Next season's show runner, as Reggie liked to be called? How about me? No reason why not.

Mercy stirred in my arms. I reached down and flipped loose the garter catches holding up one of her stockings. I slid my fingers inside the top of the hose and ran the garment down and off her leg. Mercy giggled. Her slim fingers reached out to capture my prick.

"Are you ready to fuck again so soon, you silly little wanker?"

The word *fuck* had no effect on me at all. However, moving up in the world, securing my spot on *Breaker's Heart,* becoming a show runner—now there was something to give a man a raging erection.

I moved the nylon stocking up and dragged it gently across Mercy's throat.

A Pair of Queens

Marthayn Pelegrimas

Central City, Colorado, was a boom town—again. The first time, more than a hundred years ago, involved gold in them thar hills. This time it was casinos. Legalized gambling brought new life into the worn city. Dilapidated buildings were restored and resold for ten times their value. Local tavern and restaurant owners who had managed to hold on through the tough times were now running quaint gambling halls. So far twenty-seven had cropped up along the main street connecting Black Hawk to Central City. Regular businesses managed to survive by rechristening themselves to match their fancy surroundings.

When Princess Delaney returned to work at the Pair of Queens Beauty and Tanning Salon, she knew cutting and dyeing her hair wouldn't surprise a single one of her clients or coworkers. After all, since graduating from beauty school she'd been a redhead, a blonde, highlighted, streaked, permed and straightened her hair. Sometimes she dropped down on her knees and gave thanks that she hadn't gone bald from all the chemicals she sprayed and painted on her shoulder-length 'do.

"Troy come back yet?" she asked Yvonne, the receptionist.

"Nope. Said you shouldn't expect him till next week."

Princess snapped her gum a few times. "What about Kyle?"

"Him neither. Looks like another lover's spat. You'll have to take care of things till they kiss and make up."

"Sometimes I think I'm too nice. People take advantage of me, know what I mean?" Princess moaned.

"I hear ya. But until the boss men return, you're in charge, I guess."

Princess leafed through the appointment book. "How's it looking for this afternoon?"

Yvonne took a sip of her Dr Pepper. "Slow."

"Wanna help me then? I need a change. How about something like Monique from that soap you like?"

Yvonne brightened up. "Wow, you're talking about cutting off three whole inches?"

"Let's go for it." Princess walked back to the sinks. "Come on. Time is money."

———

He should have spent the money on a real hotel room, but Bernie Creeger was a cheap bastard. Instead he pulled the dirty sheets off his own queen size and replaced them with the good ones he saved for special company. Sweeping his arm across the top of his dresser, he let the crap fall to the carpet. Then he cleaned off the chair in the corner, tossing a week's worth of dirty clothes and damp towels onto the floor. Crawling on his knees across the carpet, he bulldozed everything into the closet.

Standing back to inspect the results, he still wasn't satisfied. "It's them pictures," he grumbled. "Too personal."

Carefully folding Miss February into a flat square, he then yanked down the poster of his favorite wrestler clad in a black leather dominatrix outfit. "Sorry girls, but this is business."

Racing into the living room, he removed the paint-by-number landscape his mother had done ten years ago, before arthritis stifled her artistic career. Then he nailed it over the bed for that Holiday Inn effect. The lamps, plain brass things he'd had since high school, looked fine and the rest of the stuff wouldn't be that noticeable once the camera was positioned outside the bedroom window.

The night was cool and damp. September was shortening the days; a full moon lit up the sky. The patch of yard outside the master bedroom had long ago filled in with scraggly bushes. Thank God he'd been too lazy to trim them back. Pushing the tripod down into the grass, Bernie looked through the viewfinder of his rented camcorder. The gauzy curtains were perfect. He left the equipment and returned to adjust the bedroom lights. All he had to do now was wait for Princess to show.

———

Princess strutted out of the bathroom like she was on a runway. "How about this one? I kinda like the feathers."

Bernie sat up on the bed, still fully clothed. "What the hell ya doin'? This ain't no fashion show here."

"You said this woman was classy, didn't ya? You tell me to get my hair done short an' dark. I checked that picture you showed me, the one the guy gave ya, and it sure as hell looks to me like I'm the same size as her. I figure I got everything covered except the attitude. So I ask myself, what would she wear when meetin' her lover?"

"Jesus H. Christ." Bernie tossed the magazine he'd been reading across the room. "You're one stupid bitch, ya know that?" Walking over to her, he reached and grabbed her hands. "At least you done what I told you and took off them claws you call nails."

Princess pulled away and sat on the edge of the bed. "You're lower than dirt, Bernie. Maybe I'm gonna change my mind here. Yer awful mean tonight."

"Yeah, yeah, I'm shit on a stick." Bernie could see his bonus sprouting wings and getting ready to fly out the window. He needed Princess. "I'm sorry, baby. This has to go smooth." He ran his thumbnail across her skin, easing the feathered strap down her arm. Kneeling, he licked her shoulder, kissing his way up to her neck. That always got her.

Princess closed her eyes and moaned. "That's better."

Bernie went in for a long passionate kiss, sliding his tongue deep inside Princess's mouth. When he could feel her arch her back he disconnected and stood up. "Now take that thing off, get into bed, and I'll be right back soon as I start the camera."

"Okay."

He walked to the bedroom door, opened it, then turned back. "Thanks for helpin' me out."

Princess stood in front of him naked. "Sure. Just hurry back, it's cold in here."

Bernie ran outside, checking quickly for the freaks who lived next door. The yard and alley were quiet. Smart of him to do this thing after midnight. When he couldn't locate the tripod right away, he took it as a sign that no one else could. Glancing through the viewfinder, he watched Princess stretching out across the orange chenille bedspread. What a killer bod that broad had. Her tits were firm, thirty-six D's. No matter how many times he saw those babies, he still got hard as a nightstick. He unzipped his fly and readjusted his package with one hand while pushing the RECORD button with the other.

By the time Bernie got back inside, Princess was bending over, turning the sheets down, her smooth ass beckoning him to come in out of the cold. He couldn't help himself.

"God, baby, you get to me every time." Easing his dick out of his pants, he entered her from behind. She was ready for him, she always was. His hands reached around to fondle her breasts.

"I missed you too, Bern," she said, "you was always great in the sack, but don't go thinkin' we're gettin' back together." She pressed against him. "This here's business. And ain't ya supposed to be wearin' a disguise or somethin' now that the camera's goin'?"

He licked her ear and between thrusting and groping, he

managed to say, "Yeah, sure, but this one's for me. I'll fix the tape later."

"You think of everything."

Being the showman that he was, Bernie Creeger didn't want to ruin the mood. Their foreplay was heating the room up pretty good. All Princess had to do was look genuine. He knew what a great lay she was, but her acting abilities, those were questionable.

When Bernie was so turned on he could hardly walk, he forced himself, for the good of the video sale, to hobble to the bathroom where he'd stashed a wig. Leaving his t-shirt on to hide his Road Runner tattoo, he came back to the bed naked from the waist down.

Princess laughed at his disguise. "You look like Tom Jones. Ya know, when he was hot, not the way he looks now."

"Ya think so?" He stopped by the mirror to check himself out. "Kinda. I see what ya mean." Getting into the bed he pulled her to him. "And you, doll, with that hair ya don't look like anyone."

"What?" Princess's face dropped. "What kinda shitty thing is that to say?"

"I mean you're in a league all your own. Ya always been like that."

"Oh." She thought a minute and decided she liked the comment. Reaching down, she started massaging his balls. "Thanks, Bern."

"Better take off those rings . . . all your jewelry."

"You're the boss." She pulled off her watch and four rings, then sat up to undo three earrings hooked into each earlobe. When her hand was full of silver, she tossed everything under the bed. "What about you?"

"Oh, yeah." He yanked off his large gold pinkie ring and watch.

"Now come here." He pushed her onto her back and arranged

the pillows to shadow her face. "Act like you're havin' a real good time."

Bernie sucked on her nipples until she begged him to enter her. He covered her mouth with his own and grabbed her firm butt with both hands. Kneading the soft flesh, he could feel her positioning herself beneath him. Rising to his knees he ran his erection across her clitoris, softly, then poked inside, hitting all the good spots he could along the way.

She clawed his chest, whimpering, "Fuck me now, baby. Come on, do it to me."

He thrust into her with enough force to make her hit her head on the cheap headboard. But she was too into him to care. Lifting her legs until her ankles rested on his shoulders, she strained to get him deeper inside, gyrating her hips with each thrust until they moved like a well-rehearsed act.

"Slow down," Bernie whispered into her ear. "We got all night . . ."

". . . An' a whole tape to fill up, right?" Princess giggled. "I can last as long as you can."

———

"It took a while but I got the proof you wanted," Bernie said into the phone.

"Keep it there. I'm on a call now but I'll be finished in about an hour. Okay if I stop by your office to pick it up?"

Jeez, this guy was in a hurry, Bernie thought. But maybe he did have reason to be a little anxious, especially considering how Bernie had been stringing the poor sap along for three months. All the time charging for time and expenses he never put out. "That'll be fine, Mr. Jarrett."

"Thanks."

Bernie hung up. After finishing his sandwich, he went to the middle of the small room that had once been an assayer's office until the PI had converted it. Rolling up a corner of the carpet, he got down on his knees to open the safe. It was an ancient thing left behind by the last occupant. The lock had been busted for years but Bernie felt safer putting his valuables inside the hunk of steel than just leaving them lying around. Pulling aside his petty cash, he found the videotape his client was coming to get. Letting the door drop shut, Bernie then stood up and kicked the stained carpet back into place.

He and Princess had watched the movie several times before he'd edited out their X-rated intro.

"What if he don't buy it? Ya know, that I'm his old lady?" she'd asked.

"There's one thing I'd bet my life on," he'd told her, "and it's that people only see what they wanna see. This guy wants his wife to be guilty."

"But if she ain't cheatin', what you're gonna do to her is pretty low. Really rotten."

"You're gettin' your cut. And how many relationships you been in where you ain't cheated?"

She didn't even have to think about it. "None."

"More than 50 percent of all married people cheat anyway. It's a fact."

"Where'd ya dig that number up?"

"*Penthouse, Hustler,* one of them. Besides," he'd confided, "I gotta hunch the guy's got somethin' goin' on the side."

Placing the cassette into a manila envelope, Bernie ran his slimy tongue across the flap. All he had to do now was wait for Jarrett, then collect his money. Sometimes life could be so sweet.

Del Jarrett sat in a line of cars waiting his turn to pass the road crew. Pounding his hands on the steering wheel of his new Lexus, he shouted, "All right! I got you now, bitch!" In the security of his plush interior, he found it hard to contain his happiness.

Punching in numbers on his cell phone, Del admired his tan while waiting for the party at the other end to pick up. It only took four rings.

Anxiously he reported his news, "I got it. Yeah, I'm on my way home now. This shouldn't take too long. I'll call you after she leaves. Love you, too."

———

Linda Jarrett was surprised to see her husband's car parked in front of the house. He was always so particular about tucking it safely in his space inside their three-car garage. His business trip must have been cut short: It was a Wednesday and Del was never home on Wednesdays.

Rushing through the front door, Linda stopped short, seeing the living room littered with clothing. Thinking they had been burglarized, she stood in the doorway, wondering if she should run or stay. When she saw Del coming around the corner, she reached out to hug him. "Are you okay? What in the world happened?"

"Oh, I'm just swell." His sarcasm hung around him like armor.

Shutting the door behind her, Linda came into the room. Noticing the litter was composed of her things, she asked again, "What happened?"

Del grabbed her by the sleeve of her pink cardigan. "Come here, I want to show you something."

Still clutching her purse, Linda allowed him to jerk her to the sofa, in front of the television set. When he pushed the remote, turning the VCR on, she was more baffled than before.

"I don't get it, what . . . ?"

"Shut up and watch!" he shouted, dropping his feet onto the glass top of the coffee table. "Maybe you'll recognize someone."

She figured it was one of those porns that were being made by regular couples, sold on the Internet, but she couldn't understand why Del was making her watch it. In the middle of the day? In the middle of the mess around her? But she knew her husband's temper and sat still.

"Lookin' good there, sweetheart," he commented.

"What am I missing here, Del?" she asked, standing to take off her sweater.

"I guess it's true." He pulled her back down onto the cushions. "We never really see ourselves the way others do."

She was getting fed up with his bullshit. She was hungry and had to pee. "Meaning what?" she turned to stare him down.

"Meaning, you're too goddamn stupid to even recognize yourself and the prick you're fuckin'!"

"What?" she couldn't help but laugh. She hadn't meant to, but he was being so ridiculous the laugh just slipped out. "Are you crazy? That's not me, Del. And I sure as hell don't know who the guy is."

"You mean to tell me I don't recognize my own wife? We're married for eight years. What kind of an asshole would I be to not recognize my own goddamn wife? Tell me!"

It was her turn now and she reached out, clamping down on the soft bulge between his legs. "The kind of asshole who hasn't slept with his wife for the last three years. Jesus Christ, Del, I could have three eyes on my stomach and you wouldn't know. Also the kind of asshole husband who's looking for any excuse to force his wife out, cheat her out of everything she's helped him get. The kind of husband exactly like you, Del. The kind with no guts, no backbone, no honor." She twisted his pants.

Del grabbed her by the wrist and squeezed until she loosened her grip. "Why would I want to sleep with a bitch like you? Huh? Tell me that?"

"'Cause you don't know how to deal with a real woman. You don't know how to deal with life at all."

He raised his hand to strike her but she continued. "Now tell me, where did you get this sorry-ass piece of 'evidence'? And how much did you pay for it? 'Cause whoever palmed it off on you is gettin' sued." Linda pushed the STOP button and got up off the sofa.

She always made him feel like a dog. A stupid, shit-for-brains animal. He hated her for that. Grabbing a handful of her curly hair he pulled her toward him, until the back of her head was resting on his chest. "Not this time. You're not turning it all back on me. I want you out of here. Now! Get your crap and get out of here!" He pushed her across the room.

She hit the wall with her forehead. Her hands tried grabbing hold but she slid down the shiny wallpaper. Without a whimper, she came to a stop on her knees. Rage burned behind her eyes; her head throbbed.

Pushing her way back up to her feet, she turned and came at him. And this time when he cried for her to forgive him, she wouldn't. "If there's anyone gonna leave this house it's you! And if you don't, I'm calling the police. All they have to do is take a look at what you've done to me now and your ass is goin' to jail." She stood so close he could smell what she had for lunch.

But he didn't back off and he didn't wimp out. Not this time, there was too much at stake. "Try it, just try it! I got the tape and my lawyer will make sure you don't get shit. Not one penny, Linda, not one goddamn cent. You came into this house with nothing and that's just the way you're leaving it."

She slapped his face, hard, but he didn't budge. "I was eighteen years old, Del. Kicked out of my own house because I was dumb enough to fall in love with a jerk older than my father. You're the reason I had nothing. But I'm the reason you got all this." She spread her arms out like she was trying to fly away.

"And you can't stand that, can you, Del? It's eatin' you up. Big self-made man needs help from a high-school dropout. A kid has to help the great big man. I've worked all these years, got your life in order. And never, not one time, did I ever cheat on you. What are you gonna do without me, huh, Del? Wanna know what I'm gonna do without you? Celebrate! Fuck my brains out! Because I'm still young, I still got a chance. But look at you. That gut of yours is gonna make the ladies sick."

She wouldn't shut up, she kept coming at him, punching his body with her fists and his ego with her insults. He couldn't stand much more. "Just leave me alone. Give me a chance to think things out. Take your car, the credit cards—whatever you want—but just get out of here, will you?"

"God, you're thick. I'm not going anywhere. This is *my* house. You said you bought it for *me*. And the house in Florida, that's mine, too. Now that I think about it, I'm going after the idiot you hired to follow me. He conned you, Del, and you're too stupid to know it." She turned her back on him again.

The arrogance in her walk, the way her shoulders stiffened, infuriated him. "You're not getting a thing. Do you hear me?" Coming up behind her, he grabbed her by the throat. She kicked frantically at the air. It felt good, squeezing her neck, feeling her struggle. His muscled arms lifted her small frame easily. She sounded like she was spitting something up, but he didn't bother looking.

———

Yvonne picked up the receiver carefully, trying not to smear blue nail polish she'd just applied. "Pair of Queens Beauty and Tanning Salon, can I help you?" She listened to the guy go on and on, all excited about talking to Princess. "I'm sorry, but like I told you the last six times you called, I don't know where she is. Yes, yes, uh, uh." She shook her head and blew on her nails, hoping he'd run out of steam. "I sure will. You too. Have a nice day, okay?"

After checking that she hadn't nicked her paint job, Yvonne pushed the swivel chair away from the desk and grudgingly walked the length of the salon, stopping to knock on the door of Troy's private office. When no answer came, she turned the knob and stuck her head into the room.

"Look, you guys, that's the sixth time that creep Bernie called. He says if Princess doesn't call him back in an hour he's comin' over here."

Princess sat next to Troy, sobbing into his silk t-shirt. "What am I gonna do?" she cried hysterically.

He patted Princess's head. "Not to worry, Troy will take care of everything." Turning to Yvonne he said, "If he comes in here, call the cops. Now close that door and get back to work." He shooed Yvonne back to her desk.

"What if he gets violent?" Princess looked up at her boss; watery mascara ran black down her cheeks. "What'll I do? He's got a gun . . . I seen it."

Troy reached over for a Kleenex. Dabbing at her eyes, he reassured her, "I can certainly understand your fear. After all, the man *is* a murderer."

Princess sat up, pulling away from the large man. "Bernie never killed no one. I know that asshole husband done somethin' to her."

"Well, from what I read in the paper last night and what they said on the news this morning, the poor man came home from a business trip and found blood all over the place . . ."

"And no body," Princess said. Composing herself, she leaned over to grab a cigarette from her purse. "There's no proof Bernie killed anyone."

Troy was amazed at her nonchalance. "Well, he might as well

of, from what you told me. If he didn't pull a trigger he sure as hell handed the guy some ammunition."

Princess blew smoke up toward the ceiling. "I told you the whole thing was a scam."

"Yes you did, dear. But I think you're now what is known as an accessory . . . to murder."

"I told you, they ain't found no body. And in my book, until they do, there ain't been no one murdered here." She smashed out the cigarette in the crystal ashtray. "Jesus, Troy, I gotta get away from here. Just for a while. Think ya can lend me some money?"

Troy lifted himself up and walked to his desk. Opening the middle drawer, he took out a worn address book. "I can do better than that." After flipping through a few pages, he copied down an address. "A friend of mine runs a shop in L.A. I'll call ahead and set things up for you to start there next week. Oh, and you better come up with a new name."

Princess took the address Troy handed her. Slinging her leopard print bag over her shoulder, she stood up to say good-bye. "You're right. How about . . . Diane?"

He walked her to the door. "A D name . . . good karma."

She reached up to kiss his cheek. "Thanks, Troy, I owe ya a big one."

"Just remember, hon, the only way to save yourself is to start over—clean. As far as the police are concerned, the woman on the tape was that poor guy's wife. You don't know nothin' about nothin'."

"Sadly, that ain't far from the truth."

———

Del Jarrett had to stay in town, just until the damn police were finished with all their questions. And living in a crime scene didn't appeal to him very much. He'd have to ask how many more days that yellow tape would be plastered all over the place. It had only been two but felt more like twenty.

They hadn't discussed whether or not he should call. He thought about it for a moment, reasoning that he was at a new number and should tell someone. So he dialed.

"It's me. Don't get mad, I just had to hear your voice."

"Where the hell are you?"

"Off of 285, at the Hampton Inn."

"Feeling better? Now that you're out of that house?"

"Yeah," Del said, "you were right. You've been right about everything. Especially that Creeger guy. How'd you get so smart?"

"And gorgeous?"

"Yeah, you're a real looker, Troy." They both laughed. "But really, how'd you know the guy would come through with a video?"

"Money, baby, it always comes down to money."

"But the girl. What if she wouldn't have gone along with him?"

"He would of gotten someone else—it really didn't matter, all he needed was a certain body type. Lucky for us my Princess was so stupid and greedy."

"Well, I said it before and I don't mind repeating myself," Del said, "when you're right, you're right."

"I was sure as hell right about you, wasn't I?"

"You mean about . . . my situation?"

Troy sniffed. "Whatever you want to call it. But you know you sure as hell didn't belong with that bitch."

"I belong with you, right?"

"Forever, lover. Forever and always."

"And everything's going to be okay?" Del desperately needed a good shot of Troy's confidence.

"As long as you relax and do what I tell you. Now go take a long bath, get all cozy, and sit tight."

"I'll try."

"You remembered to give the tape to the police? Like you found it by mistake?"

"Yeah, but I still don't understand why . . ."

Troy sent a kiss through the phone line. "Just be my good boy."

———

Bernie Creeger fancied himself a careful man. The kind of man who always made sure to cover his ass. But after the police called, asking if he'd mind stopping in to answer a few questions concerning the Jarrett case, he was filled with doubts.

Rewinding the tape for the tenth time, he wasn't actually sure what he was looking for but scanned each scene, pausing and searching, making sure no one could identify Linda Jarrett's lover. Biting the fingernail of his little finger, he suddenly realized his ring was missing. Pausing the tape, he ran closer to the TV screen. "Fuck!" There was his monogrammed pinkie ring, big as day, right on the nightstand where he'd been stupid enough to leave it. "Right in plain fuckin' sight!"

Running to the phone he tried calming himself. He'd try Princess at home again. She had to be home now. When she wasn't he begged for her help after the beep.

"Princess, ya gotta go with me to the police. Tell them all about the scam we was pullin' on Jarrett. He's got them thinkin' his wife was killed by this mystery guy in the tape. They'll believe us, Princess, are ya there? Ya gotta help me out here. I'm beggin' ya."

Road Signs

Alan Ormsby

SOUTH INTERSTATE NEVADA 15—LOS ANGELES—280 MI.

You mind if I talk? I've got sort of a weird problem that I need to solve before we get to L.A. and who knows? Maybe you can help. Truth is, that's why I broke my rule about hitchhikers and picked you up in the first place. Plus, I haven't slept much lately and talking keeps me awake . . . wouldn't be too swift to doze off and crash out here in the desert, now would it? Especially at night.

SPEED LIMIT 65

Problem is, I'm supposed to get married next month, but I'm not sure I can go through with it. No, she's not the problem—I love Sheila more than I ever loved any woman in my whole life . . . and there've been plenty to choose from, know what I mean? Sure you do, good-looking guy like you. No, the real problem . . . but you can't understand unless I start at the beginning. If I knew when the fuck that was. Maybe it began in Palm Springs. Ever been to Palm Springs? No? Trust me, you should check it out.

LAST CHANCE CASINO 9 MILES—ONE FINAL SPIN

That's where I met Sheila. I'm a contractor, I was down there on a bid. So I'm heading down the main drag and I stop at a red light and Sheila crosses the street in front of my car. It was crowded and I didn't notice her at first, but then the heel of her shoe broke and she stopped and balanced herself on the hood of my car—brand-new BMW—and lifted up her foot to check out the damage.

One look and I froze.

God, she was gorgeous! Green eyes, auburn hair, copper skin, and a body like you wouldn't believe . . . most beautiful woman I'd ever seen in my life . . . and the sun coming down on her . . . she just shimmered, man, like a *vision!*

And I'm just sitting there, staring at her, and all of a sudden she, like . . . *feels* my look, you know? Like she could feel my eyes touching her . . . and she turns . . . and smiles. That smile did it.

I was toast. Gone. All over!

Then the light turned green and she whipped off her shoes and ran away, barefooted. No way I was going to let her get away, but there I am, stuck on a one-way street, can't make a U-turn, so I just *leave* the car in a no-parking zone—brand-new BMW! —and start running after her like a wild man!

I'm racing down the sidewalk, knocking aside pedestrians, and then I see her up ahead and she turns around . . . sees me . . . and stops and waits for me to catch up. Totally calm, like she was expecting me, with this look on her face like, *"What took you so long?"*

And then I'm standing there, out of breath, sweating, staring at her, and she's looking at me, smiling, like "Yes?" And I can't talk. Can't get a word out. The mouth's open but the tongue just lies there. So on impulse I reach down, whip off my shoes and offer them to her.

She laughs, says, "Thanks for your *gallantry*, but I doubt they'll fit."

My gallantry! Me! That made me laugh. So we start talking, this, that, before you know it we're walking along together, shoes in hand, like we've known each other all our lives. Like we got separated in some other life and it took this long for us to come together again. We've been together ever since. Well, until three days ago. But I'll get to that later.

WELCOME TO CALIFORNIA

We made love that first night. Hell, that first afternoon . . . couldn't even wait to get back to the hotel room! My car got towed, right? The BMW. Cops in Palm Springs don't fuck around! So she said she'd drive me over to pay the fine and we're driving along and suddenly I just have to touch her, can't stop myself. So I lean over, touch her arm. She smiles. I lean over, kiss her on the neck. She smiles again. I kiss her ear. She smiles, then takes my hand . . . and puts it between her legs . . . we pulled off the road and did it right there in the car. Then we went back to my hotel room and fucked for the next three days. It was like a drug: The more I fucked her, the more I wanted her. I had to have her within reach, man, like an alkie has to have his bottle or a junkie has to have his fix.

When I went back to L.A., she came along. Moved in with me. I thought it would taper off, but it didn't. I'd go to the office—suddenly I'd smell her on my hands, or glance at her picture on my desk, any reminder and I'd start thinking about her, didn't matter where I was or what I was doing, could be in the middle of a meeting, anywhere, suddenly I'd get a hard-on like a fucking cannon. I'd turn to the client, *"Excuse me a moment, Mr. X,"* then run out to the car, speed home, fuck Sheila, and speed back to work: *"Sorry about that, Mr. X, little emergency, uh, came up, now where were we?"*

Sometimes she'd show up at the office. Walk right in . . . *"Honey, may I see you for a moment?"* We'd go in my office, she'd shut the door, unzip me . . . Jesus, we'd fuck on the desk, on the floor, up against the wall, didn't matter! Then we'd go back out like nothing had happened. Meanwhile, everybody on my staff is lowering their eyes, clearing their throats . . . they all knew what was going on. We didn't give a shit. We couldn't help it.

But it was more than sex: We were soul mates.

Laugh, go ahead, I never believed that crap, either, but with Sheila I suddenly knew it was true. We shared the same soul and it was like we'd been separated and we were only complete when we were together. Obviously you haven't found your soul mate, am I right? Well, when you do, remember I told you so.

SPEED LIMIT 70

Tell you something else even more important: Not only is Sheila passionate, she's also—*and this is key*—the most generous woman I've ever known. Every Sunday afternoon she works at a homeless shelter; during the week, she tutors kids at the youth center, reads to the blind and takes home-cooked meals to elderly shut-ins.

And she puts her money where her mouth is: When the City Council tried to pass an ordinance banning homeless people from the streets, Sheila led a protest that defeated it and caused a new homeless shelter to be built. Naturally, being Sheila, she wouldn't take any credit for it.

What can I say? I had the perfect woman. The only flaw I could see was that she'd chosen *me* as her mate, haha! Not that I'm a bad guy, or anything, but I've been known to bend the rules when I had to. But then I figured, hey, I couldn't be that bad if Sheila chose me!

Anyway, marriage was a given. It was so inevitable that when I proposed she just said, "Of course," like it was strange I should even ask the question.

So we set the date.

I had it all, man, had it all.

. . . Until the night she had the dream.

RED ROCK CANYON/DEATH VALLEY NEXT RIGHT

It was one, one-thirty . . . she was tossing, turning . . . I put my arms around her to try and calm her down . . . suddenly she sits up, sobbing, *"Jimmy! Jimmy! Oh, Jimmy, forgive me! Forgive me, Jimmy!"*

She's shivering, in a cold sweat . . . her eyes are wild, dark, she looks at me like I'm a stranger . . . like she's in some other world.

Finally she went back to sleep, but I wasn't so lucky: see, *my name ain't Jimmy.*

Now, I'm not a jealous guy normally, but the way she called out his name, it freaked me out. I couldn't sleep, I just lay there wondering who the fuck this Jimmy guy was and how come she'd never mentioned him before.

The next day when I brought up the nightmare, she pretended like she didn't remember it. I'm like, "Fine, okay," then acting sort of casual: "I was just curious about this, uh, Jimmy character."

She froze. Turned white. Her voice a whisper: "Who?"

"Jimmy, you called out his name. Several times. 'Jimmy, forgive me,' you said."

She practically stopped breathing.

I go: "Sweetheart? What's wrong?"

She pushes me away, runs out of the room. I follow, but she runs into the bathroom and locks the door. I can hear her sobbing in there, it's breaking my heart! "Please, honey, come out, please, tell me what's wrong!"

No answer.

No matter how much I beg, no answer.

Fuck it, I go back to the kitchen and pour myself a drink. Before I can even swallow it down, I hear her car starting up, and by the time I reach the front door, she's speeding away down the street.

My first impulse was to go after her, but then I thought: No . . . better to wait.

Whoever Jimmy was, he was obviously very important to her, maybe more important than me. Words of wisdom, pal, and I quote: *"Women are adept at concealing the objects of their deepest passion"*—my first wife being a case in point. The love of her life turned out to be a guy whose name I had *never heard her mention in nine years of marriage* until the day she dumped me for him.

It took me years to recover from that bitch, no way was I going to let history repeat itself with Sheila!

I figured, wait. Wait. Give her all the space she needs. When she's ready, she'll tell me about Jimmy.

FALLING ROCKS

Next night I come home, she's in the bedroom, face all flushed, eyes red and swollen . . . she's packing a suitcase.

"I can't marry you," she says.

I couldn't respond. I stood there, numb, while she finished packing. Finally I ask, "Is this because of Jimmy?"

She won't look at me, but she nods yes.

"You still love him?"

She snaps the latches shut on the suitcase, picks it up without answering, and starts to walk out.

That's when I lost it. Slammed the bedroom door, yanked the suitcase out of her hand, threw her down on the bed . . . she fought, clawed, bit . . . I tore off her clothes, ripped off her panties . . .

I went crazy . . . somewhere in my mind I thought if I could fuck her hard enough, deep enough, I could make her mine forever, make her so that no other guy would ever be able to have her again . . .

I forced her legs apart and shoved my cock into her . . . she screamed and then . . . it was like her pussy just melted . . . she wanted me as much as I wanted her . . . she stopped struggling . . . started thrusting her hips against me, pulling me into her, nails clawing me . . . blood running down my back like sweat . . . both of us coming like volcanoes, melting into each other until you couldn't tell where I left off and she began . . .

. . . Afterward, we lay there naked, watching the sun set over the ocean (you can see it from our bedroom window). I told her there was no way I'd ever let her leave me and she said she didn't really want to leave, that she was only doing it to protect me from getting involved in something terrible that had happened in her past . . . something to do with Jimmy.

I told her I loved her and that nothing she'd done in the past could change that. Whatever her relationship was with Jimmy, all that mattered was what we had now.

I'll never forget what she said next: "Jimmy wasn't my lover . . . he was my *victim*."

"Victim? What the hell does that mean?"

This is what she told me.

EMERGENCIES—DIAL HIGHWAY PATROL ON CELLULAR

It happened ten years ago. She was eighteen, a teenager, wild, angry, spent most of her time partying, doing drugs.

She was spending Thanksgiving with her dad, at his place in the mountains. They had a fight one night, about her stepmother, and Sheila walked out. She wanted to go back to San Francisco, to the house of her real mom, who had custody, but she didn't have any money and it was snowing. She wasn't wearing boots and she was freezing, so she thumbed a ride with this guy in a truck. He said his name was Jimmy, he was Canadian, he'd driven down in his brand-new pickup to do some deer hunting with his friend Buzz. He was nice, she said, extremely polite, very sweet.

He said he was going to move to California, that Buzz was helping him find a place. He'd miss his family, of course, but sooner or later a guy had to leave the nest, that was life, it wasn't so difficult as long as you had friends, friends were very important. He asked if Sheila had any friends? You know, people she could talk to? If not, he said, he'd be happy to be her friend.

Sheila told him she didn't want any friends, that her parents were divorced and hated each other and that she hated them both and that as far as she was concerned she wished they'd both croak, the sooner the better.

She asked if he wanted to smoke a joint and of course he said no, then she said she'd give him a blow job if he'd drive her all the way to San Francisco. He got kind of embarrassed, she said, and laughed, not in a mean way, but in a brotherly, understanding way. He said he could tell from the minute he saw her that she was an unhappy person, but that she should remember that she was young and that these problems would pass and that when she got a little older she would realize how much her family really meant to her and that there was a reason she was going through all this stuff right now but that she wouldn't understand the reason until she got older.

Sheila thought all that was crap, that everything he was saying was bogus, that life was basically meaningless, that things happened at random and that she hadn't seen any evidence to the contrary.

He said he understood why she felt that way, that sometimes

it was hard to understand God's plan, but that God had one, that was for sure, she should never doubt *that*.

"Good for God," said Sheila. It was really pissing her off the way he was sitting there telling her how life was so great, while she was freezing her ass off and her whole life sucked.

Then she noticed that he had guns in the truck, a rifle and a pistol, so she asked him how God felt about him shooting animals. He said God had put those animals there for us to eat. He never killed for sport, and he always ate what he killed. Sheila said wow, that must be a great comfort to the deer when you blow his head off. Jimmy just laughed and shook his head. She asked why he needed both a rifle and a pistol and he said the rifle was for hunting and the pistol was for target shooting and did she know how to shoot and would she like to pick it up and hold it, see how it felt?

So she picked up the pistol . . . and shot him in the head.

Why?

Who the fuck knows? You think I know? *She* doesn't even know! . . . There *is* no "why"! She was in a rage, she had a gun in her hand . . . *BANG!*

WATCH DOWNHILL SPEED

The truck hit a tree and stopped. Sheila wasn't hurt, not even a bruise. She got out and walked home. All her rage was gone. She suddenly felt totally calm. The wind had died down and the moonlight made the snow look blue and peaceful, like a scene on a Christmas card.

She walked back to her Dad's house and watched TV until she fell asleep. She assumed that the cops would show up and arrest her, but they never did.

She kept checking the news for any mention of the murder, but at least a week went by before she saw one small paragraph about it in the newspaper; that's where she found out his last name was Stensen, Jimmy Stensen. The police had no clues, which made sense: She'd been wearing gloves, so she hadn't left any fingerprints, and there was a snowstorm the next day, which must have covered her tracks.

After the holiday, she went home to her mom's place in San Francisco. She kept expecting the axe to fall, but nothing happened! People reacted to her as they had before and life went on in the same old way. The murder didn't change anything! Jimmy had gone without leaving a ripple. She was right after all: Life *was* meaningless and random. Higher justice? Bullshit! No such thing! So what good would it do to turn herself in? They'd execute her and two lives would be wasted instead of one.

The only way she felt she could make up for killing Jimmy was to dedicate the rest of her life to becoming a good person and making a positive contribution to the world.

So that's what she did.

She quit drugs, quit screwing around, began applying herself in school. She set goals, made commitments and stuck to them. She became class valedictorian, got a scholarship to Berkeley, started doing volunteer work with the poor and homeless, and, ten years later, met me. *That,* she said, was when she thought that maybe Jimmy had been right; that this had been God's plan all along.

She thought she'd made up for what she did and had earned the right to love again, but when Jimmy popped up in her nightmare, she knew that it would never be over, not as long as she lived.

She cried and I held her. I told her it was okay, that I loved her and that nothing she'd ever done, or could do, would change that. Ever. I meant it, too.

WATCH FOR SLOW VEHICLES

Two days went by.

I went back to the office, Sheila did her charity thing, at night we dealt with the wedding plans, life proceeded normally. The only thing that seemed strange was how normal it seemed. I mean, here she tells me she committed a cold-blooded murder and I'm like, okay with it. At first I thought maybe this was a good thing: In my own mind it proved to me that my love for Sheila was real, that nothing could faze or destroy it, not even murder. I even felt happy. *Hey, we can do this, lightning isn't gonna come down and strike us!*

But then it bothered me that it *didn't* bother me, does that make sense? Why *wasn't* I upset that she'd killed this guy? Was I without conscience? Did I lack feeling? Or was I simply in a state of denial?

I shrugged it off: I had found the perfect woman and I wasn't going to let some long-ago crime destroy our happiness. She was a kid then, she didn't know what she was doing! Besides, Jimmy Stensen was dead and nothing we could do would bring him back!

So, fine. Forget it. Move on.

CORRECTIONAL CENTER SANDY VALLEY NEXT RIGHT

We had planned a small wedding, but even a small wedding involves a million details, and as the date approached, our lives were suddenly caught up with caterers, photographers, floral arrangements, tuxedo fittings, seating placements, honeymoon arrangements, the whole shebang. Sheila and I were rarely alone, which in a way I was glad for, because a weird thing was happening and I didn't want to worry her: I was going numb. It started in my throat. I couldn't swallow, couldn't eat. Sometimes I couldn't talk. I started to lose weight. The hint of nausea never left my gut.

My doctor told me it was just anxiety about the wedding, perfectly normal, and that was true, but not in the way he thought. My body was rebelling. My conscience had finally showed up and was forcing me to confront the truth.

I did an online search for the Jimmy Stensen case. It took a while, but eventually I found mention of him on a website devoted to unsolved murders.

Under a blurred photo of Jimmy (holding a rifle, ironically), a small paragraph stated his name, his age (nineteen), and the date that he had been found shot to death in his truck. Anyone with information about the crime was asked to come forward or call the police anonymously at a number listed at the bottom of the article. His surviving family was offering a reward. They hadn't given up: There's no statute of limitations on murder, or on grief.

I printed the article and signed off. I gazed at the photo: Jimmy's obituary shot, though he didn't know that at the time it was taken. There was his unsuspecting face smiling out at posterity. He was better-looking than I expected: blonde, cleft chin, twinkly eyes. He looked friendly. He looked "nice." I put him in the shredder.

CLOSED FOR REPAIRS

I tried to act like nothing was wrong, but that night, Sheila wanted to make love, and I couldn't get it up. This had never happened before and she knew something must be really wrong.

I told her it was nothing, that I didn't feel well, but even in the dark I could see the disbelief glittering in her eyes.

I had weird dreams all night. Next morning, Sheila's side of the bed was empty and I found her in the guest room. She claimed she had moved out there because my tossing and turning had disturbed her.

At breakfast we barely spoke and for the first time in our relationship I felt relieved to get away from her, to get out of the house and go to work.

SAFETY BELT LAW ENFORCED

All I could think about now was the murder. I kept seeing the gun in Sheila's hand, kept hearing the shot, kept seeing Jimmy's head jerk sideways on impact and the brains and the blood on the window behind him.

I thought about his family; how I had the power to call them and solve the decade-old murder that had no doubt ruined their lives.

I could bring them closure with one phone call; I could bring them justice. I dialed the number from the website, let it ring once and hung up.

Closure for them meant death for Sheila.

Sheila, who had spent the last decade atoning for her crime and becoming a force for good in the community.

Who was this "Jimmy" anyway? Some average bozo who never would've amounted to anything, no matter how long he lived! And what the hell was he doing, driving around with two loaded guns on the seat? Sheila described him as a nice guy, but how did she know what was really in his mind? Lots of rapists and psychos are "nice" and "polite" before they drop the mask and reveal the real face underneath!

Besides, if he really was such a nice guy, wouldn't he be the first to forgive Sheila?

There I sat, rationalizing it away, blaming the murder on the victim because I couldn't allow myself to judge Sheila.

AUTHENTIC GHOST TOWN 6 MILES

I have a .22 Ruger Bearcat that I keep in a box in my closet. That night, when I went to get my bathrobe, I noticed that the box was missing. A chill went through me, literally.

I tried to act casual when I asked Sheila if she'd seen the gun, but she wasn't fooled. She answered that as far as she knew the gun was still in the closet, where I'd left it. I said it wasn't. I said, are you sure you didn't move it and forget to put it back? She gave me an icy stare, and marched out of the room.

A moment later, she called me into the bedroom.

"Is this what you're looking for?" she said, lifting her hand toward me.

The gun was in it.

Pointing at me.

Her face was hard and smiling as she watched me squirm.

I tried to sound matter-of-fact:

"Where'd you find it?"

"In the closet," she said. "Under some clothes. I guess you didn't look very hard."

She handed me the gun and left the room.

SOFT SHOULDERS

After that, she began sleeping in the guest room permanently. We ate our meals in silence, although neither of us had much appetite.

Then, last Saturday, I found her sitting on the deck, staring out at the ocean. Clouds were piled up in the distance and a misty breeze swept over us. It was starting to rain. I sat beside her and we stared at the ocean together. We sat for a long time, side by side.

"I should never have told you," she said. There were tears in her eyes.

She said that it was over between us. I argued, but feebly. She was right: We couldn't continue in this atmosphere of distrust and fear. If we did, she would always be afraid that I would some-day use her confession against her, and I would always be afraid that what had happened to Jimmy might happen to me.

There was only one way to resolve it, she said, and that was to go to the police and turn herself in.

DANGEROUS WHEN WET

We drove to a small police station a mile or so from the house. The rain was heavier now and Sheila stared straight ahead, hands folded in her lap. She had refused to call her lawyer, insisting that she'd rather confess directly to the police. I tried to talk her out of it, but she wouldn't listen. She said if I didn't want to go with her, she'd go by herself. No way I could let her go through this alone.

We'd forgotten the umbrella, so we ran up to the front en-trance, past rows of parked police cars, slick from the rain. A cop who was coming out stopped and held the door open for us. We thanked him and smiled back as we entered, like we were just dropping in to get out of the rain.

The station was empty. Nobody at the desk, nobody any-where. They had these big trophy cases holding rows of bronze plaques, engraved with the names of cops who had died in the line of duty.

We stood shaking off the rain and wondering where to go when we heard voices—children's voices—and a troop of Cub Scouts emerged from one of the hallways. They were accompa-nied by two scoutmasters and a uniformed policeman, who was giving them a tour.

The cop looked at us: "Be right with you," he said, like a salesman or something, then turned his attention back to the Scouts. They were asking questions about his equipment and he started showing them his gear, piece by piece: nightstick, service revolver, handcuffs, bullets, Mace—even unbuttoned his shirt to show the bulletproof vest he was wearing underneath. He was big, with huge hands and arms and a thick neck. I looked at Sheila and she was staring at him. In the fluorescent light she looked like a ghost.

The door opened and two more cops came in: Between them was a guy in painter's overalls and handcuffs; his nose was gashed and crusted with dried blood. He struggled and cursed as they hustled him down the hallway where the holding cells were and shut the door with a clang.

One of the Scouts asked if the guy was a criminal. The guide answered that he didn't really know the details and went on talking about his gear.

I knew at that moment that I could never let Sheila turn herself in. The sight of this poor bastard in cuffs, being paraded in front of these kids, made the whole thing sickeningly real to me. I pictured Sheila being booked and cuffed and led in before a jury; I imagined her spending the rest of her life in prison, or, if the worst should happen, being strapped to a gurney for a lethal injection.

It was more than I could stomach. I grabbed her arm and hurried her out the door.

LANE ENDS MERGE LEFT

Back in the car, she goes: "Now what?"

I tell her here's what: We're going to forget about Jimmy, forget about the past, and go ahead and get married, as planned.

She laughed. Was I crazy? How could we go ahead as if nothing had happened? Even if that were possible for me, which she didn't believe for a second, it was no longer possible for her. Sooner or later Jimmy would come back to haunt us, sooner or later he'd come between us and ruin our lives. She couldn't bear to have that happen again. I promised her it wouldn't. She said she knew I meant it now, but she also knew it was a promise I wouldn't be able to keep.

No matter how hard I argued with her, she was adamant: The wedding was still off and tomorrow, or the next day, she would go back to the cops and turn herself in, period.

I begged her to give me some time. I had to go away on business for a few days and I made her promise not to do anything until I got back.

That was three days ago.

DON'T GAMBLE WITH YOUR LIVES—BUCKLE UP

I've been driving around ever since, trying to figure out what to do. I never made it to that business meeting.

Three days driving without sleep, wracking my brain, searching for an answer. Ultimately, I only came up with three options:

Option one: I confess to Jimmy's murder myself. Only problem: Sheila would never let me take the rap for her.

Option two: I kill us both. That wouldn't work, either: I can imagine killing myself, but I could never kill Sheila.

Option three . . . ah, fuck it, the whole thing is crazy! I don't know what to do. What would *you* do?

Oh, really? I see. You think she should turn herself in. You're right, of course, she killed someone, she should pay for it, it's justice, you're absolutely right, couldn't be more right, I should let her turn herself in. It's the only rational solution, isn't it?

I know that. I guess I just don't want to face it.

REST AREA NEXT RIGHT

Thank God, a rest area, I need to take a leak, how 'bout you? Where's the exit? Ah, right down this road.

Of course there's still option three . . . I didn't finish telling you that one. Well, option three didn't even occur to me until I got to Vegas. I was cruising the Strip, wondering what to do, when suddenly I saw something that made me think maybe, just maybe, it was possible to solve this problem and not lose Sheila . . .

(God, it's dark out here.)

What did I see?

(This looks like a good place to stop.)

I saw you.

That's right, my friend: *You* are option three.

Get out of the car.

Ah-ah, don't fuck around! As you can see, I have a gun.

Just open the door like a good boy and step out.

Nice and slow.

Very good.

Walk around the front of the car. Stay in the headlights. Good. Keep your hands where I can see them. That's right. Don't scream. Nobody can see us or hear us, I already checked it out.

Turn around.

Kneel down.

DO IT!

That's better.

I'm sorry about this—no, truly—but when I saw you thumbing a ride, it all became clear to me what I had to do.

I have to commit a murder of my own!

It's that simple. "His" and "Hers" murders! Then Sheila and I will be equal. She won't be able to turn herself in, because if she did, I'd turn myself in, too, and she'd never let me do that!

And I'll make up for your death, just like she did for Jimmy's. From here on out, I'm going to devote myself to charity: helping the homeless, feeding the indigent, whatever.

Don't beg, you can see this makes perfect sense: It's the only way Sheila and I can stay together, and I can't give her up, you understand that, don't you? I've tried very hard to make you understand that! Besides, I couldn't let you live now, even if I wanted to: *You know too much!* Why do you think I told you all this in the first place? It was my insurance policy, to prevent me from getting cold feet at the last minute.

Don't worry, it'll be quick and painless.

And remember, there is some consolation:

After this, I'll be a *much, much* better person . . .

EXIT

The Gold Fever Tapes

Mickey Spillane

They killed Squeaky Williams on the steps of the Criminal
Courts Building with two beautifully placed slugs in the middle of his back and got away into traffic before anybody really
knew what had happened.

But I knew what had happened and my guts felt all tight and
dry just standing there looking at his scrawny, frozen face in the
drawer of the morgue locker. One eye was still partly open and
was staring at me.

"Identify him?" the attendant asked.

"He doesn't have to," the other voice said and I turned
around. Charlie Watts had made captain since I had seen him
last, but ten years and a few promotions had only screwed tighter
the force of hate he had for people like me.

"An old cellmate of yours, Fallon . . . isn't he?" Even his voice
had that same grating quality like a file on a knife blade.

I nodded. "Six months' worth," I said.

"How'd you manage it, Fallon? What'd you have on the wheels
to get paroled out like that? What bunch of suckers would let a
damned crooked cop like you out after the bust you took?"

"Maybe they needed my room," I told him.

The drawer slammed shut and Squeaky went back into the
cold locker and the last I saw of him was that half open eye.

"And maybe you ought to come over and talk about this little
hassle in more familiar surroundings," Watts told me.

"Why?"

"Because there might be something interesting to discuss when ex-cons get shot down on public property and old buddies show up to make sure he's dead."

"I came in to identify the body. As of this morning he wasn't ID'd."

"The picture in the paper wasn't all that good, Fallon."

"Not to you, maybe."

"Knock it off and let's go."

"Drop dead," I said and held out my open wallet.

After a few seconds he said, "Son-of-a-bitch. A reporter. An *effing* newspaper reporter. Now who the hell would give you a job as a reporter?"

"Orley News Service, Charlie. They believe that criminals can be rehabilitated. Ergo . . . I have a reason for being here since I can write a great personal piece on the deceased."

"Ergo shit," he said.

"If you want to check my credentials . . ."

"Go screw yourself and get out of here."

"Ease off. The past is behind us."

"Not as far as I'm concerned," he said. "You'll always be just a lousy cop who took a payoff and loused things up for the rest of us. It's too bad that con didn't kill you up at Sing."

"Squeaky took that knife for me," I reminded him.

"So pay your last respects and blow."

"My pleasure, Captain." I put my wallet back and walked across the room. At the door I stopped and looked back. "Your leg ever hurt when it rains?"

"I don't owe you any favors for deflecting a slug for me, Fallon. I've taken three since then."

"Too bad," I grinned, "that hole in my side still bugs me."

Why some women look naked with their clothes on is beyond me, but with Cheryl I finally figured it out. She was what I called posture-naked. She always did those damn things that made a man look at her, like bending stiff-legged over the bottom drawer of the filing cabinet so that her miniskirt hiked up to her hips, or leaning across my desk in those loose-fitting peasant blouses so that I forgot whatever she was trying to point out to me.

When I walked into the office Orley News Service had provided me with she was scratching her tail with the utter abandon of a little kid and I said, "Will you stop that!"

"I'm itchy."

"What've you got?"

Cheryl glared at me a second, then laughed. "Nothing. I'm peeling. I got my behind sunburned skinny-dipping in my friend's pool."

"Great guys you go with."

"My friend is a girl I was in the chorus line with. She married a millionaire."

"Why didn't you do the same thing?"

"I have ambition."

"To be a typist?"

"Orley pays me as a secretary and researcher."

"They're wasting their money," I said.

She gave me that silly smirk of hers that irritated the hell out of me. "So I'm a sex object the brass likes to keep around."

"Yeah, but why around me?"

"Maybe you need help."

"Not that kind."

"That kind especially."

"Everybody was safer when you were a social worker."

"Parole officer."

"Same difference."

"Like hell," she said. Then her eyes went into that startling directness and she asked, "What happened this morning?"

"It was Squeaky. He's dead."

"Then write the story and stay out of it."

"Don't play parole officer with me, kiddo."

Her eyes wouldn't let me alone. "You know what your job is."

"Squeaky saved my ass for me," I said.

"And now he's dead." She studied my face for a long stretch of time, then caught her lower lip between her teeth. "You know why?"

I swung around in my chair and looked out the window over the Manhattan skyline. It wasn't very pretty any more. Absolute cubism had taken over architectural design. The city used to be sexy. Now it was passing into its menopause. "No," I said.

"In the pig's ass you don't," Cheryl told me softly. "Don't forget what your job is. You stick your neck out and everybody gets hurt."

When the door shut to the outer office I pulled the little cassette tape from my pocket and shoved it into the recorder. I wanted to hear it again just to be sure.

And Squeaky sure had a hell of a story to tell in a matter of two and a half minutes.

———

He had come out of the big house after a six-year stretch and opened a radio repair shop just off Seventh Avenue, made enough bread to consider marrying a chubby little streetwalker who lived in the next tenement and got himself killed before he got on the freebie list in exchange for marital security. But that part wasn't on the tape. That part I knew because we had kept in touch.

The tape was a recording of two voices, one wondering how the hell the Old Man was going to get eight hundred pounds of solid gold out of the country into Europe and the other telling him not to sweat it because anybody who could get it together could get it out and with the prices they were paying for the stuff over there it was all worth the risk even if five people had already been killed putting it into one lump. All they had to do was knock off the mechanic who had made it possible and they got their share and to hell with it.

The miserable little bastard, I thought. He had taken a cassette recorder with a built-in microphone into the restaurant to work on it during his lunch hour and picked up the conversation in the next booth. The trouble was he knew one of the guys by his voice and tried to put the bite on him for a lousy grand.

But they didn't call him Squeaky for nothing. His voice went across to the other end and he was staked out for a kill before he knew what was happening. All he could do was send me the tape and try to get into protective custody before they nailed him and he never did make the top steps of the Criminal Courts Building. Whoever was protecting eight hundred pounds of solid gold for overseas shipment had taken a chip off the lump and paid for a contract kill on my old cellblock buddy.

Peg it as one hundred bucks an ounce minimum and eight hundred pounds came so damn near a million and a quarter bucks. Less the cost of shipping and a few dead bodies. One was Squeaky's.

Little idiot. He was too hysterical trying to run out a few inches of tape to remember to identify the guys on the other segment. All I had was their voices and the single name, *the Old Man.*

I stuck the tape in the envelope with the graphic voice print pattern Eddie Connors had pulled for me and filed it in the back of the drawer with my bills and locked it shut. My stomach had that ugly feeling again and I was remembering how blood smelled when it was all spread out in a pool on hot pavement and that half open eye of Squeaky Williams was looking at me from under the frozen eyelid. I said something dirty under my breath and pulled the .45 out from the desk and stuck it in my belt.

Everything was going to hell and I couldn't care less. All I could remember was Squeaky stepping in front of that knife Water Head Ardmore had tried to shove into me just because I had been a cop.

————

A lot of them wouldn't look at me because I had gone sour, but there were those who had done exactly what I had done without making the mistake of getting caught and the burly lieutenant was one of them and couldn't take the chance of not meeting me without taking the chance of me pulling the string on him. He was as uncomfortable as hell because he had been forced into it, and even though he had cut himself loose, he had done it and damn well knew it.

We sat together in the back of the Chinese restaurant and over the chow mein I said, "Who's collecting gold, Al?"

"Who isn't?"

"I'm talking about a million and a quarter's worth."

"It's illegal," he said, "except for manufacturing purposes."

"Sure, and it's too heavy to ship. But that didn't stop them from forming it into aircraft seat brackets, phoney partitions, and faked machine parts."

Al Grossino forked up another mouthful of noodles and glared at me. "Look, I haven't heard of . . ."

"Don't crap me, Al. They've reopened the old mines since the price went up and technology advanced to the point where they can make them productive. Those companies are processing the stuff on the site to cut costs. It's all government supervised and if there has been any rumbles you're in the position to know it."

"Damn it, Fallon . . ."

"You make me push it and I will," I said.

He waited a few seconds, his eyes passing me to survey the rest of the place until he was satisfied. "Hell, you're always going to get the looters. Small-time crap."

"What's the rumble?"

He gave a small shrug of resignation and said, "Two Nevada outfits and one in Arizona are hassling with the unions. They started missing stuff before it got to the ingot stage. So far nothing's showed up on the New York market."

"As far as you know anyway."

"Don't lip me, Fallon."

I grinned and waited.

Al Grossino said, "We got a wire to keep an eye out but so far it doesn't look like anything. Those companies will use any excuse for a tax deduction."

"Horseshit."

"You that dumb that you don't know how the Feds cover every grain of gold mined in this country?"

"You that dumb that you don't know the difference between the official price and the black market?" I said.

"Okay, so the speculators . . ."

"Crap on the speculators. Spell it out in hard language. Who are the biggest speculators over here? Who built Las Vegas? Who handles the narcotics traffic? Who . . ."

"The mob isn't moving into gold, Fallon," he snapped. "They're too damned smart to play around with currency."

"Why do they handle counterfeit?" I asked him with a nasty grin.

He threw his napkin down and swallowed the last of his cold tea. "Make your point and let me get out of here."

"Find out how much those companies think they're missing," I said.

"Why?"

"I'm a reporter, remember?"

"It's hard to picture you that way."

"Your time might come, Al. By the way, who's the *Old Man?*"

"Hell, you're not that stupid, Fallon. You were in the army. You were a cop. Anybody who runs anything is the *old man.*" He picked up his hat, stuck me with the check, and left me sitting there.

———

I looked at the cop on the door, showed my press card, and took a handful of garbage from him until I spotted Lucas of the *News* inside and read him off with some language from the U.S. Constitution and walked into Charlie Watts running an interrogation scene on a weepy Marlene Peters. He was backed up by two detectives and an assistant DA. But the chunky little street hustler who had been slated to marry Squeaky Williams had been busted too often not to know all the tricks and, now, she was turning on her ultimate weapon of salty tears. She had the guardians of civic virtue all shook up. Lucas was there ready to put it all down and I was wondering who had the warrant or did they get themselves invited in.

Apparently I was a welcome relief and my old commander said, "I was expecting to see you sooner or later."

"Which one is it?"

"Sooner," he said. "No doubt you know the lady."

"No doubt."

"Professionally?"

"I never paid for it yet, Charlie."

The DA's man couldn't have been out of his twenties and made the mistake of saying, "What the hell are you doing here?"

I said, "I'm about to throw your ass out of here, kid. I

mean physically and with blood all over the place unless you ease on out of here on your own. And take your friends with you."

Charlie Watts made a real grin hoping something would happen, but I was right about the warrant. They didn't have one. That's why they all got up and glanced at the red-faced DA's man, and Lucas put his notes away with disgust, reading the whole thing right down to the button. I waited until the door was closed, then tossed my hat on the table and said, "How're you doing, Marlene?"

There weren't any tears now. She was dry-eyed and scared, but not because the cops had been there. Her tongue kept flicking over her lips and she couldn't keep her hands still at all. "Please, Fallon . . ."

"You worried about me?"

"No."

"You love Squeaky?"

"A little bit. He was the only guy who ever wanted to marry me."

"You know why he was killed?"

"Yes."

That crawly feeling went up my spine again. "Why?"

"He didn't tell me. He just knew something, that's all. He said he could prove it and it would make us the big bundle that could get us the hell out of this town. He had a tape recording of something."

"Oh?"

She spun around, eyes as big as wristwatches. "But I don't have it! He sent it to somebody just before he went up to see that judge who sentenced him and told me to get out quick—and all of a sudden he was dead."

"Why didn't you go?"

"Are you kidding?" She covered her face with her hands and

this time the tears were for real. "Why do you think the street's so empty for? They're outside waiting for me, that's why. Shit, I'm dead too. I'm as dead as Squeaky and I don't even know what for."

"You're not dead, Marlene."

"Go look out the window. There's a car on each end of the street. Oh, you won't see anybody. They're just waiting there for the right time and when you all leave I'm nothing more than a dead screwed-up whore who crossed up her pimp and got her throat cut for the trouble."

"So I won't leave." I pulled her hands away from her face. "Squeaky say anything at all? Come on, think about it?"

Marlene shook her head and pulled away from me. "Let me alone."

"That didn't answer the question."

"What difference does it make?"

"No sense dying, is there?"

The tone of my voice got her then and she turned around. "I'm not talking to any cops."

"I'm an ex-con," I said, "Squeaky's old roommate, remember?"

"He wanted to marry me. He really did."

"I know."

"I would have, too. He wasn't much, but nobody else ever asked me."

"Somebody will. What did he tell you?"

"Nothing. All he said was he knew who the rat was and this time he'd put him in his hole." She made a pathetic gesture with her hands and her eyes got wet again. "How am I going to get out of here?"

"I'll take you," I said.

So we went downstairs to the back of the landing and felt our way to the basement steps, inching our way past the garbage and the empty baby carriages until we made the crumbling concrete steps that led out to the rear court and the night and stood there long enough before we crossed to the rotted fence that separated her building from the one opposite, ducking under the hanging wash and skirting the crushed cartons and tipped-over garbage cans.

But they had been guarding the night longer than we had and their vision was adjusted to the dark so that when the first cough of a muted gun spit out all I saw was the flash and felt a slug breeze by. All I could do was shove her aside while I clawed at the .45 in my belt. The white spit came again, then another, but this time I had the big end of the Colt and the roar of the blast tore the night open whose only echo was a choking, gurgling gasp, until I heard the little whimper from my left and feet slamming away in front of me.

I said, "Marlene . . . ?"

And the little whimper answered, "He really would have married me. You know that, don't you?"

I lit a match and looked into blank, dead eyes. "I know, kid," I said.

Windows were banging open and someplace a woman screamed. Some guy was swearing into the night and another nut had a flashlight trying to probe into the darkness but couldn't tell where it had all come from. I walked over to the fence, found the body, and lit another match.

The guy didn't have much of a face left at all. But he did have a wallet in his right hip pocket and I put it in mine and got out just as the guy with the flashlight almost picked me out of the shadows.

Maybe my guts should have been all churned up again. Maybe that crawly feeling should have had my shoulders tight as hell. In an hour Charlie Watts would have an APB out on me and in two hours the papers would be running the old story on the front pages with my pictures in the centerfold or even splashed

on page one and there wouldn't be any place at all for me to surface.

But for the first time in a long time I felt nice and easy.

I even wished I had Cheryl handy.

Fallon, you slob, I thought, *you got a real death desire.*

Somebody else did too . . . now. They had a man dead and
knew this kind of an ex-con didn't let his old cellmate down. And
wherever he was, the *Old Man* would be sweating because the
possibility was there that a real live killer knew about all that gold
just waiting to reach the European market.

Ma Christy was one of those old-time New York pros with no
eyes, ears, or memory who ran a boarding house right close to the
docks where the Cunards used to unload and all she did was
point with her thumb and say, "The broad's in number two, Fallon."

I told her thanks and went up to where Cheryl was waiting in
the dingy room with a hamburger in one fist and a copy of the
News in the other. As least this time I was well on the inside
pages and when she looked at me over the top of the sheet said,
"You sure did it, boss man."

"Pull your skirt down. Ma thinks I rented the room for an
assignation."

"It's too short. Besides, assignation sounds like a dirty word."

"There's only one 'ass' in it."

"A pity," she said.

I closed the door and locked it, then crossed the room and
pulled the blinds closed. She still hadn't looked up from the
paper. "What did you get?"

"You're wanted for murder," Cheryl told me.

"Great," I said.

"His name was Arthur Littleworth, alias Shim Little, alias Little Shim, alias Soho Little, alias . . ."

"I know."

"Contract killer out of Des Moines, Iowa. The .357 Magnum he carried was the same one used in two other hits, one in Los Angeles, one in New York."

"Which one in the city?"

"Your friend's. Squeaky's."

"They have an angle on it, don't they?"

"Sure. He was in the can with Squeaky before you were. They were enemies."

"I don't remember him."

"He got out before you got in. I checked the dates. Your hit was pure retribution." She put the paper down and watched me with those big round eyes of hers. "You're on everybody's kill list now."

"How about that?" I said.

"Why do you have to ask for it?"

"Screw it. What do you care?"

"You don't know much about women, do you?"

"Kitten, I've been there and back."

"Learn anything?"

"Enough to stay away from you sex objects," I told her.

"One phone call and you'd be busted."

"So would you, doll."

"I'm no virgin."

"But there are other ways and the busting hurts worse."

"Sounds interesting."

"Try me," I said.

"Maybe later."

"You're lucky. Right now I'm spooky of little typists with a sex drive."

I got that silly grin again. "You bastard," she said. "Why do I have to be torn between duty and schoolgirl love?"

"What do I look like to you?"

"A big ugly bum with a record. You don't even know how to

dress properly. Ex-cop, ex-con, neophyte reporter, currently wanted criminal."

"Thanks," I said. "It's been a stinking two days."

"Can I help you out?"

"Feel like being an accessory?"

She looked at the half-made bed and grinned again. "Sometimes I wonder about myself."

"Ummm?"

"I talk better when I'm being loved," she said.

We lay there a little while afterward and she said, "You haven't got any chance at all, you know that."

"Who ever did?"

"It was all decided a long time ago."

"No Kismet crap, baby."

"Face reality. Your whole future was based on programmed performance."

"Screw it, parole officer."

"It was an assigned risk." She was looking at the ceiling, deadly serious. "They thought it would be worth it."

"They forgot about the incidental factors," I said.

"He was only a person in the same cell."

"Try living in prison. See what the person in the upper bunk is like."

"Worth dying for?"

"Isn't everybody?"

"Us too?"

"All I'm doing is screwing . . . not saying 'I love you, sweetheart.'"

"Screwing's enough for a parole officer," she told me.

"Not for a typist," I said. "Now tell me what you found out."

"Charlie thinks you'd be better off dead."

"Nice."

"He's not the only one. There's a contract out on you."

"That's what I figured," I said, then turned over and wrapped my arm around all that lovely soft flesh and fell asleep. I still was feeling nice and easy. My last coherent thought was how far a doll would go for a guy.

———

The thing they call gold fever is a thing you can't hide. Like giving the clap to your wife and the neighbor next door. So your wife won't squeal, but the neighbor will when she gives it to her husband and he's peeing red peppers in the bowl and hanging onto the rafters while he howls and he's ready to blow the whistle on everybody.

And gold sure makes them pee.

Loco Bene was so terrified of seeing a first-rate killer standing in front of his bed that he damned near browned out at the sight of the dirty end of a .45 and said, "No shit, Fallon, I never heard of nuthin' except what gets talked up on the street."

"Bene . . . you roomed with Shim Little." I was remembering what Cheryl had filled me in on.

"Yeah, yeah, I know. We wasn't no pals, though. Just because he had a couple of mob connections we were just crap to him."

"Okay, Loco, you've done your share of the delivery work in the narcotics rackets. How're the new routes set up?"

"Come on, come on! Like you're givin' me a choice between who knocks me off. If them routes get tapped, you think they won't know who was talking? Besides, they're all incoming tracks. I never ship outside."

"Loco, the word's out. There's gold going to be passed and you're a first-class route man. Don't tell me you haven't heard any buzz on it."

"Fallon . . ."

I thumbed the hammer back and the metallic snick sounded like thunder.

He swallowed first, then made a gesture with his shoulders. "Sure, I heard some talk. Like somebody wants to contact Gibbons only they don't know he's pullin' a stretch in a Mexican jail."

"Adrian Gibbons?"

"Sure. He used to handle heavy stuff, mostly expensive machine parts. He was an artist the way he could build them into cheap gizmos to fake out the inspectors. Never had a bust until he tried to rape that Mex chick."

"They won't ship gold like that," I said. "Who else are they looking for?"

"Nobody tells me . . . hell, the Chinaman turned down an offer because he's still hot from that picture deal he made with the museum. And anyway, he uses legit routes. But gold . . .'"

"Who's the Mechanic, Loco?"

"Huh?"

"You heard me."

"Like for cars . . . or a cardsharp?"

"Who would Shim Little call the Mechanic?"

His hands pulled at each other and he wet his lips down again. "Was a guy in the joint they called the Mechanic, only he used to set up cars to run hash and junk in from across the border."

"Remember his name?"

"Naw, but he had a double eight on the end of his number. He got out before me. Now how about laying off, Fallon? I gave you . . ."

I eased the hammer down on the rod and stuck it back in my belt. "Maybe I'll come around again, Loco," I said. "So keep your ears open."

————

The television and newspaper coverage I had gotten over that damned backyard shoot-out had turned me into a night person.

Every cop in the department would be alerted and there weren't many of the street people you could afford to take a chance on. Not when you knew they wouldn't mind scoring a few brownie points with the cops by pointing a finger your way. But there were a few no better off than myself and these were the ones with the best antennae in the system because it was their best survival device and they had words to say.

Cheryl's information had been exact, all right. A fat, open contract was out on me and some new faces with old reputations had shown up in places I generally frequented. O'Malley, the doorman at my apartment building who was a real, solid buddy, was glad to hear from me and was pretty damn sure somebody had my place staked out. He was going to pack a change of clothes for me and leave them in his locker in the basement, with the private rear entrance key stashed over the doorsill. Long ago I had anticipated a possible tap on the office phone line and had arranged an alternate communication system with Cheryl. She was picking up the same information, going through repeated questioning by the police, the reporters, and two of the DA's men.

There was an irritated note in her voice when she said, "You're going to blow this one sure as hell, Fallon."

"It's too late now to cut out."

"You know better than that," she said.

"Sure," I told her. "I can prove self-defense and claim the gun was one of Squeaky's but who gets that contract lifted off me?"

"That's the odd part, isn't it?"

"Damn odd. It's too high a price to pay for an ex-con who knocked off a punk hit man, but when you're protecting somebody who's sitting on a big lump of gold, it's only like paying a nuisance tax."

"Okay, don't lecture me. Just tell me what to do."

What I wanted, I told her, was to find a guy they referred to as the Mechanic. I gave her the approximate dates of his stay in the joint and the last two digits of his number. She was to get those voice print patterns and the tape from my file, that Japanese mini recorder I had, and meet me at Ma Christy's at 2:00 A.M. That gave her just four hours.

Then I went back into the night again. Somebody had to know who the Mechanic was and if the *Old Man* was scheduling him for a kill too, the quickest way to flush him out was to put the word around. Whatever the Mechanic was doing would get jammed in a hurry if he knew the payoff was to be made with a bullet. All that gold was just too big and too heavy to be moved around without somebody getting wise, so it would have to be shipped in a pretty special way. Small parcels would involve just too many different operations, too many people and accumulated risks, so my bet was that it would go as a single unit directly to a market. All I had to know was where it was, who had it, and how it was going. And what I was going to do about it if I ever found out.

Sure, I could lay the story on Charlie Watts and the good captain would dutifully process it, but if this were a possible mob operation there were always those pipelines into the bureaucratic maze of officialdom that would send out the warning signal and all that yellow metal would go right back into hiding until another time.

No, I wanted one shot at it myself first.

By midnight I had the story out in three different quarters and had picked up a little more on Shim Little. He was a loner who shuttled around between cheap midtown motels, never keeping a permanent address, always seemed to have enough money in his pocket, and didn't have any regular friends anyone remembered. A few times he was seen with the same guy, a nondescript type who didn't talk much, but Paddy Ables, the night bartender at the Remote Grill, said he knew the guy packed a gun and the couple of times he saw him he had an out-of-state newspaper with him. He couldn't remember the name, but it had a big eagle in the masthead. Paddy was pretty nervous talking to me, so I told him thanks and left.

Outside, a fine mist was blowing in from the river and you could smell the rain in the air.

I walked down Seventh Avenue to the cross street the builders hadn't gotten around to remodeling yet, sniffing at the acrid smells that were worn into the bricks like grease in an old frying pan, and turned west to the last address Shim Little had used. It was a decrepit hotel with rooms by the day or week but used mostly by the hour or minute by the jaded whores hitting the left-over trade from Broadway or the idiot tourists who thought getting clapped up or rolled in New York would make a great story to tell in the locker rooms back home.

The young kid with the dirty fingernails behind the desk made my type but not my face and was satisfied with a quick look at my press card and a five-buck tip to tell me that the cops had scoured Shim Little's room and came up with nothing but a suitcase of personal belongings and a portable radio. As far as he knew Little never had any guests and never said anything, either.

I asked, "How about dames?"

His eyes made a joke of it. "You kidding? What kind of a place you think this is?"

"So he didn't bring any in."

"All he had to do was knock on any door. This is a permanent HQ for two dozen three-way ten-buck hookers. A few even got super specialties if you're a weirdo."

I let him see another five and he flicked it out of my fingers. "What was he?"

He waved a thumb toward the tiny lobby. A chunky broad in a short tight dress was coming through the doors, her face grim with fatigue. "Ask Sophia there. She knew the guy." He made a motion with his head and when she spotted me the grim look disappeared like somebody turned a switch and the professional smile flashed across her face. She didn't even bother to be introduced. She simply hooked her arm into mine and took me up two flights to her room, unlocked the door and had her clothes off in half a minute. She turned around, held out her hand and said, "Ten bucks and take your pick."

I gave her a twenty and told her to put her clothes back on. Between the appendectomy slash, the caesarean scar, an ass full of striation marks and a shaved pussy red-flecked with pimples from a dull razor, she didn't exactly radiate my kind of sexuality.

But for the twenty she did what she was told. "You a freak?" she asked curiously. "I got some dresses if you like it with clothes on."

"Just a conversationalist," I told her.

This time her smile was tired and real. "Oh, great, mister." She flopped into a chair and yanked the black wig off her head. Her hair was a short mop of tight curls. "Tonight I'm glad to see you. It's been rough here. Now, you want dirty talk, the story of my sex life, some . . ."

"Information."

Her eyes narrowed down a little bit. "You can't be a cop because you already passed the bread."

"Reporter, Sophia."

"What the hell have I got to say? You doing a piece on whores? Hell, man, who needs to research that? All you have to do is . . ."

"Shim Little."

"Man, he's dead." Her face said that's about all she was going to say.

"I know," I told her. "I killed him."

She recognized me then. She was remembering the photos in the paper and was putting it all together and letting her imagination gouge horrible thoughts in her mind. "Mister . . ." her voice was hoarse and scared. "I only laid him twice. Just a straight job. He was . . . okay."

"He lived here for two weeks, kid. Don't tell me you don't know about your neighbors."

"So we talked a little bit. He wasn't much of a talker. In this business you're on and off if you want to make a buck."

"How much did he pay you?"

"Fifty . . . both times. He was a good tipper. You don't get many like that."

"With him you'd spend a little extra time the second time around."

"Why not?"

I grinned at her and it scared her again. "Where'd he get his loot?"

"Honest, mister . . . hell, we just . . ."

My grin got bigger and she wiped the back of her mouth with her hand. "He was . . . one of the boys. Not very big. He wanted me to think so but I could tell. He said he had a nice safe job now and laughed when he said it. Yeah, he really laughed at that, but I didn't go asking any nosy damn fool questions. He was the kind who could get mean as hell and he had that crazy gun with him all the time. He even put it on the other pillow while we were screwing."

"No names?"

"Just that it was the safest job he ever had. He kept laughing about it."

"How about friends?"

"Not around here. I saw him on Eighth Avenue once with some guy, that's all."

I got up and she shrunk back into her chair. "I don't have to remind you to forget about making any telephone calls, do I?"

"Mister," she said. "You got your conversation, I got my bread, now just let's forget it."

"Good enough." I looked at my watch. It was quarter to two.

————

Cheryl had beaten me to Ma Christy's by five minutes and had a bag of hamburgers and a container of coffee ready for me when I got there. She had deliberately dressed as sloppily as she could, using no makeup at all with a hairpiece I hated pegged to her head, but even the attempt at disguise couldn't quite hide all that woman if you looked hard enough.

I said, "Hello, gorgeous."

"Two detectives were covering my apartment. They were expecting a ravishing creature."

"No trouble?"

"They're still back watching out for Miss Ravishing. I exited through the building next door just to be sure."

"Bring the stuff?"

"Yeah, but eat first."

I had forgotten how hungry I was and wolfed down the chow. When I finished I pulled the notes from the manila envelope she had brought and spread them out on the bed. The contacts had come through and it was all there.

The guy they called the Mechanic was one Henry Borden, fifty-nine years old, arrested for possession and selling of narcotics, suspected of reworking car bodies for transportation of illegal items. By trade he was a tool and die man, sheet metal worker, and was currently employed in an aluminum casting foundry in Brooklyn. His current address was down in the Village.

Little things were beginning to tie in now. The connecting link was *metal*.

I took the package, slid it under the rickety dresser without disturbing any of the dust, and said, "Let's take a ride."

"Now?"

"Now," I told her.

"You look like you could use some rest," she said impishly.

"No. I have to keep what strength I have."

Downstairs we picked up a cab on the corner and gave an address two blocks from Henry Borden's and walked the rest of the way. The drizzle had started and we had the empty street to ourselves. We found the house number and the basement apartment Borden occupied and didn't have any trouble getting in at all because whoever had been there before us didn't bother to lock up on the way out.

He had just left the Mechanic lying there with his throat cut almost all the way through in a huge glob of blood that was draining toward the back of the room on the warped floor.

The apartment was too small to take long to search, but the frisk had been efficient enough. Everything was turned inside out, including the pockets of everything he owned, with an empty billfold lying in plain sight to give the earmarks of a robbery. Even the lining of Borden's work jacket had been torn loose and the zipper pocket yanked off. Still dangling from the flap were two ballpoint pens and a small clip-on screwdriver. I tugged them off, tossed the screwdriver on the chair and stuck the pens in my own pocket. Borden wasn't going to use them again.

In back of me, Cheryl was beginning to gag. I got her outside, walked her until she felt better, then grabbed a cab and got her back home. She went in through the other building and I went back to Ma Christy's. Nobody followed me.

For a little while I sat on the edge of the bed and listened to the tape again on the mini recorder. The voices were talking about knocking off the Mechanic, which completed the job and the stuff would be ready to ship. Well, now it was ready to go and I'd fall with it. I took out my pen and jotted down a few notes for tomorrow. It skipped on the paper so I put it down and used the other one. I finished what I was doing before I saw the printed name on the pen. It read, *Reading Associates, Rare Books, First Editions.* The address was on Madison Avenue in the lower fifties. I looked at the other pen. It was another cheap giveaway with *MacIntosh and Stills, Aluminum Casting* printed on it. I shrugged and flopped back on the bed. I was asleep in a minute.

———————

So the old cop instinct comes out and you check all the possibilities, but the con instinct was there too and you do it as unobtrusively as possible because you know about the eyes that are watching and how fast it could end if you weren't careful.

I checked the papers, but the morning editions didn't have anything at all about the body down in the Village and unless somebody purposely checked in on Henry Borden he might not even be found until the odors of decomposition started to smell up the neighborhood.

At ten-thirty I took the elevator up to the fourth floor of the building that housed *Reading Associates.* It was a multi-office operation with a staff of a dozen or so and already getting some traffic from some elderly scholarly types. A few collegiate types were browsing through the racks and examining manuscripts in the glass-topped cases.

I wasn't much of an authority on rare books, but apparently the collectors were a breed apart and assumed anyone there had to be an enthusiast. A tiny old guy gave me a friendly nod and immediately wanted to know if I were going to exhibit at the show. I faked my way around the question and let him do the talking. He had already attended the one in Los Angeles, was going to be at the one here in New York next week, but unfortunately had to skip the one in London the end of the month. Of course, the main event would be the Chicago showing in six weeks where it was hoped some new finds would be put on display.

I even shook hands with Mr. Reading himself, an owlish man in his middle thirties with thick glasses and a bright smile who was in the middle of three conversations at once. The main topic seemed to be the surprise he was preparing for the Chicago exhibit.

When I broke loose I roamed around long enough to get a quick look into the offices, but there was nothing more than the crackle of papers coming from any of them. The door to Reading's office stood wide open, a book-lined room with a single antique desk stacked with papers and an archaic safe with the door swung out stuffed full of folders.

I was about to leave when a pair of magazine photographers I recognized came in and I squeezed back behind the shelves, backing into a smudged-faced girl in a smock and knocking the wastebasket out of her hands. She let out a startled, "Oh!"

I said, "Sorry, Miss," and bent down to put the junk back in the basket.

She laughed and brushed her hair out of her eyes. "Here, let me do that. You'll get your hands all dirty and you know what Mr. Reading thinks about that." She picked up the used carbons, stencils, wrapped a paper around the mimeograph ink cans and the two paint spray cans, dropped the empty beer bottle on top of the lot and edged around me.

The photographers were clustered around Reading, pointing out something in the cases, and when I had a clear field I went back to the corridor and punched the button for the elevator.

It was a good try, but that's all it was. A real, fat fizzle.

When I reached the street the rain had started again, but it gave me a good excuse for keeping my head tipped down under my hat. I went across town to the big newsstand that carried out-of-state papers and scanned the racks without finding any with the big eagle in the masthead. I tried one more and didn't make it there either. The later local editions were out, but there still wasn't any mention of Henry Borden's death.

Time was always on the side of the killer when these things happened. You can't just let them drop when you trip over them no matter what the score is. I found an empty booth in a Times Square cigar store, looked up MacIntosh and Stills in Brooklyn and got an irritated manager on the other end. When I asked him if Borden had been in he half-shouted. "That bastard hasn't shown all day and we're sitting here with an order ready to go out."

"Maybe something's wrong with him," I suggested.

"Sure. We let him use our tools to do a moonlight job and now he forgets where they belong. He's the only guy here who can handle this damn job, but if he doesn't get his ass in we'll damn well do without him."

"I'll go check on him."

"Somebody oughta," he said and hung up.

I checked by calling 911, the police emergency number, and told them where to look for a mutilated corpse and didn't bother to leave my name. I made one more call to Al Grossino and arranged for a meet at nine o'clock. That was still a long way off and I didn't want to go prowling around the city in daylight. The answer was in a crummy little bar on Eighth Avenue that didn't believe in overlighting and didn't care how long you sipped at a beer as long as you kept them coming.

By six o'clock I was starting to feel bloated and was ready to cut out, but the TV news came on and the preshow rundown made a big splash about another gruesome killing in Manhattan, so I called for another brew. It was great coverage, all right. They didn't show any body shots, but the announcer on the street was giving a running commentary on what the police had found after an anonymous tip. Half the residents in the neighborhood were gawking and waving into the camera or pointing at the rubber body bag being loaded into the morgue wagon, but by that time I had stopped listening and was watching the background, because there was one character there standing on his toes to look over the heads in front and folded in his pocket was a newspaper with a big, rangy eagle in the masthead. He walked out of camera range as I was leaving for the phone booth in the back of the room, and this time I didn't have to leave my name because Charlie Watts recognized my voice the second I said hello to him.

"You coming up, Fallon?"

"You want another commendation in your file, Charlie?"

"They don't give out medals for nailing people like you."

"How about that body with its throat cut?"

Charlie let a beat go by, then: "I'm listening."

"Your guy got himself on television tonight without realizing it. A real good shot, front face and profile. He's on the six o'clock news with a newspaper in his pocket . . . one with an eagle across the front."

"How do you know?"

"Check him out, buddy. You'll have his mug shots somewhere. If that's his hometown newspaper you can go through his local department. I got the feeling this guy's still got some of the amateur left in him. No pro is going back to make sure the body is growing cold."

"You ought to know."

"Get with the legwork, Charlie. You don't have to say thanks." I cradled the receiver before he could get a trace through, left a buck on the counter for the bartender and went out to join the rush hour crowd getting home. I had spent too much time in the same clothes and was getting sloppy and soggy looking. Right then I could smell myself and I didn't feel like getting tapped for being a bum, so I hustled up the avenue, turned east where the buildings partially kept the rain off me and headed toward the street that ran behind my building.

It took better than a half hour and nobody was around to see the underground route I took to my own place. I crossed the yard behind Patsy's, pushed the boards in the fence out so I could squeeze through, and went in the rear entrance to the service personnel's locker room.

O'Malley had left everything I needed, including a shaving kit and a towel. When I had showered and gotten the beard off my face I changed into my fresh clothes, packed the old stuff back into the locker and slid the .45 under my belt.

Outside the thunder rumbled and I slung my raincoat on. Something was bugging me and I couldn't quite reach out and touch it. Squeaky had handed it to me on a platter, but killing one lousy punk had thrown the whole thing out of kilter. All I had to do was sit through an interrogation by the cops and everything would have been blown sky high. Routine police work could have jammed the entire operation, but Squeaky had to go and try to take a bite out of it. Damn it, that nice little guy was a born loser and he went down the hard way, scared half out of his mind with no way out. He didn't even have sense enough to let somebody else make that call to Shim Little, and him with a voice you could spot like a snowball in a coalpile.

Now the operation had bought its time and I was the only one who could stop the clock. But I couldn't surface very easily and they'd know that too, so all the options were on their side.

That little bug inside kept nagging at me. It had a big grinning face like it knew all the answers and I did too, only I couldn't put it together like the bug did.

Darkness had finally settled in and I went into it gratefully. I edged around the row of plastic garbage bags and headed for the fence, my hand feeling for the loose boards. I was halfway through when I realized how stupid I had been, because there were other people who thought like I did too.

But this one's stupidity was not putting the boards back the way I had left them and I had the bare second to dive and roll under the knife blade that hacked a huge sliver out of the post above my head and there wasn't a chance in the world of reaching for the gun I had buried under my clothes.

He didn't get a second chance with the blade because this was my kind of fight and my boot caught his elbow and the steel clattered against the concrete walkway. I had a fistful of hair, yanking his face into the dirt beside me, one fist driving into his ribs, and he tried to let out a yell but the ground muffled it all.

For ten seconds he turned tiger, then I flipped him over, got my knee against his spine, my forearm locked under his chin, and arched him like a bow until there was a sudden crack from inside him and he went death-limp in my hands.

He should have used the gun he kept in the shoulder sling, or maybe he just enjoyed the steel more. Or he never should have gotten into the pro ranks in the big town. There wasn't any wallet on him, or any keys, but he wouldn't be too hard to identify. The newspaper was still in his pocket, a three-day-old weekly from a small town in Florida.

What really was interesting came out of his side pocket. He had sixty bucks in tens and fives and ten one hundreds. Only the C notes had been torn in half and somebody else was holding the other sections. I had to grin at that old dodge. It was a neat piece of insurance to make sure somebody got a job done and could prove it before he collected the other part of his loot. I took the sixty bucks, two of the torn bills and tucked them in my billfold.

I almost missed something else, but it flashed in the light and I took that too and the little bug inside me grinned bigger.

————

Al Grossino huddled behind the wheel of the car, filling the interior with foul-smelling cigar smoke. He handed me two sheets of paper, but I said, "Just tell me, Al."

"Those companies keep up a constant weighing system. That gold got lost before it was poured into ingots. The Nevada bunch think they figured it out. It was siphoned off with the same vacuums they use to pick up the residue on the floor."

"Somebody would be checking the containers."

"They found a by-pass."

"Yeah?"

"Three guys walked off the job a month ago. Security ran checks on their job records and they were all phoney."

"So it was engineered," I said.

Al wouldn't commit himself besides a shrug. "Could be. It's a federal case now."

"What was the final count?"

"About a thousand pounds."

"That's one hell of a bundle of loot."

He took another deep pull on the cigar and looked at me. "Who's got it, Fallon?"

"You want to be the hero?"

"Why not?"

"Let's make it some other time."

"You're getting to own me this time, buddy."

"Fine. I'll make you half hero." I told him where to look to find a dead man and how he could play it if he were smart, then I backed out of the car and watched while he drove off.

When I called Cheryl from the booth on the corner I gave her the code message that meant an immediate meet and in twenty minutes I saw her coming toward me. She passed me in the doorway while I made sure she wasn't being followed, then when she crossed and doubled back I went over to join her.

"Any trouble?"

"That car was still there."

"Charlie's men?"

"Department registration. I checked."

"What about the office?"

"They have a man there too."

"Any squawks from Orley?"

"I didn't want to give you the bad news," she said.

"So?"

"You, my friend, are under the boom. They're about to lower it."

"A hell of a way to end a career," I grinned at her.

"Well, if the worst comes to the worst, I'll support you." She kissed her fingertip and touched my mouth with it.

"I like it better the other way around. Maybe Orley will see it my way." Then I told her what had happened and even in the dim light from the street I could see her go pale.

She shook her head a little sadly. "They won't see anything now. You know how fast Charlie can work when he wants to. He'll pull out every stop just to nail your hide."

"But if I come up with the big package it won't hurt so bad." I gave her hand a squeeze. "Your training with parolees ever teach you anything?"

"Just to keep my skirt down and my blouse buttoned up with the ones fresh out."

"How about breaking and entering?"

"I've read up on the subject."

"Let's give it a try." I took out the two half bills, scribbled a note across one, and told her what to do. She repeated the instructions back to me, her mouth tight with worry, but she knew the score and she knew the alternatives and didn't question what

I told her. The thing could go two ways now, but when you consider egos or fear or reprisals you could place your bets with the odds slightly in your favor and hope Lady Luck would give you the edge you needed. At least she seemed to frown on trivial stupidity and minor coincidences when they both locked hands to build a beautiful infield error.

I rang the night bell in the building and the sleepy-looking watchman unlocked the door and said, "Yeah? The place is closed up."

I showed him my press card and he shook his head. "That don't mean nothing."

Fifty of the sixty bucks I had taken from a corpse did mean something though, and he agreed to a five-minute talk because his coffee would get cold.

"There been any night work going on here?" I asked him.

"Sure Maintenance, cleaning . . . all the time."

"How about Reading Associates?"

"Night deliveries sometimes. They had their shelves reworked two months ago."

"I mean lately."

He thought for a moment, then nodded. "Some guy was let up to install new glass cases in the place, only Mr. Reading was with him most of the time."

"Use much equipment?"

This time I got a frown. "Yeah, a big toolbox and a small crate. Wooden one with steel bands around it. The day man said they had some welding bottles up there too. Why? They finished all that stuff the other day. Nobody's been here since."

"You like to make a hundred on top of that fifty?"

He started to get pictures in his mind then and his eyes got a flinty look in them. "Like hell, mister. You get your tail out of here like now. Come on, buddy, scram."

I took off my hat and let him see the edges of my teeth.

"Take a good look, feller. You might have seen my picture in the paper recently." When I held my coat open he saw the gun in my belt too and it all came through fast and he wore the same expression Loco and Sophia did when their mouths went suddenly dry.

I looked at my watch. "I won't be long. You'll get your hundred on the way out. But if I were you I'd stay right in the doorway where a buddy outside can see you, and if anybody comes in here you just ring that office once. Just once, understand?"

He couldn't talk. My reputation and the big story in the paper had put a knot in his belly and a lump in his throat. He nodded and I walked to the elevator, took it up to the floor I wanted and pushed the down button to get it back to the ground floor before I got out.

Getting into the office wasn't hard at all. It took two minutes with the picks and I was inside with all the musty paper smell and when my eyes were adjusted I went across to Reading's office and sat down behind his desk. If the schedule worked out I was twenty minutes early.

But the little Lady of the Luck was on my side for a change and I was only two minutes early, because the desk phone rang once and quit and I knew he was on the way up. I heard the keys work the lock, saw a single overhead light snap on, and heard him come into his office. He had a gun in his hand, but it was dangling while mine was aiming for a spot right between those owlish eyes of his and he just stood there because a face-to-face shoot-out wasn't that end of his job at all. He had planned on an ambush and could have made it stick with me as a prowler but it hadn't worked out at all.

I said, "Drop it, Reading."

He let the gun clatter to the floor.

"Sit down. Over there."

"Listen, you came for a payoff. All right, I'll . . ."

"It's going to be more than the six hundred you offered your boy to wipe me out."

"Okay, we'll deal. How much?"

"All of it."

At first he didn't get what I meant, then the message went through, but a wily expression clouded his eyes and I knew he was thinking of his insurance policy. Too bad he didn't know about mine. "You're not very smart, Fallon."

"Cutting in on mob money isn't supposed to be, buddy. But neither is killing a guy's old pal very smart either. And I don't think organizing a few extra kills on your own without authority from higher headquarters is very bright thinking."

"You're out of your mind."

"Finding those torn bills under your door has made you pretty skitterish, pal."

"What torn bills?"

"The ones you knew had to come from a dead man. But before that man was dead he talked to me and told me who gave them to him. That's what you thought. So it was just fine to meet with me right here and lay me out when I came in because the story would look good. Hell, man, you had me pegged when I came in today. Oh, you were cool about it, but you knew you had to work fast. There were others that saw me and could identify me as having looked over your collection and a heist of a few of those first editions of yours could net me a bundle in the right places. Yeah, it really would have looked good. And that hood you picked was a little smarter than I thought he was. He had the stakeouts pegged and knew I'd probably make a try to get back home some way. I was beginning to look too seedy to be roaming the streets anymore."

"Fallon . . ."

"Your own men blew it on you, kiddo." I was remembering what Shim Little had told the whore in the hotel. "But the big blooper was your own. You had those giveaway pens lying around and it's just natural for people to pick them up."

"Those pens are distributed in every bookstore in town."

"But they don't turn up in the pockets of dead people," I told him.

His smile was hard, going over the technicality, and he knew damn well it wouldn't stand up as evidence at all. He was still banking on his own insurance.

I said, "All of it, Reading. I want it all."

We both heard the door slam open and the pounding of feet on the floor. He let out a little laugh and said, "None of it, Fallon," then called out, "In here, officers."

They came through the doors in a rush and I nodded to Charlie Watts and the other three and laid the .45 on the top of the desk. "You took long enough to get here."

I was staring at all those police .38s and it wasn't a very pretty sight at all. "You're finally down, Fallon. You're finally going to get that great big fall."

When I smiled at him he didn't like it a bit. There was just too damn much confidence in it and he turned to tell Reading to shut up because he was cop enough to get a smell that wasn't supposed to be there at all. It hung in the room like smoke and he was the only one who could smell it.

"Read me my rights, then let's give it fifteen minutes and we'll do it all downtown like the old days. Later they'll give you and Al Grossino that new commendation and everybody will be happy."

I was thinking of what he was going to say when he heard the tapes, when they did voice prints from interrogation tapes on Shim Little and his dead buddy and tied in the dead Mechanic, then got a statement from little squat Sophia and tied it all in with the double-edged hook I was ready to throw.

So he gave me the fifteen minutes, which was exactly the

right amount of time for Cheryl to get there, escorted in by another patrolman.

Reading was still making noise, insisting I had called him under the pretense of blackmailing him for holding stolen rare books and like a good citizen had immediately called the police to intercept the action. The gun on the floor was his and he had a license to carry it, but I had gotten there first and was threatening his life.

Sure, it was true enough. It was what I had figured he'd do. I said to Charlie, "You get the rest of those torn bills from Al?"

The captain watched me a moment and nodded. "I have some more on me." I glanced over at Reading. "He has the other halves."

Once more I got that crafty look and he stated with indignant sincerity, "That's ridiculous!"

"Cheryl?"

"After I delivered the first two I watched through the window. He got an envelope out of his desk drawer and tossed it in the fireplace. He made one phone call then got out of there in a hurry. I went in through the window and pulled the envelope off the fire. It's under the rug in his den right now."

"Money doesn't burn very easily, Reading," I said.

"You're not planting evidence on me, Fallon. I demand . . ."

"Shut up," I said. "Charlie, come here."

My old commander walked across the room and I took out my wallet. I opened the back compartment and showed him something new. "For your eyes only, Captain. Orley News Service is just a staged setup for this outfit. My being busted out of the department and doing that short stretch was all part of the staging."

I almost wanted to laugh because although he'd check it out in detail later he knew every part of it was true and he was hat-ing himself for never having given me any benefit of doubt at all.

Reading was having a fit in front of the other officers, demanding to call a lawyer, and I said nice and loud and clear, "He's holding the gold, Charlie. It was going to be shipped out of the country right along with him and his little prized book collection and when he gets ready to talk you'll get all the names you want because Mr. Reading here doesn't want to get any contract put out for him for gross negligence in handling mob cash and prison walls are a lot thicker than the ones he has here."

But Reading was thinking he still held the trump card. I reached for the .45 on the desk and asked Charlie, "Mind?"

He didn't say anything, but the other cops were still holding hard on me. "Shim Little said he was on the safest job in the world. Let's see if he was right."

I thumbed the hammer of the .45 back and aimed it at the open door of the archaic safe and touched the trigger. The roar in the room was momentarily deafening and the stink of cordite was sharp.

Everybody had jerked back waiting to hear the whistle of a ricocheting slug bounce off the steel, but there wasn't any at all. There was just a neat hole punched in the door and under the dull black finish was the shiny yellow that only gold can reflect and over in the corner Reading slumped into the chair and began to choke on his own fear.

"Downtown now, Charlie?"

He smiled at me for the first time in years. "Yeah, you bastard."

"Let's keep it that way if we can. It's better for our business."

"The broad too?"

"She's one of us, buddy."

"I'll be damned."

Downstairs I paid the night watchman with a hundred bucks of Cheryl's money and we all went out to the cars together. I never thought it would happen again, but this time I got to ride in the front seat with my old commander. Just this once. Washington wouldn't approve of the fraternization after all the work they went through.

When we were getting in, Cheryl said, "We can't even hire a hotel room tonight, you slob. You took all my cash."

"There's always home," I told her.

She grinned and squeezed my hand. Like a little trap. And I was caught in it. But it felt good anyway.

Research

Jeff Gelb

*T*he nude and gorgeous girl writhed in front of me on the silken sheets of her bachelorette pad bed. I grabbed her dual domes of delicacy and began to mash them, like sweet potatoes. I swirled my tongue around a red gumdrop nipple until it grew as hard as a cherry.

She grabbed at my love gun and I let her take me in her mouth, her tongue playing with me, taking me to places I'd only dreamed of. Meanwhile, I was fingering her nipples, teasing them, tugging them, twisting them here and there, like the controls of a stereo system, until she groaned for me to take her, to slake her. I was willing and more than able to oblige. My pulsating manhood slid—

Joe Price looked up at his client. "Jesus, Bill, I can't sell this."

Bill Hammerhoff squirmed in the worn chair across the desk from his longtime literary agent. Price sighed. "This kind of writing went out with free love. Where'd you get this manuscript— the back of your closet?"

Hammerhoff looked down at his clenched hands. "I need the money, Joe."

Price slowly shook his head. "No one's buying this kind of stuff anymore, Bill. Not in years. Decades."

Hammerhoff looked around Price's one-room office. Books and magazines were piled everywhere. The walls were filled with photos of clients, some famous, some once-famous and now all-but-forgotten. Outside the single grimy window he could see palm trees lining the hillsides of Hollywood.

He screwed up the courage to look at Price. "But there are more men's magazines than ever . . . and the Internet. My God, half the Internet is porn sites. Don't they need some fuck fiction?"

"Sure, but not something that sounds like it was written when James Bond was still just a series of paperbacks."

"You used to like my sex stuff."

"I used to like my Betamax too, but they don't make 'em anymore."

"I'm desperate, Joe," he all but whispered.

Price waved off the comment. "Look, you're the one who dropped out of this twenty-five years ago to become a teacher. What happened?"

Hammerhoff shrugged. "I got sick of the little teenaged brats. At first I thought maybe it was just the school district, so I kept switching schools. But after all those years, all those thousands of kids, nothing had changed. From Beverly Hills to Compton, they're all the same. They're not there to learn English, they're there to get each other pregnant, make drug deals, and drive their teachers to drink." He paused and licked his lips. Under his breath, he added, "Little bastards used to call me Mr. Hemorrhoid.

"So a few years back, I gave it up and tried early retirement. But there's not enough money for . . ."

". . . your habit," Price finished the sentence. "Still drinking, Bill?"

"Oh, here and there."

"Right." Price sighed. "Well, I can't help you if you're gonna hand me outdated stuff like this. This isn't real sex, Bill. It's pure fantasy. When was the last time you got laid, anyway?"

Now Hammerhoff really squirmed in the uncomfortable wooden-backed chair.

"Sorry, don't answer that," Price said mercifully. "Look, you're right about one thing: Sex still sells. And you used to be a great writer of this stuff, one of the best. But times change, people's tastes change. It's a whole new millennium, you know? If you want to write some sex stuff, get back in practice. And I don't mean writing practice. Do some research. Go out and find a hottie, or whatever they call them these days. Get laid a few times, and then write me some really sizzling stories. I guarantee I can sell reams of sex stuff for you, but only if it's more up-to-date, more—I dunno—edgy."

————

Bill Hammerhoff stared at the streets of Hollywood with a new set of eyes. Price had nailed him. Hammerhoff didn't know how to write about sex anymore because he hadn't had sex in years. Mabel had divorced him in the mid-seventies when his teacher's paychecks had failed to keep up with her tastes in fashion, and Hammerhoff had had little luck with the opposite sex ever since. He'd become a hermit, rereading the hundred-plus books he'd written back in the sixties, when he could stay up a few nights, write a complete book, and pocket two hundred dollars. Not bad money for the time. He recalled one year when he'd turned out fifteen books under a variety of pseudonyms, and cowritten five or six more. Some of those books were pretty good reads. But even then he had faked much of the knowledge behind the sex scenes that made up every other chapter of these books, written for a variety of fly-by-night publishers.

The bitter truth, Hammerhoff thought as he stepped into the cool of the early Hollywood evening, was that the manuscript he'd shown his old literary agent was a brand-new work. Hammerhoff had sweated over it not for nights or weeks, but for six painful months. Woefully out of practice, it was the best he could do.

He had to admit: He really was out of touch with the times,

and especially with its women. He began walking down the crowded city street, looking at each woman who passed him in a new way. How could he even start a conversation that would lead him to have sex with anyone young enough to teach him the ropes, as it were? There was a whole new generation of sexual perversions that he had to learn, so he could turn them into a series of new books that would put him ahead of his bills for the first time in years. And that would also pay for "his habit," as Price had called it. Yeah, he drank, and too much for his own good. But that was just because his life sucked, and he had nothing better to do. Or so he told himself during his frequent drunken stupors.

The reddish hues of the sunset were blending with the neon above storefront windows on Hollywood Boulevard, creating a patchwork quilt of colors that made Hammerhoff's eyes hurt and made him long for a drink. He stepped into a darkened bar and was greeted by a topless waitress. Hammerhoff noted that her breasts were shaped like pears, with tiny corn-kernel nipples and massive aureoles. They were ugly but they were real, and they were not at all the way he'd written about them in his failed attempt at a new novel.

"I'll have a whiskey," he stuttered, unable to lift his eyes from her sweating breasts.

"We don't serve alcohol here," she said. "Otherwise you couldn't stare at these the way you are," she said as she cupped her uneven-sized breasts and pointed them at him like guns.

"Sorry—I didn't mean to . . ." He let the sentence trail off as he stepped back outside, eyes blinking rapidly to adjust to the shift in light. This was not going to be easy, he thought as he began walking down Hollywood Boulevard. He saw some women whom he supposed were hookers. They were certainly dressed that way, thigh-high skirts caressing bubble butts, thick nipples poking their way through tight t-shirts advertising some heavy metal band or another. He cleared his throat and approached one.

"Excuse me."

The closest girl gave him the evil eye.

"Are you working?" he stammered.

"What do you mean?" she challenged. A joint drooped from her mouth, its odor sickening Hammerhoff, reminding him of too many bad memories from his teaching days.

"How much . . ."

"For what?" Now her voice was raised to a high pitch.

He nodded in the direction of her breasts.

"Say what?" the teenager shouted, her spittle hitting Hammerhoff's chin. He backed off as a massive black guy in leather pants and torn muscle shirt strode out of the nearby CD store. "Whassup, girlfriend?" His eyes shot daggers at Hammerhoff.

"This ASS-hole asked me how much these cost!" She lifted her t-shirt and two small, perky breasts popped out.

"Why the fuck you do that, motherfucker?" He approached Hammerhoff, who turned tail and ran down a side street, as their fading taunts stung his ears.

Three blocks later he slowed, thinking he might throw up in fear and exhaustion. He stopped to catch his breath, balancing against a wall, and looking back to see if anyone was chasing him. Mercifully, no familiar faces were following him. Regaining his composure, Hammerhoff looked at the headlines of the newspapers in a series of nearby boxes that fronted the sidewalk. Two were legit L.A. newspapers, but two others were obviously sex rags that were just shills for ads for sex businesses.

Hammerhoff blinked. Here was his answer—a sex supermarket all wrapped up in newsprint. He dug a quarter out of his pocket and put it in the machine. It would not open to his touch. He banged on it angrily while a passing couple made disapproving noises in his direction. One called him a "lousy drunk." Well, fuck them, Hammerhoff thought, as he dug out another quarter and put it in the second box, which harbored a stack of something called The *LA-XXX Weekly.*

This newsbox opened and he pulled out a copy of the rag, thumbing through it. Sure enough, there was page after page of ads for strip clubs, massage parlors, and escort services. The last half of the newspaper was nothing but one-inch by one-inch photo ads for private dancers who would come to the reader's own home to strut their stuff. Hammerhoff looked at the photo ads, mesmerized by the sea of faces. Some were fresh-faced, some hard-nosed, some desperate, others haughty. Each ad announced the girl's name, measurements, sexual proclivities, or other hook to use as bait for guys like Hammerhoff. He studied each ad in the blinking neon light of the liquor store behind him. The girls' features turned orange and purple, orange and purple in its shifting glow. He was searching for some indefinable quality in one of the ads, something that would grab him by the balls. Finally, one ad made him stop his visual search.

Its headline read "Young schoolgirl needs to be punished for turning in her homework late." The photo showed someone named "Amanda" who could have passed for eighteen but was probably older. There was something about her, something behind her glazed eyes that suggested every teenaged twat who'd ever sleepwalked through his high-school English courses over the decades. She'd be perfect, he thought, as he stepped into the liquor store for some bottled courage.

———

"Nice place," Amanda said with a hint of sarcasm as she stepped into Hammerhoff's small apartment. After calling her number in the ad, he'd spent the next hour cleaning the place, opening the windows in hopes he could get the stale booze smell out of the apartment before he brought her here.

They'd met at an out-of-the-way coffee shop, haggled over prices, and then he'd driven her back to his place. Hammerhoff studied her more closely as she walked around his apartment.

"Looking for something?"

"Hidden cameras," she said.

Hammerhoff laughed. "Do people do that?"

"Hey, you wouldn't believe what people do." Apparently satisfied, she returned to his side. She was pretty in a girl-next-door way, but also already hardened in a way he'd seen over the years many times in his classes. Was it life with cruel or absent parents? Mean classmates? Or just life itself in these crazy times that pre-aged all kids anymore? Physically she'd do just fine. As her photo promised, she had pouty lips, long dark hair, large breasts, and a shapely figure, just barely hidden behind a very tight summer dress. He guessed she was not wearing panties, or at least that would be the case in the story he'd start to write later that night.

"Let me see your driver's license," Amanda demanded, her hand out.

Hammerhoff frowned. "Is that necessary?"

"If you want us to have fun, it is. I gotta make sure you're not a cop." Reluctantly, he dug his wallet out of his pants pocket, took out his license and showed it to her.

"Mr. . . . Hammerhoff," she read aloud slowly. She made a face, nodding to herself.

In person, she looked younger than her newspaper ad photo, young enough to be his daughter. "You sure you're old enough to be doing this?"

She smiled humorlessly. "Does it matter? I mean, we're not exactly gonna be doing anything legal here anyway, right?" She squeezed his crotch as she said it, and he gasped in surprise and pleasure.

She laughed. "Well, I won't show you my driver's license, but

I'm twenty-four. I can pretend I'm younger if you like—a lot younger. Would you like that?" She fondled him through his trousers and he could feel fluid leaking out of his penis and into his underwear. She'd been here three minutes and he was already about to explode, before he'd even started his research. He pushed her hand away and retreated to his weathered couch, where he sat down.

"Come over here," he said as he patted the patched cushion beside him.

"Why?"

"I want you to . . . do things to me."

"What kinds of things?" she asked as she approached the couch, while stepping out of her summer dress. Hammerhoff had guessed wrong: She was wearing underwear, though in truth, it was little more than two strings and a minute patch of cotton. He could see everything but the inner folds of her vagina while she stood in front of him, proudly showing off.

He cleared his throat. "I . . . I want you to show me how you fuck your boyfriend."

She cradled the back of his head with her hands and brought it forward, so that he was nestled between her breasts. He could smell her scent, a potent combination of smoke, cheap perfume, and musk. He was dizzy with sexual energy and the drinks he'd consumed while he'd straightened up his place. She whispered throatily, "You can be my boyfriend for the next hour."

He backed away. "No, I want you to show me what you and your boyfriend do . . . sexually. What turns you on. What gets you off."

"Why?"

"Just research," he answered truthfully.

She laughed. "Sure, Mr. Hemorrhoid."

"What—what did you say?" he stammered, scarcely believing he'd heard the old hated nickname.

"Didn't think I'd recognize you? It's only been six years since you kicked me out of your English class. Remember, Mr. Hemorrhoid? Just because I wrote an essay on what it felt like to get assfucked by my boyfriend?"

Hammerhoff stared at the girl, really seeing her for the first time. My God, he did recognize her, the little bitch. No wonder her ad had grabbed his attention. She was the embodiment of everything he hated about all the kids he'd tried to teach for so long, who didn't care to learn.

He smiled at her with as much phony pleasantness as he could muster. "Maybe we should revisit that essay tonight."

She laughed. "You're a kinky bastard, ain't you?"

"You'll find out," he promised.

————

Price set down the new manuscript and regarded his client. Hammerhoff seemed looser, more self-confident than he had the last time Price had seen him, just a week ago.

"I have to admit," Price said, "that when you left my office, I never thought I'd see you again, let alone so quickly."

Hammerhoff shrugged. "I got inspired."

Price nodded. "I'll say. Honestly, I didn't think you had it in you to change, to update yourself and your writing.

"But this"—Price shook the manuscript pages—"is seriously great stuff. Sexy as all get-out, a real turn-on." He laughed. "I hadda take a couple of showers last night while reading it.

"But more than that," he continued, "it's entirely fresh, up-to-date, exciting . . ."

"Edgy enough for you?"

"My God, yes. The girl's murder came as a complete surprise. I don't recall you ever doing a murder mystery way back when."

"Can't say that I did." Hammerhoff looked down at his hands. He noticed there still were dark stains under his fingertips.

"What inspired you?"

Hammerhoff thought about it for a long moment before answering. "My research."

Price all but ignored the response. "Because if you think you can write more of these sexy murder stories, they're all the rage. I'm positive I can sell them. Maybe even hardcover. A three-book deal. Big money, Bill. Big."

"That would be . . . nice."

Price stood up and held out his hand, signaling the end of their meeting. "So get outta here and start writing your next sexy murder mystery, okay?"

Hammerhoff smiled softly as he shook hands with his agent. His mind was already elsewhere. "Yeah, sure."

He left the building, stretched, and gazed at the setting sun. Night was coming soon, and with it, the heady promise of a new adventure. He found a row of newspaper boxes and fished out two quarters. With one, he retrieved a new copy of *LA-XXX Weekly*. With another, he bought the day's paper. A small headline at the bottom of the front page caught his eye: "Police Seek Public's Help in Disappearance of Call Girl."

Yes, he'd write another sexy murder mystery for Joe Price. But first he would have to do some more research.

Death on Denial

O'Neil De Noux

> The Mississippi. The Father of Waters.
> The Nile of North America.
> And *I* found it.
> —Hernando de Soto, 1541

The oily smell of diesel fumes wafts through the open window, filling the small room above the Algiers Wharf. Gordon Urquhart, sitting in the only chair in the room, a gray metal folding chair, takes a long drag on his cigarette and looks out the window at a listless tugboat chugging up the dark Mississippi. The river water, like a huge black snake, glitters with the reflection of the New Orleans skyline on the far bank.

Gordon's cigarette provides the room's only illumination. It's so dark he can barely see his hand. He likes it, sitting in the quiet, waiting for the room's occupant to show up. Not quite six feet tall, Gordon is a rock-solid two hundred pounds. His hair turning silver, Gordon still sees himself as the good-looking heartbreaker he was in his twenties.

He wasn't born Gordon Urquhart those forty years ago. When he saw the name in a movie, he liked it so much he became Gordon Urquhart. He made a good Gordon Urquhart. Since the name change, he'd gone up in life.

He yawns, then takes off his leather gloves and places them on his leg. He wipes his sweaty hands on his other pants leg.

The room, a ten-by-ten-foot hole-in-the-wall, has a single bed against one wall, a small chest of drawers on the other wall, and a sink in the far corner. Gordon sits facing the only door.

He closes his eyes and daydreams of Stella Dauphine. He'd caught a glimpse of her last night on Bourbon Street. She walked past in that short red dress without even noticing him. As she moved away, bouncing on those spiked high heels, he saw a flash of her white panties when her dress rose in the breeze. He wanted to follow, but had business to take care of.

Sitting in the rancid room, Gordon daydreams of Stella, of those full lips and long brown hair. She's in the same red dress, only she's climbing stairs. He moves below and watches her fine ass as she moves up the stairs. Her white panties are sheer enough for him to see the crack of her round ass.

They're on his ship from his tour in the U.S. Navy. Indian Ocean. Stella stops above him and spreads her legs slightly. He can see her dark pubic hair through her panties. She looks down and asks him directions.

Gordon goes up and shows her to a ladder, which she goes up, her ass swaying above him as he goes up after her, his face inches from her silky panties. Arriving at the landing above, she waits for him atop the ladder. He reaches up and pulls her panties down to her knees, runs his fingers back up her thighs to her bush and works them inside her wet pussy. She gasps in pleasure.

A sound brings Gordon back to the present. He hears footsteps coming up the narrow stairs up to the hall and moving to the doorway. Gordon pulls on his gloves and lifts the .22-caliber Bersa semiautomatic pistol from his lap. He grips the nylon stock, slips his finger into the trigger guard, and flips off the safety as the door opens. He points the gun at the midsection of the heavyset figure standing in the doorway.

Faintly illuminated by the dull, yellowed hall light, Lex Smutt reaches for the light switch. Gordon closes one eye. The light flashes on and Smutt freezes, his wide-set hazel eyes staring at the Bersa.

"Don't move, fat boy!" Gordon opens his other eye and points his chin at the bed. "Take a seat."

Smutt moves slowly to his bed and sits. At five-seven and nearly three hundred pounds, Smutt knows better than to think of himself as anything but a toad. He runs his hands across his bald head and bites his lower lip. Wearing a tired, powder-blue seersucker suit, white shirt, and mud-brown tie, loosened around his thick neck, Smutt is as rumpled as a crushed paper bag.

"Keep your hands where I can see them." Gordon rises, his knees creaking, and closes the door. In his black suit, Gordon wears a black shirt and charcoal-gray tie.

Yawning again, Gordon says, "Long time, no see."

Smutt lets out a nervous laugh.

Gordon's mouth curls into a cold grin. "Lex Smutt. That's your real name, ain't it? It's a stupid name. You stupid?"

Smutt shakes his head slowly, his gaze fixed on the Bersa.

"You know why I'm here."

Smutt's eyes widen as if he hasn't a clue.

"Give me the fifteen thousand. Or die."

A shaky smile comes to Smutt's thin lips. "I don't have it."

"Then die." Gordon cocks the hammer—for effect—and points the Bersa between Smutt's eyes.

Raising his hands, Smutt stammers, "Come on, now. Gimme a minute."

"You'll have the money in a minute?" Gordon's hand remains steady as he closes his left eye and aims careful at the small, dark mole between Smutt's eyebrows. The loud blast of a ship's horn causes Smutt to jump. Gordon is unmoved.

As long seconds tick by, Gordon takes the slack up in the trigger and starts to pull it slowly. Staring eye-to-eye, Smutt blinks.

"I got six grand," Smutt says.

Gordon's trigger finger stops moving, but his hand remains steady. He blinks and nods.

"Where?"

"On me."

"Where?"

Smutt wipes away the sweat rolling down the sides of his face and exhales loudly. "For a minute there I thought—"

"Where?" Gordon interrupts.

Leaning back on his hands, Smutt looks around the room.

Gordon raises his size-eleven shoe and kicks him in the left shin. Smutt shrieks and grabs his leg. He rocks back and forth twice before Gordon presses the muzzle of the Bersa against the man's forehead.

"Where?" Gordon growls.

"Under the bed." Smutt rubs his shin with both hands. "Under the floorboard."

Gordon grabs the seersucker suit collar with his left hand and yanks Smutt off the bed, shoving the man to the floor. Kicking the bed aside, Gordon orders Smutt to pull up the floorboard.

"Come up with anything except money and you're dead."

On his hands and knees now, Smutt crawls over to where his bed used to stand. Reaching for the loose board, he looks up at Gordon and says, "We have to come to an understanding."

Gordon points the Bersa at the floor next to Smutt's hand and squeezes off a round. A pop is followed by the sound of the shell casing bouncing on the wood floor.

Smutt looks at the neat hole next to his hand, looks back at Gordon, then yanks up the loose board. He reaches inside and pulls out a brown paper bag. He hands it to Gordon without looking up.

Snatching the bag, Gordon takes a couple of steps back. He opens the bag and quickly counts the money. Six grand exactly.

"You're nine thousand short."

Smutt rolls over on his butt and sits like a Buddha, hand on his knees. He wipes the sweat away from his face again and says, "Mr. Happer will just have to understand. You just came into this but it's been goin' on awhile. I need time. Most of the fifteen is vig . . . interest. You know."

Gordon points the Bersa at the mole again. "You're certain this is all you have?"

Smutt nods slowly, looking at the floor now. He waves a hand around. "Does it look like I got more?"

"Try *yes* or *no!*"

"No!" Smutt's voice falters and he clears his throat.

"I heard you won more than this at the Fairgrounds."

"Well, you heard wrong."

Gordon waits.

Smutt won't look up.

So Gordon asks, "Why deny it? You cleared over twenty thousand."

"I had other bills to pay."

"Before Mr. Happer?" Gordon's voice is deep and icy.

"I told you this has been going on awhile. I need time."

"You shoulda thought of that before. Now look at me." Gordon closes his left eye again.

Smutt looks up and Gordon squeezes off a round that strikes just to the left of the mole. Smutt shudders and bats his eyes. Gordon squeezes off another shot, this one just to the right of the mole. Smutt's mouth opens and he falls slowly forward, face first, in his lap.

Gordon steps forward and puts two more in the back of the man's head.

Then he carefully picks up the spent casings, all five of them, and puts them in his coat pocket. The air smells of gunpowder now and faintly of blood. He searches the body and finds another four hundred in Smutt's coat pocket. Still on his haunches, Gordon looks inside the hole in the floor, but there's nothing else there.

He ransacks the room before leaving.

The night air feels damp on his face as he walks around the corner to where he'd squirreled away his low-riding Cadillac.

––––––––

Gordon checks his watch as he ascends the exterior stairs outside the Governor Nicholls Street Wharf. It's 9:00 A.M., sharp. He looks across the river at the unpainted Algiers Wharf. Shielding his eyes from the morning sun glittering off the river, he can almost make out the window of Smutt's room.

At the top of the stairs, he enters a narrow hall and moves to the first door. He knocks twice and waits, looking up at the surveillance camera. He straightens his ice-blue tie. This morning Gordon wears his tan suit with a dark blue shirt. Before leaving home, he told himself in his bathroom mirror that he looked "spiffy."

The door buzzes and he pulls it open.

Mr. Happer sits behind his wide desk. Facing the TV at the far edge of his desk, next to the black videocassette recorder, the old man doesn't look up as Gordon crosses the long office. Happer looks small, hunkered down in the large captain's chair behind the desk.

The office smells of cigar smoke and old beer. The carpet is so old it's worn in spots. Gordon takes a chair in front of Mr. Happer's desk and pulls out an envelope, which he places on the desk.

Raising a hand like a traffic cop, Mr. Happer leans forward to pay close attention to the scene on his TV. Gordon doesn't have to look to know what's on the screen. It's Peter Ustinov again and that damn movie Mr. Happer watches over and over. By the sound of it, Ustinov and David Niven are slowly working their way through the murder on the riverboat. What was the name of that French detective Ustinov plays? Hercules something-or-another.

Mr. Happer suddenly turns his deep-set black eyes to Gordon.

Pushing seventy, Mr. Happer is a skeleton of a man with razor-sharp cheekbones, sunken cheeks, and arms that always remind Gordon of the films of those refugees from Dachau. Mr. Happer reaches with his left hand for the envelope on his desk, picks it up with his spider's fingers, and opens it.

"That's all Smutt had on him," Gordon volunteers.

Mr. Happer nods and says, "Four hundred?" He focuses those black eyes on Gordon and says, "What about the twenty grand from the Fairgrounds."

Gordon is careful as he looks back into the man's eyes. He shrugs. "He said he had other bills to pay."

"Before me?"

"That's what I said to him."

"So?"

"So I took care of him. Tossed the room and that's it."

Mr. Happer shakes his head. Gordon watches him and remembers the man's name isn't Happer either. The old bastard was born Sam Gallizzio and tried for most of his life to become a made man, working at the periphery of La Cosa Nostra. Trying to be a goomba, Happer failed. He did, however, manage to remain alive, which isn't easy for an Italian gangster who's not LCN, even if he's only a semi-gangster.

Shoving the envelope into a drawer, Mr. Happer pulls out another envelope, which he slides across the desk to Gordon.

Gordon picks it up and slips it into his coat pocket. He doesn't have to count it. He knows there's a thousand in there—the old bastard's cut-rate hit fee.

Mr. Happer picks up a stogie from an overflowing ashtray and sticks it in his mouth. He sucks on it and its tip glows red. He shakes his head again.

"It's worth it," Mr. Happer says, as if he needs convincing. "The word'll get out. Make it easier later on. That's what the big boys do."

Gordon nods.

"He woulda never come up with the fifteen," Mr. Happer says, and Gordon wonders if the old man is baiting him. "He woulda never paid me."

Fanning away the smoke from between them Mr. Happer says, "You sure you tossed the place right, huh? You weren't in no hurry."

"No hurry at all." Gordon feels the old man squeezing him.

Mr. Happer raises a hand suddenly, leans to the side to catch something Ustinov says. He nods, as if he's approving, then props his elbows on the desk. He looks at Gordon.

"You sure?" And there it is. *The* question.

"I'm sure, Mr. Happer." Gordon likes the way his voice is deep and smooth.

"I gotta ask you straight up, you know that, don't you?" The old coot's face is expressionless.

Deny. Deny. Deny. Gordon doesn't even blink. He feels good.

Finally, the old man blinks and Gordon says, "Mr. Happer. I've always been straight with you. You know that."

Mr. Happer waves his hand again as he falls back in his chair.

"Son-of-a-bitch dumped the money awfully fast." Mr. Happer looks again at the TV.

Gordon stops himself from reminding the old bastard that their agreement was simple. Find Smutt, get as much as you can from him, then whack him and leave him where he'll be found. He did his job. A contract is a contract.

Gordon waits. He wants to say, "Well, if that's all—" but knows better. He waits for Mr. Happer to dismiss him.

The old man turns around and looks at the windows that face the river. He takes another puff of his cigar, lets out a long trail of smoke, and then says, "That's what I get for dealing with bums like Smutt. At least he got his."

Turning to Gordon, the old man smiles, and it sends a chill up Gordon's back.

"I was thinking of asking you if you happen to know where Smutt used to hang out. Maybe he had another place. But the money's long gone."

When the old man looks back at his TV, Gordon casually looks at the windows. A gunshot rings out and excited voices, including Ustinov's, rise on the TV. Gordon waits.

Finally, after the commotion on the riverboat calms down, Mr. Happer looks at Gordon and says, "I know where to get you."

Gordon stands and nods at the old man and leaves, Mr. Happer's dismissal echoing in his mind. He knows where to get me. Good-bye and hello at the same time.

Stepping out into the sunlight again, Gordon squints and stretches, then walks down the stairs. He looks at the brown, swirling river water and laughs to himself. Ustinov is still on the riverboat, floating on his own brown water, trying to solve the murder with Mr. Happer watching intently. It strikes Gordon as very, very funny.

Before pulling away in his Caddy, he slips on his sunglasses and looks around. He spots the tail two minutes later, a black Chevy.

———

Gordon Urquhart's bedroom smells of cheap aftershave and faintly of mildew. Waiting in the darkness, Stella Dauphine sits on Gordon's double bed, her .22 Beretta next to her hand.

She wears a lightweight, tan trench coat and matching tan high heels, a pair of skin-tight gloves on her hands. A young-looking thirty, Stella has curly hair that touches her shoulders. For a thin woman, she's buxom, which made her popular in high school but proved a hindrance in the mundane office jobs she held throughout her twenties.

Beneath the trench coat, she wears nothing except a pair of "barely there" sheer thigh-high stockings. She runs a hand over her knee and up to the top of her left thigh-high, pulling it up a little as she waits.

Closing her eyes she listens intently.

She didn't used to be Stella Dauphine. Born Carla Stellos, she changed her name after a year in New Orleans. After seeing a late-night movie on TV—*A Streetcar Named Desire*—and after parking her car on Dauphine Street, she decided on the change. She felt more like a Stella Dauphine every day.

Her eyes snap open a heartbeat after she hears a distinct metallic click at the back door. The door creaks open. Standing at the foot of the bed, Stella picks up her Beretta, unfastens the trench coat, her gun hidden in the folds of the coat as she waits.

She feels a slight breath of summer air flow into the room and hears a voice sigh and then light footsteps moving toward the bedroom. A figure steps into the doorway.

The light flashes on.

Gordon Urquhart's there, a neat .22 Bersa in his hand.

Stella opens the trench coat and lets it fall off her shoulders.

As Gordon looks down at her naked body, Stella squeezes off a round, which strikes Gordon on the right side of his chest. He's stunned, so stunned he drops his gun. Gordon's mouth opens as he stumbles into the room, falling against the chest of drawers. Blood seeps through the fingers of his right hand, which he's pressed against his wound.

"You shot me!"

"Kick your gun over here."

Gordon's face is ashen. He blinks at her, looks at his chest and stammers, "You *shot* me!"

"If you don't shut up, I'll shoot you again." Stella's mouth is set in a grim, determined slit. "Now kick the gun."

Gordon swings his foot and the gun slides across the hardwood floor. Stella steps forward and kicks it back under Gordon's bed.

The big man is breathing hard now. Blood has saturated his shirt.

"I think you hit an artery," he says weakly.

"Then we don't have much time, do we?"

"For what?"

Stella points her chin at the bed. "Sit, before you collapse."

Gordon moves to the bed and sits.

Stella moves to the doorway between the bedroom and kitchen, the Beretta still trained on Gordon.

"So," she says. "Where is it?"

He looks at her as if he hasn't the foggiest idea.

"Mr. Happer told me to give you ten seconds to come up with the money you took off Smutt." Stella narrows her eyes. "One. Two. Three—"

"I gave him the four hundred."

"Four. Five. Six—"

Gordon raises his head and says, "Go ahead and shoot me. There's no money."

"Seven. Eight. Nine—"

"If I had it, you think I'd be dumb enough to have it on me? I spotted your Chevy as soon as I left the Governor Nicholls Wharf."

Stella squeezes off another round, which knocks the lamp off the end table next to the bed.

"Dammit!" Gordon groans in pain. "I don't have any more money. Smutt blew it all."

Stella brushes her hair away from her face with her right hand and tells him, "Mr. Happer doesn't believe you and I don't believe you."

Gordon clears his throat and says, "Mr. Happer and me go back a long way, lady. He knows better."

A cold smile crosses Stella's thin lips. "I'll just whack you and toss the place. I'll still get my fee."

"This is crazy. I tell you, there's no more money."

Stella aims the Beretta with both hands again, this time at Gordon's face. She says, "So you and the old man go back a ways, huh? Well I'm the one he calls when things go badly. And you're as bad as they come."

Gordon nods at her. "I seen you around. I know all about you. And you got me all wrong, lady."

Stella watches his eyes closely as she says, "When Smutt left the Fairgrounds, he went straight to his parole officer's house and paid the man off. Three grand. Stiff payoff, but Smutt figured it was worth it. Then he went to two restaurants, gorged himself. Then dropped some cash at the betting parlor on Rampart."

She watches Gordon's pupils. A pinprick of recognition comes to them as soon as she says the words, "Six grand. He had about six grand left. You took it off him."

"No way."

Stella fires again, into Gordon's belly, and he howls.

"That's it." Stella's smile broadens. "Keep denying it."

"I don't have it!" Gordon slumps backward.

Stella levels her weapon, aiming at Gordon's forehead. She pauses, giving him one last chance.

"I don't!" He screams.

She squeezes off a round that strikes Gordon in the forehead. Stepping forward, she puts two more in his head before he falls back on his bed. For good measure she empties the Beretta's magazine, putting two more in the side of the man's head.

She picks up all eight casings and slips them into the pocket of her coat. She leaves his Bersa under the bed. Let the police match it to the Smutt murder. Then, slowly and methodically, she tosses the place.

An hour later, she finds the six thousand in the flour container on Gordon's kitchen counter. The giveaway—what man has fresh flour in a container?

———

Mr. Happer, sitting back in his captain's chair, bats his eyes at the TV as Peter Ustinov taps out an S-O-S on his bathroom wall, a large cobra poised and ready to strike the rotund detective. Stella, standing at the desk's edge in the trench coat outfit from last night, recognizes the scene and waits for David Niven to rush in with his sword to impale the snake.

When the scene's tension dies, Mr. Happer turns his deep-set eyes to Stella and says, "Okay. You got the money?"

Stella shakes her head.

Mr. Happer's eyes grow wide. "It wasn't there?"

"I tore the place apart. If he had it, he stashed it."

"Dammit!" Mr. Happer slaps a skeletonic hand on his desk. He picks up the remote control and pauses his movie. His black eyes leer at Stella's eyes as if he can get the truth just by staring. She bites her lower lip, reaches down, and unfastens her coat. She opens it slowly as Happer's gaze moves down her body.

Stella lets the coat fall to the floor and stands there naked except for the thigh-high stockings, which gives her long legs the silky look. Rolling her hips, Stella sits on the edge of the desk. Mr. Happer stares at her body as if mesmerized. It takes a long minute for his gaze to rise to her eyes.

"You sure you tossed the place right?"

Stella nods.

Mr. Happer picks up the remote and looks back at the TV.

The riverboat is moored now, against the bank of the wide Nile River.

"Well, the word'll get out. Make it easier later on," Happer says. "That's what the big boys do."

Stella climbs off the desk and picks up her coat. As she closes it, she looks at the old man. Mr. Happer turns those black eyes to her and says, "You *sure* you tossed the place right?"

She's ready, her face perfectly posed. "I'm sure."

"Okay." Mr. Happer looks back at the TV and mouths the words as Peter Ustinov speaks. Without looking, he opens his center desk drawer and withdraws an envelope. He slides it over to Stella, who picks it up and puts it in her purse.

"Good work," Mr. Happer says.

"Thanks." Stella turns and leaves him with his Ustinov and David Niven and riverboat floating down the Nile.

On her way down the stairs she looks at the dark Mississippi water and whispers a message to the dead Gordon, "So you and Mr. Happer go back a long way. Well, we go back a longer way."

And I have tools, plenty of tools to work against this man, against all these men.

Three minutes later she spots the tail, a dark blue Olds.

Talon's Gift

Stephen Mertz

Talon sat alone, nude, at Evie's vanity, chambering rounds into the .38-caliber revolver. For some damn reason, as he slid each cartridge into each chamber, he thought of himself sliding into his hot, willing wife. A flick of his wrist snapped the cylinder shut, and it made a sound that was a small metallic explosion, strangely contrasting the intimate warmth of the bedroom.

He had given Evie a free hand in the furnishing and decorating of their house. She'd exhibited an artistic, deft touch. The living room was friendly, hospitable. The kitchen was where love was *created* more than *made* through the magic of her cooking, where scents and tastes were as much a part of sexual foreplay as the intimate caress.

But here in the bedroom. Ah, here in the bedroom, thought Talon. Talk about cooking. Here in the bedroom, love was always *made* amidst tangled, perfumed sheets to the scent of incense, but even incense could not match the sweet scent of Evie's sweat at those times.

Everything about Evie was sweet. Sweet and hot.

She had a peppery side, and Talon liked it. His wife was every man's fantasy, a pert brunette with a hard, shapely little body, insatiable between their silken sheets after two years of marriage. Evie was a hot-assed little bitch. Not politically correct, but true. He'd never had better, and never would. He understood this.

With the .38 loaded, he palmed a spin of the cylinder, checking the action, then he set the revolver upon the vanity. He stood and began dressing, realizing that he was half erect. He willed himself into asexual consciousness and donned the black jeans, black T-shirt, leather gloves, and black sneakers.

Talon was thirty-five years old, dark-haired, well-muscled, a big man exuding feral, economical grace in his every movement. By the time he was garbed, sexual thoughts and images of Evie were gone. He was sharp and focused again, the way you had to be when you whacked someone, which was what he was about to do. He grabbed the .38, curling his index finger around the trigger. He left the bedroom.

Evie wouldn't be back for another three hours at least. She'd left a half hour ago to see a movie at a cineplex across town with her girlfriends from church. Talon chuckled and shook his head. Church, he thought.

She was twelve years his junior.

Her lovely, fresh child-woman face had expressed the cutest indecision. "I hope you don't mind, honey." The touch of her fingertips, like scented feathers, caressed his cheek. She gazed into his eyes with that sweet-as-hell, puppy-dog devotion he'd come to adore. "If you want me to stay home, sweetie, I'll just fib and tell them I'm not feeling well. Are you sure you don't mind me going out?"

He'd given her a hug, a kiss and slipped her a fifty.

"Babe, you and your girlfriends have yourselves a night at the movies. Enjoy."

Before Evie, the only women he'd known were professionals or the wives of associates. Evie awakened something within him, call it love, that he'd never known. He had grown to love her. She must never find out what he was about to do.

He left the house, and the dark colors of his clothing melded him at once to the night.

The suburban neighborhood had that 9:30 P.M. feel to it, a dog barking here and there, voices carried on the summer night, the scent of a neighborhood barbecue, and of new-mowed lawns. The evening was beginning to wind down in a neighborhood that was like any middle-class suburb of any American city. The pre-fab houses followed two basic designs. The streets were winding and sedate, the houses on half-acre lots. A suburban dream or a suburban nightmare, depending on how you looked at it, thought Talon.

He quit the shadows of the ranch-style home where he and Evie lived and bolted, practically invisible, like a commando clos-ing in on a target, across the expanse of dark lawn toward the split-level-style, neighboring house.

He remembered the time he'd taken out Studs Pokowski, who'd been stupid enough to think he could skim off the Fam-ily's take and then exhibited double stupidity in thinking that he could hole up in his mansion up the river with enough protection so that no one could whack him. Talon had made that hit his own, accepting it as a personal challenge, penetrating Studs's heavily guarded estate under cover of night just like this. It had been a long time before anyone else tried to skim off the Family.

Damn, thought Talon now. Damn.

He'd made his bones with the Family when he was a teenager, and during his "career in crime" had tucked away more than a few wiseguys for their dirt nap. But tonight would be his first hit in years. Something he thought he would never do again.

But tonight, he had no choice.

He had not thought of himself as Talon in two-and-a-half years. Even "Talon" wasn't his real name, but a bastardization by Don Venucci, shortened from Tallone. He had been the Don's enforcer, but the day arrived when the hammer came down big-time and by the time the dust settled, Talon had turned state's witness to save his own ass and his Don had gone up for life without parole. The Feds kept their word, entering Talon in the witness protection program, providing him with a new identity, telling him that his relocation and "reinvention" was less of a hassle than usual because he'd been single with no kids.

So here he was, living seven states away from his past, the proud owner of a carpet-cleaning business in this suburb outside a medium-sized midwestern city, married to a girl-next-door-beautiful wife. He'd met Evie after relocating here as "Tim Madsen." Evie knew nothing of Talon's past. His government-supplied, fabricated personal history had satisfied her curiosity.

Yeah, he had it made.

Except for two things.

One. He could never safely show himself beyond a self-determined perimeter around his chosen city and its environs. A lifetime shoot-on-sight order was out on him from Little Joey, who had inherited the old Don's far-flung empire. Talon knew the rules. The Family never forgave, never forgot, never stopped trying to track down witness protection snitches.

Which was why he had to kill Pete Rogers, and why he had to do it tonight. That was problem number two.

Pete Rogers. Neighbor. Friend. *Best* friend.

He reached the impenetrable shadows at the side of Pete's house.

It was his own damn fault. Last night, he had drunk more than he should have with Pete. He'd allowed his defense and survival skills to deteriorate, obviously, and he was not at all pleased with himself about that. But first things first.

No man being an island, he'd early on felt the need for some sort of male companionship in this "new life." He did miss the rough-hewn male camaraderie that had so been part of being a Family soldier. In his new world, he could hardly consider friendship with the college kids and day laborers who composed his workforce at the carpet-cleaning service.

Pete had seemed like—and, in fact, was—a 100 percent nice guy—square-jawed, sandy-haired, husky, with an easygoing manner and self-confidence. Talon's age, he'd started some sort of successful, small Internet company that supplied software or something. Talon wasn't sure, and didn't much care. "Tim Madsen" and Pete's friendship was anchored by a shared passion for sports. Also, the "Madsens" had moved in next door while Pete was going through a messy divorce, and Pete had needed a pal too. He and Talon talked sports, laughed, and argued about just about anything, and Evie had been sweet enough not to mind. The three of them enjoyed regular barbecues and social outings, teaming up about once a month with Pete and one of his numerous current girlfriends for a double date. Pete never seemed to lack for female companionship.

Last night, though, it had been just Talon and Pete. They watched a game, after which they sat around bullshitting, the way guys do, as usual about everything under the sun, yukking it up, drink after drink lubricating words and thought that flowed too freely in good-natured banter until somehow, late in the night of drink and rambling conversation—Talon still couldn't remember exactly how it happened—the subject of his own past somehow became grist for the conversation mill and, without thinking, he'd alluded to an obscure piece of personal information. Obscure, that is, except for the fact that it *could* conceivably lead to that Family shoot-on-sight order being some day carried out, to his past catching up with him and finding him here in suburban Middle America and blowing all to hell his cushy lifestyle with his hot-assed little churchgoing wife.

It had been nothing, really.

He'd made some comment about growing up in the city he'd been born, raised, and worked in until he'd been relocated . . . not realizing, until thoughtless words slipped from him, that a completely different city of origin was part of the cover story he'd told Pete and Evie and everyone else.

He'd caught Pete's blink of confusion.

"Hey, buddy, I thought you always said you were from up north."

Talon had done his best to shrug it off, but it felt like cold water flushing through him, though he made sure not to let that show.

"Uh, I knew that." He laughed if off. "That's what I meant to say." He'd grinned in that offhanded manner of anyone who's merely misspoken and took another sip from his bottle. "Couple more of these beers and I won't even know where I am, much less where I've been!"

But he'd seen clearly that the seed for potential serious damage had been sown.

With the discrepancy seemingly idly shrugged off, the conversation last night had continued to ramble on. But Talon didn't miss the subtle flickers of curiosity in Pete.

He always trusted his instincts, and had since his days as a runner at the bottom of the Venucci organization. He trusted those instincts now. He could not allow the possibility to exist that Pete could in some way take it upon himself to dig into his past. Knowing Pete, it would only be out of curiosity over the discrepancy revealed in that slip of the tongue. Talon didn't know anything about computers or the Internet except that, supposedly, a bright, inquisitive guy could learn anything he wanted to know about anyone. Pete was a bright, inquisitive guy.

He was going to have to whack his buddy.

A protective survival measure.

He wished that he did not have to do this, but he saw no alternative, not from any pragmatic point of view.

Fast and painless, that's how he'd make it.

He had taken out guys with gut shots, and that was the worst, a protracted, hideous, screaming death by inches, minutes that must have been a hellish forever to the ones Talon had seen, curled up in a fetal ball, squealing and pleading to God because of the pain, because they couldn't hold in the gooey red slop that burbled out from between clenching fingers. The worst way to die, and he'd only capped guys like that when ordered to do so because the manner of death was meant to be a message.

With Pete, he'd make it fast and painless, messy but quick, the way head hits always are.

Pete was a good guy—intelligent, witty, worldly. But Talon would allow *nothing*, not even the life of a friend, to in any way jeopardize, in reality or potentially, the life that was now his. It struck him that this was a testament to how much he'd come to love Evie. He could walk away from this city, if survival at any cost was the name of the game. He had money stashed. You always left yourself an escape hatch, rule number one. And he knew every trick of the game of surviving in the cold, of reinventing himself. He and Evie *could* begin anew, somewhere else. But Evie would want to know why, reasonably, and would demand truthful answers, and what could he tell her?

He edged along the length of Pete's house, his back to the wall, the short-barreled .38 up and ready, his every sense probing the night.

Nothing seemed unusual. Crickets chirped everywhere, merrily, or at least relentlessly. The barbecue nearby was breaking up, voices calling goodnight, some inebriated. Car engines were starting.

He gained a corner of the house and peered around the front.

The porch light was off. There was no guest car in the driveway. The tail of Pete's sporty red Triumph, the one he'd bought after his divorce, was visible, extending from the carport on the far end of the house. Good. Pete was alone, forgoing an evening with one of his lady friends.

Talon knew the layout of the house from his years of regular visits. Lights illuminated the drawn curtains of the den, where Pete had his home entertainment center: a wide-screen TV, the

works. He retreated to the rear of the house, away from the occasional passing car on the street, to impenetrable shadows sur-
rounding the back door, the one that, he knew, Pete never locked
when he was home.

He also knew Pete's habits. Pete would be sitting in front of
his wide-screen TV right now, watching one of his favorite sit-
coms. The one tonight starred a curvaceous comedienne he was
always fantasizing about aloud to Talon.

Talon intended to make the murder appear as if a burglar had
reacted when surprised by a homeowner. A common scenario.

He entered the house.

Sounds of the night vanished when he eased shut the back
door without any noise. He discerned the shapes of the washing machine and a dryer, a half-filled laundry basket, the five-
speed bicycle, in the feeble light, from the front room, that
reached this far down to the end of a hallway that bisected the
house.

Hugging one wall of the hallway, he moved with brisk stealth
to the archway of the den, the pistol remaining raised from force
of very old habits, the knuckle of his index finger white around
the trigger. He was mildly surprised that he didn't hear the tele-
vised clamor of witty one-liners, canned laughter, and applause
from the TV. Pete was obviously at home, what with the front-
room lights on and his Triumph in the carport. Maybe the TV
was broken, thought Talon. Maybe Pete fell asleep early. Maybe
he's reading a good book. Whatever he's doing, it's about to
end . . .

Puzzled, he peered into the den.

Empty.

Then he heard something so imperceptible that at first he
couldn't determine either the origin of the muffled sound or its
nature.

He stepped past the den, into the front room, a comfortably

upholstered male retreat. A short stairway led to the second level of the home.

The nature of the vague sounds became apparent while remaining indistinct. From their nature, he knew where they came from.

The bedroom.

Upstairs, a man and a woman were engaged in enthusiastic lovemaking. They'd left the bedroom door open, believing that they were alone in the house, and so did not much care how much noise they made.

Talon paused where he was. He decided to bail. He started to withdraw the way he had come in, feeling his heartbeat already beginning to slacken to normal, feeling the inner cold begin to thaw. He needed Pete alone. Pete *had* to be alone. Whacking him would be unpleasant enough. There was no reason for anyone else to die. Another time, he decided. Soon, but another time. There had been no visiting car, so a cab must have dropped off tonight's hot and willing bedmate, or else a randy housewife from the neighborhood was making the old back-door creep, he thought with the start of a grin.

The grin died, and he felt his eyes and mouth become tight slits.

Faint as they were, for the first time he heard, well enough to recognize them, those female moans, because the lovemaking was becoming more enthusiastic, increasing in intensity and volume. He heard the mewing, commanding, demanding little-girl pain-pleasure noises that he had only ever heard from one woman and could have identified in a million.

Damn, he thought again. *God*damn.

Pete and Evie.

He stepped swiftly then, cat-like, up the stairway, into the second-level hallway, toward the bedroom. The ice was back, even though, unlike any hit since his first, his heartbeat was pounding in his ears like a bass drum. But his mind was clicking coolly, calculating his options for the next step, for after he left here. He obviously could not continue *this* life. By the time neighbors and the police responded, he'd be blocks or more away and he would not stop. He would begin anew, somewhere else. Alone.

Evie's mewing moans, the heaving bedsprings, Pete Rogers's rasping, labored grunts became louder to him with his every step.

Then he was standing in the bedroom doorway, and there they were.

God*damn* them.

He saw nothing but what they were doing, there on those tangled silken sheets, making their primal pleasure noises that had drawn him, going at it with little Evie on top like she always liked with him, riding with her back erect, hips pistoning, head thrown back, long black hair falling, and her hard little breasts bouncing, fists clenched to either side, reveling in carnal celebration of her power, energetically possessing, riding Pete like the horny goddess she was.

Bitch goddess, thought Talon. There was a bitter taste in his mouth.

The worst part was that he could *smell* the arousing musky-sweet sweat scent of her—talk about *primal*—and he could identify that anywhere, too. Her sweet bitch-in-heat smell when she rode was stronger than any incense, but not strong enough to stop him now.

They became aware of him, standing squarely in the doorway, tracking his revolver in their direction, and their energetic screwing ceased.

Frantic.

Screaming.

Pete unceremoniously dumped Evie and leaped to his feet on the far side of the bed, oblivious of his nakedness.

"Tim, *wait!*" was all Talon gave him time for.

Talon placed a .38-caliber round right through Pete's gut, just below the navel, and Pete went down squealing like a tortured animal, vanishing from sight on the far side of the bed where he continued to squeal, an unholy sound.

Evie wore the red lace camisole that Talon had bought her for Valentine's Day. She was crazy, panicky wild. Down on her knees in front of him. Her hard little body quaking with her panic and fear. Trembling arms grasped the calves of his legs for dear life, and her beautiful child-woman beauty, obscenely flushed, tear-streaked beyond recognition, jabbered hysterical pleas for forgiveness, of repentance.

And because he loved her, Talon killed Evie with a single shot to the head.

Bullet Eyes

Jon L. Breen

Y ou got another one for me, Johnny?"
Kimball McDermott leaned back in his worn swivel chair,
his feet on a corner of the desk, a Camel in the corner of his
mouth, the telephone receiver tucked under his right ear. He
wore his usual uniform of scuffed loafers, worn jeans belted
under his protruding stomach, and loud Hawaiian shirt. At the
desk across the room, his younger and thinner partner, Rick De-
Witt, who doggedly insisted on wearing a coat and tie to work,
groaned audibly. Kimball smirked at him, blew a smoke ring, and
tossed his apple core at the wastebasket next to Rick's desk. It
missed, landing at his partner's feet. *You're aching to pick it up,
DeWitt. But you won't give me the satisfaction, will you?*

The single office of McDermott-DeWitt Productions, a large
room in a nearly empty and soon to be demolished Hollywood office building, was smoky, shabby, and cluttered, the carpet soiled
by cigarette burns and past wastebasket misses, film cans
stacked in two out of four corners, scripts strewn on all three
desks, an ugly gouge in the door to the bathroom (the product of
an over-the-hill actor's chair-throwing tantrum) only partly covered by the 1963 *Playboy* calendar. Pictures of the producing
partners with second-line celebrities like Zsa Zsa Gabor, Edd
Byrnes, and Francis X. Bushman occupied every part of the wall
not papered with B-minus movie posters. Only one of the pictures featured, *Teen Motor Rumble*, cheaply made and profitable,
had actually been a McDermott-DeWitt production, but the oth-

ers (*Teenage Caveman, Twist Around the Clock, Riot in Juvenile Prison*) fit right into the decor.

"What's this one like, Johnny?" Kimball asked. He extinguished the butt of his cigarette in the remnants of coffee in the Styrofoam cup on his desk.

On the other end, agent Johnny Fleagle snorted. "You know what she's like. Midwestern beauty barely off the Greyhound, did Emily in *Our Town* in community theater back home, now works at Disneyland. How many of those have you seen? They've been invading this town since Clara Bow."

"Clara never played Emily or worked at Disneyland. The play wasn't written yet, and Walt was just a kid doing his own drawing."

"Thanks for the history lesson. Anyway, you know what I'm sending you." *Don't we sound disapproving though? Nothing more irritating than a sanctimonious pimp.*

"But, Johnny, can she act? Will she come across on screen?"

"Will she come across where? Oh, I get it. Rick's in the office, huh? Don't know how that poor bastard stands working with you, but tell him hello for me. What do you care if she can act?"

"Oh, Ricky, Johnny says hello!" His partner ignored him. "Johnny, you misjudge me. We *are* casting a picture here, and we start shooting in ten days. There's no time to fool around. You know, this represents a big step up from our usual stuff, hardly a teenager or rock-and-roller in it. This one's a nitty-gritty crime flick for adults, and the casting has to be just right."

"Private eye thing, right?"

"Right. Oh, did I tell you we got a title for it?"

"No, you didn't."

"Yeah, Ricky came up with a great one: *Bullet Eyes*, sort of violent and sexy and menacing all at the same time, don't you think? My partner's a genius, you know." Rick glared at him.

"Sounds like a piece of shit."

"Thanks for the vote of confidence, Johnny. Really makes us want to hire one of your clients, you know?"

"Private eye stuff is dead in the water, gangsters too. Spies are the only thing now, I keep telling you. Ever heard of James Bond?"

"Yeah, yeah, I know. The president loves him. But about this girl you're sending me."

"Right, the important stuff. Her name's Fawna Blair. She'll be there in about fifteen minutes."

Kimball looked at his watch. "Fifteen minutes. Good."

"Be nice to her, McDermott."

"When am I ever otherwise?"

When Kimball McDermott hung up, Rick DeWitt looked at him balefully for a moment, then got to his feet. "I'm going to lunch. A long lunch, so take your time. You don't need me here."

Kimball shrugged. "I'm not kicking you out."

"Just remember what you told Johnny. We are making a picture here, aren't we? At least, that's why I come to work every day."

"And so do I," Ricky said.

"Uh-huh." *The name Ricky annoys him, like I'm the adult, he's the kid. Never mistake me for Ozzie, though.*

"I have a good feeling about the girl Johnny's sending over today. Maybe she'll be a real find. Plenty of gorgeous broads in Hollywood, but so few can act. Makes it tough."

"Yeah, I know you find it a real pain in the ass, this endless talent search of yours."

"Think I'll try her out on the nude scene. That'll show if she's a real pro."

Rick's mouth tightened. "There's no nude scene in *Bullet Eyes*. Not in the script I read."

"Maybe we oughta add one. Give us an extra edge out there in the marketplace." He waved a hand at the pile on his desk.

"Nude scenes are the coming thing. More and more of these scripts have 'em. We'd keep it tasteful, of course. Artistic. Up to your high standard."

"Right. I know what you're doing with all these girls that come up here, you know. But just watch it. Nothing criminal, okay? Nothing that can come back to bite us both. Don't break any laws."

"Break any laws?"

"Yeah, laws. Rape laws, for example."

"When did rape become necessary in the motion-picture-casting process?"

"I want to work in this town, Kimball. I want to work here for a long time."

"*They* want to work in this town. They'll never say a thing. These girls may say yes, they may say no. They may think I'm out of line, or they may think my cock's better than an Oscar Mayer hotdog. But either way the girls who come up here know how things work in Hollywood."

"Right. And that's why you prefer girls fresh off the bus from Podunk."

"I really wonder about you, Rick. Where's your outlet? I never see you with broads. I never see you with guys, either, and you don't act like a fairy. I can't figure you out."

"Not everybody carries on his sex life at the office, Kimball. Some do it on their own time. Some picture people do it with civilians, marry them even. But hell, you have to have your fun, don't you. And I owe you my career, as you keep reminding me. Here, why don't I help you?" Rick rolled the chair over from behind the usually unoccupied secretary's desk and placed it carefully opposite Kimball's desk. "How's this? Shall I sit down and cross my legs so you can tell if the angle is right?"

Kimball offered his ugly smile. "I play my own angles, pardner. I don't need you setting up my shots for me."

"You're an asshole, Kimball." *Strong language coming from Rick.*

"Yeah, but I'm your asshole. We need each other, pard. You do what you can do, and I do what you can't do."

"Or won't do."

"Okay, or won't do. But it still needs doing. So have a nice lunch. Go be creative while I tend to business."

Rick almost slammed the office door on the way out but stopped himself at the last second. *Poor guy is holding his anger in too much, just asking for an ulcer.*

There wasn't much Kimball needed to do in preparation for Fawna Blair's audition. He found the script with the scene he wanted in the pile on his desk and bookmarked the page. He checked his bottom drawer for a necessary prop. He took the *Playboy* calendar off the door of the john and glanced around inside to make sure it was at least as clean as the average service station rest room.

Almost exactly fifteen minutes after Johnny Fleagle's call, there was a tentative knock on the door. Kimball could see the agent's new client through the frosted glass, which was one of the few reminders of what a classy office building this used to be. The image in the doorway was distorted but promising. Apparently not another blonde. That was good. He was getting tired of faux Monroe.

He opened the door and ushered her in. *Thank you, Johnny!* She was tall and slender, a raven-haired beauty special even for Hollywood. Her dark brown eyes were penetrating, like they looked right through you, saw all your secrets. Fit their title. *Bullet Eyes.* Her outfit wasn't expensive, but she knew how to dress, in a pastel-green formfitting suit, the skirt knee-length, showy without being flashy. Very high stiletto heels, showcasing the trim ankles and well-muscled calves. Clearly of age but still very young. For all the carefully applied makeup, apart from those special eyes, there was a blank-slate girlishness to her face. Sweetly innocent head on a provocative woman's body. Her manner said it all to Kimball McDermott. Thin veneer of Hollywood sophistication over deep Middle American naïveté. It was just what he liked and so rarely saw in the girls who came through here.

She extended her hand. "I'm Fawna Blair. Is it Mr. McDermott or Mr. DeWitt?"

"Do I have the pleasure of addressing Mr. Scrooge or Mr. Marley?" McDermott said, mimicking her tone. It didn't seem to throw her. She just smiled, a very nice smile. "Okay, I'm Kimball McDermott."

"And is Mr. DeWitt dead these seven years?" *Quick, baby. Very quick. You can match wits with anybody, can't you?*

"Very much alive, but we have a strict division of labor. He's the idea man, the artistic type, you might say. I'm the money man. I don't have it, you understand, but I'm pretty good at finding it. Also, though I'm not that creative myself, I know a good idea when I hear it and I know talent when I see it. Mr. DeWitt leaves the casting decisions to me for the most part. System works very well for us. Won't you sit down?"

She sat primly in the secretary's chair opposite Kimball's desk, knees together, nervous and expectant but poised. "I love that story," she said.

"What story's that, Miss Blair?" *The story of our company? The story of my life? Did you read our script already?*

"You know, *A Christmas Carol*. We watch it every Christmas at home. The Alastair Sim version."

"Oh, yeah. A classic, I agree." He sat back in his chair and gazed across at her, as if expecting her to carry the conversation. He liked to test people, throw them off balance, put them at a disadvantage. But once again, she wasn't rattled. She just looked around the office, her expression subtly commenting on the shabby chaos.

"Showplace, ain't it?" he said.

She laughed. "I think it's a little spooky. Aren't there any other tenants in this building?"

"Not many. Of course, we won't be here long."

"Going out of business?" *Some guys might not like that sharp tongue of yours, baby. But I'm ready for it.*

"No, no, not that, but the building's been condemned. I don't mean it's in danger of collapsing or anything, but they're going to tear it down, put up a high-rise. We have to get out in another few weeks. Most of the others have moved out already."

She shivered. "It would give me the creeps to work in an empty building, but I guess it's different for men."

"No, I feel the same way sometimes. But we can't be choosy about office space. We aren't MGM, you know. Mr. DeWitt and I are what you call independent producers. We don't have a bunch of people under contract. We don't have a studio commissary. Hell, we don't even have a studio. We don't even have a secretary most of the time, just an occasional temp. That third desk is mostly another broad surface to stack things on. Every production is a start from scratch, and every penny we spend has to show on the screen."

"Yes, I understand that, Mr. McDermott. I find the idea of independent filmmaking very exciting. Superficial frills don't impress me." *Yeah? How about unsuperficial frills?*

"So you're an actress."

"Yes." *Very good, kid. Decisive, determined, confident.*

"Any credits?"

"Not that would mean much, I'm afraid. Not yet."

"Johnny said you did Emily in *Our Town*."

"For my hometown theater group."

"And is your hometown bigger than Grover's Corners?"

That smile again. "Only a little. But we were good." She crossed her very nice legs and leaned back in her chair, getting more comfortable with him. "We had a professional director in town. He used to work in Chicago. We did community theater of a very, very high standard." Pause. "Really, we did."

"So how do you like working with Johnny Fleagle?"

"Oh, he's sweet. Very protective, you know? Like a mother hen. It's almost like I never left home."

"Really?" *Doesn't sound like Johnny.*

"Well, no, not really, but he is very nice. He seems to understand the pressures on girls like me trying to make it in Hollywood. He had a niece who wanted to be an actress, but I don't think she had a happy experience. He seems kind of sad about it, and even more protective of his clients."

"And what'd he say about me?"

"Oh, he thinks you're terrific. He says working with you would be a great opportunity for me." *Johnny, you're a conscienceless hypocrite, and I love you.*

"Fawna's an unusual name. How'd your parents happen to come up with that?"

A sly and knowing look. She knew he knew better. "They didn't. They named me Linda Grace Swackhammer. Don't get me wrong. I'm proud to be a Swackhammer. It's a very honored name in Creston Falls. But I don't see it on a marquee, do you?"

"But you do see Fawna Blair on a marquee?"

"Oh yes." *And so will the world! Touching confidence.*

"Would you change that, too, if I asked you to?"

"Don't you like the name?"

"It's okay, but would you change it if I could think of something better?"

"Maybe. I'd want to ask Johnny's opinion, of course, and it would depend on why and to what. I like the name Fawna Blair, but I'm not married to it. It's just a label, not the essence of me as a performer or as a woman." She leaned forward, earnestly. "I do consider myself a real actress, Mr. McDermott. I didn't just play Emily back home. I did Juliet and I did Madge in *Picnic*. I've learned my craft and I approach it with the seriousness of a pro, even if I don't have any professional credits. I've been studying with Miles Barnard since I've been here in Los Angeles." She said the name as if playing her ace, but Kimball McDermott knew Barnard was at least a semi-con man. "He's considering me for a workshop production at his theater." *His theater huh? What theater is that?*

"No local work at all yet, huh?"

Rueful grin. "Unless you count an auto show. Oh, and I've been working at Disneyland the last few weeks. In Fantasyland. Loading kids on the Mr. Toad ride mostly. They call us cast members, but I'm afraid there's not much acting to it."

She paused, but he didn't fill the breach. She kept looking at him steadily, meeting his gaze with those remarkable eyes. He let her look. *Cool. The long pauses usually fluster them.*

Finally she said, "Did you want me to read something for you? Something from the picture you're casting, maybe? I read cold very well."

"No, let's just talk awhile longer, shall we?"

"All right."

"Fawna—I can call you Fawna, can't I?"

"Certainly."

"Call me Kimball, if you're comfortable with that. Fawna, it doesn't take me long to size somebody up, to know if they have what it takes or not. Just from our brief talk here, I think you might be one of those lucky few. It's not just a matter of looks or just a matter of personality or just a matter of intelligence or even acting ability. It's something that takes in all of those things, but it's hard to put your finger on just exactly what it is. Usually I know it when I see it, though, and I'm very rarely wrong about it." He paused again. She looked impressed, excited, midwestern dreams come true shining in those dark eyes. "Fawna, I hope you realize you've come to Hollywood at a very exciting time."

"For someone like me, I can't imagine Hollywood at an *unex-citing* time."

"Yes, but things are different now from what they were ten or twenty years ago. Change is in the wind. The studio system is breaking down. Fewer and fewer artists are under contract. In-dependent production, the kind of thing DeWitt and I do, is going to become more and more important in the days ahead. When you looked around the office"—he waved an arm at the walls—"you may have been looking at these posters and think-ing, well, this may be a place to break in, but these guys are just out to make a buck, these guys are not real cinema artists."

"I didn't say that, Mr. McDermott."

"No, but you thought it, didn't you? Come on, admit it. And you thought wrong. A picture like *Teen Motor Rumble* was just a means to an end for us. These other posters are things we picked up cheap to decorate the office, make it clear to the visitor we make movies. They aren't really our kind of pictures. Do we want to make money? Sure. But we also have a vision. We want to make good pictures, great pictures if we can, and we're in busi-ness at a perfect time for that. The old taboos are falling all around us. We can do things on the big screen they can't do on TV. That big-screen freedom is what will save the picture busi-ness. It's a great time for us, and it can be a great time for you, too."

She was looking at him with unfiltered respect now. *Naked re-spect?* "Yes, that's just what I want. If it's not too presumptuous to say it, I think I share your vision, Mr. McDermott."

"Please, I said to make it Kimball."

"Kimball, then."

"You say you have the attitude of a professional."

"I hope so."

"And the training?"

"All I can afford, and I'm working at adding more all the time."

"Can you ride a horse?"

She looked surprised, a little amused. "I've ridden some. Are you doing a western?"

"No, there's no riding in this picture. But it's an important skill to have in this town. And something else you need to learn, something that's particularly hard for a beautiful girl like yourself, is you can't be a slave to vanity. Answer me honestly. Would you mind looking less than beautiful on screen? Dowdy even?"

"If it was necessary to the character, of course. Is that what you're looking for?"

"No. If I were, I wouldn't be considering girls who looked like you, believe me."

"Thank you, I think."

"Do you sing?"

"Church choir at home."

"Dance?"

"I took some ballet. Is this a musical?"

"No, it's a crime story. We call it *Bullet Eyes*."

"What an intriguing title. Are you shooting it in color?"

"No. We thought about it, of course, kicked it around, but we decided on black and white."

"I suppose color would be too expensive." *You got that one right, baby.*

"That's not it at all. Color would be all wrong for the mood of this picture. It's what the French critics call *film noir*. Can you imagine *The Maltese Falcon* or *Double Indemnity* in color?"

"No, I suppose not."

"Just a few more questions. Do you have any objection to working long hours?"

"Not at all."

"Can you take direction?"

"Absolutely."

"Does criticism bother you?"

"Not from someone I respect. If it comes from someone more experienced than I, it can only help me."

"Are you athletic at all? Play any sports back home?"

She gave him a don't-be-silly look. "Not after about the age of ten. I was a cheerleader, though, if that helps. Are you looking for a stunt woman, Kimball?"

"Not a stunt woman, no, but there is some action in this picture, and in an independent production you might have to do more in a physical way than you would over at one of the big studios where they can afford a lot of doubles. Nothing really dangerous, but you have to be ready to risk the occasional scrape and trust the people you're working with."

"I think I can do that. I twisted my ankle cheerleading once and didn't even cry." Mockingly, starting to have fun with the give-and-take.

Now get the big question in. Offhandedly. Matter-of-factly.

"How would you feel about doing a nude scene?"

That got her, smearing the carefully applied sophistication at least for a second. She looked like she wanted to run out of the office. She was embarrassed, reddening under her makeup. In an almost involuntary motion, she tugged at the hem of her skirt. McDermott thought he could read her mind as she tried to regain her composure. She hadn't expected this, but she was in Hollywood, not Creston Falls. She was a worldly woman, not a farm girl. She gathered herself until she was able to speak without a quaver.

"What are you making here, stag films?" *Just the right note of superiority and derision. Best defense a good offense. Perfect.*

Kimball McDermott put on his hurt face. "That's a rotten thing to say, Fawna. What do you know about stag films?"

"Well, there are such things, aren't there? I've never seen one, but my brother told me about them when he came home from college. They must make them somewhere. And they don't make them at MGM, do they?"

"Look, I told you we're interested in creating art." Working up a fine state of indignation now, stoking his self-righteous fire. "Ever been to an art gallery, Miss Blair? Don't they have nudes in the art galleries where you come from? Do they put fig leaves on the statues in Creston Falls? Was Michelangelo a pornographer to you? Maybe you'd better get back on the Greyhound."

She looked just a little chastened and a little more amused by his outburst. "I'm sorry if I misjudged you, Mr. McDermott. It's just that I never thought about serious motion pictures having nudity in them."

"I guess they don't have an art house in your town, Miss Blair. You obviously haven't seen many European films. Plenty of nudity in them. If it's part of life, why shouldn't it be on the screen? Did you know that Hedy Lamarr—?"

"*Ecstasy,*" she said. "I'm not totally ignorant of film history, you know. It's just that I didn't know American movies could have nudity in them. Don't they have something called a Production Code?"

"Ah, but that's just it. The Code is breaking down. Its days are numbered. Pretty soon you'll be seeing nudity in mainstream Hollywood films."

"You make that sound like some kind of a victory."

"It is, in a way. For the First Amendment. Didn't they teach you about the Constitution in your civics class back in Creston Falls, or is that too controversial a document?"

"They didn't teach us the First Amendment was written to protect the rights of pornographers. And along with the nudity in these brave new films, will there also be cursing and drugs and sex and all those other good wholesome things?"

"There might, and maybe an occasional idea, too. Maybe the kind of important themes that novelists and playwrights can address and American films have never been able to, at least in the last thirty years. That's why I say this is an exciting time to be beginning a career here."

She smiled disarmingly. "But I'm not sure I want to be a pioneer. Maybe when the first real American movie star shoots a nude scene, I'll think about it."

"It's already happened. Natalie Wood shot a nude scene in *Splendor in the Grass*."

She looked puzzled. "I saw that movie, and I don't remember any nude scene. I'm pretty sure I'd remember, too."

"They didn't leave it in the final print. But they did shoot it. It's only a matter of time before—" He broke off shaking his head, looking across at her with sad resignation. "This is no good. I think I owe you an apology. You're not ready for this. You're a nice, innocent, churchgoing small-town girl, and you must think I'm some kind of evil white slaver or something. I'm sorry, Miss Blair. I've wasted your time. Go back and work at Disneyland, do some workshop productions, get some credits. Commercials are good, no nudity there. Maybe when you really achieve this professional status you claim, we can work together."

Ooh, that one stung her. "I am a professional. At least I hope I am. You were calling me Fawna before, Kimball."

"I thought I was getting too familiar. Maybe it's better to keep it more impersonal under the circumstances. I hate people to get the wrong idea about me."

"I hate that, too. I hate people to assume I'm not a professional."

"Okay, Fawna, if you're a professional, do a scene for me right now."

"I said I'd read—"

"There's not much dialogue in this scene. It's mostly action. But it involves taking your clothes off."

"Well, uh, I can sort of pantomime that part, can't I?"

"What would that prove? About your talent, I mean."

"Are you interested in seeing my talent or seeing my body?"

"If you're an actress, your body is part of your talent." Apologetic smile. "That's the way of the world, not just Hollywood. Do you want to do the scene or not?"

"What? Here in the office?"

"This is where we do our casting, Fawna. I warned you it isn't MGM, didn't I? If you're a professional, then show me some professionalism."

"All alone with you in your office in a practically deserted building, you want me to take my clothes off?"

"Look, it'll mean nothing to me. Sexually, I mean."

"Why not? Are you a homosexual?" *So we know about fags in Creston Falls, too. Ooh, we are sophisticated.*

"No, but in matters like this, I'm like a doctor. I've seen it all before. I approach it with a professional eye, a business interest." He turned his tone sarcastic. "I wish I could afford a nurse to chaperone you, but like I said, everything we do has to show on the screen. We don't have money for the niceties."

"Everything has to show on the screen. Yes, I get it." *Very good, sweetheart. Match me sarcasm for sarcasm.*

"Look, I can see you still have the wrong idea. Let me clear one thing up. I'm not asking you to strip naked in front of me. Not at all."

She looked relieved but puzzled. "But didn't you just say—?"

He took a script off the top of his desk, leafed through it to the appropriate page and handed it to her. "This is the scene."

She looked at the script, turning to the title page. "*Rumble, Baby, Rumble*," she read. "Is this the picture you're casting?"

"No, I told you, ours is called *Bullet Eyes*, a much classier property, believe me, and one you'd be perfect for. Your eyes would anyway. This is just a scene that works well for auditions. I have a prop you'll need." He opened the bottom drawer of his desk, drew out a huge pink bath towel and handed it to her.

She looked at the towel suspiciously.

"It's clean, don't worry. Now, that door there leads to our humble powder room." He pointed to the scarred door across the room. "There are hangers for your things. Take the script in there, read it through, see what we're looking for, memorize the little bit of dialogue, and when you're ready, come out and do the scene with me."

"*With* you?"

He laughed. "You see a double meaning in everything, don't you? Relax. I'll read the guy's lines, but I'll be all the way across the room from you, nowhere near you."

She looked from him to the script to the towel to the gouged door. She was obviously torn between her good-girl modesty and her eagerness for work.

"What happened to the door?" she asked. *Delaying tactic, but she's almost hooked.*

"An actor drawing Social Security who thought he could play a teenager in one of our pictures. He got mad and took it out on the door. Look, are you going to do this or not?"

"I don't know, Kimball."

"You don't need the work?"

"I don't know if I need it quite that badly."

"Look, I know you're embarrassed, but if you want to be a pro, you have to overcome that and do the scene as if you're enjoying it. That's if you're the real actress you say and not just a nice lit-tle girl from the Midwest who should have stayed home and worked in her father's drugstore."

"My father's a dentist!" she retorted fiercely. Then she seemed to sense the absurdity of the exchange and smiled a little, reluc-tantly.

He waited a few beats, then said softly, "You're going to do it, aren't you?"

"I guess I am."

"You trust me, don't you?"

"Well, I'm sure Johnny wouldn't have sent me here if—yes, sure, I'm going to do it. I'll do my best. Remember this is my first time. It may take me a little while to study the scene and get ready."

"Take all the time you need, Fawna."

She took the towel and the script, walked across to the bath-room door, and, after another distasteful look at the gouge in the wood, walked inside, closing it behind her.

Kimball felt himself getting excited, breathing more shallowly. This girl was perfect. Most of the others were *too* knowing, too ready to play the game. *Take it easy, boy. Be cool. You're a profes-sional, too.*

Sometimes if they were nervous enough, they had to pee be-fore they could attempt the scene. Even a professional stripper who auditioned for him had done that. He was glad Fawna Blair didn't. The sound—you could hear everything through the thin door—would get Little Kimball too excited too soon.

Kimball stayed in his chair, slipping off his loafers, unbuck-ling his belt, carefully pulling off his trousers and briefs and leav-ing them in a heap under the desk.

He had her figured to gut it out, humiliation or no, not like that one girl (what was her name? Judy something) whose nerve had failed the second she dropped the towel, who'd wound up sobbing in the corner desperately trying to cover herself. He'd got her dressed, called her a cab, written it off. That hadn't been much fun, and the professional strippers weren't much fun either. So far this Fawna Blair, this Linda Grace Swackhammer, tasted like Mama Bear's bowl of porridge. Just right.

The script called for the girl to come out of the closet, listen to the adulterous lover who was self-righteously telling her of his plans to go back to his wife and children, and convince him in the most dramatic and provocative way possible that he really wanted to stay.

It was only a few minutes before the door to the john opened a crack. "I'm ready," said an only slightly quavering voice.

"Okay, Fawna. Action."

The door opened all the way. She stood there in the doorway, hands behind her back, the towel wrapped around her, tied under her armpits and covering her down to below the knees. Very nice shoulders. Beautiful bare feet. And she was acting up a storm. She was the perfect good girl's version of the bad girl, the sulky lower lip, those knowing bullet eyes in contrast to the all-body blush.

Kimball recited the man's line from memory. "I'm leaving, Alexis. I'm going back to Barbara."

"You're not, Charlie," she said, steadily, decisively. *Look, Ma, I'm acting. This one is game all right.*

"I am. I've come to my senses at last. This isn't my kind of life. I'm leaving, and you can't stop me."

She smiled an evil bad-girl smile. "I can't, huh?" *Seems to be getting into it.*

"No, you can't."

The moment of truth. Suddenly her bravery seemed to fail her. She swallowed and a panicked look flickered in her eyes. She waited a beat or two too long for the character she was supposed to be playing.

Would she do it? Would she drop the towel?

She did.

The script called for the towel to fall all at once, but she did it in stages, like a bather creeping gradually into a cold swimming pool. This was undoubtedly a product of her nervousness and reluctance to bare all rather than a calculated acting choice, but it was still a nice touch. Her left hand came from behind her back, undid the towel from her shoulder and let it drop to her waist, held there by her right arm. His eyes focused on her breasts, big, firm, young, pink nipples erect. A beat later she released it further, revealing the rest of her body to his hungry eyes but keeping the towel draped over her right arm.

"Look, Charlie. Have one last look." Even with the distraction of those breasts, of her nearly flat belly with deep-dish navel, her dark pubic triangle, he noted in one corner of his mind that the line reading wasn't bad. Maybe he really would cast this one. But first there was other business to take care of.

The script next called for her to walk across the room to him, slowly, provocatively. If she had the self-assurance to manage that part—and most of them didn't—it would make things easier for him, but in this isolated office, he could perform his part regardless.

She was doing it. She was starting toward him. She hadn't completely vanquished her pained self-consciousness, but this one was a gamer, projecting scripted seductiveness and unscripted humiliation simultaneously. She still held the towel, though, dragging it from her concealed right hand, a security blanket in case she decided to opt out of the audition and flee back to the bathroom.

When she got close to his desk, staring straight into his eyes, her own brown eyes smoldering with what might have been lust or hatred or any other hot emotion, he stood up from his chair and moved around the desk. Now there would be no concealing from her what was going on. She would see rising up under the Hawaiian shirt an engorged penis straining for action. He had to be ready to grab her and pull her to him, ready to stifle her scream, but she wasn't reacting as he expected. She seemed transfixed by the sight of his cock, she seemed ready, she seemed not at all what she seemed, she must want him, she and her bullet eyes.

She let him draw her to him.

She dropped the towel from her hand.

He felt something cold on his thigh. His eyes dropped to that right hand and saw the pistol she held for just an instant before she fired once into his crotch.

She heard his satisfying scream, she read her line ("This is for Judy!"), she fired again into his chest. "Do I get the part?" She left him bleeding and dying on the floor.

She had to wash a little blood off before she could get dressed and get out of the office.

———

"Yes, Johnny, the audition went fine, just the way you said it would. Having me drop that crook Miles Barnard's name was an especially nice touch."

"Was your prop where Rick said it would be?"

"Yep. Inside the toilet tank. I met the cleanup crew on the stairs. That building's practically empty, so they shouldn't be disturbed. Next time you go up to Camarillo to see your niece, tell her I delivered the line you wrote me with feeling."

"I will. Thanks."

"So, you guys should be happy. You defended the family honor, and Rick's out from under that turd. Now what about me, Johnny?"

"You'll be paid, Linda. We won't welsh on our arrangement."

"That's not what I mean. I want more work from you, but not

this kind. I know I'm good at it, but it's almost never as satisfying as it was today. And I don't want to take any more calls, either."

"Linda, look on the bright side. You're multi-talented. You have a range of career options few women can match."

"Hit woman or whore? I know you're being funny, but notice I'm not laughing. Johnny, I'm a real actress. I proved it in Mc-Dermott's office. I had to make that snotrag believe in me, and I did it. You should have seen the layers I gave him in that performance. I could give the fuckin' Actors' Studio lessons. I want you to get me a real job now, an acting job, a bit, a commercial, anything. I've turned enough tricks for a lifetime, and there aren't many men rotten enough to deserve what I just did to Kimball McDermott. Not even in Hollywood."

"Are you sure about that?"

"I'm not kidding around, Johnny. I want a real acting job."

"Honey, I'm sure you were great. But I'm getting out of the talent agency business. No stomach for it anymore."

"Well, before you go, can't you just get one door open for me and let me do the rest?"

"Maybe. If you'll do one more thing for me first."

"You got another one for me, Johnny?"

Pickup

Martin Meyers

I

*I*was drinking Roy Glass's famous Irish coffee. I figured that way I could make the drunk last.

The ceiling fan in Glass's Bar turned slowly in a weak attempt to cool and dispel the beer-soaked steam heat caroming off the old fleur-de-lis-stamped tin walls and ceilings from the overproductive radiator along the wall opposite the age-burnished mahogany bar and suck the smoke out of the air.

Outside, it was the end of February. The weather, and how I felt, seemed colder than the proverbial witch's tit.

All the fan did was circulate the heat and vaguely disturb the ashes and butts in the ashtrays Roy or May never seemed to find time to empty.

That didn't bother me. But the stupid neon sign in the window was making me nuts. The G and the L and the final S were out, but not completely; they kept flickering, bouncing off the glimmering mirror behind the bar, and no matter where I sat, into my eyes.

Now the sign read ASS BAR, which on Friday and Saturday nights brought every horny snot into the place.

My boss, Sol Schiff, and I had gone down to Chelsea that morning. We raided the Viking Realty Office looking for Stanley Purcell, who was working a credit card scam. We found a cache of phony cards, but no Stanley.

Back in the office Sol stepped into my cubicle.

"We've got a problem, Neal. That pack of phony credit cards we turned up at Viking is gone."

"It's a terrible world, Sol. Thieves everywhere."

Sol shook his head.

"What?" I asked, daring him. "I didn't take the cards. Gilly was the outside man. He saw me taking them out. Zola saw me bringing them in. Ask Gilly. Maybe Gilly or Zola took them."

"They've been with me for years."

"You want me to empty my pockets?" I did just that.

"I'm going to have to lay you off. My niece needs a job."

"Yeah, sure," I said, cleaning out my desk.

I never took those cards, but there was no way for me to prove it. Sol's word against mine. So he could give his lousy niece a job. Why didn't he come out and say it? More likely, she wasn't his niece and he was looking to screw her. That was it. Niece was in at the Victory Investigation Bureau and I was out.

I went home, made a few phone calls. No one was hiring. I'd bum for a week and look again. Maybe take a month or two off.

I usually pack a weapon everywhere I go. But not when I intend to do some serious drinking. The only thing more dangerous than a drunk with a car is a drunk with a gun. I figured on starting in Yorkville and drinking my way downtown and home.

In Glass's Bar I put on my sunglasses to ward off the neon flare, which was giving me a headache, tore the filter off my Marlboro, and lit up. Just for something to do, I got up and pushed some coins into the jukebox near the door. Louis Armstrong started playing something bluesy. Fit my mood completely. I was about ready to switch from Irish coffee to shooters.

The cold, clammy blast across my knees let me know the front door was opening. At first all I saw was the glistening wet street. Then, there she was. Also glistening and wet.

She pulled off her red kerchief and brushed a stray strand of spiky blonde hair back in place so it stood at attention with the rest of the spikes.

Her skin was fair, pale, as if dusted with rice powder. There was a certain indifference about the woman that made you believe nothing ever mattered to her one way or the other.

She was perfect. Not in the movie-star way. Her nose was not perfect. The flaw was slight, a bit of swelling on either side. I had the feeling it had been broken at least once. Her two front teeth, a slight gap between them, slanted toward each other. Not unattractive. A pretty, but used face. A peasant, not a lady.

She was small; obviously she didn't think of herself as small: Her clothes declared that. Under the wet trench coat she wore a black suit over a Chinese-red blouse. Her gloves were black with red slashes and the heels on her black patent pumps were red. Lips and fingernails shimmered vermilion.

Glass's Bar was almost empty. Still, she walked directly to the space alongside me at the bar, heels clacking even though they were wet and the tile floor had sawdust on it. Her voice was surprisingly gruff. "A shot of Irish, neat."

There was a contradiction in her voice, an ardent tone that I would learn was a siren's song. But I was more than ready. For what I didn't know. Didn't care. I was ready, even eager, for anything. "I'll have the same, Roy."

Roy's a short, big-chested guy with a dour mouth. "You got it," he said, wiping the bar with his towel, taking a good look at the new woman. I believe a smile broke his sour lips, but I wouldn't swear to it.

From her station at the other end of the bar, May, the big redhead who's married to Roy, sailed forth to pick up the two ashtrays flanking me and the blonde. May not only emptied them, she wiped them clean.

Roy set the drinks on the fresh cocktail napkins May supplied.

I stuck a cigarette between my lips and torched it.

"My treat." The blonde settled herself on the bar stool. "Vera. Vera Tallaferro."

"Neal Thomas." I nodded and parked my cigarette in the ashtray. Things were looking up.

"Can I have one of those?" She nodded at my box of Marlboros.

Ignoring the cigarette smoldering in the ashtray, I pulled two fresh from the box. "With or without protection?"

She smirked. "What the hell. Without."

I tore off the filters, shoved both cigarettes in my mouth, and flamed them. Vera's hand lifted to my mouth and took one. Her touch made me shiver even more than the damp, icy wind that came through the front door as someone new entered.

She sat there next to me, smoking and drinking. Next, she was singing. Softly, under her breath, but I could hear it plain as a bell, same thing that Louis was playing on his horn, an old tune from the forties. Something about things happening again. I was in love. Hook, line, sinker, and rod.

She could ask me anything and I would do it.

Louis's muted trumpet moaned plaintively in the night.

We drank, we smoked, listened to Louis.

Somewhere along the way I said the fateful words. "I'm a good listener; tell me about it."

Glancing nervously out at York Avenue, she said, "I don't know how to begin."

"Who are you afraid of?"

In the dim light I saw her pale complexion flare red. "I didn't know it showed." She composed herself. Her skin reverted to its normal tone. "I'm being stalked."

"By . . . ?"

"A man I used to know."

"An ex-lover."

She shuddered. "Oh, God, no. Just a man. He's obsessed with me."

"Can't say that I blame him."

"What?" Her eyes narrowed. "Thank you."

"My pleasure." Outside, the streetlamps cast a pocket of light on the wet sidewalk. "Stalking? You mean following you?"

"Sometimes following. Mostly calling."

"Have you gone to the police?"

"I can't." She drained her drink and tapped the bar with her glass for another.

I drained my glass and did the same. "Why not?"

She sucked in a great big breath, her breasts heaved. I was in love. "He has pictures."

"Oh." Our new drinks arrived. I sipped a small taste. "If he's not an ex-lover, how did he get them?"

"He stole them from my husband."

My ardor cooled, but not by much. "Your husband?"

"He's dead."

Sad to say I was not ashamed that I felt so glad about another human being's death. "I'm sorry."

"I'm not. He's the reason I'm in this mess."

She turned and gave me the full benefit of her brimming eyes, a million watts, at least. "Phil Shore, my husband, and Charlie El-gart, the man who's stalking me, used to be partners."

I nodded.

Vera didn't miss a beat. "Real estate. They owned buildings to-gether." She shook her head. "He and Phil were equal partners." Her husky voice grew more strident with each syllable. "Will you explain to me why I ended up with one falling-down tenement and he ended up with three prime income-generating buildings?"

"Have you talked to a lawyer?"

She nodded and gulped the remains of her new drink. "Kosher and ironclad. Apparently Charlie put up most of the money."

Signaling for two more shots, I finished what was in my glass.

When May moved away Vera said, "I've got Irish whiskey and Louis Armstrong at home."

"Sounds good," I murmured. My heart beat like a hammer.

———

"Two stops," she told the cabby. "First, down Broadway. I want you to drive by a restaurant off Fifty-third Street."

The ride had no talking, only long, drawn-out kisses.

She broke our lip-lock. "Turn here. Drive slowly."

An impatient horn sounded behind us.

"Never mind that. Stop the cab. Keep the meter running." Vera stepped out and walked to the restaurant where diners sat by the window. She said loudly, "See that bastard sitting there?"

"Calm down," I said, catching up to her.

"Don't want to calm down."

I could see the man as clear as day. Black hair that looked dyed. Black sports coat and a black polo shirt. His trim swimmer's body and silver-rimmed sunglasses completed the Hollywood look.

He was scarred on the right side, from hairline, across his eye, his nose, through his mouth, and to his chin.

It looked like somebody had cleaved his face with an axe, then rejoined it. However, the pieces didn't quite line up. In spite of the milky glaze over the damaged right eye it moved and appeared to be functioning. When he spoke to the waiter, he talked out of the down side of his lopsided mouth.

"That's the kind of arrogance he has," Vera shouted.

"Shh," I whispered. "Doesn't the management object?"

"He is the management, that split-faced bastard. He owns the place." She raised her voice, louder than before. "A place that should rightfully be mine."

The split-faced man spotted us. He threw his napkin on the

table and came barging out the door toward us. "What the hell do you want?"

"I want what's mine," Vera screamed.

He shoved a fist in her nose. "I'll give you what's yours."

"Hey," I said, stepping between them.

"Who's this, your latest hero? You want some of this, asshole?"

"Manners," I said, setting my feet. He was as tall as I was and outweighed me, but I figured I could take him.

"I'll give you fucking manners." He tried to kick me in the shin.

I stepped away, nullifying his kick. He nailed me with a left hook, nearly tearing my head off.

Adrenaline pumped. I shook it off and was ready to give a little back. He sneered at me and marched into the restaurant.

"Come back here, you bastard," I cried. "I'm going to kill you."

"Shh," Vera was now saying. "Let's get out of here."

People in the restaurant and on the street were staring at us. Looking at me as if I was the maniac who had started all this.

Vera led me to the cab. Once we were inside she opened my shirt and put her cold hands on my chest. "Mmm," she murmured, fingering the chain hanging around my neck. "I like a warm man."

When I made no move she shook her head and sucked my tongue till I thought she'd pull it out of my mouth. She whispered in my ear. "You know what my dream is? Lying on the beach in Havana. Want to go to Havana with me?"

I rubbed her nipples; they were hard. "Why not?"

"Would you really kill him for me?"

I pulled away from her.

Vera shook her head again. "Just playing. You're an idiot. A wonderful idiot, but an idiot." She leaned toward the patient cabbie. "We're going east." She gave him an address on Fifth Avenue.

The cab dropped us at what looked like a modest apartment building. Bars on outside glass door, iron grate on inside glass door.

The elevator took us to the fifth floor. I had assumed wrong. Not modest, merely subdued. The entire floor was dedicated to this one apartment. I never did figure out how many rooms there were.

To the left, coming off the elevator, was a small sitting room. Expensive wallpaper, paintings on the walls. Couches, chairs, the rest.

Three large windows overlooked Central Park. I walked to the center window, looked down at the park, the street, buses rolling by, people, lovers.

I turned back to the room and the most prominent item in it: a black-and-white Deco bar, including a modern refrigerator tarted up to be Deco. The space the bar and its accessories took up was about half the size of my apartment.

Vera stepped behind the bar, pulled down two large highball glasses from the overhead rack, and chunked each with ice from the refrigerator's icemaker.

"Leave room for the booze," I said.

She dumped the contents of the glasses into the sink. "Just to cool the glasses. How about you? Do you need cooling?"

She poured.

We drank.

"I love ice." She scooped some cubes from the sink and tossed them from hand to hand.

We drank a few more rounds.

In between, she played ice games, rubbing some on her mouth, her neck. She opened a button on her blouse, improving my view of the swell of her breasts. She caressed her breasts with the ice, then sucked the ice.

"You like ice," I said moronically.

Vera nodded. "There are lots of things you can do with ice."

She was driving me crazy. I knew what I wanted from her. What did she want from me? I was aware of the answer; I just didn't want to admit it. Killing another human being was too high a price for a piece of tail.

I grabbed her, started pawing.

"Not like that."

"Huh?"

"Haven't you ever heard of foreplay?"

"I thought we had that in the cab."

"I'm not a piece of meat. Talk to me. Tell me what you want."

"You're beautiful."

"And . . . ?"

I licked my lips, feeling somewhere between a pimply-faced adolescent and a dirty old man. "I've been thinking about your breasts."

Her cheeks were sprinkled with drops of rain. She removed her gloves, dropped them, wiped her face, licked vermilion lips. "Look at me. Talk to me."

I stared at her breasts under the red blouse.

"Pig. Right to the tits." She removed the jacket, let it join the other clothes on the floor and ran her vermilion nails down each breast, shivering at her own touch. I could see her nipples pushing at the red silk.

"Your . . ."

"Shut up." She opened her blouse.

I could barely swallow. "Your nipples are purple peaks . . ."

"Awful. But I appreciate the attempt. Well, what are you stalling for? Do you intend to keep me waiting all night? That's no way to treat a lady."

Vera led me into the bedroom. She stroked me. Here. There. She smelled of rain. And sex. And underneath, something vaguely rotten. I was exhausted, but ardent. We kissed, animals feeding at the trough, as we fell to the floor. I hoisted her skirt, tore her panties. Vera fell on me, a wrestler pinning me to the mat.

The fairy web brush of her nipples against my chest revived me. Gone was the exhaustion. I was about to explode.

"Bite me," she cried.

Countdown. Not yet, I thought. Too good to waste.

I bit her. She bit me.

Now!

No, not now. I needed to, I wanted to. I couldn't.

What was holding me back? A warning? A sign?

Then, unsatisfyingly, it was over. What the hell.

Panting, I lit a cigarette. I turned to her and offered her a toke.

"Thanks, you are a sensitive soul."

I cradled her in my arms. Too late. Stiff with anger, she smoked the cigarette. Next, she stood, removed the rest of her clothes, got into bed, and was immediately asleep. I had to redeem myself. I crawled into the bed, kissed her, groping, frantically.

She awoke, calm. "Get me a drink first."

I looked around, the village idiot.

"In the bar, stupid."

Dutifully, I fetched the bottle and a bucket of ice.

She granted me a smile. "You're learning."

I joined her in bed. Eager. As I was considering how to have her next, much to my despair, I zonked to sleep.

But there is no stopping a determined woman. There are more things in this world that you can do with ice than you've ever dreamed of. It was in her mouth. Her mouth was on me.

The bedroom door crashed open and Split-Face charged into the room. At first I thought I was hallucinating, but Vera's shriek changed my thinking.

The man had a large hunting knife in his hand.

Vera grabbed a gun from the drawer in her night table, shoved the gun into my hand. Next thing I knew she was out of the bed, clawing at him, confirming what I'd sensed about her. The damn woman had a death wish.

Split-Face seemed willing to accommodate Vera. He stabbed at her. Blood misted the air as she screamed, "Kill him. He's killing me. Kill him."

I fired. Rat-tat-tat. Split-Face grabbed his gut. The gun jammed, but my target was down. Blood streamed from Split-Face's mouth and from between his fingers at his stomach. He fell in a dead heap.

When I leaned over Split-Face's body, gun still at the ready, to assess the damages, the bastard lashed out with that big hunting knife.

I fired. With no results. Like shooting the Frankenstein monster. He was slashing as he got off the floor.

Arms up in defense, I pulled back.

He cut me. Hands. Arms.

I decided to run.

Not in time.

The son-of-a-bitch cut my throat.

II

My name is Sol Schiff. I own and operate the Victory Investigation Bureau out of the Chanin Building, a sad, gray structure that sits across the street from Grand Central Station, on East Forty-second Street.

The transcription you've read is from Neal's tape that Paul Gilys found.

The day after Neal met Vera, I, completely unaware of the previously mentioned events, was in my office. My office, like me, is ordinary. Cherry wood panels and glass partitions. My permanent staff is small. When I need more, I have a group of free-lancers I rely on.

The investigation business is just that, it's a business. Forget all that glamorous crap they feed you in the movies and on TV and in books.

Pat Hardy and Selma were in the field playing catch-up on the credit card thing. I was doing paperwork.

The large righthand drawer to my desk was stuck. I gave it a tug. Out it came. Behind it, causing the jam-up, were the missing credit cards.

"Damn." I called Neal Thomas's apartment. No answer.

I buzzed Zola, my receptionist. "Everyone has an answering machine. Why doesn't Neal?"

"I have no idea, Mr. S."

"Keep trying him," I said. "I owe the poor bastard his job back."

"If he's dumb enough to take it," she said, switching off.

"Yeah, that too." I scrambled through the drawer I'd just pulled out, found house keys, tagged 3F. Neal's. One of the requirements of the job is for employees to leave a spare set of keys. He'd forgotten to take them back when I canned him.

I buzzed Zola again.

"He's still not answering," she said.

"Do I have anything?"

"Nothing till two."

I grabbed my coat.

"Be back before two," I called over my shoulder.

I caught the 7 to the West Side, then downtown on the 9 to Neal's apartment on West Nineteenth Street in Chelsea. It was an old walk-up, pre–World War II. I had Neal's keys ready for the front door, but it gave with a push. I climbed to the third floor. Two doors, 3F and 3R. This time I needed the keys.

Three-F was about six hundred square feet. Medium-sized by New York standards. I entered directly into the kitchen.

The living room was on the right. I fumbled for the wall switch. Useless. The only source of light came through the one shadeless window.

Brick walls. A fireplace that hadn't been used since Franklin D. Roosevelt lived in the White House. Probably no chimney, anyway.

An Ikea table and armchair were the only furniture.

The sole item on the table was a rotary dial telephone. To describe the place as spare would be painting the lily.

Under the table, a trove: Four used Duracell AA batteries and a torn section of cardboard with the letters TDK. Safe to assume Neal owned a tape recorder. Where was it?

In the small john, a toilet and a narrow stall shower. Looked like the kind the military use in the field. No medicine cabinet, only a shelf and a mirror. No wastepaper basket.

In a denim laundry bag on the doorknob, two soiled shirts and a damp washcloth stained blue-red that smelled like a hospital.

A glimpse of orange behind the toilet bowl caught my eye. I snagged the capsule. Tetracycline. I put it in my pocket.

While I was down on the tile, I spotted one small drop. With my Swiss army knife I scraped it up. I sniffed this too. Blood.

I secured the blood drop in the folds of a small sheet of paper from my memo pad and parked it with the tetracycline.

Back to the kitchen. The refrigerator was empty. I shined my small flashlight into the few cabinets. Cans of chili. But no garbage. In the hall, the large plastic garbage can was empty.

A broom closet next to the bedroom, used as a clothes closet. Socks and underwear on a shelf. One jacket and a pair of pants on the only wooden hanger. Three shirts. A pair of jogging shoes.

No suitcase. No toilet kit. And no tape recorder or cassettes. I looked around the pitiful place. I hadn't realized Neal was that up against it. I vowed not only to offer him his job back but to give him a bonus.

The bedroom was so small you couldn't swing a cat in it. No night table, no closet. The bed was up against two walls and almost touched the other two. Going to sleep had to start with a leap from the doorway.

The overhead light worked dimly. I sat on the bed, scooted my hand under the pillow, flicked my flashlight, and peered under the bed. No corpse. Neal's or otherwise. I did find a scrap of paper with blue printing. "One sterile gauze pad. 4"x4". 12 PLY."

Near the gauze my hands discovered a box of .38 shells and a Police Special, a .38, four-inch barrel, six-shot cylinder with fixed sights. Neal's gun, loaded, but with the chamber under the hammer empty. I sniffed; the weapon hadn't been fired recently.

Blood, gauze wrapper, tetracycline. If Neal wasn't dead, he was hurt. And not carrying his weapon.

In the living room I called Bonnie MacRae, a friend of mine at One Police Plaza. When Bonnie answered I didn't identify myself.

"You know Neal Thomas?"

"Yes." The response was more cautious than I'd expected.

"I can't find him. He's been gone for a day. Any of the John Does in the system or in the morgue sound like him?"

"You know about the killing of Charles Elgart yesterday?"

"Only what I've read in the papers."

"He was shot with a nine-millimeter."

"The most popular gun on the street," I said.

"Either a Sig-Sauer or a Glock."

"And you're talking to me about this, why?"

"The shooter most likely still has the weapon."

"And?"

"We believe the shooter is Neal Thomas."

———————

The meeting was in our conference room. Me, Paul Gilys—Gilly—he's one of my permanents, Pat Hardy, my best freelancer.

Bonnie MacRae had confirmed pretty much what was in the newspapers. Vera Tallaferro called it in. Brian Markoff, the vic's lawyer, lived in the building.

I'd told Zola that none of us would be available for new cases until further notice. Gilly and Pat sat on one side of the long table in the dumpy leather chairs that came with the office when I'd opened it years before.

Computers are great; we have them. I prefer my trusty double-faced blackboard for working out problems. My two operatives were studying it while I chalked out what few facts we had.

1. CHARLES ELGART. SHOT TO DEATH IN HIS APARTMENT ON FIFTH AVENUE OPPOSITE CENTRAL PARK.

2. POLICE LIKE NEAL THOMAS FOR THE SHOOTING.

3. VICTIM'S PARAMOUR, VERA TALLAFERRO, ALLEGEDLY WITNESSED THE SHOOTING. SHE ADMITS THAT SHE PICKED NEAL UP IN A BAR AND BROUGHT HIM HOME TO THE APARTMENT SHE SHARED WITH ELGART.

4. ACCORDING TO HER, ELGART CAME HOME AND SURPRISED THEM. NEAL PULLED OUT A GUN AND KILLED ELGART, THEN TOOK OFF. THE VIC WAS SHOT WITH A GLOCK NINE OR A SIG-SAUER.

"Long as I've known Neal he's carried a Police Special. It was in his apartment. Not fired recently." I resumed writing.

5. VIC'S LAWYER, BRIAN MARKOFF, LIVES ONE STORY UP FROM THE MURDER SCENE!

My pounding that exclamation point broke the chalk. I dropped the two pieces on the blackboard ledge and dusted my hands.

"Very convenient," Gilly said. "How often does the sucker come down to borrow a cup of sugar?"

I like Gilly. The tall, thin, cocoa-colored man and I go back to when I was a cop. The ear-to-chin scar on his face is his souvenir of when he ran with the bad guys. He looks tough. He is.

"Good point," Hardy said. Hardy looks like an aging football player. He's fifty and. Maybe six feet, two-fifty, two-sixty pounds. His gray sports jacket was open, evidence that he was off his diet. Hardy is partial to bright yellow shirts; when I see him I think of Big Bird from *Sesame Street*. Still, he gets it done.

"Which means?" I asked.

Gilly jumped in. "Only two theories fit. One, Neal done it."

"Or two," Hardy said, "the wife killed her lover and is dumping the crime on Neal. And the lawyer's in on the scam."

Gilly leaned his long body against the horizontal limits of his leather chair. "Exactly."

"Okay. We dig. I'm on Markoff. Gilly, you take Neal."

"And I," Pat said, standing, beaming, "get the girl."

Gilly leaped to his feet, causing the chair to squeak and groan in relief. "Not at the end you won't." He cackled.

"Four more items." I dealt three photos onto the table, one facedown. "I have copies for each of you. Brian Markoff and Vera Tallaferro. He's the lawyer upstairs, she's the dead man's cheating lover." I turned the third picture over. "That's the vic, Charles Elgart, when he was alive and kicking."

"Ugly bastard," said Gilly, fingering his own scar.

Hardy picked up Elgart's photo. "Looks like he was in a very serious accident." He turned to Gilly. "Car crash or knife."

"Plural. I'm betting knives," Gilly said. "What kind of business was this character in?"

"Real estate."

"Hmph." Gilly sneered. "Nastier business than I thought."

Hardy examined the scarred face in the photo, then gently laid it on the table. He had memories of his own. Like a bullet in his gut years and years before. "You said four items."

"Item two," I said. "A tetracycline capsule, a gauze wrapper and signs of blood. My bet is Neal is worried about an infection."

"Shit! To state the obvious, Neal's been shot or cut." Gilly grinned. Not at Neal being hurt, but at the game. It was a high.

"What else?" Hardy asked.

"Batteries and cardboard left from a cassette package," I said. "No tape recorder or cassettes. Finally, an off-the-wall theory, but worth considering. The dead lover was in real estate. The day Neal supposedly did the deed, he and I busted a real estate office and came up with a fistful of bogus credit cards."

———

Brian Markoff's office was on Madison Avenue, in the forties. A far cry from Stanley Purcell's Viking office Neal and I'd raided. Markoff was a one-man operation that seemed to cover a potpourri of practices. Real estate. Estates. Divorce. Criminal law.

"May I help you, sir?" the gum-chomping receptionist asked.

"Sol Schiff," I told her, displaying my old cop badge. "Investigating Charles Elgart's death. Mr. Markoff, please."

"Yes, sir." Blowing a mini-bubble, she pressed a button. "Detective Sol Schiff. Investigating Mr. Elgart's death."

She led me down a short hall.

"Thanks, Sandra."

Pop. Sandra's bubble popped. "Sorry, Mr. Markoff."

He didn't seemed fazed. Perhaps he liked dumb. His desk, mahogany and leather-topped, gleamed, smelled of polish. Excluding a telephone and a computer, the surface was bare.

The lawyer, lounging in a recliner a few feet away, was movie-star handsome, tan and empowered, as if he felt the world owed him something. He had a runner's spare body and sun-blonde hair and wore a black blazer over a deep-purple polo shirt. Glancing up from a thick file, he pushed silver-framed eyeglasses down from the top of his head, smiled affably, and swung to a sitting position.

"What can I do for you, Detective Schiff?" he asked, fretting his forefinger with his thumb.

"Just a few questions about the shooting," I said, glancing at his hands. The finger he'd been fussing with had touches of black in the cuticle. Ink, I concluded. From his pen. Or maybe the cops had printed him to eliminate prints. I let it go.

He snagged a cell phone from the floor and set it on his lap.

"Where were you when Mr. Elgart was shot?"

"In my apartment, one flight up."

The cell phone rang. He showed me a smile. "Hello." He listened, disconnected. "The police. You're not a cop. Get out."

————

At the office Zola told me Hardy was waiting.

"Gilly?"

"He called from Chinatown. Said he was following a lead."

I made a face. "I hope so."

Hardy was in the conference room, reading the *Post*. I said, "Tell me about the woman."

"She ditched me." Hardy took a Palm Pilot from his case. He turned the small computer on and read the screen. "So, if I couldn't find where she was going, I'd find out where she'd been. The doorman happened to know the cabdriver he flagged for her on the day in question—cost me fifty bucks to get the guy's number."

I waved my hand impatiently. "Cabby recognize Vera's photo?"

"You bet."

"Where'd the cab take her?"

"Would you believe Viking Real Estate?"

I smiled. I happen to enjoy irony. "Yes. Go on."

"The cabby said she was watching a dude. His word, not

mine. Very tan, with sunglasses—the sun kept glinting off the silver frames—then a couple of other dudes came out."

I had not stopped smiling. "I've got a thousand dollars that says that those dudes were me and Neal. And five hundred that says the tan watcher with the shades was Brian Markoff."

Hardy nodded. "The woman used her cell phone. The tan dude answered his cell phone. Short conversation. The tan dude walked away and the woman told the driver to follow the other two dudes."

"Hunch," I said. I picked up my phone and dialed.

"Brian Markoff's office."

"Isn't this Viking Real Estate?"

"No. That's Stanley Purcell. Let me give you his number."

I scribbled the number, hung up. Thank God for stupid people. "Go on," I told Hardy.

"Peter Castellano—the cabby—followed you here. After Vera left his taxi, he stopped for a large pizza, which he ate all of while parked." Hardy added with envy, "And skinny as a rail . . ." Hardy buttoned and unbuttoned his jacket. "He saw Vera follow the dudes into this building. It wasn't till Castellano was down to his last slice that one of the men came out."

"Neal?" I asked.

Hardy nodded. "She followed. Castellano got another fare."

My phone rang. "Yes."

"Gilly," Zola said.

"Yeah?" I put him on the speaker.

"I found him," Gilly said. No doubt how excited he was.

I was concerned about Neal. I'm not saying Gilly wasn't, but to Gilly it's a big wonderful game that he gets off on. "Neal's hurt but alive," Gilly said. "The doctor's called Butcher. Get this, his clinic is connected to a mortuary."

"I know the man," I said. "Lost his license in New York for patching up bad guys. Hymie Butcher Pampanelli."

"You know him?" Gilly asked incredulously. "You should see. Older than God. Butcher?"

"Nothing murderous. He ran the only Kosher Italian butcher in New York while he was going to med school."

"You're kidding," said Zola, still on the line.

"Pampanelli was my mother's meat man where I grew up on the West Side. How bad is Neal?"

"He might just make it. Sol?"

"Yeah?"

"There's a tape."

"And Neal?" I asked, pondering the news about the tape.

"Throat cut. Not deep, just a razor slice. Lucky. He was wearing a cross on a chain around his neck. It snagged the knife. Saved his life. Missed the carotid and the windpipe. Had enough bandage around his neck to wrap a mummy. Hands and arms covered with bruises and cuts. Can't believe he didn't go to a real hospital. Can't believe he's alive."

"Because he was wearing a cross," Zola murmured.

"So he's going to make it," I said, riding over her.

"I think so."

"How'd you pick up his trail?" Hardy wanted to know.

"Starting on Sixth Avenue, I went to a few locals, showing Neal's picture. One witness in Hogan's Grill told me Neal had been in, saying he was on the job, and looking to connect with Butcher Pampanelli. Finally, in bar number six I met a drunk who told me about Butcher's mortuary and clinic—don't that take the cake? That's why I'm in fucking China-fucking-town."

"Are you going to cut to the damn chase?"

Gilly played the tape.

III

"Wow," Zola said softly. She had joined us in the conference room.

"Exactly," Gilly said.

"How are the facilities?" I asked.

"Not the most modern, but clean. In a boarded-up dump on Mott Street. You don't even know it's there. Bunch of Third-World types who seem to know their stuff."

"That's Butcher," I said. "What I don't get is why he extended himself to Neal."

"That's easy," said Gilly. "Neal promised you'd pay."

I groaned, then smiled. "He'd be right about that."

"Good." The guttural voice exploded in my ear.

"Hello, Butcher."

"Hello, Sollie. For old acquaintance sake, a hundred grand."

"Fuck old acquaintance. Twenty-five."

"Good, now we have a basis for negotiation." A loud click and I presumed he was off the line. But with Butcher Pampanelli you never know anything for sure.

"Come on in, Gilly. We've got work to do." I hung up. "Hardy, find that damn woman. Find Vera."

I sat in a blue funk. Too much data. It should be typed and put in order so I could read it. I pressed the button. "Zola."

"What?" She was just the other side of my desk. Scared the hell out of me.

"I need you to type . . ."

She was shoving Markoff's photo at me. "Want to hear something stupid?"

"Shoot."

"This clown, he dated my cousin Carmen."

I squinted at her. Neal had said something on the tape. About Charles Elgart wearing a black sports coat and a black polo shirt.

And sunglasses with silver frames. Charles Elgart and Brian Markoff could have been dressed from the same closet. Another thought, still unformed, niggled at my brain.

Zola said, "His name is Tom Luciano. An actor. Worked on those trucks bringing the Spanish Theater Group to the barrio."

"Impossible. Too coincidental. You know that." While I was protesting I was remembering the traces of black on Markoff's cuticle. Not ink. Hair dye when he played Split-Face for Neal.

I punched up Bonnie MacRae's number.

"Hi," she said. "You calling to turn someone in?"

"Not hardly. But I do have something to run by you."

"Yes."

"I remember a scam going down when I was at the Seven. This woman stood by while her boyfriend shot the husband, then packed him in the freezer till she could sucker a dupe to take her home. She got the dupe coked up, took the corpse out of the deep freeze, woke the dupe, play-acted a shoot-out, so the neighbors could hear, cut the dupe's throat, put the murder gun in the dupe's hand, the knife in the dead husband's hand. When the husband was room temp, they called the cops."

"Did that really happen?"

"Could have."

"You always did have a vivid imagination."

"Is there a freezer in the murder apartment?"

"Not big enough for a corpse. There is an ice maker. And the downstairs neighbor complained of a leak in one of her bathrooms."

"You might check if Tallaferro or Markoff bought a knife." Bonnie didn't answer. I said, "So I guess we'll talk again."

"In the very near future."

IV

Ten minutes later I was still sitting at my desk. I knew what had happened. I even knew what had to be done.

Zola buzzed.

"Yes."

"Call for you. I think it's Neal."

"Sol Schiff here."

"You know who this is?"

"Yes."

"Meet me at the Butcher's, so I can fill you in. I'll need some cash to get out of town. Can you spare five thousand?"

The too-familiar guttural tones of Butcher Pampanelli broke in. "I'll need some cash, too."

"You'll get yours, Butcher. Off the line."

"Ten grand, at least." The click was no guarantee he wasn't still listening.

I sent Gilly as advance while Hardy and I walked to the bank.

Hardy hailed a cab.

"No. We'll take the Lex to Canal Street. Faster."

A train was waiting. Canal Street in ten minutes. Mott Street and Pampanelli's Funeral Parlor were barely a walk. Traffic along Canal was jammed as usual.

The supposedly abandoned five-story, redbrick building dated back to the nineteenth century. The front door was locked.

A shot echoed across Mott Street as if we were in some sort of canyon. No reaction. No lights went on, no sirens blared.

While I checked out the fire escape, Hardy applied his battery-powered lock-pick to open the lock.

"I'm in," he said.

I joined him. The place was dark. He shone his light to reveal narrow halls and stairwells.

"Gilly?" I whispered loudly. No response. "Which do you hate worse, heights or rats?" I asked Hardy.

Hardy's yellow shirt seemed to shimmer in the flashlight's amber glow. "Hobson's choice is not a choice," he muttered. "I'll take these stairs. You can have the fire escape."

I was more than halfway up the fire ladder when it began to drizzle. And when I heard two more shots.

My instinct was to get out of there. But you know the old gag about detectives and their partners. Or their employees. I had to keep going. I owed it to Neal. I scrambled up as fast as I could.

Two stories later, as I peered over the edge of the roof, I saw the glint and heard another shot.

I was on the roof and running, my gun in my hand. Faint silhouettes appeared to be corpses of defenders at the battlements.

A noise like rat claws scratched the tar surface of the roof.

"Pat?" I asked, hopefully, crouching and moving to my left.

"No," he whispered. "Pat's behind you."

"Hello, Gilly."

"Right."

We waited perhaps five minutes before we all shone our lights and checked out the roof. No one.

"Look at this," Gilly said, plucking something out of a fallen brick chimney. "There's blood on it."

"Neal's tape recorder?" Hardy said.

"Do you smell something?" I asked.

"Rat shit," Gilly said.

I disagreed. "Smoke." My comment was made all but inaudible by the clamor of the sirens.

Gilly, tucking the cassette recorder like a football, ran for the fire ladder. Pat, for all his weight, was a close second. I didn't mind being third. But only when my feet hit the sidewalk.

The fire was a four-alarm blaze. Two hundred fire fighters.

The drizzle became a major torrent. The air smelled of smoke and rain. And death. This time we took a cab.

V

We were in the office. Gilly, Pat Hardy, Zola, and I.

I played the new tape.

Neal's voice.

Split-Face's nose was peeling, milky glaze pouring out of his right eye. Greasy stuff from his cheek came off on my finger. "Vera!" I swayed over the body. "Sweetheart, get me a doctor."

"All right, honey." But Sweetheart wasn't reaching for the phone, she was reaching for the damn knife in Split-Face's hand. The bitch swung the blade at me underhanded, like a street fighter.

She tried to gut me. I feinted to the left, slipped in close, and punched her in the mouth. Down she went, next to Split-Face.

At last, wary, I ran my fingers through supposed gore on her stomach. No wound. Fake blood. I knew Split-Face's bullet wounds were the same bogus crap. A variation on the old badger game. Any reasonable man would have called 911, explained it to the cops. I was not in the mood for reason. I snatched my clothes and ran.

My mind raced, going nowhere, like a hamster on that damn wheel in the cage. The deceitful bitch had suckered me easier than a three-card-monte dealer nails a mark. She was silk, pure silk.

And hot. She had me going the first minute. Outwardly very sophisticated. Very Upper East Side. The type of soigné I never in a million years thought I could approach. There was something in her eyes. Honest and deceitful at the same time. A whore.

The sophisticate was the woman I wanted. The whore, the woman I knew I could have. What I failed to take into account was that she was smart. Smarter than I was. And she loved playing games.

In the stairwell I carefully ran my fingers over my throat. Bleeding, but not gushing. Finally, good news. I wrapped my shirt around my throat to stanch the blood, put on the rest of my clothes, and forced myself to walk down the stairs, slowly. I didn't want to get my blood pumping faster than it had to.

All I got from the doorman was, "Good night, sir."

On Fifth Avenue, lamplight got lost in the rain. A cab bounced through a pothole and sprayed me.

I kept thinking how Vera had played me for a sucker as a taxi took me to my place on Nineteenth Street. I should have switched cabs but I wasn't in the mood for good procedure nuances.

I cleaned up, iodined hands and arms, and tied a temporary rag around my throat. Though I needed medical attention, I took the time to clean the blood from the bathroom floor and change the batteries in my cassette recorder. Funny what seems important during a situation like that. At least I had the sense to swallow a bunch of tetracycline capsules.

Exhausted, I crawled onto the bed before I pulled off the rag and taped a four-by-four of gauze on my throat, which was in better shape than I had any right to hope for.

When I searched under my bed for my Police Special, I got dizzy. I took a deep breath and kept probing, coming up only with a box of rounds. Nine-millimeters. They'd work for the Glock. Figuring two guns better than one, I searched harder for my .38. But I got dizzy again and I think I passed out. When I opened my eyes, I knew I was pushing my luck hanging around. I stowed some stuff in my small flight bag and got the hell out of there.

I had a raw hamburger at Hogan's Grill. Not daring to check in at any hospital, I started playing cop, asking about Butcher Pampanelli, a cut man Sol had told me about.

After a couple of drinks, I felt better, but shaky. I lucked on a dipso who said he was starving to death, would do anything for a corned beef sandwich. Even offered to have sex with me. I told him I was flattered but not interested. I said, "You tell me where Butcher Pampanelli has his clinic and I'll buy you your corned beef."

"With fries?"

"And cole-slaw."

"Throw in a beer and we have a deal."

But he made me wait till he was chowing down before he told me that Butcher had a safe clinic on Mott Street in Chinatown.

Problem: The torn awning on Mott Street said Pampanelli's Funeral Parlor, but the building was boarded up. Another problem was the two cops patrolling Mott Street.

Three buildings away I found an open front door and camped on the roof. I now had a way in and out of Butcher's building.

I spent a fitful, paranoid night. Split-Face had to be after me. He had to kill me before I talked. The safest and smartest thing for me to do was go downstairs and turn myself in to those cops. But while I think I'm smart, I've never been accused of taking the safe route. Besides, the cops would never believe me.

Dawn came noiseless and nasty. Grinding pain in my head and belly that threatened to turn me inside-out woke me. First I couldn't remember anything except being in the bar with Vera.

Then, with my aching throat and the feel of the blood-clotted gauze on my skin, the fiasco with the knife and the bullets that didn't work came to me full force.

I was drenched with sweat. Each move was agonizing.

No cops on the street, but I waited, figuring the scam. The makeup on the fake Split-Face was the key. The real Elgart was most likely dead before Vera and I even met. She'd been hunting for a sucker, and I was it. He'd been in the freezer or in a tub packed in ice. The gag was simple. I shoot blanks at lover boy disguised as Split-Face. With a mug like that, makeup was easy.

Pretend-Split-Face was supposed to cut my throat, killing me, or I was supposed to run. But I was supposed to run immediately. Not stick around to try and kill Split-Face again. Or to discover he was made-up.

After I was dead or running, the corpse would get up, put real bullets in the gun, toss a slug into the wall for verisimilitude, and get the real body from cold storage. Presto: instant frame.

Except, I didn't die. Or run, according to the script. Yeah. But I was still the patsy. They probably switched to plan B.

Vera's story was now that Elgart cut me but I'd shot him and run. My prints were in the apartment. I was seen going in and coming out. Seen arguing with him earlier in front of the restaurant. My only proof was the gun with blanks in it. I popped the magazine of the Glock.

Three impotent slugs left. I took the blanks out. I had live rounds in my pocket. I reloaded the blanks. They were the only evidence that my story was true. But they were not proof. I could have put them in myself after killing Elgart.

This had to be the murder gun. My best move was to toss it in the river. The question was to stash it now or keep it with me. If I was caught with the murder weapon, it would be all she wrote.

Casually as a bum with a bloody neck could, I ambled to the torn awning of the boarded-up Pampanelli's Funeral Parlor. A short, mild-looking old man sitting on the stoop gaped amiably at me. His physical appearance certainly didn't live up to his name.

"You Butcher?"

"You Neal Thomas?"

"How'd you know?"

"I got ways. Your room's waiting."

He led me up some stairs to a clean room where an Asian man in a white coat checked me out and bandaged my neck.

A short pause in the tape. Then, Neal spoke again. Whispering. But he sounded stronger than in the previous section.

I'm on the roof of Pampanelli's Funeral Parlor. What's this thing I have for roofs lately? I'm one big ball of paranoid wax. The Filipino patched me with clean bandages, gave me blood, and pumped me full of antibiotics.

After a bowl of soup I slept. Woke to see Gilly smirking at me. I gave him a quick rundown and the tape. Not this one, of course. Slept, I don't know how long, woke again just when all the lights in the building went out. I heard footsteps on the stairs, doors slamming, then a single pair of feet in the hall. My stalker and I were alone. And the gun I had held blanks. Time to take care of that. But first I hightailed it to the roof.

Damn place looks like a fort. But I don't have any cannon. To think: I'm up here on this dumb roof with a hole in my throat and the cops after my ass. All I'd wanted was a couple of drinks, to get laid, and to listen to Louis Armstrong.

No more sentimental shit. My scheme works, I'm in the clear.

A husky voice, but a woman's: *"How're you doing, Neal? It's me, Vera. Butcher sent me."*

A scrambling sound.

The husky voice again: *"Cost me ten thousand. Don't hide, lover. What are you going to do? Shoot me?"*

"Everybody dies."

Hardy shook his head. "That's a line from an old John Garfield movie that goes with the one she just used."

"Shh," I said, rewinding the tape to where Hardy had interrupted.

The female again: *"I'm going to kill you, lover, and I'll get away with it. You're the man who killed my Charlie. They'll never believe your cockamamie version that I did it and framed you."*

On the tape a round went off.

"Damn." That was Neal.

"I'm having the hardest time killing you, hero," a new male voice said.

There were scraping rat-claw sounds. And heavy breathing. I pictured Neal dragging himself across the surface of the roof.

"The night is old," Neal whispered. *"Shadows upon shadows seem to be scheming . . . ."*

Neal broke off as if whatever delirium he'd been experiencing had passed. *"Fucking Markoff finally got me. It won't kill me. But Markoff is sure to if he wins this round. Got to lay low until I can get it together."*

Except for Neal's breathing the next minute or so was silent. Two more shots. What sounded like two cries of pain. Male. Female.

"You dirty son-of-a-bitch." That was Neal.

"Brian's dead," the female voice cried. *"I'm bleeding. How . . . ? I loaded that gun myself. Blanks, all blanks."*

"I know, lover. I reloaded."

"You smart-ass son-of-a-bitch."

Vera's words were the last on the cassette.

But. There was one more shot.

I guess it was the one I'd heard coming onto the roof.

I have no idea what happened to Butcher, that Judas bastard. I'm sure he survived. Brian Markoff's burned body was found on the roof. But not Neal's or Vera's. Anywhere.

END OF REPORT.

CLIPPED TO THE BOTTOM OF THE REPORT WAS A POSTCARD WITH A PICTURE OF HAVANA BAY ON ONE SIDE AND A CUBAN POSTMARK

ON THE OTHER AND THE MESSAGE, SCRAWLED IN NEAL'S HAND-
WRITING: *"Having a wonderful time."*

UNDER THAT IN SOL'S NEAT CURSIVE:

*This came in May. No signature. But it was Neal's hand-
writing, sure enough. I couldn't help but wonder if Vera was
with him. And how long it would be before one of them killed
the other.*

S.S.

Many Happy Returns

Catherine Dain

The woman stood with her toes on the edge of the cement, as far as she could get from the wire gate without stepping onto the asphalt drive. Her body was angled as if she were willing it to leave the spot.

She shifted restlessly from one foot to the other, uncomfortable in her shoes, the heels higher than she had grown accustomed to wearing. In other shoes, she might have started walking. She wasn't certain how much longer she could stand and wait, patiently and quietly.

The road in front of her curved and headed downhill less than a quarter of a mile from the fence. She closed her eyes briefly, to rest them, then focused again on the curve, not wanting to miss the first glimpse of the car. The sun was too bright. She wished she had asked for dark glasses.

"Are you sure she's coming?" the guard called.

The woman glanced back at him and nodded.

"I could make a phone call for you," he added.

"No." The woman said it too softly and had to try again. "No, thank you. I'm certain she'll be here."

"Do you want to wait inside?"

"No. No, thank you."

God, no. She didn't want to wait inside.

The sun outside was no brighter than the sun inside had been, she knew that. No warmer, no different in any way. Nevertheless, she was beginning to feel a fragile power from standing in its light, its too-bright light, and going back inside, even for a moment, even to cool off in the shade of the guardroom, would erode that little bit of strength.

For much of her life she had been powerless, never more so than in the last year. But now it was over.

A drop of sweat extended the dark circle under her arm, and she tugged at the lilac silk blouse, trying to keep it away from her skin. She had gained weight, overeating institutional food, and it was too tight now. The light-gray slacks had barely stretched around her waist when she put them on early that afternoon, once she had finished packing the few belongings from her cell.

Food had been the only sensory pleasure available to her for more than a year. But that was about to change. Soon.

A black bus with a sheriff's insignia on the side came rolling up the hill, and a surge of adrenaline forced her back from the driveway, almost to the fence. The shadow of the bus skirted her feet. She looked up to see the bus pass through the parking lot, watched the gates open, then swallow it up.

Dark streaks rose from the silk around her waist to touch the ones falling from under her breasts. She searched in her purse for a tissue to blot her face, but she hadn't thought to include one.

The black bus had brought her up the hill a year ago. She had a sense of shifting reality at the curve in the road, even before the bus reached the gates. The stench of the other women in the bus, a combination of alcoholic sweat and poor hygiene, had been so overwhelming that she almost vomited. Since then her nose had become less sensitive.

She tugged at her blouse again, trying to make it fit, trying to keep the dampness away from her skin. It was over. Kickout day, she reminded herself. She had survived the year.

The scrub on the hill had turned yellow again in the September sun. She had watched it through an entire cycle of seasons, waiting for this day.

The sun was almost hidden, the dry hill beginning to darken, before the car she was expecting nosed around the curve. She recognized the silver BMW 325i even before it slowed, then stopped, in front of her.

The engine kept puffing.

No one got out.

The trunk lid flipped open, and she heaved the suitcase in, fighting the urge to slam the lid back down. She closed it as softly as she could.

The door on the passenger side was locked. She had to wait for the driver to let her in. She arranged herself quietly, fastened her seat belt. The blast from the car's air-conditioning made her shiver. The damp silk stuck like glue.

She had to touch the surfaces—the silvery-gray leather of the dashboard, the gray plush of the seat. She thought about closing the louvered vent but didn't do it. She would get used to air-conditioning again.

"I'm sorry I'm late, Lynn, but the freeways were jammed."

The woman in the driver's seat kept both hands on the steering wheel as she said it. She looked straight ahead as she pulled away from the curb.

Lynn. Annie was the only person who had called her Lynn for months, ever since the last of her former friends stopped visiting. She had been Marilyn in the jail, not Lynn.

That was something she would have to decide, whether she wanted to be Lynn or Marilyn. She had a lot to decide, really, although most of the big decisions were already made, had been made a year ago so that she hadn't had to think about them in jail. She wondered if she could ever possibly be Lynn again.

She looked at Annie, the woman in the driver's seat, and decided not to bring up the name question. The identity question. Annie hadn't been perspiring, and her clothes fit, and her auburn hair had been cut by someone with a license.

Annie, her sister, who didn't want to look at her.

The BMW smoothly completed the circle of asphalt and headed back around the curve, down the hill.

Marilyn—she discovered that she thought of herself as Marilyn—leaned forward, watching for the first house. When she saw it, white stucco with red tile roof, just as it had been when she had ridden up the hill in the sheriff's bus, she realized that she had been holding her breath, afraid too much had changed, in just one year, for her to even recognize a house.

She wanted desperately to see something familiar in this decaying neighborhood of graffiti-covered garages and boarded-up gas stations. All she saw was one frail, ragged, brown-skinned man pushing a frozen fruit cart. She would have to wait.

They paused for the light at Eastern. Annie glanced at her, then moved into traffic and signaled for a left onto the freeway.

"There are a few things I need to tell you," she said. "The family has decided against a celebration. We felt it would be awkward."

"Celebration?" Marilyn realized that she had forgotten to think about what would happen when they reached the house. She had spent her first months in jail training herself not to think beyond the moment. It was only during the last week that she had allowed herself to remember the future. She hoped she hadn't lost the ability to plan, the thing that happens to people with frontal lobotomies.

"Your birthday."

Marilyn shut her eyes.

"I'm sorry—I really am." Annie's voice rose. "Turning forty has to be rough under any circumstances, and this—"

Marilyn could feel Annie's struggle for control, but she couldn't find the energy to help her. She had to conserve her energy to hold on to that tiny bit of power she had received from the half hour of waiting in the sun. She leaned her head against the window. Her window. This was her car. Two years ago it had been her birthday present.

"It was all I could do to convince Karl that you should have dinner and spend the night with us. I'm sorry, I really am," Annie repeated. "I'll help you find another place to stay tomorrow."

"I'm not sure I can find a place in one day," Marilyn said. She wasn't ready to tell Annie, but she had another place to spend the night, a night that had been planned a long time ago. She remembered that—she had remembered it a lot the last few days, remembered that she had something to look forward to. She could feel the blood surging in her veins, and she was glad her face had been already flushed from the heat, so she didn't have to explain. "Debbie and Buddy will probably want to stay close to the school, and there aren't that many rentals in the area."

"That's another thing." The other thing had to wait until Annie was in the right lane for the Hollywood Freeway. "You don't need to find a place for three. Debbie and Ross have decided that they want to stay with us, and Karl and I are happy to have them. So is Meryl. She likes having her cousins living with her. We all think it's the best way to go."

Marilyn froze at the name Ross. Then she realized that Annie was referring to Buddy—her son, not his father. She couldn't think of her son as Ross. And Annie didn't know that she wanted a place for four, not three.

"Why? Why is it the best way to go?"

Annie concentrated on her driving.

"Why?" Marilyn repeated.

"Come on, Lynn. You know why. You murdered their father. They haven't forgiven you for that."

Murder. Both the word and the coolness of Annie's voice jolted her. It wasn't murder, Marilyn thought. It wasn't murder. It was voluntary manslaughter with the special circumstance the lawyers call extreme emotional disturbance. Everyone had agreed to the plea bargain. She opened her mouth, but there was nothing she wanted to say to Annie about it.

Annie glanced at her stiffly, reprovingly. Annie had probably expected her to cry, she thought, would have been happier if she were crying, but she felt too relieved to cry. Ross was dead, after all, and she was free.

"Maybe I should stay in a hotel," she said. Saying it was easier than she feared. "I need to talk with Debbie and Buddy—need to explain to them. I could do that tomorrow. But maybe tonight I should stay in a hotel."

"Okay. If that's what you want. Where?"

"I'll let you know. Someplace where they will take care of me. Someplace where I can get a facial and a manicure and a massage." Did the Chateau Marmont have a spa? She wasn't sure. If not, she could take care of those things tomorrow.

"I don't think that will help you with Debbie and Ross," Annie said. "They're looking for signs of remorse."

Remorse. Marilyn had to think about remorse.

"I'm not sorry Ross is dead." She searched for the right words. "I know you want me to say I am, but I'm not. I am sorry I couldn't come up with a means of getting away from him that didn't include bashing his head with an iron sculpture. But I don't think about that night anymore. I haven't thought about it for a long time."

She had a flash of memory, of Ross, naked, throwing her down on the bed. Then another flash of Ross covered in blood, and a surge of joy. That was enough. She turned back to Annie.

"What did you think about?" Annie asked. "You spent a year in a cell. What was more important?"

Marilyn was startled by how angry Annie was. What did Annie have to be angry about?

"I didn't think about the past. I survived, that was all I could do. I wish we could go back to where we were, though. You and I. Can we be friends again?"

"We can't go back to where we were as long as Ross is dead."

"I didn't do very well, did I? Letting you know what it was like?"

"What what was like? Marriage to Ross? What's to understand? That he screwed around? That he had too much to drink a couple of times and threw you against the wall? I can understand that. Shit happens, and Ross was a bright, funny guy, but he wasn't always a nice guy. So if you had divorced him, I would have been with you every day in the courtroom while you fought for custody and child support. That would have made sense. Murdering him didn't."

"Voluntary manslaughter," Marilyn whispered. She would have said more if she thought Annie could hear.

"They could have had you on second degree, but nobody wanted the trial, least of all Ross's partners. Ask Karl. They just wanted the scandal to go away before it ruined the firm. Temporary insanity would have been even better, but the DA's office wouldn't go for it." Annie's face twisted. She concentrated on changing lanes on the freeway, then continued more softly. "People can't just kill people, damn it. We live in a society that's falling apart, and it's all because people kill people."

"I'm sorry you were hurt." Marilyn was tired of apologizing, and she stifled an urge to respond with anger of her own. That had been a useful skill in jail, stifling anger. It was one she had acquired as a child, and she had only lost it that single time with Ross.

"Unintended consequences," Annie said. "We all have to live with the unintended consequences of what we do."

"You're making it sound simpler than it was—divorcing him. What you don't understand—what I don't know how to explain— is how powerless I felt. Until I picked up that small iron torso and hit him. He looked so stunned—so incredulous—so amazed that I might fight back—that I had to hit him again. And then when he was lying on the floor—when he was powerless—I hit him again."

"Stop." Annie's face had turned white. "I don't want to hear this. Please just sit quietly until I can get you to a hotel."

"But this is my car. Did you forget? I didn't. This is my car. I'll leave you at your house. And call you tomorrow. We can talk then."

"Oh, God. You think you got away with it. One year in county jail wasn't punishment. You think you got away with it."

Marilyn was silent. They were leaving the freeway on Highland, skirting the edge of Hollywood to get to Hancock Park. She wanted to see the buildings, the people, the trees.

Annie turned the car onto a street with houses set back from the street, houses with landscaped grounds. She paused in front of a gated driveway.

"Thank you for picking me up," Marilyn said. "And for taking care of Debbie and Buddy. I'm not sure I ever really thanked you for that."

"You're welcome." Annie said it stiffly, without looking at her. "You'll need money to stay in the hotel. I picked up fifteen hundred in cash to tide you over. I was going to give it to you in the morning."

She took the bills out of her purse and handed them to Marilyn. Then she got out of the car and walked around it toward the house, leaving the engine running.

"Thank you again," Marilyn called to Annie's back.

Marilyn slid into the driver's seat. She touched the steering wheel and carefully released the parking brake. She eased the car away from the curb.

Freedom. She could sleep wherever she wanted. Stay wherever she wanted. Starting tomorrow, anyway. She had definite plans for tonight.

"Mrs. Bradford!"

The voice startled her. A short, dark, middle-aged woman in a pink uniform with two shopping bags at her feet was standing in Annie's driveway, waving. It took a moment for Marilyn to recognize Consuelo.

She pulled over to acknowledge the maid's greeting.

"Welcome back, Mrs. Bradford," Consuelo called.

"Thank you. Do you need a ride somewhere?"

"Just to the bus stop on Wilshire, if it isn't out of your way."

"No, not at all."

Marilyn leaned over to open the door.

Consuelo tucked the shopping bags under the dashboard and sat heavily.

Marilyn again eased the car out into the street.

"It's good to be careful," Consuelo said. "It takes a while for things outside to feel normal."

"How do you know?"

"My nephew robbed a 7-Eleven. He was in county jail for three months."

"What happened when he got out?"

"Nobody cared. Everybody robs a 7-Eleven, nobody cares, except people who hire you. When he got out, he came home. His mother was glad to see him."

"And he promised her he would never do it again?"

"No. The next time it was an ARCO AM–PM. Don't tell Mrs. Stenner, okay?"

"I won't tell Annie. Where is your nephew now?"

"Back in jail, waiting trial. It's bad, you know? He robbed the 7-Eleven because he couldn't find a job, and he wanted money for clothes and stuff. Then he had a jail record, so he couldn't find a job, so he robbed the ARCO. What does he do next?"

"I don't know." Marilyn concentrated on the signal light, on making the left turn on Wilshire.

"Who will hire him? His life in prison, that's what he's looking at. His whole life in prison."

"I'm sorry."

"Could you maybe talk to somebody? To give him another chance?"

"I'd be happy to, but I don't know anybody."

"Mrs. Bradford, forgive me. But you got a year in county jail for a crime I would have got life in prison for. You know somebody."

"I'll try to think." Marilyn frowned, not certain how one went about helping a petty thief. "I'll let you know if I can help."

"Okay. Thanks. The stop is at the corner."

Marilyn pulled over and Consuelo got out. She smiled at Marilyn the whole time she was retrieving her shopping bags.

"I believe you will help, okay?" Consuelo gave her a little parting wave.

"I'll do what I can." Whatever that was.

She drove down Wilshire toward Beverly Hills, wondering if anyone she knew would help Consuelo.

Then she turned north to Sunset. She had a date, a date set over a year ago, a date to meet at the Chateau Marmont. Blood surged in her veins again, the feeling of being alive. The blood in her head, in her fingertips, in her thighs, was arousing her. She had to concentrate on driving.

The traffic was picking up, and she had to drive slowly. Carefully. She didn't want anything to happen to the car.

Seeing the hotel turrets was a relief. She eased the BMW into the narrow driveway that led down to the parking garage.

The young man in uniform opened the door and smiled at her.

"Are you staying with us?" he asked.

Marilyn did her best to smile back.

"Just for the night."

She took the claim check and left the car.

Dealing with the clerk in the lobby was a little harder. But the reservation was there, in her name, guaranteed with a credit card number, even though hers had been canceled long ago.

"Do you need help with your suitcase?" he asked.

"No. Thank you."

The clerk directed her up the staircase to the second floor.

The room was disappointing. Marilyn wasn't certain what she had expected, but something with a little more glamour. A newer bedspread, better upholstery on the chair. And a little less street noise. Sounds filtered up from Sunset Boulevard. Still, there was space. Space to swing her arms. A bowl of fresh fruit. And a framed poster from the Matisse exhibit on the wall, one of the pictures he had painted from inside a room of the view out the window, and she liked it better the more she looked at it.

There were no bars on the window in the Matisse poster. The artist was inside looking out, but he could leave. Now there were no bars on her windows, either.

She placed the few items of clothing from her suitcase in the dresser, her toothbrush and makeup in the bathroom, and lay down on the bed, enjoying for a moment the luxury of being alone, knowing she wouldn't be alone for long.

In the morning they could make the next round of decisions. Where to live, how to tell people about the relationship. How to tell Debbie and Buddy. The rare moments when she had envisioned her new life, it had included Debbie and Buddy. Somehow she had thought they would understand and forgive, and she still thought that. It would take a while, but someday she would explain it and they would all understand and forgive her, Annie too.

She was still lying on the bed, staring at the ceiling, when the telephone rang. It had to ring three times before she remembered that she was supposed to answer it.

"Lynn? Lynn? I thought you were going to call me at the office when you got to the hotel."

She panicked for a moment, struggling to recognize the voice, one she hadn't heard in over a year. But it wasn't Ross. Ross was dead.

It was Ed. Yes. They had agreed that he shouldn't come to the jail, but they would meet at the Chateau Marmont the day she got out. And he hadn't forgotten.

"Ed. I'm just settling in."

"Don't get too settled. I'll be there in less than an hour."

"I don't have anything to wear to dinner."

"Hell, Lynn, we'll order room service."

"I'll see you in an hour, then."

Marilyn hung up the phone. Ed Bradford was Ross's half brother. And he had hated Ross almost as much as she had. That was what had first drawn them together. Mutual revenge against Ross for being Ross. Then it had become much more.

Divorcing Ross had crossed her mind, but Ed had argued against it. They had so much more to gain with Ross dead.

By the time she heard a knock at the door, Marilyn was show-ered and dressed in her one change of clothes. Another blouse and slacks that were too tight. She was annoyed that she had to see Ed with a bad haircut, no manicure, and ill-fitting clothes. But they had both waited long enough for this night.

"Lynn! You look great!"

Ed walked in and kissed her on the cheek.

His lips were full and rough. She turned her face, wanting more.

"Easy, Lynn," he said. "Somebody's coming."

She pulled back and looked at him.

There was a faint resemblance to Ross, especially around the deep-set eyes, the same ones Buddy had inherited. Ed's eyes were bright blue, though, and there was no anger in them. The suit he was wearing looked like one Ross might have worn, Ital-ian silk, tailored to fit. Ed was shorter and heavier than Ross. But Ross would have envied his thick, dark hair.

"I've been called Marilyn for the past year," she told him. "Would you have a problem calling me Marilyn instead of Lynn?"

"Not a problem, but you might have to remind me a couple of times," he answered. "Everyone in L.A. changes something. You might as well change your name."

She smiled at him.

Another knock at the door made her lose the smile. But Ed had said he was expecting someone.

Ed opened the door to display a young man with a ponytail and too many earrings holding a tray with a champagne icer and two glasses.

"Come right in," Ed said.

The young man set the tray on a table between two chairs.

"Do you want me to open it?" he said.

"I'll take care of it. Here you go." Ed handed him a folded bill. The young man glanced at it.

"Thank you, sir. Anything more, just give us a call."

He slipped discreetly out the door.

Ed twisted the cork from the champagne, poured two glasses, carefully letting the foam settle, and handed one to Marilyn.

"Happy birthday," he said.

"To freedom," she responded. "And to us."

He clinked her glass and took a sip. "To us. It's been a hell of a long year, but I haven't forgotten. And you haven't either, or you wouldn't be here. You'd be celebrating with Annie and Karl and your kids instead."

Marilyn opened her mouth to tell him that they hadn't wanted her, but she decided that could wait. They could talk about Debbie and Buddy in the morning. She took a sip of the champagne.

"I want to be with you," she said.

"Come here." Ed put his glass down. "Let's start the celebration now."

Marilyn took another sip of the champagne. The wine was cool and bittersweet and the bubbles made her nose itch. But she wanted more, she wanted more of everything. She held up her hand to hold him off so that she could drain the glass. Then she put it down next to his and held out her arms.

"Now," she whispered.

Ed took off his jacket and dropped it on the chair. Marilyn was tugging at his tie, then the buttons on his soft white shirt.

"Slow, kid," he said, laughing lightly. "I'll meet you on the bed."

Marilyn stepped back long enough to get rid of her own clothes, tossing them so that they mixed with Ed's on the chair. She reached the bed before he did, and when he sat down to get rid of his shoes and socks she began kissing the back of his neck.

"I've waited so long," she whispered.

He stood up to get rid of his trousers. Then he was on top of her, kissing her with that wonderful rough mouth, kissing her face, her eyes, her neck, lingering on her breasts, sliding down over her stomach, and the blood was flowing in her veins so that she could barely contain herself, forcing herself to slow down, not wanting to spend too much too soon, but giving in to the surging waves of pleasure almost at once.

He worked his way just as slowly back up her body.

"I'll get us more champagne," he said.

"You don't have to stop," Marilyn said. "Please don't stop now. I want more."

"We'll do more. But let's take a break."

It was only then that she realized that he wasn't aroused.

She pulled her knees up to her chest.

"I've gotten ugly," she said. "You don't want me."

"Lynn, honey, it isn't that. I do want you." He poured two more glasses and brought them back to the bed. He sat down next to her and handed her one. "But I'm not as young as I used to be."

Someone else had said that to her, those same words.

Ross. And the words had always meant that he was having an affair, had slept with another woman the night before.

"Who is she?" Marilyn asked.

"What?"

"The woman you're sleeping with. Who is she?" She brought the glass inside her knees, so that she could hide her body and drink at the same time.

"A friend. Someone I've been seeing. She's not important." His voice was tight, though, and she didn't believe him.

"Does she know about us?"

"No. No one knows about us. We agreed."

"We agreed to wait."

"Come on, Lynn, you didn't think that meant I'd be celibate, did you?"

"I thought you'd wait." She had to stop herself from screaming at him. "How are we going to look for a place to live tomorrow morning when you have a girlfriend who doesn't know about us?"

"A place to live?" He moved away from her. "I think it's a little soon for that, isn't it? I thought we were going to wait."

"I did wait. I did my time. And now I want to get on with my life. If you don't want to be with me, get out."

"Get out? You don't mean that."

"I mean it. I changed my mind. I don't want you after all." She began to sob as she realized it was true. "I killed Ross for you, oh, God, I killed Ross for you. And now you can't even get it up for me. I mean it. Get out."

"Not so fast." Ed's voice was cold, unloving. "I'm not ready to leave. You killed Ross for you, not for us. Although I won't say I haven't benefited. But don't forget that I'm the one who brokered that plea bargain, so you only did a year. Let's not quite say you owe me. Still, I've looked forward to tonight, and I'll be really disappointed if you send me away too soon."

Ed's face had changed. His eyes had become icy with anger. He grabbed Marilyn's arm, holding on too tightly. And his anger was arousing him. Like Ross.

Her heart was pounding, no longer from joy, though, and she couldn't think of anything to say to him.

His grip was bruising her as he pulled her closer.

She forced a smile, stopping him long enough to place her glass on the table. She looked at the champagne bottle, but she wasn't certain it was heavy enough. The lamp on the bedside table was a Tiffany replica with an iron base. The lamp might be better.

It would mean another plea bargain and another year before

she was truly free. Surely she could negotiate the sentence her-self this time.

"Whatever you want, dear," she murmured in Ed's ear.

She felt him relax just a little as they began to kiss. She pulled him close, allowed him to slide into the warm, moist place be-tween her legs.

"Oh, yes," she whispered, as his thrusts became urgent.

Her right hand closed around the lamp.

Top of the World

Bill Crider

I heard the song everywhere I went that spring. It was popular for months. It came out of the greasy jukes in the burger joints, and it was playing on every staticky station that the car radio picked up. "Sittin' on Top of the World," it was called, but at one point it surely sounded to me as if the woman singing it was saying "settin'." I knew that was wrong. Vicky always corrected my grammar, which I have to admit ain't—*isn't*—the best, and she'd never let me say a thing like that. "How many eggs are you setting on, you old hen?" That's what she'd have said to me if I'd made a mistake like that.

But it didn't seem to matter to the people who bought the records because, as I said, the song was everywhere. It was even playing on the cheap plastic radio in the little hotel room where Vicky and I were staying while Vicky sat on the edge of the bed and rolled her stockings down over those fine calves of hers, with her dress pulled up so that I could see the flash of her white panties.

She knew I was watching. And I knew she liked for me to watch, even though it made me feel rotten inside, sweet and rotten at the same time like a bruised, overripe peach lying in the sun.

It wasn't sunny outside. It was rainy and dark, and the lights were on in the buildings across from the hotel. The room we were in felt clammy and damp. I could smell the musty wallpaper.

And I could smell Vicky.

She knew that, too.

I felt my throat getting tight. I tried to swallow, but I couldn't. My throat was too dry. The blood was rushing in my head, and I couldn't hear the radio any longer.

Vicky kicked the rolled stockings off her feet, then stood up. She reached down and grabbed the hem of her dress, straightened up, and pulled the dress over her head. She tossed the dress on the bed and smiled at me.

"Not bad for an old broad, huh?" she said.

I couldn't answer, so I just nodded.

She unhooked her bra and threw it on the bed with the dress. Her breasts were round and firm, tipped with dark nipples that stiffened as I watched. Something else was stiffening, too, and I tried to turn away, but I couldn't. She knew I couldn't, and her smile grew wider. She hooked her thumbs in the elastic band of her panties, still smiling, and slid them slowly down over the burning bush, still a flaming red, though she'd dyed the hair on her head jet black. She kept right on smiling as she kicked the panties away from her and fell back on the bed.

"Come to Mama," she said, and, God help me, I did. It wasn't long before she was clawing at my back as I plunged between her legs, the rotten feeling welling up inside me, nearly choking me, but what we were doing was so sweet that I could ignore it until it burst from me and filled her and she cried out as I collapsed on top of her and lay there panting, wondering when she'd try to kill me.

Or whether the cops would get us first.

———

Sam Cobb was the one who introduced me to Vicky. He came in the shop early one day when I was lying on a creeper under a '50 Ford, putting a new muffler on it. He kicked my left foot, and I turned my head so I could see his shoes and the bottoms of his pants.

I knew who it was right off because nobody else I knew kept his shoes polished so bright or had such sharp pleats in his britches.

I rolled out from under the car and looked up at him while I wiped my hands on a rag. He was tall and thin, and he looked even taller from down there on the floor. I sat up on the creeper and said, "Hey, Sam. What brings you in here? That Merc' of yours giving you trouble?"

I knew that wasn't it. He took better care of that Merc' than most people take of their homes.

"Might have a job," Sam said. "You want in?"

I looked around the shop. There was no one there but me and Sam and the oil and grease stains on the concrete floor. Which was a good thing, considering what he was talking about.

"Let's go in the office," I said.

I got up from the creeper, and Sam followed me into the little room that I called the office but that wasn't much more than some sheet-metal siding put up like a couple of walls jutting out from the walls of the shop. There was a doorway but no door.

We went inside, where there was an old desk covered with repair forms and receipts, a chair on rollers, and an old couch. Neither one of us sat down.

"What about a job?" I asked.

"Got it from a woman named Vicky." Sam looked at me speculatively. "She's got red hair like yours. Looks a lot like you, in fact. She's not your mother, is she?"

"I don't have a mother," I said.

"Everybody's got a mother."

"Not me. I was what they call a foundling. I grew up in an orphanage in Dallas."

"Sorry to hear it. My mother was an angel on earth."

I didn't want to hear about his mother.

"They taught me to work on cars at the orphanage," I said. "Tell me about the job."

He did, and it sounded sweet: a bank in a little cotton town that was taking in tons of dough while the farmers were selling their crops at the gin.

"Not a lawman in the whole town," Sam said. "Maybe not in the whole county."

I knew better than that, and so did he, but he was making it sound easy because he wanted me in.

"So you need a driver," I said.

"Yep. And you're just the guy for the job. What do you say?"

I'd driven for Sam before, and the money had always been good, just the way he promised. I figured that in a couple of years, I'd have enough money to open a really nice shop, hire some mechanics, and make a straight living. I might even be able to get a dealership. That's if we didn't get caught. But we'd never even seen a cop, not a single time. But then we'd never worked with anybody named Vicky before.

"She's okay," Sam told me. "I met her in church."

I thought he might even have been telling the truth. Sam was the kind of guy who met women everywhere. They liked him a lot, and he liked them.

But Vicky wasn't like anyone Sam had met before. Or anyone I'd met, either.

————

Sam and Vicky did the inside work at the bank, him with his hat pulled low and her wearing dark glasses, with a scarf tied over her red hair and a big floppy sun hat over that. Me, I just sat in the car and waited for them. I didn't have anything to do with what went on inside. I was just the driver.

When the two of them came running out and jumped in the

backseat, I took off, fast at first and then just like a guy out for a pleasant drive. After all, I didn't want to get a traffic ticket.

Before long we were out of town and into the country. I'd scouted the dirt roads around there for a couple of days, and I knew no cops would ever find us now, not unless they got awfully lucky, which I didn't figure would happen.

What did happen was that my eyes met Vicky's in the mirror as I was driving along, and that was that. She grinned at me, and I grinned back, and we both knew what was going to happen between us without either one of us saying a word.

Two hours later we'd dumped the car, split the dough, and gone our separate ways. Or Sam had gone his separate way in the Merc', while Vicky and I had gone off together. I was supposed to drop her at her car, but we went straight to a little hotel I knew where the desk clerk never asked questions.

It didn't matter that she was a lot older than me or that we'd hardly spoken more than two words to each other. We both knew what we wanted, and it didn't take us long to find out that it was going to be even better than I'd thought it would. What she lacked in youth, she made up for in enthusiasm and experience. I rode her hard, and she wrung me dry.

"Slap me!" she said at one point, when I was too far gone to know any better.

She laughed when I did, and as the imprint of my fingers reddened on her face, she grabbed my hand with both of hers and bit it so hard that the blood ran out and over her chin and dripped on her breasts. But I didn't even feel it because all my feeling was concentrated so intensely somewhere else that my lips were peeled back in an insane grin.

Later we lay on the bed and smoked Luckies while we listened to the radio playing "Sittin' on Top of the World." My hand was throbbing, but it wasn't bleeding any longer, and I felt like the song was a good sign.

I was wrong about that, of course.

"Sam's going to be upset, you know," Vicky said as she blew out smoke and watched it rise up toward the ceiling. "He thinks he owns me."

"It's not like Sam to get hung up on one woman," I said.

"He's hung up on me."

"Then what he don't know won't hurt him."

"*Doesn't* know," Vicky said.

"Huh?"

"*Doesn't*, not *don't*. What he *doesn't* know."

"Oh. I get it."

"And don't say *huh*. It's vulgar."

"Is this vulgar?" I asked, rolling toward her and pinched the soft flesh between her legs. "How about this?"

"No. No. It's lovely. And don't stop."

I didn't, not until we were both too tired to move.

"Sam will find out," Vicky said, much later.

"I can handle Sam," I told her, and I was sure that I could.

———

"I know what's going on, son," Sam told me a month or so later.

I wasn't surprised. I'd been with Vicky more than a dozen times since the bank job. It would have been a miracle if Sam hadn't figured out what was going on by that time. I wondered what had taken him so long. Maybe he just didn't want to admit it to himself.

"I swear to God, I don't know what you're thinking about," he said. "You're a young guy. She's old enough to be your mother, for Christ's sake."

We were in the shop again, back in the office. I was leaned back in the chair with my feet up on the desk. Sam was standing there with his hat in his hands, turning it around and around.

"What difference does it make that she's older?" I asked.

He shook his head. "None, maybe. But it worries me, the way you look alike and the way she's been asking me things about you. Anyway, you stay away from her from now on. I've got another job lined up, and I don't need you thinking with the little head instead of the big one."

I swung my feet to the floor. "It's none of your business how I think."

"It is when you're doing a job with me. Or maybe you don't want to do that anymore. Maybe you want to spend your time in Sunday School."

"Fuck you," I said.

He shook his head again. He didn't look mad, just kind of sick, or maybe just sad, and he turned and left the garage, settling his hat down carefully on his head.

———

"He's going to kill you," Vicky told me.

We were lying in bed, which is where we usually were when we were together, buck naked, sweating like pigs, drained and drooping. Or at least I was. Vicky wasn't drooping, or drained, either. Just bruised a little, and she liked that. As far as I could tell, she never got tired.

"Sam?" I said. "What the hell would he kill me for?"

"Because he's jealous. He wants me for himself. I told you that."

"He won't kill me. He needs a driver."

"Anyone can drive."

"Not the way I can."

"I like a man with confidence."

I was confident enough about my driving, but not about other things. I didn't like guns, and I didn't like the people who used them, except for Vicky. That's why I was a driver. I'd never been inside a bank during one of Sam's jobs, and I never planned to be.

Vicky was different. She liked guns. I'd seen her running her fingers over the barrel of the .38 she carried in her purse, caressing it the way she sometimes caressed me.

"You're shivering," she said. "Are you cold?"

"No," I said. "I'm hot. Hot for you."

"I can see that," she said, looking down.

We didn't talk much after that.

———

Sam tried to kill me right after the next job. I let him out of the car at a deserted house in the country. No one had lived there for years. There was no paint left on the boards, and the windows were all broken. Sam's Merc' was in the dilapidated barn, and Vicky and I were going on to ditch the one I was driving in a city about fifty miles away. But Sam wanted Vicky to stay with him.

The wind was blowing dust down the road and tossing the trees near the old house. It was whipping Sam's suit coat, and he had to hold his hat down on his head with one hand.

He leaned down to the car window and said, "Get out, Vicky. You'll be going with me this time."

"We're not supposed to stay together," she said. "You've got the money. What more do you want?"

We always met later to divide the money, usually a week or two later, after the excitement had died down. I'd trusted Sam with the money before, though I wasn't so sure that I could do that anymore. But then I cared more about Vicky than the money by now.

"You know what I want," Sam said.

"You can't have it," Vicky said.

He opened the door and dragged her out before I could do

anything about it. He twisted her arm when she struggled with
him, and she raked his face with the fingernails of her free hand.

He let go of her arm, and she stumbled backward and fell to
the road. Sam just stood there, his hand up to his face. I could
see blood seeping around his fingers. His hat had blown off and
was tumbling down the road, but he didn't even look to see
where it was going.

I was out of the car by that time and heading around to the
other side of the car. I couldn't let Sam manhandle Vicky like
that, even if it didn't seem like she needed my help.

Before I got to him, though, Sam had his pistol out, and it was
pointed right at me.

"Stay right there," he said. "Don't come any closer. There's
something you have to know."

He didn't have to tell me twice to stay where I was. If there's
anything I like less than a pistol, it's a pistol that's pointed at me.

But he didn't want me to stop because of anything he had
to say. He just didn't want a moving target. I saw his eyes
widen, and I knew he was going to shoot, but I couldn't move.
It was like I was wearing concrete blocks on my feet instead of
shoes. I remember wondering if the bullets would hurt me
when they hit.

There were two shots, but neither one of them hit me. I kept
my eyes closed, waiting for another one, but it didn't come. The
next thing I heard was Vicky's voice. She was talking fast and
breathlessly, as if she'd just run a couple of miles carrying a heavy
suitcase.

"It's okay," she said. "You don't have to worry about Sam anymore, baby. I took care of him for you. It's okay."

I blinked my eyes and then opened them all the way. Sam was
lying right about where he'd been standing. He was on his back,
looking up at the sky. His jacket was flopped open, and there

were two dark-red stains on his white shirt. His gun was still in his hand, but he wouldn't be using it again.

I walked over and looked down at him. His eyelids flickered, and his lips moved. I couldn't quite make out what he was trying to say. It sounded a little like *Dallas*.

He didn't get a chance to say it again. Vicky stood beside me and shot him in the head.

"Get the money," she said, but I couldn't move. I just stood there, looking down at Sam, at the little round hole in his head, at the stuff that was leaking out the back of it on the ground.

Vicky grabbed my arm and jerked me toward the car.

"Get in," she said. "I'll get the money."

I got behind the wheel and sat there, staring out through the windshield. The back door opened, and Vicky threw the money bag in the backseat. I didn't look around, but I knew it was a black leather bag, like the ones doctors carry.

"You have to help me," Vicky said. "We can't leave him lying there like that."

I didn't move.

"Do you hear me?" she asked. "We can't leave him, and I can't move him by myself."

I nodded and got slowly out of the car, moving like a very old man. I let her lead me over to Sam.

"You get his shoulders," she said.

I took a deep breath, knowing that sooner or later she was going to talk me into doing it. There was no use putting it off. So I grabbed Sam's shoulders and lifted. I tried not to let his head touch me, but it did. I didn't look down, but I knew I had blood on my clothes. Blood and maybe a little something else.

Sam was heavier than he looked, but between the two of us, we managed to get him into the barn and into his car. When we slammed the door on him, Vicky said, "Does anyone ever come here?"

"How would I know?" I said. Then I relented a little. "Sam wouldn't pick a place where anyone would stumble on his car by accident."

"Good. Then we don't have a thing to worry about."

Right, I thought. Not a thing. Not us. We're sitting on top of the world.

———

It's always the little things, the ones you never think of, that come back to bite you. This time it was something as small as a hat, the one I'd seen bouncing along the road when it blew off Sam's head and never thought of again.

It was the hat that led the cops to Sam, less than a day after we'd left him there in the barn. I should have thought about the hat, but after we left Sam, I wasn't thinking about anything at all. Seeing a man shot down and then having to drag him off to a barn will make you forget a lot of things.

Vicky couldn't complain. She hadn't thought about the hat, either. All she could think about was the money. She kept telling me over and over not to worry about Sam because we didn't need him anymore. We had plenty of money, and it was all for the two of us. Besides, she knew where Sam kept the rest of it.

"He doesn't spend it?" I managed to say.

"Well, he spent some of it on me," she said. "But not enough. I don't think he really liked having the money, anyway. All he cared about was robbing banks. It gave him a thrill."

It had never given me a thrill. And it wouldn't be giving Sam one any longer. It thrilled Vicky, though. I could see that now, and I could see that killing Sam had been an even bigger thrill for her. She was so excited that she could hardly stop talking. She was bouncing around in the car seat like the steel ball in a pinball machine.

"You know what gives me a thrill?" Vicky asked.

I thought she'd been reading my mind, but that didn't seem possible. So I just shook my head as if I didn't have a clue.

"Fucking you," she said. "That's what gives me a thrill."

I was almost as shocked as I'd been when she killed Sam. I'd never heard a woman use that word before, not even in bed.

"As soon as we get that money, I'm going to fuck your brains out," she said.

But she wouldn't have to. She'd already done that, a long time ago.

———

I read all about the hat in the papers.

Some farmer was driving along the road, and he happened to see what looked like a really nice man's hat that had blown up against a fence post and hung there. He thought maybe it had blown off some guy's head, but he wondered why anybody would be driving on those back roads in a convertible. And he wondered why anybody would be so careless as to leave a nice hat like that behind. So he looked around a little, and he found the place where Sam had been killed. It wasn't hard to find, he said. There was a buzzard pecking at something on the ground.

I tried not to think too much about that, but the farmer thought about it, and he did a little more looking. When he found the Merc' and Sam's body, he drove to town and went straight to the police.

So now they knew about Sam. Which meant that they might also know about me. Sam and I had kept our business as secret as we could, and I'd certainly never told anybody that I was driving for a bank robber on the side. That didn't mean Sam hadn't told anybody, though.

And it didn't mean that the cops didn't know about Vicky. They found out about her within another day because of her connection with Sam, and there was her picture on the front page of the papers, along with her name and all the reporters could find out about her, some of which was very interesting. Especially the part about where she was from: Dallas. That was probably what Sam had been trying to tell me before he died. I had a feeling I knew why he'd wanted to tell me, a feeling that made me slightly sick and excited at the same time.

I didn't say anything about it to Vicky. Somehow I couldn't bring myself to talk about it.

We were staying at my place, and I was going in to the shop every day, working on cars the way I always had, even though there was more than twenty-five thousand dollars in a couple of black bags stuck under my bed.

Vicky wanted us to take it all and run away to Mexico.

"We can live for the rest of our lives down there with that kind of money," she said, and I knew she was right.

And I knew it was time to go when the cops found out about me.

———

I'd been careful not to let people see me with Sam, but Vicky and I hadn't been nearly so discreet. It took the cops a while, but they're always patient. Someone finally must have told them about the young guy who'd been seen with Vicky. They got a description, I guess, and then they got more than that. And then they tracked me down one morning at the shop.

They weren't sure about anything even then, but they were persistent. I answered all their questions politely, and they left without arresting me, but I could tell they weren't satisfied. I waited around until lunchtime, just in case they were watching, and then I locked up and went to my place.

Vicky wasn't there, which was just fine with me. It was time

we split up, long past time, and it would've been next to impossible for me to tell her that. She had a powerful hold over me,
even though I knew it was wrong, and more than wrong.

If she wasn't around, though, I could just leave. It wouldn't be
easy, and I couldn't have done it if I'd had to face her. I wasn't
planning to take all the money, just half of it. I figured that was
my share. I got one of the leather bags from under the bed, stuck
some underwear, a couple of shirts, a toothbrush, and a razor in
on top of it, and I was ready to go.

I was almost to the back door when Vicky came in.

"Where do you think you're going?" she said.

The bag felt like lead in my hand.

"Nowhere," I told her.

"The hell you weren't. You were running out on me."

"I left your half of the money."

"I don't give a damn about the money. I just care about you."

"I know," I said, and wished I hadn't.

She gave me a look that lifted the hair on the back of my neck,
and I felt my eyes widen in fear and surprise, exactly the way
Sam's had widened just before she shot him.

Two things occurred to me then. One was that Sam hadn't
been afraid of me at all. The pistol might have been pointed in
my direction, but only to threaten someone else. The second
thing I realized was that Vicky may very well not have killed Sam
to protect me from a bullet. She hadn't been afraid he was going
to shoot me. She'd been afraid of what he was going to tell me.

She kept on looking at me. Finally she said, "I don't know
what you mean, but I do know I'm coming with you."

I tried to keep my shoulders from slumping. Maybe I was
even successful.

"Get your things," I said.

And that's how we wound up in that little hotel room on a rainy, musty spring day. Eight or ten more hours of hard driving and we'd be in Mexico, if the police didn't catch up with us or if Vicky didn't kill me. Because I knew now that she was crazy.

I'd seen the way she fondled pistols like a lover, and I'd seen her nearly delirious with excitement after we did a job. I'd heard her voice, full of breathless exhilaration after she shot Sam. And then there was the way she acted with me, the way she talked, the things she made me do. It had finally dawned on me that what had taken me so long to figure out, well, that was something she'd known all along, or at least for a good while. I was sure Sam had told her what he knew about me, which wasn't much but which was enough.

She came out of the dinky little bathroom with a towel wrapped around her.

"Aren't you going to scrub my back?" she said.

I got off the bed, feeling as if I'd turned to stone. I was surprised my legs and arms would move.

"Sure," I told her, and I tried to smile. I don't think I managed it, though.

I followed her into the bathroom, and she dropped the towel to the floor before she stepped into the bathtub. The porcelain was cracked. The rust that had formed in the cracks looked like dried blood.

I worked up a good lather on the washcloth and began soaping Vicky's back. She sighed and closed her eyes, and I worked my way around front to her breasts. There was a light coating of freckles across them, and I rubbed them gently. She sighed again and started to lean back in the tub. When she'd rested her head against the back of it, I climbed in on top of her, got my hands around her throat, pinned her arms and legs, and took her under.

She kicked and thrashed for a while, but not for long. I was a good bit heavier than she was. I tried not to look at her face when it was done.

I got out of the tub, took off my clothes, and toweled dry. I found myself talking to Vicky, explaining why I'd had to kill her. I'm sure she would have understood.

Then I changed clothes and packed the bags with everything in the room. I didn't want to leave anything that would identify either of us. We were in a small town a long way from where we'd killed Sam. The cops there might never make the connection.

When I left, I checked the map. I wasn't too far from Dallas, so I decided to make a stop at the old home place.

———

Nothing much had changed. The grounds were still neatly cut, and there were a few flowers already blooming in the beds. There'd be a lot more later on.

I didn't know the woman at the desk, but when I mentioned to her I was a former resident, she told me that one of my teachers was still around.

"Miss Arnold. She's in class now, but if you'd like to wait a few minutes . . ."

I said I'd wait, and I walked back into the classroom wing. It still looked and smelled the same. Maybe the floor had been worn a little smoother by all the feet passing up and down the hall. I stood by the wall until class was over and the kids came out the door. Then I went inside.

Miss Arnold hadn't changed much, either. She still wore her hair pulled back in a bun, though it was gray now instead of black, and she had on a pair of little half glasses on her sharp-featured face. She peered at me over the top of the glasses.

When I told her who I was, she said, "Of course. I remember you now. How could I forget that red hair?"

It wouldn't be red much longer, because I had Vicky's hair dye with me, but I didn't tell Miss Arnold that.

"I remember the day you came here," she said. "It must have been more than twenty years ago."

"It was," I said. "Do you happen to remember anything about my family?"

"We don't give out that kind of information," she said. "Besides, I don't have it."

"I didn't think so. I was just wondering."

Her face softened a little then, which surprised me. I don't recall that she'd ever softened when I'd been in her class.

"I do remember your father, though," she said. "I don't know his name, of course, but he had red hair, just like yours. I remember his saying that they'd never give you up if only they could afford to keep you."

I had an uneasy feeling.

"You said *they*. What did my mother look like?"

Miss Arnold stared off over my head as if the shadowy corner of the room might hold a preserved image of the past.

"She looked nothing like you. She was a cute little thing, short and blonde, with pretty blue eyes. You do have the blue eyes, however."

I felt hollow inside, all the way down to my toes, and I stood there looking stupidly at Miss Arnold for a few seconds while she waited for me to make some kind of comment. But there was really nothing for me to say, except that I'd been wrong about Vicky, fatally wrong, and I wasn't going to mention that to Miss Arnold. Or to anyone. I left as soon as I could and got away from there.

———

Mexico isn't so bad. The climate's nice, and the ocean's pretty and blue where I am. I don't speak the language very well yet, but I have a lot of money, and that pretty much takes care of the language problem. There's plenty to drink, and there's—there are— plenty of women. Funny, but I can't seem to get interested in them. And when I do get interested, nothing happens, if you know what I mean. There's no shame in that, they tell me, and I guess they don't care, as long as I pay them. Maybe if they were redheads it would be different, but I try not to think too much about that. So all in all, things are going great. I guess you could say I'm sitting on top of the world.

Just Kryptonite

Jeremiah Healy

I

"Awright, people, listen up."

Detective Sergeant Ellen O'Hare watched Captain Cotter arrange his notes on the podium in the Squad Room. The rest of the Boston homicide detectives broke off their chatter with the reinforcements from the state police, all in plainclothes. Nudging each other and settling with coffee into chairs, they centered the cups on the little half desks attached to the arms. Jaded seniors stuck in a poor high school.

Cotter looked out at them. Dour, seeming five years older than three weeks ago. O'Hare thought, the Cap doesn't think we're going to catch this guy.

"We're at the one-month mark, eight days since he killed the last one. For you people joining us from the State, similarities first. All three victims were female, thirties, between five-two and five-five in height. Black hair, brown eyes. All businesswomen, reasonably successful, sharp dressers but not flashy. All met the guy in a bar, took him back to their place. All strangled in the bedroom."

Cotter paused for a moment. "All Jewish."

A state trooper grunted, everybody looking over at him except Moss Aaron. Cotter had been having Aaron interview the surviving families. Aaron just kept his eyes on Cotter, on the podium really, his bald head catching the fluorescent light like a puddle of rainwater.

Cotter said, "Now the differences. Each woman from a different business: advertising, retailing, law. Only one was religious, and then only sometimes. The first in her own house, the second in her condo, the third in her apartment. So far as we can tell, none of the vics knew any of the others. Also a different bar each time, but he always leaves a trademark on the nightstand. A matchbook from whatever bar it is."

The captain paused again. A statie, not the one who'd grunted, said, "Forensics?"

Cotter looked at the trooper a minute, just to let him know that next time he should wait, then said, "Greer?"

Giles Greer from the Identification Lab stood up but didn't move to the podium. O'Hare caught Jack Drury flopping his wrist over. The guy next to Drury stifled a laugh. Ellen O'Hare thought, if there was one thing I could change about Drury, it would be his attitude toward gays. O'Hare had been interested in Drury ever since they'd gone through the academy together, just after he'd gotten back from the Army. After a while, though, she decided it was like Barbra Streisand in *The Way We Were,* chasing after BMOC Robert Redford. She'd never catch him, and if she did, she'd never be able to change him. Or hold on to him.

Greer straightened his tie and took a breath. O'Hare always liked Greer. He wouldn't stand out in a crowd, but he never wore anything but a sport jacket until after Thanksgiving, always saying the cold Boston winds never got to him. She also liked the way he didn't let the hazing get to him. She never thought he was gay, either, just a quiet, sensitive guy who did a miserable job well.

Greer said, "The victims all experienced intercourse shortly before their deaths."

Some of the staties smiled behind their coffee cups. Greer's voice was high and a little squeaky, like the guy who always was editor of the yearbook.

Greer appeared not to notice the smiles. "Each was found in bed, strangled by a towel from their own bathrooms. The killer twisted the towel into a braid and left it around the throats. None of the victims had skin under the fingernails, and apparently the perp used a condom each time."

A third statie, a black woman wearing an elaborate watch, said, "Prints on the foil?"

Greer said, "Just the victim's. He apparently has her, each one, open them and takes the condoms themselves away with him."

The statie didn't say "neat," but Ellen O'Hare thought that's what the woman was thinking. It was what O'Hare had thought after the first one.

The statie who'd grunted tried to redeem himself. "Pubic hairs?"

"Only from the victims. The guy combs them afterward."

"Combs them?"

"That's right."

"Christ."

The statie who'd asked about Forensics said, "Anything from the bartenders or waitresses?"

From her chair, Ellen O'Hare said, "Not much."

Heads swiveled to look at her. "Each woman sat at the bar. The perp came over, sat down, bought them a drink or two, then they'd leave."

O'Hare anticipated the next question she'd get from one of the staties. "None of the women were hooking on the side, none of them were regulars in the places he found them. All of them were on a quiet night, Tuesday or Wednesday."

O'Hare noticed the black woman glancing down at her fancy

watch. O'Hare didn't have to. She knew it was Wednesday, 3:00 P.M.

Captain Cotter said, "Another thing."

Everybody turned back to him.

"Apparently the guy slips the women a mickey. Greer?"

Greer reeled off a twelve-syllable phrase that had the staties exchanging shrugs.

Cotter said, "Works fast, makes them just a little groggy. That might be a help to you."

The black woman said, "How do you mean?"

Cotter said, "So far, we've had Aaron on the families, Drury on the vics' employers, and O'Hare on the bars."

Ellen O'Hare held her breath and sat a little higher in the chair.

Cotter engaged their eyes. "And that's the way it's gonna stay."

O'Hare exhaled and settled back.

"We want you State people out redoing the house-to-house."

No groaning, a credit to Cotter's command presence.

"Somebody in one of the neighborhoods or buildings must have seen or heard something. No more questions, I'll divide you up."

There were no more questions.

———

Jack Drury set his cup on O'Hare's desk and said, "Cap's loyal, you shouldn't have sweated it."

It made Ellen O'Hare angry that Drury could read her so well, until she realized that meant Drury had been watching her during the briefing.

"Jack, the Cap's very loyal, only he can't wait forever on getting these closed."

"Look, El, the first one, it seemed like maybe it was family or work, so he put Moss and me on those and you on the bars. Made sense, we've got seniority on the squad. But then when it seemed like the bars were the thread, he kept you on them."

Moss Aaron said, "And he was right to do it. You'll maybe see something they would have and we wouldn't."

O'Hare was pleased that Drury and Aaron were backing her up, even just to herself. Especially pleased that Drury was. She was about to suggest a drink, knowing that Aaron would beg off, Wednesdays being the night he had visitation with his kids. Then Cotter came around the corner, a sheet of yellow paper in his hand and another year on his face.

The captain said, "We got number four."

II

The uniform said, "Chain on the door wasn't engaged."

Jack Drury took out a notepad in the living room and said, "How'd you get in?"

"Superintendent has a key to every unit in the building."

"Doorman?"

The uniform shook his head. Ellen O'Hare hadn't asked about a doorman because there was no desk for one in the foyer or lobby of the building. Drury missed things like that, but at five-eleven and maybe one-eighty, he looked like a homicide detective, so he'd gotten to be one a good two years before Ellen O'Hare had. She knew she couldn't complain about making it by age thirty-three, and she wouldn't, even to herself, if Drury hadn't beaten her to it.

Walking deeper into the apartment, O'Hare adjusted the shoulder strap of her handbag, a big Dooney & Bourke that set her back over two hundred dollars. It was worth it, though, allowing her to appear to be any kind of professional woman while still having plenty of room to carry a six-round Detective's Special, two autoloaders, handcuffs, and a leather sap.

O'Hare drew even with a skinny ID man named Tuohey bending over the breakfast counter. O'Hare couldn't ever remember meeting a fat ID officer.

Tuohey was dusting the countertop for prints.

O'Hare said, "Anything?"

"Maybe. Looks like Ms. Deborah Shapiro was a good housekeeper. Everything's pretty clean, so maybe." `

"But probably not."

Tuohey shrugged. "She gave him a drink, she washed the glasses and dried them before hitting the sack."

"Or he did afterward."

Tuohey shrugged again.

O'Hare moved toward the bedroom, dreading the view once she got past Moss Aaron at the threshold.

Aaron turned his head halfway as he felt her close on him. "Consistent bastard."

Deborah Shapiro. She had pointy breasts that hadn't yet gone flaccid. The towel around her neck was burgundy, the cheeks blue and bluer as they shaded into the dark-blue lips, tongue protruding, eyelids at half-mast. God, Ellen thought, why don't they ever look even just a little alive.

Aaron said, "Medical Examiner figures last night, midnight onward."

Tuesday into Wednesday. O'Hare said, "We know what she did for a living?"

"Computers."

"Designing them?"

"Selling."

O'Hare moved to the nightstand. In a small, clean ashtray was a box of matches with the word "Jeeves" in flourished script.

Ellen thought, another trademark.

From the hall, O'Hare heard Greer's voice, echoing as if he were in a sound chamber.

Aaron and Drury were both turned and on their way to the bathroom door by the time O'Hare got to them. She elbowed Drury a little so she could see around him.

Greer was scrunched under the sink, both legs folding around the pedestal and arching on his back like a wrestler. O'Hare thought, he's in better shape than I thought.

Greer used a short plastic dowel to hold up the toilet seat while he shined a penlight on the underside. "I think I've got something."

O'Hare could see Greer's leg spasm under him. "Greer, you all right?"

"Just a cramp." In a singsong voice, he said, "Definitely a latent, though. Nice one, tented arch, maybe the left middle finger after touching something sticky."

"Bingo," said Drury.

"Just one marker, actually," said Greer.

O'Hare said, "I've got to hit the bar she was at. You've got a latent, maybe you should come with me."

"I'll be a while. Take Tuohey. The experience should broaden his horizons."

On the way out, Drury said, "I don't want to know what Giles Queer thinks broadens somebody's horizons."

O'Hare said, "Jack, I wish you wouldn't say that," knowing it did no good.

III

Jeeves turned out to be a butcher-block-and-fern joint around the corner from a bank building. As Ellen O'Hare stopped inside the door to let her eyes adjust to the dim lighting, Tuohey bumped into her with his sample case.

"Sorry."

"That's okay," said O'Hare, rubbing the back of her thigh and picturing the bruise she'd have within hours.

A hearty male voice said, "You can take any table. We won't be crowded till five or so."

O'Hare walked up to the bar and opened her identification. "Police. Got a minute?"

The bartender was a young surfer-boy with nice forearms, the blonde hair curling over corded muscles. Then he moved his lips as he read her ID. Ellen thought, the lights are on but nobody's home.

He looked up seriously. "What can I do for you?"

"What's your name?"

"Billy."

"Billy what?"

"Oh, sorry. Billy Bucholz."

"Mr. Bucholz—"

"Billy, please."

"Billy . . ." O'Hare noticed a fishbowl of matches on the bar-top near a laminated post. "You know a woman named Deborah Shapiro?"

"Don't think so."

O'Hare took out the Polaroid of the head and neck of the body on the bed. "I'm sorry, Billy, but this is kind of rough."

"Jesus," said Bucholz.

"Recognize her?"

"Yeah, just. She was like in here last night."

"Alone?"

"Came in that way. Left with a guy."

"Did you recognize him?"

"No. Never saw him before."

"You talk with either one of them?"

"Not really. When she sat down I said, like 'I'm Billy,' and she said her name was Debby."

Inspired, thought O'Hare. "And the guy?"

"He didn't say anything to me except his drink order."

"Which was?"

"Beer. Draft."

Consistent, like Moss Aaron said. "And hers?"

"Sex-on-the-Beach."

O'Hare had tried one once. It was so sweet it made her teeth hurt. "Tell me what happened."

"Well, like I said, she came in and—"

"When?"

"When? Like, around now, four, four-thirty tops."

"And him?"

"Not sure. Maybe around the same time. He was just a regular-looking guy, didn't pay any attention to him."

"What about her?"

"Her?"

"How was she dressed?"

"Oh. Like for work, only . . ."

"Only what?"

"Only maybe like, a little special, you know?"

"Like she was meeting a date?"

"No, no. They didn't seem to know each other ahead of time. More like, she wore a little something extra to work because she was hoping to pick somebody up, maybe they'd take her to heaven."

O'Hare moved her tongue around inside her mouth. "So she was sitting here and he did what?"

"Don't know. I mean, like he must have come sit down and started talking with her, you know, but I didn't actually see him take the stool."

"Where?"

"Where what?"

"Where were they sitting?"

"Oh. Over by the pole there."

Bucholz gestured toward the fishbowl.

O'Hare said, "You clean the fishbowl or the pole?"

"Clean it?"

"Yes. Wipe them off or—"

"Oh, yeah. Well, kind of. With the Windex on the bowl, any-way. Otherwise, it looks like hell, all the people handling it to get matches and all. Don't know why they do it."

"Do what?"

"Take the matches. I mean, like nobody smokes anymore, right?"

O'Hare nodded to Tuohey. He looked dubious, but he started setting up to dust the bowl and pole.

The bartender said, "So, like what happened, anyway?"

O'Hare said, "Can you describe the man who sat down next to the woman?"

"Describe him? Wow, like average, you know?"

"Height?"

"Average."

"Weight?"

"Average, medium whatever."

"Age?"

"I don't know. Maybe a little older than you."

O'Hare stopped for a moment, but the kid was just being re-sponsive. Tuohey wanted to laugh but didn't. O'Hare knew he'd save it for back at the lab.

"Hair color?"

"Brown. It was a rug, though."

"A toupee?"

"Yeah. Probably a bald guy. They always wear these stupid rugs, like it makes them look young, I guess they think."

O'Hare took him through eyes ("Didn't notice"), mustache ("No"), scars ("Like, how would I see any of those?"), and everything else she could think of without much help. "How about his voice?"

"Couldn't tell you. Low, maybe?"

"You mean deep?"

"No, not like some opera guy. I mean like, he didn't talk loud but it sounded smooth, like one of those guys on the easy-listening stations."

"You hear anything at all he told her?"

"Sorry. I had like customers, you know?"

"I know."

"I didn't even hear the joke."

"The joke?"

"Yeah. The guy, he must have made a joke, because all of a sudden she laughs and says 'Just Kryptonite.'"

"Wait a minute. She says, 'Just Kryptonite'?"

"Yeah. Like, it's the punch line of some joke he tells her, and she says it back to him, like to let him know she thinks it's funny. That's when I knew she was over the limit."

"Drunk, you mean?"

"Yeah. Funny, too. She seemed fine when she came in here, otherwise I don't serve her to start with, not with all the drunk-driving stuff around. But the guy bought her the second round, and she goes off to the bathroom, and she's maybe halfway through the drink tops when she laughs like that and two minutes later she's climbing all over him as they head on out."

The mickey. "Anything else you remember?"

"Nope."

"Anything at all."

"Sorry, ma'am."

This time Tuohey did laugh.

————————

Ellen O'Hare locked and bolted the door to her apartment. From Jeeves, she'd given Tuohey a lift back to the lab, him telling her he couldn't get anything usable, her not being surprised. As she'd typed up her report of the interview with Billy Bucholz, that's what she told herself was the problem with life. No more real surprises. At least, no more good ones.

The bathroom was right off the bedroom, which O'Hare liked even though most people would have wanted it off a hallway. She liked being able to just pop in and pop out without going into a corridor. O'Hare turned on the hot water halfway but didn't put in the plug, since it took a good five minutes for the really hot water to reach her floor no matter how many times she complained to the super about it.

Back in the bedroom, O'Hare put her Detective's Special in the drawer of her night table. She didn't envy the cops with kids, who had to keep their weapons unloaded at home and even then lock them away. Out of everybody's reach, unfortunately so if needed.

O'Hare stripped in front of the full-length mirror on the bathroom door, noticing, as she knew she would, the bruise on the back of her leg from Tuohey's sample case. Otherwise, though, she thought she looked pretty good. Black Irish hair, not "big" hair, but full and lustrous. Shoulders maybe an inch too wide on each side, but tapering down to a real waist and reasonable hips for the kind of job she had. Striking, if not beautiful. Then she remembered somebody saying that about the second vic and shivered.

Back in the bathroom, O'Hare plugged the tub and turned the faucet on full blast, sprinkling in some bubble bath that had the word "Aspen" on it, for "Relaxing After a Difficult Day at Work." Not waiting for the tub to fill, she climbed in, the hot water rising around her making Ellen think about Billy Bucholz and his nice forearms. Forgetting the crack about her age and the "ma'am," she gave him a brain and let him take her to heaven.

IV

Moss Aaron sat on the corner of O'Hare's desk and said, "The mother just kept crying. It gets to me."

Jack Drury said, "What does?"

"The sight of another human in grief. The bodies, they long ago lost the ability to shock, get me? But the people, the families, that's what turns you over inside."

Drury said, "You get anything from them?"

"Zip."

"El, how about the bar?"

"Like the others. Off-day, off-peak. He sidles up to one by herself, not a regular. He talks to her, quietly. Then he manages to slip her a nighty-night, and pretty soon he's taking her home. Seems he's also got a sense of humor."

Aaron said, "How do you mean?"

O'Hare told them what Bucholz had said about Kryptonite.

Drury said, "I don't get it."

O'Hare sighed. As Moss described the Superman story, Ellen thought, maybe Jack isn't worth catching.

Then Drury said, "I still don't see how that's gonna help us. But here's something that might. I go to Shapiro's computer place—it's a whole building, like three hundred employees. Takes me maybe an hour to get that one of these three hundred just got passed over for a job on account of the vic."

Aaron said, "I thought she was in sales?"

"Yeah, well. It seems like a month ago she got the promotion this guy—Richard Womack—had his heart set on."

O'Hare said, "A month."

Aaron said, "Nice coincidence, we're about a month into these killings."

"Nice timing, anyway. So I see this Womack, and he's diddling with his coffee mug, one of those Cape Cod things you see at all the tourist traps? Well, he's turning it around and around in his hands, and he starts complaining. Complaining about his car bills, complaining about the stock market, complaining about this other guy two days ago who was wasting his time, handing him a résumé with two typos in it and Womack throws it back at the guy."

O'Hare said, "This taking us somewhere good?"

"Then I show Womack the photos of the other vics, and he says to put them down on his desk, so I do that, and he stands up and looks from one to the other. Kind of lingering over them, cool as you please, and then he says, no, he doesn't recognize any of them."

Aaron said, "Neither did Shapiro's family. Or any of the families, for that matter."

"Then this Womack says, 'If there's nothing else? . . . ' So I tell him, no, there isn't, and he lets me gather up the photos and put them back in the envelope."

Drury stopped, looking from one to the other.

Ellen O'Hare said, "He didn't want to touch the photos."

"Bingo."

Aaron said, "The way those women looked, who would?"

O'Hare said, "The point is, the guy throws a résumé back at some idiot, but didn't want to put his prints on something a cop's going to take away."

Drury crossed his arms and rocked back in his chair, a big grin on his face.

Aaron said, "So?"

Drury said, "So, I had a talk about this guy with Giles Queer over at the Lab."

O'Hare said, "Jack . . ." as Aaron said, "Again, so?"

Drury looked at him. "So, little Miss Apprentice and I are going calling."

O'Hare felt Aaron glancing at her, expecting her to take offense. "Why?"

"Because I need somebody with a pocketbook."

O'Hare said, "Handbag."

"Whatever."

Aaron said, "And you need a handbag for . . ."

This time O'Hare smiled at Drury and thought, maybe there's hope.

V

Richard Womack said, "I thought we were all through?"

"Not quite," said Drury.

O'Hare watched Womack as Drury explained the probationary detective scam. Womack was about the right medium-everything to fit each description of the perp. He spun the mug around constantly, even though it appeared empty.

Womack said, "I don't get it. Why wasn't she here with you first time around, to learn how you ask questions?"

Drury didn't answer, so O'Hare did. "Detective Drury is trying to spare my feelings, sir. You see, I'm not experienced enough yet to watch an initial interrogation without getting some sense of what you already said."

Womack said, "Jesus Christ, let's get on with it, then. I've got product to try to move over the dead body of the last person who couldn't move it."

O'Hare bit back a response and put a smile on her face as

Drury took Womack through the motions. When Drury got Womack to move over to the cabinet to pull out a file on Deborah Shapiro, O'Hare used a handkerchief to switch Womack's mug for the one she'd bought and scuffed up and carried in her handbag to Womack's office.

————

Jack Drury leaned toward the teller's cage and said, "What do you mean, Greer's off?"

Tuohey blinked at him, pointing to a watch that said 5:20 P.M. "Just what I said. His dinner break."

Drury hefted by a corner the baggie with Womack's mug in it. "We got something here he's gotta check against that latent from the Shapiro scene."

"I can do that."

Drury said, "No, better it's Greer."

Tuohey's face showed he'd taken offense.

O'Hare said, "It was Greer's idea, that's all. When will he be back?"

Tuohey pouted a little. "Hour maybe. I can check your elimination prints there, tell you whether any's a possible, okay?"

O'Hare looked at Drury. "Okay, Jack?"

Drury handed over the bag by the corner. "No. Let it wait for Greer. I've got other things to do, anyway."

————

Two hours later and upstairs, Captain Cotter said, "Greer's sure?"

Drury grinned. "Positive. Fifteen points of comparison when we left him, and he was still counting."

O'Hare said, "I looked through the glass, too, Cap. No question."

Cotter frowned. "The guy worked in the same office as she did. Maybe he stopped in one night, used the john."

"Ten people at their company say they wouldn't have said two words to each other since a month ago."

"The print could be that old."

O'Hare said, "Could be, but Tuohey said the rest of the house was immaculate, and Greer seemed as convinced."

Cotter was still frowning. "We can't go in at night without a warrant."

Drury said, "We wouldn't want to."

Cotter and O'Hare looked at him.

Drury said, "I just got the record check back on him. He's got a permit for household."

Cotter said, "Computer tell you what he's got?"

"Walther, PPK."

"Swell."

O'Hare said, "Doesn't mean he hasn't bought something bigger out of state."

Cotter said, "The Walther's big enough. Kevlar vests all around."

Cotter got on the phone to the emergency assistant district attorney while Drury called to get some uniforms over to Womack's apartment house right away. O'Hare took her weapon from her handbag and clipped it on her skirt over the right hip and under her blazer.

———

At ten minutes past midnight, Aaron arrived at the stakeout with an arrest warrant. Cotter and Aaron went up the front stairs, O'Hare and Drury the back, each team with two uniforms behind it. Womack didn't answer, one of the uniforms using a fourteen-pound sledge borrowed from Narcotics to go through the door.

They needn't have rushed.

VI

The first reporter, from one of Boston's two dailies, asked, "Was there any motive for the crimes?"

Ellen O'Hare thought Captain Cotter was trying to speak over the thicket of microphones in his face. "No motive that seems to link all of them, unless the rest were cover for the one that mattered to him."

The second reporter, from a television station, asked, "Did Womack leave any note?"

"No."

The third reporter, from a radio station, asked, "Did he use his own gun?"

"The preliminary indications are that he did. We'll have to wait until—"

"Did he know any of the victims?"

"—until we have a full report from the Medical Examiner and from Ballistics. And yes, he knew at least one of the victims."

"The last one, Deborah Saperstein?"

"Deborah Shapiro, madam. She's murdered, you could at least—"

"What was the nature of their—"

"—get her name right. They—Womack and Ms. Shapiro—worked at the same company."

"Was there some kind of political infighting then as motive?"

"We haven't come to any firm conclusions at this—"

"What does her family think?"

"I'd say ask them except I don't think you should."

"What was it that sent Womack over the edge?"

"If you mean why did he commit the crimes—"

"I mean why'd he commit suicide?"

"Good police work. Now if you'll excuse me."

"Captain Cot—"

"Just one more—"

"Jesus, how does a jerk like that get to carry a badge."

Ellen O'Hare slipped through a corridor door before the pack could turn.

———

"Jack?"

Drury swung his head toward O'Hare and pointed to the phone cradled on his shoulder. Ellen waved that she could wait and did.

Drury hung up and said, "How was the press conference?"

"Pretty tame. You up for a drink after all this?"

Drury looked up at the clock on the wall over his desk. "Can't, El. Got a date."

"Oh. No problem."

"With all the overtime on this mess, it's really cut into my social life, you know?"

"Yeah. Mine, too."

"See ya."

Ellen O'Hare slumped into a chair and tried to remember her last meal. Dinner last night? Yeah. And a stale doughnut on the stakeout about—

"Ellen?"

She looked up into Giles Greer's composed face. "Oh, sorry. Daydreaming."

"You sure you're all right?"

O'Hare started to snap, then pulled it back in time. "I'm fine, Greer."

"We should talk."

"Fine, but not now, okay. I'm—"

"Ellen, there was something wrong with the latent."

O'Hare thought that if the doughnut was still there, it had just turned over.

———

Greer came back to the small, round table with their drinks, a light beer for him and a piña colada for her.

O'Hare said, "Thanks for keeping the little umbrella out of it." She took a swallow. "God, that's good. But I've got to have some munchies, too."

"In a minute." Greer lowered his voice and leaned over the table. "We've got to talk."

O'Hare decided his voice wasn't nearly as squeaky as it sounded trying to fill a room. "About the latent."

"Right. Remember when I found it, I thought it seemed a little sticky around the edges?"

"I remember you saying something like he stuck his finger—"

"Yes, well, after you and Drury left me last night, I ran some chemical analysis on the print."

"And?"

"And. . . Ellen, the print was lifted."

"From where?"

"I don't mean stolen. I mean the latent on the toilet seat was lifted from somewhere else and put on the seat."

"Oh, Greer, come on."

"I didn't believe it myself, not until I started studying it back in the lab. Then I realized I'd better keep it to myself, until I was sure. Now I'm sure and I realize I'd better keep it to only a few people."

O'Hare felt a little foggy. "Why?"

"Ellen, who do you know who could lift and transfer a print like that?"

A shrug. "Lots of people."

"Like who, for example?"

"Like any cop . . . Jesus."

Greer just looked at her. She felt it sinking in.

O'Hare took another jolt of the drink. "Sweet suffering Jesus."

Greer said, "I don't know what to do."

"Wait a minute. Last night, you said the prints matched."

Greer lowered his voice again, patiently. "The prints do match, Ellen. That's the point." He hesitated. "The latent was set up to match this Womack's prints."

O'Hare could feel the fatigue getting the better of her and shook her head to clear it. "But why?"

"Maybe to cover his tracks, give us a killer who conveniently commits suicide."

O'Hare could see it, barely. "Maybe."

"Or maybe just to set us up to look bad when he starts in again after we supposedly closed the case over Womack's grave."

O'Hare went to stand, her knees feeling a little wobbly. "We should talk . . . again tomorrow."

"You're beat, Ellen. I'm sorry. Let's get you home."

VII

When Ellen O'Hare awoke, it took a minute to remember she was in her own bed, glowing. Her arms and legs felt deliciously heavy, her head pounding just a little. She could just hear the shower going through the bathroom door. If she had to pick one word for the way she felt, it would have been dreamy.

God, was Jack Drury wrong about Giles Greer.

Greer had gotten her home, and in the door, and kissed her. His tongue came alive in her mouth, and hers in his. They practically stripped each other coming through the living room, clothes and guns and shoes scattered along the trail. Once in bed, though, he was sweet and slow, gentle and teasing. He almost made you ache for it, but when it came . . .

Ellen shook her head, which made it hurt, but only a little. She was just thinking about getting up to fix something for them to eat when the bathroom door opened and Greer came out, hair wet, a towel clutched sarong-style around his waist.

He said, "I'm sorry. I was afraid the shower would wake you up."

"That's okay, Giles. A nice change of pace for me."

His smile toward her was shy. "You're a nice change of pace for me, too."

O'Hare just lolled her head on the pillow, watching him take off the towel. Greer was in great shape, much better than she'd have guessed. "Was the water hot?"

The smile got even shyer. "Not very."

"Jeez, Giles. I'm sorry, the landlord—"

"Don't worry about it."

O'Hare levered up onto an elbow to check the time, thinking about Greer in only his sports coat in late November and not registering the matchbook from the bar next to the clock radio. "Doesn't anything ever bother you?"

"Just kryptonite."

As Ellen O'Hare watched him twist the towel into a braid, she tried very, very hard to remember where she'd left her gun.

Twilight's Last Gleaming

Michael Collins

The moans and cries of violent passion reached like a searing tongue of flame into the dark silence of the storage room where they had me locked. From the bedroom on the far side of the small cabin, intense and urgent. Almost savage. Even huddled under the two blankets in the cold of the cabin, my head on a hard sack of rice, I could not escape the gasps and groans and soft, ecstatic screams. I closed my eyes, but that made it worse. My mind saw the shine of slick bodies, the thrusting and lifting in locked rhythm, the slow and liquid dance of entangled skin and flesh in the night cabin. A heedless and ancient animal intensity in the cries and moans. A long, piercing shriek and guttural cry. Then silence.

And after a time the low delight of small laughter, and quiet murmur of far-off voices, rising and falling in the silent cabin with only the mountain wind outside.

They were not the sounds I had been afraid I would hear in the remote forest cabin. Not the terrible screams of pain and death, but the ecstatic screams of passion. A different violence. A smaller death.

The kidnaping had been all over the headlines and TV news. Gretchen Bayer, nineteen, super athlete, magazine cover model, Olympic skier, and rookie professional soccer player, had been kidnaped in broad daylight from a shopping mall in Carter

Creek, Nevada, by two men who had vanished into the Sierras, with her kicking and cursing in the back of their old and battered Ford Bronco. No one in Nevada had a clue who the men were, or why they had kidnaped the young woman. The FBI had taken charge.

Klaus Bayer, her distraught father, paced his Los Angeles office in front of walls of framed photos and magazine covers of Gretchen in action. "It's been twenty-four hours, Mr. Fortune, and neither the FBI nor the cops have a goddamned clue."

"No ransom calls? No note?"

"Nothing," Klaus Bayer raged. "They're combing the mountains with helicopters and dogs, but so far zilch, *nada*. If she isn't dead, she will be soon, unless someone stops those monsters."

I tried to calm him. "The FBI knows its work, Mr. Bayer."

He snorted in derision. "I don't trust them to think of Gretchen first, or even last. FBI, BATF, state police. You know their record. Waco, Ruby Ridge, Attica."

When he had asked the LAPD if they knew a PI experienced in the mountains, a detective who knew me had told him about the time I had to chase a man through the Guatemala mountains, and then make my way out alone. Bayer had immediately summoned me to the L.A. office.

"Go up there, Mr. Fortune. Find her first. Make a deal with those criminals. Name your price. Whatever it takes. Spread money around. All expenses. She's my only daughter."

And, I thought, somewhat unkindly, his only meal ticket. But the money was right, and the location, Carter Creek, made me remember another LAPD detective who knew me: Detective-Sergeant Leonard Tucker, who had retired from the Los Angeles Police Department six years ago. He and his wife had moved to Carter Creek to join the growing colony of ex-LAPD officers there. Tucker and I didn't think much alike, and he had never been exactly a friend, but we had worked cases together, I had held up my end, and we got along. It gave me an idea of how I could possibly do the job Klaus Bayer wanted.

I've been in enough small towns to know they tend to be suspicious of strangers, and protective of their own. Especially Carter Creek—a right-wing bastion highly distrustful of government. They don't love the FBI or BATF in Carter Creek. If the kidnapers were locals, the Feds weren't going to get much help.

But if they were locals, someone up there would know where they were, or, at least, where to look.

———

Deep among the first row of mountains of the Sierras, Carter Creek was a mining town once, silver and copper, but now lived on tourists who came for the boating and fishing in summer, the skiing and hunting in winter. Klaus Bayer had first taken Gretchen there in the summers for the water sports, then for the winter sports, and finally to protect her from the temptations of Southern California. When you're nineteen, and earning millions, the temptations are many, but from what I had already heard, and what I read flying up, Gretchen Bayer was all sports and business, day and night.

When I drove into Carter Creek there were so many suits, stenciled jackets, and uniforms, it looked like the FBI, BATF, and Idaho police were occupying the town, with the newshounds buzzing around them. The locals were conspicuous by their absence.

I checked into a rustic motel and called ex-detective-sergeant Tucker. He agreed to meet me at a roadhouse outside town.

———

"Why do you want to find these guys, Dan?"

He's a big man, Tucker, burly and gruff in the way all cops used to be before the college grads and women moved in. I had bought him a Coors. I took a Red Tail ale. He noticed the difference.

"Her father hired me to find them first. He's frantic about the lack of any word, and he's worried about the Feds."

"Yeah," Tucker said. He had had his own problems with the Bureau. "If you found them, then what?"

"I try to talk them down. Buy them off. Scare the hell out of them. Make them realize what real deep shit they're in."

Tucker shook his head. "Not these guys, Dan."

"Then you *do* know who they are?" It was what I had counted on. Or at least hoped for. Tucker was one of those old cops who made it their business to know everything that happened on their tour. "They're locals?"

"I know *about* them," he corrected, "and they're not exactly locals."

"What the hell does that mean?"

"It means they live alone way back in the Sierras, and not many people in town have a clue where, or give a damn. One of them's pretty much a total nut."

"What kind of nut?"

"The father's a right-wing survivalist, government-hater, and loner. Can't even get along with the radical antigovernment militia types we have here. The son's only half as nutty."

"Father and son?" It had more than a whiff of the Old West. Tombstone. The Clanton clan. "They have names?"

"Carter, that's the father, and Sepp Mason. They hunt, fish, live off the land, don't show up in town more than once, twice a year, if that. Sometimes you don't see them for two or three years." He drank his beer. "The Feds're gonna have their hands full just finding them, and then it'll really get hard. They're armed, paranoid, and dangerous as all hell."

The grim possibilities of an almost certain bloodbath when the FBI and BATF found the kidnapers lay between us on the scarred tavern table. I ordered another round. The barman who brought our beers watched me stone-faced. He knew I wasn't any kind of police, not with one arm, but I was a stranger talking to an ex-cop.

I waited until the barman left, lowered my voice. "Then I really need to talk them down before the Feds find them. I know how it works in a place like Carter Creek, Lennie. Some people up here have to know where the Masons would hole up."

He rotated his beer glass in his hands and looked back toward the bartender. Then he stood up. "I'll see what I can do. Where do I contact you?"

I told him the name of my motel.

————

The numbers on the dashboard clock changed from 1:32 to 1:33 A.M. in the dark interior of the mud-caked Jeep Cherokee. The three of them had picked me up at my motel five minutes earlier. I kept my hand on the little Sig-Sauer in my pocket.

The tall, wiry man wearing surplus forest camouflage fatigues sat beside me in the gloom of the backseat. The driver, an equally skinny guy, half the size and age of my companion, also wore forest camos, and had trout flies in his floppy hat. The man in the front passenger seat shifted sideways to look back at me. Large and muscular in blue sweatpants and a red sweatshirt with Carter Creek High lettered on it, he was clean-shaven and losing his hair.

"Tucker says you want to talk to the kidnapers. Why?"

"Because the woman's father thinks it could get ugly if someone doesn't find them before the Feds do."

"He doesn't trust the Feds?"

"He doesn't trust the Feds or the kidnapers."

"What does he expect you to do if you find them?"

"Make sure she's okay." I repeated what I had told Tucker,

even though I was pretty sure Tucker had filled them in on our entire conversation. They were testing me. "Negotiate. Pay them off. Find out what they want and talk them out of it. Whatever I can. At the very least, her father figures if I'm there the Feds'll think more about the woman's safety, and not be so trigger happy." The two in camos snorted. I took that as anti-Fed encouragement of Klaus Bayer's point of view, and went on. "If Tucker talked to you folks, I guess that means he thinks you can get me to the kidnapers."

The spokesman said something low to the driver, and the Cherokee pulled off the road into an open field silver in the moonlight. Tall trees rose dense around the clearing, and mountains towered pale blue in the moonlight. All three of them got out, and walked away to confer.

When they finally stepped back to the Cherokee, the spokesman said, "We want you to understand something, Fortune. Me, and Ben," he nodded to the tall, wiry one, "and Samuel," a nod to the scrawny driver, "we respect the Masons, even honor them. Carter and Sepp live their own lives their own way, and don't give a damn about what anyone else thinks or does as long they're left alone."

"Patrick Henry and the antifederalists," I said.

"What?"

"Back at the time of the Revolution, Patrick Henry and others had the same idea. They hated the Constitution and everything in it. They wanted to live by their own rules, and to hell with everyone else. I guess bad ideas never die."

For the first time the driver spoke. "Shit. This guy's a goddamn lib—"

The spokesman snapped, "Shut up, Sam. This isn't about philosophy or politics. We agreed on that." He glanced away toward the shadows of the mountains where one distant peak poked a snowcapped summit above the lower ones. "You better know exactly why we're going to help you, Fortune."

"Because kidnaping's a little too much rugged individualism?"

The driver growled, but the spokesman ignored him. "Because the Masons have no use for money. The old man says it's the root of hell. They hate money, and everything it represents. If they need anything they can't make, grow, or kill, they come down and trade for it or steal it."

"Then why . . . ?" I stopped. All three of them were watching me. I didn't feel too pleasant. "What do they want with a young woman?"

"Yeah," the tall, wiry one said. "What."

———

For the first half of the next day, the surly driver bounced and bumped the Cherokee along rutted dirt roads deep into the Sierras. Toward 3:00 P.M. we parked, and the tall, wiry one named Ben, nearly invisible in his forest camos, led me up, down, and around mountain slopes through the thick stands of Ponderosa pines. It was near dusk, a sharp wind rising, when he located what he thought was the Masons' cabin. In the twilight, an enormous Stars and Stripes whipped at the top of a flagpole, and a Confederate battle flag blew below it.

Ben scouted, and when he returned, nodded to the flags. "It's the place, all right, and they're here. I didn't see the woman, but the Bronco is hid in the trees out back. You're on your own from here, Fortune. Be careful."

He did not shake my hand or wish me luck, we were not on the same side except for this one instance, and I watched him vanish through the Ponderosas in the fading light feeling alone, exposed, and vulnerable.

When my nerves had calmed down, and I finally recovered

from the long half-day climb, I worked my way cautiously along the edge of the tall pines trying to see if the girl was there too. It had been more than two days now since the kidnaping, and I did not know what I was going to find.

I neither saw nor heard the man until he stood behind me like an apparition.

"Stand up."

He was not a big man. Youngish, five-eleven, 170 pounds. He looked bigger. It was in the shoulders. In the slim waist, no hips, flat ass. He wore mismatched bits and pieces of surplus German army uniform from World War II. Desert boots, field-gray service jacket, khaki drill shorts tight against his powerful thighs, and the 1943 replacement field cap. Afrika Corps. He would be Sepp.

He held an M-16, the muzzle pointed at me. I stood up slowly.

"FBI?" he snapped. "BATF?"

"Private investigator."

He liked that even less. "Bounty hunter?"

"Working for her father," I said. "He's worried about when the Feds find you. He's scared. He doesn't want her dead. He'll pay—"

"They won't find us."

"Yes they will," I said. "I did."

That was when he patted me down, took my little Sig-Sauer and my wallet, and marched me ahead of him into the cabin shadowed deep among the Ponderosas on the slope of the mountain and nearly invisible.

Another man, who had to be the father, stood at a front window looking out from the cover of the wall, a big old Colt .45 1911 held like a toy pistol in his enormous hand. He *was* a big man. Well over six feet tall in his fringed buckskin, and nearly as wide. A full gray beard hid most of his face, and he wore high moccasins. A mountain man with the layers of fat and massive belly to carry him through the winter when there were few animals to kill, and the berries and roots were under the snow.

Sepp Mason said, "Name's Dan Fortune. A private eye."

The whole cabin was one medium-large room, with a kitchen and dining area at the right rear, and an interior door on the left into what was probably a bedroom. Another door in the kitchen had to be a storage room and pantry. There were two front windows, and a single long, narrow window high above the kitchen sink. A scarred and chipped refrigerator stood next to the sink, and a rough-hewn log table took up most of the open space in the kitchen.

Gretchen Bayer sat in a straight chair against the rear wall, still wearing the full summer skirt and halter top she had been kidnaped in. Her hands were tied behind the chair back. Her skirt was stained with pine sap, and her short dark hair was tangled. If I had expected a scared, tearful girl filled with gratitude and hope at seeing me, I was wrong. She gave me a baleful glare, and snarled, "You know what these Neanderthal clowns want? A fucking squaw! Can you believe that? They'll rot in hell first."

It was pretty much what I, and the three militia-types in Carter Creek, had feared. The Masons had not wanted money, they had wanted a woman. Any woman, and probably for both of them. But as near as I could tell, she was unmarked and appeared unharmed. Rape doesn't show, and few women are going to let a stranger know they've been raped, especially by two men. But rape and fear do show in the eyes, and what was in Gretchen Bayer's eyes was neither rape nor fear. It was anger, hate, and a grim and watchful violence waiting its chance to explode.

It was at that moment I saw the two sleeping bags on the floor of the main room, open and slept in. The implication, that the two men had slept alone on the floor of the main cabin while the girl had the bedroom, was a long way from rape. It looked like at least one of the pair was reluctant. I felt a surge of hope that there could be a way out of this for the girl, and for me.

I decided to attack them head on. "So what happens now? You kill me?"

Carter Mason growled, "What we got to lose, Fortune?"

His bearded face was as full of anger as Gretchen Bayer's, but his was directed at the world in general, at everyone but himself and his son.

"You have everything to lose. Kill me, and you have to kill her, and then it's over. You're dead too. Both of you. You know the Feds. Even if you keep the girl alive, she'll probably get killed in the cross fire. They'll take no chances. You've seen them in action. If you murder anyone, it's all over."

"We can take care of ourselves," Carter Mason snarled.

These first ten minutes were critical. I needed to keep them talking, find out which one was not so sure of what they were doing.

"Maybe," I told the older man, "but I found you, and they will too."

Sepp said, "How did you find us?"

He did not ask how come I let him catch me. He knew why he had caught me—he was a better man.

"It wasn't all that hard." I told him about Tucker, Ben and the driver, and the spokesman in the sweatshirt.

"The high-school coach," Carter Mason said grimly. "Damn. Knew he had the spine of a jackal. Probably told the Feds too. We better get the hell out of here. You grab the woman, Sepp, and I'll take care of Fortune." My fate was clear in his voice.

Sepp disagreed. "We'll take him with us, too. He's right, we kill anyone, and they—"

Before he could finish, Gretchen Bayer was all over him. Unseen, she had managed to slip her hands out of the rope, and moved faster than a mountain lion leaping on an unsuspecting mule deer. Her athlete's muscles coiled and corded, and then she sprang. Her charge knocked Sepp Mason flat on his back, and before he hit the floor she had the M-16. She stepped backward. "Tell your old man to put that cannon on the floor!" Her eyes flickered to me. "You, whatever your name is, get the old man's gun, and—"

In a single fluid motion, Sepp Mason rose to his feet, walked straight toward her and the rifle. I saw her finger tremble on the trigger of the M-16 as if she wanted to squeeze it but couldn't make her finger move. Her feet tried to move. But his reckless speed paralyzed her mind, or maybe it was that she had never shot anyone before.

Whatever it was, he plucked the rifle out of her hands like a feather, and slapped her hard enough to knock her down.

Carter Mason's .45 Colt dug into my back.

For a second Gretchen Bayer lay on the floor, shocked.

But only for a second. "Son-of-a-bitch!"

As fast as he had jumped up to take the rifle from her, she came off the floor swearing and throwing punches at his face. He picked them off effortlessly. She swung a knee up into his crotch. He blocked it with his left hand, and her right fist went in over his lowered left hand and slammed full into his face. Blood spurted from his nose, and he staggered backward. His back hit the wall, and in the split second his shoulders rested against the wall, his hands lowered in surprise, I saw a light in his eyes. I saw amazement, and . . . What? Admiration? Revelation?

She rushed him to follow her advantage. She aimed another hard right, he stepped inside her punch and his fist hit her flush on the chin. She went down again, her full skirt flying up over her face exposing bare thighs and blue bikini panties. Sheer blue panties with the dark wedge of hair clear under the thin cloth. Sprawled on the hard wooden floor, she wiped a slow trickle of blood from her mouth, and I saw the same light in her eyes. Amazement, admiration, revelation.

Sepp reached down, hauled her to her feet, and pushed her back into the chair.

"Stay there."

She struggled up again. "Shit I will! You goddamn bast—!"

His hand pressed down, squeezed, and forced her back into the chair as their eyes locked. Time stood still. Then he released her shoulder and stepped away. Blood still trickled from his nose.

She made no attempt to get up again. Only stared at his face. "You're fucking going to rot in prison. They'll fucking throw away the key. Maybe they'll fry you. Both of you. I'm going to watch and laugh."

"Shut your goddamn face." Carter Mason strode toward her with the .45 raised to hit her.

Sepp stopped him with his hand. "No."

Carter blinked at his son. They stood that way for a moment, then the old man turned away. "It's damn near dark. We better finish off Fortune and get the hell out of here if we're going to make—"

"Not tonight," Sepp said. "Tomorrow."

"Sepp—"

"Not tonight," Sepp said, "and we kill no one. That's not what this was about."

The old man licked his lips and stared at his son. So did Gretchen Bayer.

"Tomorrow," Sepp Mason said, stepped to Gretchen Bayer in the chair, and in a quick fluid motion picked her up in his arms. I saw the young athlete's body stiffen, go rigid, prepared to resist, to fight. Then she let go and buried her face in Sepp Mason's chest.

He carried her into the bedroom, kicked the door shut behind them.

———

Alone in the main room of the cabin with Carter Mason, I found myself staring at the bedroom door.

I forced my mind to turn away, and I looked at the old man. Carter Mason still watched the silent door, except he did not really see the door. He saw a distance that existed somewhere deep inside his own thoughts. But the .45 remained ready in his hand, and he was too far away for me to jump him.

He continued to gaze at the door with his unseeing eyes. "Sepp's mother walked out four years ago. You live off the land out here, it's hard when you got no woman in the house. I been doing it forty years, I can handle it alone. But Sepp, he needed a woman so we got him one."

"You got something," I said. "I'm not so sure it's what you had in mind."

His massive head and beard turned slowly to study me. He did not erupt in the rage that existed only millimeters beneath his skin, he did not do anything. Only sat there looking at me.

"They'll find you sometime," I said. "The FBI. BATF. What do you do then?"

Now he did explode. "We fight the bastards! We're free men, we've got our rights no matter how hard the fucking government tries to take them away."

"The right to kidnap a wife when you want one?"

"If we goddamn have to," the old man roared. "A man makes his own life. They show up here, we fight them and we beat them!"

He was crazy, yes, but it wasn't a medical insanity. It was the insanity of pushing an idea, a theory, as far as it could go, and then going farther. The insanity of frustration, of being left out.

The insanity of feeling you don't count, that the world you be-lieved in is being taken away from you.

"You can't beat them," I said. "You know what cops are. Their job is to protect those in power, and the laws they make to stay in power. It doesn't matter who's in power. The cops defend what exists today, keep order, control the citizens. Any cops, any time, any place. They can't allow you to defy the law. You're in rebel-lion, if not revolution, and no government, nation, or tribe ever made rebellion or revolution legal. You want to change the world, you better be ready to die."

Carter Mason sneered. "You think that scares us, Fortune? A free man fights for his rights. If we die, we die."

"The woman too?"

He suddenly stood. "You talk too much. Get up."

He marched me into the storeroom and locked the door. An hour later he threw in a bag of homemade trail mix and beef jerky, and soon after I finished eating the wild cries of lovemak-ing began to echo through the cabin.

———

Now, in the dark storeroom, I tried to block out the sounds from the distant bedroom. The images of every woman I ever made love to were filling my mind, when I needed to think of how I would get out of this alive. I finally went to sleep without any ideas, the cries from the bedroom still in my mind.

I woke up to pitch dark, looked at my watch. It was barely midnight. At first I heard only silence, but as I lay there in the dark storeroom I began to hear a different set of sounds. Voices, talking softly and quietly. Talking on and on some-where in the cabin. I was still listening to them when I fell asleep again, and when I awakened once more the cries of pas-sion were back.

When I woke up the final time in the darkness, my watch

read 3:47 A.M., and the voices were talking again, low and steady. I lay awake listening and thinking about those quiet voices, hearing the earlier passion, and wondering.

In the morning the FBI was there. And the BATF.

From the dark of the storeroom, a thin line of light under the door, I heard the old man's voice, "Sepp, we got company."

The storeroom door flung open. "Get out here, Fortune."

Blinded by the glare of the morning sunlight, I stepped out into the main room. When my vision finally cleared, I saw Carter Mason at his post beside the front window, his .45 in his hand, but staring back into the room to where Sepp Mason stood in the open bedroom door, the M-16 down at his side, and Gretchen Bayer beside him. She had both hands on Sepp's arm, and looked as belligerent and protective as he did.

As I watched, the old man seemed to shrink, to become smaller. His eyes above the thick, gray beard were suddenly dull and tired. As if he knew all at once that something he had long been afraid might be true, was true.

I watched him, and watched Sepp and Gretchen Bayer, and if what I thought I could see was right, I knew the way out of this.

I crossed to the corner of the second window. The Feds were at the edge of the Ponderosa pines in full assault gear: Three FBI, two BATF, and a single Nevada cop with a dog. An advance unit. There would be more soon. They acted as if they had just arrived, lurking inside the edge of the Ponderosas, and were not yet sure this was the right cabin.

I turned from the window quickly. "Okay," I said, "what's it going to be? Fight them, or give it up? You don't have a lot of time to make up your minds."

One arm around Gretchen Bayer, Sepp Mason said, "We can

talk to them. It's changed. You go out, Fortune. Tell them Gretchen wants to stay. Tell them she doesn't want their help."

Gretchen Bayer said, "Or my father's. I stay with Sepp."

It had been there, not in the cries and moans of last night, but in the voices talking softly and quietly between the bouts of passion.

"They won't buy it," I told them. "They'll say you're another Patty Hearst, a brainwashed woman under psychological duress. It's a kidnaping, and the victim doesn't get to call it off."

"I'm not going to prison," Sepp said, his voice flat. "And I'm staying with her."

"She's got her own life," I told him.

"No," Gretchen Bayer said, "I don't. I've got a career, a bank account, a famous name. I never needed any of it. He did. My son-of-a-bitch father. If I'm famous, he's famous. If I'm rich, he's rich. He told me it was what I wanted, and made me believe it. I never really did, but I had nothing else. Now I do."

"With him?"

"Him, the mountains, a life," she said, her voice as fierce as her eyes.

I shook my head. "They won't let you. They can't. They've spent a ton of money to rescue you, and they can't let Sepp and Carter walk away. It's prison for sure. Ten years at least. You can wait—"

Gretchen Bayer was enraged, "Then we'll fight them! The three of us. If they go down, I go down too. How's that going to look?"

"No," Sepp told her. "You're a woman, it's not your job. I'll go to pris—"

She rounded on him. "In a pig's ass it isn't! I can fight as good as you! And I say what I damn well do and don't do!"

I saw that admiration on his face again, but his voice was iron. "No."

All the while Sepp, Gretchen, and I had been talking, I had kept sight of Carter Mason. The old man stood silent the whole time, listening, watching, the .45 hanging down toward the floor, forgotten.

I hoped I was right about what that meant, and took a breath. "They have to jail someone. It's cost too much, there have been way too many headlines and TV news bulletins, and they'd look stupid. They can't lose all the way."

There was a silence. When the old man finally spoke, his voice was clear, his decision made. "It was all me, Fortune. Sepp didn't know I was going to do any of it. He only went along after because I'm his father, and I brought him up to respect his father."

"Dad—!"

Carter Mason tossed the .45 onto the table, and dismissed his son with a wave of his giant hand. "I don't have a life, boy. I've known that for a long time. All I've got is an attitude. I hate everyone not like me. Everyone who doesn't think like me is the enemy. Other people ain't really people. Alone against the world and proud of it. No wonder your mother left me. I've gone from one damned hate to another all my life. You got a chance for a real life, boy. Never saw you take to a woman like you done with her. Or her to you. You take this chance, you hear me?"

For a time no one said anything more, and then from outside a voice boomed through a bullhorn, "You in there! This is the FBI. Release your prisoner, and come out with your hands up!"

The old man turned to the cabin door. "I'll go out."

"Not you," I said, "me."

I faced Sepp and Gretchen. "I'm pretty sure the cabin isn't surrounded yet. There're too few of them, and they're not absolutely sure we're in here. Is there a window in the bedroom?"

"No," Sepp said.

"Can the two of you squeeze through that narrow kitchen window?"

Sepp and Gretchen looked at the long, high window above the kitchen sink, and nodded in unison.

"Okay. As soon as I go out, and they're all watching me because they don't know who I am, you two go out that window. Go somewhere you know you're pretty safe, but no one else knows about, not even Carter. Stay there. Start whatever new life you've got in mind."

I turned back to Carter Mason. "You wait here. Just sit tight and don't do a damn thing."

I stepped to the door, opened it, and shouted. "Okay, we're coming out!"

With my lone hand held high, I stepped out and walked straight toward them. There are times being a so-called cripple comes in handy. A one-armed man is not especially threatening, and no one-armed man was part of the kidnaping, so who was I? Their weapons tracked me all the way, but I could see them looking at each other, then back at me, then at a tall, gray-haired man in full FBI field gear.

When I was five feet away, three of them jumped out, grabbed me, dragged me into the cover of the first line of Ponderosas, and patted me down. They seemed disappointed to find no weapons. They hustled me to the tall FBI man.

"Who are you?"

"Dan Fortune. Private investigator working for Klaus Bayer."

"What the hell were you doing inside that cabin? Are the kidnapers there? Who are they? Where's the woman? Is she alive? Have they harmed her? If they have . . . Goddamn it, talk to me. You're in deep trouble, Fortune."

"No I'm not, you are. You ready to listen, or do you want to talk some more? I've got all day."

He almost strangled. "Talk."

"Their names are Carter and Sepp Mason. Father and son. Local survivalists. I found them yesterday, twenty-four hours before you did." I exaggerated, but I made my point. "That's going to look pretty lame. Especially since Gretchen Bayer doesn't want to be rescued, and won't testify against them."

"Goddamn it, For—"

I cut him off, "The girl and Sepp Mason have found each other. It's as real as anything I've seen, believe me. She says she's ready to die with them in a hail of bullets and a river of blood if that's how you want to play it. If you don't like that scenario, try this: Carter Mason will swear the whole thing was his idea. Sepp went along only to protect the girl. Carter Mason grabbed her to get a woman for Sepp. They didn't touch her, and Sepp told her if she didn't like the life out here after a while, they'd send her home. You get the picture?"

He had stopped sputtering about a minute back. I waited, but he only scowled at me now, so I continued. "The Bayer woman and Sepp Mason are already gone. Carter Mason will confess to doing the whole thing. Neither the son nor Gretchen Bayer will testify, even if you find them. If you do find them, they'll fight. So, either you leave Sepp and the Bayer girl alone, and go home in triumph with Carter Mason in tow and confessing to everything, or you try to find Sepp and the girl and end up in a bloody shoot-out probably killing them both. Your call."

"I could kill you and this Carter Mason, then go after the son and the girl."

"Too many people know what I'm doing and why. Especially Klaus Bayer. Gamble on getting away with killing me, if you want to, and take a chance on not killing the girl when they fight you, but the folks back in Washington must be getting awful tired of the FBI coming home with nothing but corpses to show for the money."

He thought that over. "Who handles Klaus Bayer?"

"I do. You can deal with the media."

It killed him. "Get the goddamn father out here."

It killed Klaus Bayer too, when I told him, but I remembered what Gretchen had said and convinced him if he ever wanted the girl to make him a buck again, he had better let her go.

Contributors

Paul Bishop

Paul Bishop is a twenty-five-year veteran of the L.A. Police Department, currently assigned as a senior detective supervising the Sex Crimes and Major Assault Crimes unit in the West Los Angeles area. Twice named LAPD Detective of the Year, Bishop is the author of nine novels, including *Chalk Whispers*, the fourth book in his Fey Croaker series. A collection of his short stories, *Pattern of Behavior*, has also been published.

Jon L. Breen

Jon L. Breen, the author of six novels and more than eighty short stories, reviews crime fiction for *Ellery Queen's Mystery Magazine* and has won two Edgar awards for his critical writings. Among his recent books are the short-story collections *Kill the Umpire: The Calls of Ed Gorgon, The Drowning Icecube and Other Stories*, and the second edition of *Novel Verdicts: A Guide to Courtroom Fiction*. He lives in California with his wife and sometime collaborator Rita.

Matthew V. Clemens

Matthew V. Clemens is the coauthor of the bestselling true crime book *Dead Water* and has contributed stories to several anthologies, including *Private Eyes* and *Murder Most Confederate*. He is the author of numerous magazine and newspaper articles and has collaborated with Max Allan Collins on several previous short stories. He is the publisher of Robin Vincent Books and lives in Iowa.

Max Allan Collins

Max Allan Collins is the author of the Shamus Award–winning "Nathan Heller" historical detective novels, most recently *Angel in Black.* He is also the author of such bestselling tie-in novels as *The Mummy, Air Force One,* and *Saving Private Ryan.* Collins has also written comic books, trading cards, and film criticism, and is the writer/director of three independent features, including the innovative *Real Time: Siege at Lucas Street Market.* He lives in Iowa with his wife, writer Barbara Collins.

Michael Collins

Michael Collins is the author of the nineteen Dan Fortune detective books that began in 1967, the most recent of which is *Fortune's World.* A collection of stories, *Spies and Thieves, Cops and Killers, Etc.,* was published in 2001. He has won the MWA Edgar for a novel, and has been given PWA's Lifetime Achievement Award. Under the names of Mark Sadler, John Crowe, William Arden, and Carl Dekker, he has published another eighteen crime novels and thirteen juvenile crime novels. Under his real name, Dennis Lynds, he has published two novels and two collections of short stories.

Bill Crider

Bill Crider is the chair of the Division of English and Fine Arts at Alvin Community College. He is also the author of fifty published novels, including ten mysteries in the Sheriff Dan Rhodes series (*A Ghost of a Chance* being the latest, with *A Romantic Way to Die* due in fall 2001), five featuring Galveston private investigator Truman Smith, and three starring English teacher Carl Burns. *A Knife in the Back,* featuring Sally Good, community college department chair, will appear in 2002. Crider has coauthored two mystery novels (*Murder in the Mist* and *Murder under Blue Skies*) with famous weatherman and TV personality Willard Scott. He won the Anthony Award for "best first mystery novel" in 1987 for *Too Late to Die* and was nominated for the Shamus Award for "best first private-eye novel" for *Dead on the Island.*

Catherine Dain

Catherine Dain is the author of the Freddie O'Neal series, which were nominated for two Shamus awards from the PWA. Titles include *Lay It on the Line* and *Lament for a Dead Cowboy.* Her prolific short fiction has appeared in *Cat Crimes Goes to Court* and *Marilyn: Shades of Blonde,* among others. *Angel in the Dark* is the latest novel from this popular speaker at mystery writers' seminars and conferences.

O'Neil De Noux

A cop-turned-writer, O'Neil De Noux is the author of five novels, one true-crime book, and over one hundred published short stories. His recent short-story collection, *LaStanza: New Orleans Police Stories,* has received critical praise, including an "A" rating by *Entertainment Weekly.*

Jeff Gelb

From *Dick Tracy* to *Sin City,* from *Double Indemnity* to *Body Heat,* from Cain to Connelly, if it's noir, California's Gelb devours it. He has often introduced noir elements in his stories for the award-winning *Hot Blood* series and other books. As for the erotic elements, he blames Hugh Hefner and Larry Flynt, not necessarily in that order.

Jeremiah Healy

Jeremiah Healy is a former professor at the New England School of Law and the creator of the John Francis Cuddy mystery series. His books include *So Like Sleep, Swan Dive, Right to Die, Shallow Graves, The Stalking of Sheila Quinn,* and his latest Cuddy novel, *Spiral.* He served as president of the PWA for two years and is the current president of the International Association of Crime Writers. He has spoken about mysteries at conferences around the world.

Mary Kay Lane

Mary Kay Lane's short fiction and poetry have appeared in various publications, including *Transversions, Nightmares, Out of the Cradle, Lyrical Iowa,* and the webzine *Dragon Soup.* She lives in Missouri.

Wendi Lee

Former associate editor of *Mystery Scene* magazine, Wendi Lee writes a female PI series starring Angela Matelli. Titles include *The Good Daughter, Missing Eden, Deadbeat,* and her latest, *He Who Dies . . .* She has just finished the fifth Matelli mystery, currently titled *Ph.Dead.* She lives in Iowa with cartoonist husband Terry Beatty and daughter Beth.

John Lutz

John Lutz is the author of more than thirty novels and two hundred short stories and is a past president of MWA and PWA. His novel *SWF Seeks Same* was made into the hit movie *Single White Female,* and he coauthored the screenplay for the movie *The Ex,* adapted from his novel of the same title. He is the recipient of the Edgar Award, Shamus Award, PWA Life Achievement Award, and the Trophee 813 Award for best mystery short-story collection translated into the French language. Lutz is the author of two private eye series, one featuring Fred Carver and set in Florida, the other featuring a detective named Nudger and set in St. Louis. His latest novel is the suspense thriller *The Night Caller.*

Stephen Mertz

Stephen Mertz has written novels, under a variety of pseudonyms, that have been widely translated and have sold millions of copies worldwide. His latest, written under his own name, is a Vietnam murder mystery, *The Golden Triangle.* Steve lives in Arizona and is always at work on a new book.

Martin Meyers

Writer/actor Martin Meyers is the author of five detective novels featuring private detective Patrick Hardy, including *Kiss and Kill* and *Spy and Die.* In collaboration with wife Annette Meyers, as Maan Meyers, he wrote a series of history mysteries, including *The Dutchman, The House on Mulberry Street,* and *The Lucifer Contract.* His short fiction has appeared in the *Crime Through Time* anthologies and others.

Richard S. Meyers

Richard S. Meyers is an eclectic writer, film consultant, and media personality. His novels, credited to several variations on his name, include *Murder in Halruaa, Fear Itself, Living Hell,* and *Doomstar.* He has been twice nominated for the Mystery Writers of America Edgar Award and has been inducted into both the World and the Worldwide Martial Arts Hall of Fame. His most popular nonfiction books are *Murder on the Air, For One Week Only: The World of Exploitation Films,* and *Great Martial Arts Movies: From Bruce Lee to Jackie Chan & More.* He can be seen on the A&E, Discovery, and Bravo cable channels and heard on more than a dozen DVD audio commentaries.

Alan Ormsby

Californian Alan Ormsby works full-time in the TV and movie industry as a screenwriter in various genres. His credits include *My Bodyguard, Cat People, The Substitute, Mulan,* and *Nash Bridges.*

Marthayn Pelegrimas

Marthayn Pelegrimas is the author of numerous short stories in the horror and dark fantasy genres, including works in the *Hot Blood* series, *UFO Files,* and *Love Kills.* Under the pseudonym Christine Matthews, she has written mysteries and was the coeditor of *Lethal Ladies II.* Her first novel, *Murder Is the Deal of the Day,* written with Robert J. Randisi, was published in 1999. She is working on her next novel with Randisi, *The Masks of Auntie LaVeau,* and her first thriller, *Scarred For Life.*

Bill Pronzini

A full-time professional writer since 1969, Pronzini has published fifty novels, including three in collaboration with his wife, novelist Marcia Muller, and twenty-seven in his popular "Nameless Detective" series. His is also the author of four nonfiction books, six collections of short stories, and scores of uncollected stories, articles, essays, and book reviews, and he has edited or coedited numerous anthologies. He has received three Shamus awards and the Lifetime Achievement Award from the PWA.

Mickey Spillane

The recipient of grandmaster awards from both MWA and PWA, Mickey Spillane is the bestselling author of private eye fiction of all time. His character Mike Hammer has appeared on the radio, in comics and TV, and on the silver screen, including the celebrated 1955 film noir, *Kiss Me Deadly.* In addition, Spillane is the only mystery writer to portray his own detective, appearing as Hammer in the 1963 film *The Girl Hunters,* and he spoofed his own tough image in a long-running series of Miller Lite Beer commercials. Though his writing output has slowed in recent years, Spillane—who lives in South Carolina—still occasionally publishes a Hammer novel. He is the subject of coeditor Collins's award-winning documentary, *Mike Hammer's Mickey Spillane.*